Extraordinary Praise for
DALE BROWN

"**D**ale Brown is a superb storyteller."
—W.E.B. GRIFFIN

"**E**xciting and intelligent entertainment."
—MARK GREANEY,
#1 Bestselling Author of *Mission Critical*

"**B**rown puts readers into the cockpit. . . .
Authentic and gripping."
—*New York Times*

"**B**rown's look at the future of the military
and potential conflicts with new technology
and warfare continues to be engaging. . . .
Fans . . . will love this latest installment."
—*Booklist* on *The Kremlin Strike*

"**B**rown has long been a master at high-tech
thrillers, and . . . there is no denying that he
knows his stuff. . . . Even with a long-running
series, he continues to find ways to keep the
action lively and relevant. For the Tom Clancy
crowd, Brown remains the go-to guy."
—*Booklist* on *The Moscow Offensive*

"**S**pectacular . . . The action builds to
an exciting climactic battle. . . . Brown
shows once again why he stands out in
the crowded military thriller genre."
—*Publishers Weekly* on *The Moscow Offensive*

By Dale Brown

DALE BROWN

THE KREMLIN STRIKE

A NOVEL

WM

WILLIAM MORROW

An Imprint of HarperCollinsPublishers

THE KREMLIN STRIKE. Copyright © 2019 by Creative Arts and Sciences LLC. All rights reserved. Printed in the United States of America. No part of this book may be used or reproduced in any manner whatsoever without written permission except in the case of brief quotations embodied in critical articles and reviews. For information, address HarperCollins Publishers, 195 Broadway, New York, NY 10007.

First William Morrow premium printing: March 2020
First William Morrow hardcover printing: May 2019

Print Edition ISBN: 978-0-06-284303-6
Digital Edition ISBN: 978-0-06-284304-3

Cover design: Richard L. Aquan
Cover photograph: Moscow © MazzzaO/Shutterstock
Cover illustration: plane © Kollected

William Morrow and HarperCollins are registered trademarks of HarperCollins Publishers in the United States of America and other countries.

20 21 22 23 24 QGM 10 9 8 7 6 5 4 3 2 1

This novel is dedicated to the visionaries: the leaders and innovators who see beyond fear and mistrust, the ones who aren't afraid to challenge conventional thought and strive to build something greater for the future.

Space is one such place where we need fresh ideas and action. I've written about a Space Defense Force for many years—and now a sixth branch of the U.S. armed forces, the Space Force, has been proposed.

Naturally, the howls of fear, distrust, outrage, and anger are sweeping around the world. But space is too important for the United States to ignore. It's time to plan, organize, build . . . and act.

Let your plans be dark and impenetrable as night, and when you move, fall like a thunderbolt.

—Sun Tzu, *The Art of War*

ACKNOWLEDGMENT

As always, thank you to Patrick Larkin for his hard work and skill.

CAST OF CHARACTERS

AMERICANS

JOHN DALTON FARRELL, president of the United States of America

ANDREW TALIAFERRO, secretary of state

DR. LAWRENCE DAWSON, PH.D., White House science adviser

ELIZABETH HILDEBRAND, CIA director

SCOTT FIRESTONE, admiral, U.S. Navy, chairman of the Joint Chiefs of Staff

AMANDA HAYES, major general, U.S. Air Force, U.S. Strategic Command Missile and Space Warning CENTER

THOMAS NISHIYAMA, commander, U.S. Navy, White House military aide

DANE "VIKING" THORSEN, commander, U.S. Navy, F/A-18E Super Hornet squadron commander, USS *Ronald Reagan*

JOINT SKY MASTERS AEROSPACE, INC.—SCION SPACEPLANE PROGRAM

HUNTER "BOOMER" NOBLE, PH.D., chief of aerospace engineering, Sky Masters Aerospace, Inc., lead pilot for the reactivated S-series spaceplane program

BRAD MCLANAHAN, spaceplane pilot and Cybernetic Orbital Maneuvering System (COMS) pilot

MAJOR NADIA ROZEK, spaceplane pilot and COMS pilot

PETER CHARLES "CONSTABLE" VASEY, former pilot in the Royal Navy's Fleet Air Arm, spaceplane pilot and COMS pilot

JASON RICHTER, PH.D., colonel, U.S. Army (ret.), chief executive officer of Sky Masters Aerospace, Inc.

SCION

KEVIN MARTINDALE, president of Scion, former president of the United States of America

PATRICK MCLANAHAN, technology and intelligence expert, former lieutenant general, U.S. Air Force (ret.)

IAN SCHOFIELD, Scion deep-penetration expert, former major in Canada's Special Operations Regiment

SAMANTHA KERR, operative, Scion Intelligence

MARCUS CARTWRIGHT, operative, Scion Intelligence

DAVID JONES, operative, Scion Intelligence

ZACH ORLOV, computer operations specialist, Scion Intelligence

LIZ GALLAGHER, lieutenant colonel, U.S. Air Force (ret.), copilot, S-29B Shadow spaceplane

JAVIER REYES, data-link officer, S-29B Shadow spaceplane

PAUL JACOBS, defensive systems officer, S-29B Shadow spaceplane

JILL ANDERSON, lieutenant commander, U.S. Navy (ret.), offensive weapons officer, S-29B Shadow spaceplane

RUSSIANS

GENNADIY ANATOLIYVICH GRYZLOV, president of the Russian Federation

COLONEL GENERAL MIKHAIL IVANOVICH LEONOV, commander, Aerospace Forces, head of the Mars Project

VIKTOR KAZYANOV, minister of state security

DARIA TITENEVA, foreign minister

MAJOR GENERAL ARKADY KOSHKIN, chief of the Federal Security Service's Q Directorate

CAPTAIN DMITRY POPOV, aide to Arkady Koshkin

LIEUTENANT COLONEL VASILY DRAGOMIROV, field operative for Russian military intelligence (GRU)

MAJOR EDUARD NAUMOV, technical officer, GRU Ninth Directorate

COLONEL VADIM STRELKOV, Space Forces cosmonaut, Mars One commander

MAJOR GEORGY KONNIKOV, Space Forces cosmonaut, Mars One sensor officer

YURI KLEMENTIYEV, launch director, Vostochny Cosmodrome

ALEXEI GREGORJEV, launch director, Baikonur Cosmodrome

MAJOR ALEXEI RYKOV, Su-27 pilot, former Mars Project cosmonaut candidate

CAPTAIN SERGEI NOVITSKI, Su-27 pilot

LIEUTENANT COLONEL PAVEL ANIKEYEV, Space Forces cosmonaut, Mars One second in command

MAJOR VIKTOR FILATYEV, Space Forces cosmonaut, Mars One chief weapons officer

CAPTAIN LEONID REVIN, Space Forces cosmonaut, Mars One deputy weapons officer

MAJOR PYOTR ROMANENKO, Space Forces cosmonaut, Mars One engineering and special action officer

LIEUTENANT NIKOLAY KHRYUKIN, Air Force meteorology officer

COLONEL VLADIMIR TITOV, commander, 1529th Guards Air Defense Missile Regiment

LIEUTENANT GENERAL SEMYON TIKHOMIROV, second in command, Aerospace Forces

COLONEL IVAN FEDEROV, Su-35 pilot and commander, 23rd Fighter Aviation Regiment

POLES

PIOTR WILK, president of Poland, former general in the Polish Air Force and commander of the First Air Defense Wing

KAROL SIKORA, sergeant, Polish Special Forces

TADEUSZ DOMBROWSKI, sergeant, Polish Special Forces

CANADIANS

CHARLES COSTELLO, brigadier general, duty controller, North American Aerospace Defense Command

REAL-WORLD NEWS EXCERPTS

U.S. MILITARY IS PREPARING FOR THE NEXT FRONTIER: SPACE WAR—CNN.com, 29 November 2016—Since man first explored space, it has been a largely peaceful environment. But now US adversaries are deploying weapons beyond Earth's atmosphere, leading the US military to prepare for the frightening prospect of war in space.

. . . China and Russia are taking aim at America in space with a dizzying array of weapons seemingly borrowed from science fiction. Russia has deployed what could be multiple kamikaze satellites such as "Kosmos 2499"—designed to sidle up to American satellites and then, if ordered, disable or destroy them. China has launched the "Shiyan"—equipped with a grappling arm that could snatch US satellites right out of orbit . . .

SPACE WAR IS COMING . . . AND THE U.S. IS NOT READY—Politico, 6 April 2018—War is coming to outer space, and the Pentagon warns it is not yet ready, following years of underinvesting while the military focused on a host of threats on Earth.

Russia and China are years ahead of the United States in developing the means to destroy or disable satellites that the U.S. military depends on for everything from gathering intelligence to guiding precision bombs, missiles and drones . . .

. . . There is the potential for an actual physical attack—with a missile or laser—to destroy space assets. Some experts worry the most about that scenario, which was exemplified by a 2008 test in which China tested an anti-satellite laser to blow up one of its own satellites . . .

Space As a War-Fighting Domain—Air and Space Power Journal, Summer 2018— . . . In the future, our potential adversaries will have the capability to hold every one of our critically important national security satellites at risk . . .

. . . The best way to prevent war from extending to space is: to prepare for that possibility, deter aggressive action in space, and if deterrence fails, be ready to fight and win . . .

THE KREMLIN STRIKE

PROLOGUE

Flanked by a pair of heavily armed Ka-52 Alligator gunships, a twin-engine HeliVert AW139 helicopter clattered low over a forest of birch and pine, slowing as it turned toward a small clearing in the woods. Its tricycle landing gear swung down and locked in position. Rotors whirling, the helicopter flared in and settled onto a concrete pad painted to look like a natural blend of rock and grass from high altitude. The two Ka-52s veered away, climbing steeply to circle overhead.

Along the horizon, several dozen buildings rose among the trees. Until recently, Akademgorodok had been a booming center for venture-capital-funded research and development—a place tagged as Russia's "Silicon Forest." But now Moscow ran the science city's labs and research institutes with an iron hand. The billions of rubles allocated to cybernetics, high-powered lasers, and other top secret weapons programs brought with them ever-tighter restrictions. This entire area southeast of the industrial city of Novosibirsk was now forbidden to those without the highest security clearances. And huge efforts were being made to conceal the existence of new factories and other facilities from foreign spy satellites.

As the AW139's rotors slowed, soldiers doubletimed across the concrete and fanned out to form a defensive perimeter. When the helicopter's passenger cabin door slid open, they snapped to attention—presenting arms with a polished flourish as Russia's president emerged. Gennadiy Gryzlov returned their salute with easy grace and dropped lightly down onto the camouflaged landing pad. At forty-five, he retained the rugged good looks that had won so many votes from his own people and, at least early on, the fawning admiration of gullible Western journalists.

The middle-aged military officer who stepped forward to greet him was cut from a very different cloth. Shorter than his commander in chief, though broad-shouldered and barrel-chested, Colonel General Mikhail Leonov would never be mistaken for a movie star. But any illusion that his round, open-featured face was that of a simple peasant or factory worker was dispelled by the intensity of his cold, appraising gaze. Recently promoted to head Russia's aerospace forces, the tough-minded fighter pilot and cosmonaut had cut his way to the top of his profession by outflying, outfighting, and out-witting a host of peers and rivals.

"Welcome to the Special Devices Test Center, Mr. President," Leonov said. He snapped a crisp salute.

With a short, sharp laugh, Gryzlov clapped him on the shoulder. "Come now, Mikhail! Why so formal? We're not still junior cadets on parade, marching around like we've got sticks shoved up our asses. Those days are long behind us, thank God."

"Old habits die hard, Gennadiy," Leonov said, donning a dutiful smile at the other man's crude humor. After all, he and Gryzlov *had* been class-mates for several years, first at the Yuri Gagarin Military Air Academy and later at the Military Space Academy in St. Petersburg. Unlike the president, though, Leonov had completed his cosmonaut training and flown Soyuz spacecraft on several missions to the old International Space Station before transitioning back to fly conventional fighters like the MiG-29 and Su-27.

"True enough," Gryzlov agreed. His expres-sion hardened. "But die they must, Leonov. Old habits. Old ways of thinking. Old men unwilling to adapt. All of them. Russia needs agile, innova-tive warriors who aren't afraid of the future. Men ready to seize every military advantage new tech-nology offers. For too long, slow-thinking fossils like your late and unlamented predecessor wasted our resources on incremental improvements to existing aircraft, missiles, and other weapons, only to fail miserably against the Americans, the Poles, and their mercenaries when put to the test. The time for half measures and caution is over."

Leonov nodded. Gryzlov meant what he said. One by one, the advisers who'd tried to temper his aggression and willingness to run risks had fallen by the wayside. Some of them were dead. The rest were disgraced or in prison. Of course, he thought coolly, the same fate awaited those who carried out the president's bold plans . . . and still failed.

Serving Gennadiy Gryzlov was a high-wire act, one with very little margin for error.

"So," the president said impatiently. "What do you have to offer me, Mikhail?" He waved a hand at the forest around them. Apart from a few ventilation and exhaust pipes disguised to look like trees and a dirt-and-log-covered bunker, there were no other signs of human handiwork. "The wonders of Siberian nature?"

Smiling more genuinely now, Leonov shook his head and ushered Gryzlov toward the bunker. "What you are about to see *is* wonderful, Gennadiy," he said. "But I assure you that nothing about it is at all *natural*."

His meaning became clearer when they pushed through an opening in the camouflage netting draped over the crude-looking shelter and were immediately confronted by a solid steel door. Leonov swiped his ID card through a reader next to the door. It beeped once. Then he pressed his palm against a biometric panel set into the door itself.

"*Leonov, Mikhail Ivanovich. Positive identification,*" a computer-generated female voice said with careful precision. "*Mars Project Level One security clearance match.*"

He turned to Gryzlov. "Now it's your turn."

The president raised an eyebrow. "You're joking."

"No, sir," Leonov said. "No one is admitted to this facility without confirming his or her identity and required clearance level. Not even you, sir."

"And if I refuse?"

Leonov shrugged. "Alarms will sound. That door will stay locked and sealed. And within moments we will find ourselves answering questions asked by some very unsympathetic security officers."

"*Otlichno*, Mikhail," Gryzlov said. "Very good. Security lapses have cost us dearly in the past. It's high time somebody besides me understood the necessity of keeping secrets." He took out his own ID card and followed the same procedure.

The massive steel door slid aside, revealing a waiting elevator car. As soon as the two men entered, the door closed. "Place defensive systems on standby," Leonov ordered. "And then take us to the control level."

"*M. I. Leonov command authority confirmed. Defensive systems are on standby,*" the computer acknowledged.

The car descended smoothly, swiftly dropping deeper into the earth. Holding on to a railing, Gryzlov turned his head. "Defensive systems?" he asked.

"A final precaution," Leonov told him. "Should an enemy force breach the facility's outer security, there are explosive charges set along the elevator shaft—rigged to kill any intruders and seal off the lower levels."

Gryzlov whistled softly. "Entombing everyone inside?"

"There is a carefully concealed emergency exit," he said calmly. "But if necessary, yes. The work being done here is vital to the defense of the Motherland. It would be better to sacrifice a few scientists and engineers than risk seeing the Americans or the Chinese get their hands on it."

"You are one coldhearted son of a bitch, Mikhail," Gryzlov said with evident approval.

The elevator slowed and came to a stop, nearly two hundred meters underground. When the door opened, they stepped out into a corridor guarded by a squad of tough-looking soldiers. Beyond the security post, another massive steel door blocked access to the control center. Though it was clear that the officer in charge recognized them, their ID cards were again closely scrutinized before they were allowed through.

Inside the control center, Gryzlov eyed his surroundings with evident interest. Computer consoles set on three stepped tiers faced a cinema-sized video screen showing the image of a huge, brightly lit chamber. Dozens of civilian scientists, technicians, and engineers wearing headsets manned the consoles, along with a handful of young-looking military officers. Intricate graphs and readouts blinked on each console. An air of keen anticipation filled the room.

Leonov turned to one of the scientists, an older man with a shock of thick, white hair. "Are you ready to proceed, Dr. Savvin?"

"We are, General," the other man said with quiet confidence. "All systems are functioning perfectly." At Leonov's silent nod, the scientist spoke into his own headset mike. "All control stations, this is Savvin. Commence weapons test."

Immediately Gryzlov heard a muted, high-pitched whine and felt a faint vibration coming through the floor. On the video screen, the appearance of the bright lights illuminating the huge chamber went oddly *flat*.

"High-efficiency pumps are emptying the test chamber's atmosphere," Leonov explained. "When they finish, it will be in a near-perfect vacuum."

Gryzlov nodded. Without air molecules to diffract the light, no wonder it seemed so strange. He focused his attention on the screen.

At the far end of the chamber, he could see the full-scale mock-up of an American reconnaissance satellite—complete with fully extended solar panels, GPS receivers, downlink antennas, and radar dishes—hanging in midair, attached by wires to the ceiling, walls, and floor. Closer in, a maze of power conduits and fiber-optic cables surrounded a complex assembly of electronic equipment. To his untutored eye, this machine resembled a massive, upright, six-armed starfish with a short, stubby rod projecting from its center.

The shrill whine died away, along with the vibration. "Pump cycle complete," one of the controllers reported. "Atmospheric pressure now less than one hundred nanopascals."

Gryzlov was impressed. That was roughly one-hundred-millionth of the air pressure at sea level. In effect, atmospheric conditions in that vast chamber now closely approximated those of outer space.

Savvin glanced at another technician. "What is the weapon's energy status, Andrei?"

"Our high-energy graphene supercapacitors are at full charge and holding."

"Very good." Savvin turned toward a trim aerospace forces officer seated at the nearest console. "You may fire when ready, Captain Kazantsev."

"Firing now," the younger man acknowledged. He leaned forward and tapped a glowing icon on a touch-screen control panel.

Instantly, the center of the large starfish array emitted a blinding white pulse. The satellite mock-up at the far end of the chamber shuddered violently—wreathed in a shimmering orb of lightning for just a split second. Shards of shattered solar panels and antennas spiraled away.

"That's a confirmed kill," another controller said exultantly, studying data from sensors attached to the satellite.

Gryzlov blinked. "What just happened?" he demanded.

Leonov grinned. "It will be easier to see in slow motion, Gennadiy. Fortunately, we have the entire test chamber covered by ultra-high-speed cameras." He signaled Savvin. "Replay the attack sequence, Doctor."

This time, Gryzlov watched closely, mesmerized by the otherworldly imagery. A glowing, meter-wide toroid of plasma emerged from the stubby cylinder in the middle of the array and streaked toward the target satellite—slamming into it with a blinding flash. When the lightning faded away, it left the satellite replica a blackened, half-melted wreck.

He shook his head in disbelief. "What the devil is that device?"

"Our new weapon, Mr. President—a coaxial plasma rail gun," Leonov told him proudly. "We call it *Udar Molnii*, Thunderbolt."

Gryzlov's eyes narrowed in thought. "Go on."

Leonov pointed to the cable-draped, starfish-shaped machine on-screen. "Using energy stored in the supercapacitors lining that six-armed structure, Thunderbolt creates a ring of extremely dense plasma, effectively a form of ball lightning, and then accelerates it with a powerful magnetic pulse."

"At what speed?"

"Up to ten thousand kilometers a second," Leonov said flatly. "Which is why these plasma toroids explode on contact with significant thermal and mechanical force. Those explosions also produce destructive electromagnetic pulse effects and high-energy X-rays."

Ten thousand kilometers a second? Gryzlov was staggered. That was faster by orders of magnitude than any other missile or projectile ever invented by man. Only lasers, which struck at the speed of light, were faster. He dragged his gaze back to Leonov. "What is the effective range for this weapon?"

"At least several thousand kilometers," the other man replied. "Perhaps more. Supercomputer simulations suggest the plasma toroids could remain stable for almost a full second." He shrugged. "We would need operational testing in space to confirm those numbers, of course."

For a moment, Gryzlov bared his teeth in a wolfish grin. Wicked glee danced in his pale blue eyes. *Screw the naysayers who moaned and bitched about extravagant spending on what they called wildeyed schemes*, he thought. Together with the other advanced weapons, energy technologies, and space launch systems he'd championed as part of *Proyekt Marsa*, the Mars Project, this new plasma rail gun had the clear potential to make Russia the world's unchallenged superpower. After all the narrowly disguised defeats and Pyrrhic victories of the past several years, he could at last sense his long-held ambitions and plans coming to fruition.

But then his predatory smile faded as he was struck by a sudden and very unwelcome possibility. "What about the Americans, Mikhail? Especially that damned company, Sky Masters. What if they're working on a plasma rail gun of their own?"

"They are not," Leonov said confidently.

"How can you be so sure?" Gryzlov snapped.

"Because the Americans themselves first tried to develop this weapon long ago—as part of their

President Reagan's so-called Strategic Defense Initiative. They named it MARAUDER, which stood for 'magnetically accelerated ring to achieve ultrahigh directed energy and radiation,'" Leonov told him. "They even powered their experiments using capacitors in the same six-armed shape, something they called the Shiva Star."

"And how, exactly, is learning that the Americans are potentially decades ahead of us supposed to comfort me?" Gryzlov said acidly. "In an arms race, victory does not go to those who lag so far behind."

"That is the point," Leonov said with a wry smile. "There is *no* arms race in this case. After a few small successes, a later American administration canceled the MARAUDER program—both to save money and because it opposed the whole concept of space-based weapons. So the Americans classified their research and then locked it away out of sight and out of mind . . . which is exactly where our spies uncovered it a few years ago, gathering dust and cobwebs."

"So by the time our enemies realize their folly and scramble to restart their own long-mothballed program—" Gryzlov realized.

"It will be too late," Leonov agreed. "Russia will own the very sky itself."

CHAPTER 1

JEDNOSTKA WOJSKOWA KOMMANDOSÓW (MILITARY COMMANDO UNIT), COMBAT TRAINING AREA, NEAR LUBLINIEC, POLAND
Several weeks later

Seen through a thin screen of pine trees, the little village looked abandoned. Except for a few dingy, off-white curtains wafting in the gentle breeze, nothing moved among its cluster of drab one-story houses or along its rutted dirt streets. Old-model civilian cars and light trucks, more rust and dents than anything else, were parked outside some of the homes.

Crouched in cover near the edge of the forest, Polish Special Forces Major Nadia Rozek slowly lowered her binoculars. According to the intelligence briefing for this special training exercise, a simulated force of Russian Spetsnaz commandos was holed up in the town—probably using its inhabitants as human shields. Which meant appearances were deceiving. A slight frown creased her attractive, tanned face. More than one hundred meters of open ground separated these woods from the nearest houses. No competent enemy commander would miss the chance to turn that clear stretch into a killing zone.

"*Ryś Jeden do Ryś Trzy,*" she radioed. "Lynx One to Lynx Three. Report."

Lynx Three was her two-man sniper team. They'd infiltrated in ahead of the rest of the assault force. By now they should have settled into a concealed position that offered them a good view of the town and its immediate surroundings.

"Lynx Three to One." Sergeant Karol Sikora's calm voice crackled through her earphones. "We see no sign of the enemy on this side of the village. There are no thermal traces in the buildings we have eyes on. Repeat, none."

Nadia bit down on the urge to tell him to look harder. The sergeant wasn't a rookie. Like her, Sikora was a veteran of the Iron Wolf Squadron—an elite, high-tech force of pilots, intelligence operatives, and special-operations soldiers that had helped defend Poland and its Eastern European allies against periodic Russian aggression for several years. Originally, the squadron's men and women were all foreign-born, mostly Americans. In fact, she'd first been assigned to Iron Wolf chiefly as a liaison officer for Poland's president, Piotr Wilk. But as casualties mounted, more Poles joined the unit in combat roles—accumulating valuable experience and technical expertise before rotating back to their nation's regular armed forces.

So when the sniper sergeant said there weren't any Spetsnaz troops deployed in the houses with fields of fire covering this approach, she could take it to the bank. Which left one big problem. Where in hell were the Russians she'd come to kill? Were they really foolish enough to let her soldiers push inside the town without a fight? *No*, she decided, somehow she was still missing a piece of this tactical puzzle.

Nadia's frown deepened. The clock was running. Every second she spent now trying to decide what to do next would cost her dearly later—on the back end of this mission. But while speed was life when you were already under fire, attacking blindly, without thorough reconnaissance, was usually a recipe for disaster.

Her mind ran faster. By refusing to defend the edge of the village, her Spetsnaz opponents clearly wanted to lure her into risking a quick dash across that wide-open ground ahead of them. Which meant—

"Lynx Three, this is One," Nadia said into her headset mike. "Check out the tree line on our right and left flanks. Don't rush it. Take your time and do a thorough job."

"Understood, Lynx One," Sikora replied. "Scanning now." In these conditions, the SCT-2 thermal sights he and his spotter were using should be able to pick out a human-sized target at well over a thousand meters. If the Russian troops were sheltering under anti-infrared camouflage cloth, it would be tougher to spot them. But nothing short of the highly advanced camouflage systems used by Iron Wolf's combat robots could render a target effectively invisible . . . and those were systems Russia still could not replicate.

Nadia glanced over her shoulder. Her assault force, broken into three six-man sections, squatted among the trees close by, waiting for the order to go in. Bulky in their body armor, tactical vests, Kevlar helmets, and shatterproof goggles, most of her Special Forces soldiers cradled short-barreled Heckler & Koch HK416 carbines. She could sense their eagerness. Like wolfhounds scenting prey, they were keyed up, straining at the leash.

"Three to One," Sikora said suddenly. "You were right, Major. There's a Russian weapons team dug in on the edge of the woods, about two hundred meters off on our left flank. I count two Spetsnaz troops with a PKP machine gun sited to sweep the clear ground."

Nadia breathed out. The PKP Pecheneg light machine gun was a fearsome weapon, designed especially for Russia's Spetsnaz units and mechanized infantry. Capable of firing between six hundred and eight hundred 7.62mm rounds per minute, that belt-fed automatic weapon would have cut her men to pieces the moment they left the cover of the trees. "Take them out on my signal," she ordered.

"Understood."

Carefully, she rose from her crouch and checked over her own HK carbine and other gear one last time. Soft rustling sounds indicated that the rest of the assault force was following her lead. No one wanted to find out the hard way that some vital piece of equipment had gotten tangled up or gone missing while they'd slogged their way through a couple of kilometers of dense forest to reach this position.

Of course, Nadia thought wryly, sometimes there was nothing you could do about things that were missing. She glanced down at where her feet should be—and no longer were. Instead, she saw the twin tips of her black carbon-fiber prosthetic running blades. Though the sight was no longer alien, she still couldn't pretend that it felt natural. Not even after almost a full year.

Last summer, while defeating a Russian attempt to assassinate the man who was now America's president, she'd been badly wounded. To save her life, trauma surgeons had been forced to amputate both of her maimed legs below the knee. Weeks of agonizing hospitalization had been followed by months of exhausting and painful rehabilitation. First, she'd relearned to walk using conventional prosthetics. Then more months had been needed to master the use of these agile, incredibly flexible running blades—and to rebuild her lost strength and endurance. And all of it—all her hard work, all her sweat, all her pain—had been driven by a single, overriding imperative: to prove that she was still fit for active service in Poland's Special Forces, even without her legs.

Well, today is that day, Nadia told herself. Win or lose, this was the chance she'd fought for.

"Lynx Three, this is One," she snapped. "Nail that machine-gun team." She started forward. "All other Lynx units. Follow me!"

Two muffled cracks echoed through the nearby woods.

"Enemy weapons team down," Sikora reported. "We have your back, Major."

Good enough, Nadia thought. Now to cross that killing zone before the Russians realized their ambush had been blown. She moved faster, accelerating from a deliberate, almost gliding walk to a tooth-jarring, equipment-rattling jog. Then, as soon as she broke past the last few trees and came out into the open, she sprinted onward at top speed—bounding forward on her prosthetic blades toward the center of the little village.

Two of her assault sections peeled away, moving off to the left and right. They were tasked with fighting their way into the town from opposite sides—in a pincer movement intended to spread the enemy's defenses and smash any attempted retreat. The six men of the third section stuck with her.

Nadia darted past the first row of empty houses and dropped into cover behind an old, banged-up Tarpan pickup truck. Her troops spread out around her, weapons up and ready to fire at the first sign of any hostile movement.

Voices flooded through her earphones as the other section leaders provided a running commentary on their progress. Their units were systematically clearing houses, going room to room in a hunt for Spetsnaz holdouts and any hostages. Stun grenades exploded with ear-piercing bangs, followed almost instantly by short, sharp bursts of assault-rifle fire.

"House One clear. One hostile down. No civilians present."

"House Five clear. Two hostiles dead. No civilians here."

"House Nine clear. No contact."

Comparing their reports with her mental map of the town, Nadia realized that roughly half of the estimated Russian commando force was still unaccounted for . . . along with around a dozen innocent men, women, and children. Realistically, there was only one place left that was big enough to hold that many people. She risked a quick glance around the pickup truck's rusting bumper.

The village's largest building sat not far away down the street. According to the quick-and-dirty intelligence briefing she'd received, that gray cinderblock eyesore served as a kind of community center—a place for celebrations, day-care classes, local meetings and political rallies, and even a small, bare-bones health clinic staffed by a visiting nurse. Its main entrance, a set of big double doors, looked out onto the road.

Nadia snorted. There was no way in hell she would lead a charge through those doors. *The easy way is always mined*, ran one of Murphy's half-humorous, half-serious laws of war. Or, in this case, probably rigged with a booby trap and zeroed in on by a couple of cold-eyed Spetsnaz bastards just itching to even today's score by killing a few Poles. Even though it would cost her more time, they needed to find another way inside.

Swiftly, she led the way around one of the

abandoned houses and then along a narrow alley crowded with bags of garbage, old mattresses, and waist-high stacks of worn-out tires. The alley opened onto a small cross street paralleling one side of the community center. And there, flanked by overflowing trash bins, was another door—narrow, dingy, and looking as though it was almost never opened. *Perfect*, Nadia thought.

Using quick, silent hand signals, she deployed her small force, stationing two soldiers to provide covering fire while the rest lined up behind her in a tactical stack next to that side door. Satisfied, she tapped the section's breaching expert, Sergeant Dombrowski, lightly on the shoulder. "Make us a hole, Tadeusz," she murmured, easing a flashbang grenade out of one of her assault-vest pouches.

With a nod, he moved around her and racked his Mossberg 500 twelve-gauge shotgun to chamber breaching rounds. Angling the shotgun down at a forty-five-degree angle, he jammed the muzzle tightly against the door—aiming halfway between the knob and doorframe. *Wham. Wham.* Two quick shots blew a hole through the door and smashed its lock.

Without pausing, Dombrowski kicked the door open and whirled away. In the same split second, Nadia leaned forward and lobbed her grenade through the opening.

BANG.

The stun grenade detonated with a blinding flash. Smoke and dust eddied out of the doorway.

"*Go! Go! Go!*" Nadia shouted. Tucking her HK securely against her shoulder, she rolled through the swirling smoke and into the building—sliding right to clear the way for the other Polish Special Forces soldiers pouring inside after her.

They were in a large room filled with over-turned tables and chairs. Through the gray haze hanging in the air, she could make out indistinct shapes sprawled across a scuffed-up linoleum floor. Frowning, she glided sideways, keeping her back to a wall. Her eyes scanned back and forth, alert for any signs of movement.

Abruptly, motion flickered at the right edge of her vision. She spun in that direction, seeing what looked like a Spetsnaz commando holding a rifle pop up from behind one of the overturned tables. Trained instincts took over. She squeezed off a three-round burst.

Pieces flew off the mannequin and it flopped backward. Its helmet spun lazily across the floor.

"One hostile dead and down," she said coolly, already swinging back to hunt for another valid target.

More HK carbines stuttered as some of her troops spotted different figures representing Russian soldiers and opened fire. The others barked orders, warning the simulated civilians trapped inside this room to "get down and stay down!"

Nadia kept moving, advancing deeper into the tangle of tables and chairs. Part of her admired the illusions created by those who'd put together this combat exercise. Another part felt frustrated. Shooting up silhouettes, mannequins, and pop-up targets was never as satisfying as facing off against live foes. As Whack Macomber, one of the Americans she'd served with in the Iron Wolf Squadron, would often growl, "These frigging battle simulations are a lot like kissing your sister."

Clearing the rest of the shooting house reconfigured as a "community center" took several more minutes of close, effective teamwork—carefully working through a labyrinth of rooms filled with a mix of targets dressed as both Spetsnaz soldiers and innocent Polish civilians. When they were finished, she ordered everyone back outside.

Once there, they regrouped with the rest of the assault force.

"Training Command, this is Lynx One," Nadia radioed, scowling down at her watch. They were running very short on time. "We've cleared the village. All hostiles eliminated. No friendly casualties."

"Acknowledged, Major Rozek," a laconic voice replied. "We show Phase One complete. Proceed immediately to Exercise Area Bravo."

She sighed inside. Area Bravo was more than a kilometer away. *Good Christ*, she thought. This was going to be tight. Very tight.

Concealing her worries, Nadia issued out a set of rapid-fire orders that deployed her troops into a column of fours and put them in motion. With her in the lead, they set off at a fast trot—hurrying back into the forest and down a winding dirt road in a rattle and clatter of weapons and equipment.

Ten minutes later, they broke out into the open again. A three-meter-high log wall stretched across their path. After they'd spent hours tramping through the woods in full battle gear and then fighting their way through a mocked-up village, the obstacle looked as tall and imposing as the Great Wall of China.

Nadia took a deep breath. This was it. She turned her head. "All right, guys. Let's go! Up and over and through!"

She set off at a dead run. Just short of the wall, she leaped upward, grabbing a handhold between two logs near the top and planting one of her blades on the narrow edge of another log, lower down. Then, pushing off with the flexible prosthetic limb, she jumped again and got both gloved hands on top of the obstacle. Breathing hard, she swung herself up and onto the top of the wall—using her arms and upper-body strength to compensate for her missing legs.

Without pausing, Nadia lowered herself down the other side and dropped the last few feet. She rolled over and came up facing a wide field crisscrossed by barbed-wire entanglements and shallow, muddy ditches. Instructors manned machine guns set on fixed mounts along one edge of the field.

Gritting her teeth, she scrambled upright, ran forward, and then dove headlong into one of the ditches. Cradling her carbine in both hands, she wriggled forward using her elbows and knees for leverage. Her blades, perfect for running on firm ground, were virtually useless now . . . deadweight. Their slick, carbon-fiber surfaces couldn't get enough traction in the soft, sticky mud.

The machine guns began firing. Live tracer rounds whipcracked low overhead—drawing lines of glowing fire across the field just a few centimeters above the razor-sharp coils of barbed wire. Soldiers started to pass her on both sides. She was falling behind the pace. Nadia swore silently and pushed on, straining to crawl faster.

WHUMMP.

A fountain of mud erupted a few meters away. Seconds later, more small explosions rippled across the obstacle course. *Wonderful*, she thought grimly. The trainers were setting off buried pyrotechnics to simulate mortar rounds, grenades, and mines. That was all she needed now.

Tucking her head low to snake under a wire entanglement, she squirmed onward. Barbs snagged at her tactical vest and then tore loose. She raised up slightly, spat out a mouthful of mud, and risked a quick look ahead.

The edge of the field was just twenty meters away.

WHUMMP.

Another pyrotechnic went off close by, spattering enormous clumps of mud and dirt into the air. The blast knocked her sideways . . . right into another coil of barbed wire.

Caught in the entanglement, Nadia strained to move. Barbs jabbed and tore at her sleeves, ripping through the tough camouflage cloth and drawing blood. A loose strand had even wrapped itself tightly around her prosthetic blades. Ignoring the pain, she yanked a pair of wire cutters out of one of her equipment pouches, curled up, and went to work—grimly slicing through the metal strands pinning her in place. She needed to free herself as fast as possible and keep going.

But it was too late. Whistles blew shrilly, signaling the end of the exercise.

"Shit," Nadia muttered. Suddenly exhausted, and fighting down tears of frustration, she sat up and finished cutting herself free. Despite her best efforts, she'd failed to complete the course in the required time.

CHAPTER 2

JEDNOSTKA WOJSKOWA KOMMANDOSÓW HEADQUARTERS BUILDING
The next day

Perched on a chair, Brad McLanahan saw the door to Colonel Henryk Pietrzak's office swing open. He stood up, straightening to his full, broad-shouldered height.

Neat and trim in her Special Forces dress uniform, Nadia Rozek stepped out into the hall-way and quietly closed the door behind her. As always, he felt a warm glow inside at the sight of the beautiful, dark-haired young woman—coupled with a lingering sense of awe that he'd been lucky enough to win her affection. When he'd joined the fledgling Iron Wolf Squadron four years ago, he'd thought their relationship would just be a short, fun romp for both of them. A sort of "pretty local girl has a wild fling with a lonely expatriate American" deal. But now he knew differently. Nothing about Nadia was frivolous. She was tough-minded, intensely passionate, and totally fearless . . . and he couldn't imagine life without her.

"How did it go?" Brad asked gently, already suspecting the worst from the distant look in her blue-gray eyes.

"Not well," Nadia admitted. "Though he wishes otherwise, Colonel Pietrzak will not return me to active-duty status, at least not as a combat arms officer." Her mouth turned downward. "In light of my injuries, he believes the risk to me and to those under my command would be too great." She shrugged her shoulders. "Apparently, the best I can hope for is a rear-area headquarters staff post . . . or perhaps an assignment as a tactics instructor at either the Kościuszko Land Forces Military Academy or the National Defense University."

Internally, Brad winced, imagining her reaction to the suggestion that she spend her days pushing paper from one side of a desk to the other or delivering lectures to bored junior officer cadets. "Ouch. So . . . did you leave the guy in one piece . . . or should I call for medics and an ambulance?"

For a moment, the shadow of a smile ghosted across her face. "Despite my fearsome reputation, I do have *some* sense of military decorum, Brad. The colonel is alive and quite well. For the moment."

"Then what did you tell him?"

Nadia sighed. "I asked for more time to consider

my other options." Her expression darkened. "I only wish I knew what they were."

Get your game face on, McLanahan, Brad thought. This was his big chance. He cleared his throat nervously. "Yeah, well, see, as it happens, that's kind of something I've been talking over with a few folks."

"Oh?" Her mouth tightened slightly and she folded her arms. "And which *folks* are those, exactly?"

"Me, for one," someone said from over her shoulder.

Caught by surprise, Nadia spun around. And then she stiffened to attention. The newcomer raised a hand with a nod and an easy grin, silently ordering her to stand at ease. "Mr. President?" she stammered. "What are you doing here?"

Piotr Wilk shot her an easy grin. "At ease, Major Rozek." Wiry, fit, and not quite fifty, Poland's president still looked more like the veteran fighter pilot and charismatic air-force commander he'd once been than the political leader he'd become. His eyes twinkled with amusement. "I flew here from Warsaw this morning at Captain McLanahan's suggestion."

Recovering quickly, Nadia looked skeptically from one man to the other. She raised an eyebrow. "Oh? And should I understand then that the two of you have been settling my future for me? Behind my back?"

Still smiling, Wilk shook his head. "Not at all, Major," he replied. "Consider this more of a brainstorming session." His expression turned more serious. "Colonel Pietrzak is a good man and a fine soldier. His determination to maintain the highest physical standards for the officers and soldiers under his command is commendable."

Reluctantly, Nadia nodded.

"But Pietrzak is *not* Poland's commander in chief. That is my role," Wilk continued. "What is more important is that I know you better than he does. I have seen your abilities with my own eyes. So in this narrow case, I believe it might be reasonable, even just, to waive certain standards—"

"*No*," Nadia interrupted fiercely. "With respect, Mr. President, you must *not* pull strings on my behalf in this matter. Not for any reason. You would harm the good order and discipline of our armed forces."

Wilk shook his head. "I doubt any damage would be lasting, Major. Remember, you are one of our nation's most decorated and accomplished soldiers. No one of consequence would resent a small accommodation on your behalf."

Nadia was silent for a long moment.

Brad held his breath.

"But *I* would," Nadia said finally. She swallowed hard. "I do not want special treatment . . . or pity." She straightened her shoulders. "Colonel Pietrzak's tests were fair. In certain ground combat conditions, my prosthetic legs clearly put me at a severe disadvantage." She blinked hard, her eyes bright with unshed tears. "And though I wish with all my heart that were not so, it is obvious that the real world will not yield to my wishes."

"Very well." Wilk smiled. "Your courage and honesty do you great credit, Major." He glanced at Brad and nodded slightly, acknowledging that the younger man had been right about how she would react. He turned back to Nadia. "Which means we must find another way to use your skills in Poland's service."

"That might be difficult," she said, not bothering to conceal a touch of bitterness. "I can run, but I can't crawl. I can shoot, but I can't overcome obstacles that keep me from closing with the enemy. Of what use is a soldier unfit for combat? How can I serve my country now?"

"You can fly," Brad said simply. He brushed his fingers across her helicopter pilot's badge, the *gapa*, a silver eagle with a golden laurel wreath clutched in its bill. "Remember?"

Bewildered, Nadia stared back at him. While she could certainly fly helicopters, even with her prosthetic legs, the same limitations that kept her off active-duty status would still apply. No one would risk sending her behind enemy lines where she might be shot down—and forced to evade capture on foot. "Poland has plenty of civilian transport pilots," she said, choosing her words with care. "I do not think she needs another."

"I agree," Wilk said. "But that is not what Captain McLanahan and I are proposing, Major Rozek."

"Sir?"

"Our strategic situation has changed," he reminded her. "And for the better. Which is something I would have believed impossible all but a short time ago."

Now *there* was an understatement, Brad decided.

Four years before, America's then-president, Stacy Anne Barbeau, had refused Poland's call for help when Russia's ruthless leader, Gennadiy Gryzlov, launched a war of aggression. Even Article Five of the North Atlantic Treaty Organization would not dissuade Barbeau—and if the U.S. wouldn't respond, neither did any other member nation. Only the advanced combat robots and other high-tech weapons, innovative tactics, and intelligence expertise provided by the Iron Wolf Squadron and its corporate parent Scion, a private military company, had allowed Poland to survive. But the cost in lives and equipment had been painfully high.

Barbeau's callous and cowardly inaction had shattered NATO. Abandoned by the larger Western powers, the Poles and their Eastern European neighbors had formed a new defense pact, the Alliance of Free Nations. Still aided by the Iron Wolf Squadron and Scion, the AFN had staved off Gryzlov's repeated attacks—in the air, on the ground, and even in cyberspace—though always by the narrowest of margins.

Then, last year, the biggest bill for Barbeau's strategic blindness and short-term political expedience had finally come due. The Russian president attacked the United States itself with his own mercenaries—using war robots reverse-engineered from captured Iron Wolf equipment. For weeks, Gryzlov's hired killers had spread death and destruction everywhere they went. They'd even tried to kill Barbeau's November election opponent, Texas governor John D. Farrell, plotting to sow political chaos that would cripple America for years to come. Only a risky covert intervention by Nadia, Brad, and Whack Macomber, piloting their own Iron Wolf combat machines, had saved Farrell's life. In a brutal battle across the Texan's sprawling ranch, they'd destroyed Gryzlov's robots . . . but at a horrific price . . . a price that included her own amputated legs.

Watching Nadia closely, Brad saw the memory of that blood-soaked night rise in her mind. *Probably for the millionth time*, he thought sadly. The pain she still felt and might always feel was reflected in her taut, motionless face.

Despite that, he knew that Poland's leader was right. Good *had* come out of all that carnage and suffering. The American people, finally fed up with Barbeau's blunders, had tossed her out of office in the 2020 presidential election—replacing her with John D. Farrell.

And now Farrell, a man who viscerally understood the threat posed by Russia to the whole free world, was working hard to repair the damage inflicted by Barbeau's shortsighted administration. Already, the United States had renewed its military, economic, and political ties with Poland and the other members of the Alliance of Free Nations. Despite protests from Moscow, American troops and aircraft were flowing into AFN bases. From now on, any further aggression by Gryzlov against the smaller Eastern European states would run the risk of sparking a war between two of the world's great powers.

"This arrival of U.S. forces on Polish soil opens many doors," Wilk explained. "Among them, it allows us to make significant changes to the composition of the Iron Wolf Squadron."

Hearing that, Nadia looked surprised and slightly guilty. For months, she'd been focused almost entirely on her own efforts to regain her strength and endurance. Understandably, she just hadn't had the time or energy to keep track of events in the larger world, even when they concerned old friends and comrades-in-arms. "What kind of changes?" she asked quietly.

"The squadron is transitioning from being a mixed unit of Polish and foreign volunteers to becoming a predominantly Polish force," Brad told her. "Sure, a few Scion advisers and technical experts will stay to help out with some of the high-tech weapons and sensors you've bought. But the rest of us expats aren't really needed here any longer. Your own guys are more than ready to take over."

She looked stricken. "You're leaving?"

"I've been offered a slot with a new Sky Masters–Scion private space enterprise," he said evenly. "Before Stacy Anne Barbeau, in her infinite lack of wisdom, mothballed the whole program, we were flying S-19 and S-29 single-stage-to-orbit spaceplanes—which are incredibly advanced spacecraft that revolutionized manned space operations.

Well, President Farrell wants those birds back in operation and flying. And pronto."

Nadia swallowed hard. "Sky Masters has asked you to be among those who will fly these spaceplanes?"

Brad nodded. "Yep."

"*Gratulacje*," she said softly. "Congratulations. That is a wonderful opportunity. A . . . a once-in-a-lifetime chance. Of course, you must go. I . . . I . . . understand." Tears glistened in her eyes. "But I will miss you."

"Not so fast, Nadia Rozek," Brad said flatly. "I haven't said I'd take the job yet."

Taken off guard, she stared back at him. "Why not?"

He grinned down at her. "Because Sky Masters doesn't want just me. They want you, too."

Her eyes widened. "They want me? To fly in space? To become an astronaut?"

Brad nodded again. "If you take the gig, you're slated for training as a spaceplane copilot and EVA specialist."

"EVA?"

"Extravehicular activity," he clarified. "A spacewalker."

"Walking in space?" Awkwardly, Nadia glanced down at her artificial legs. "Even with these?"

"Your prosthetics won't be a hindrance. Not in zero-G," Brad assured her. "They might even be an advantage. I've read a bunch of reports by astronauts with a lot of EVA time. They say most of the work is done with hands and forearms, and that legs often just get in the way. One NASA astronaut, a guy named Doug Wheelock, actually described a spacewalk as less a 'walk' and more like a space ballet danced on your fingertips."

Nodding thoughtfully, she turned to Piotr Wilk. "What do you think, Mr. President?"

"I hope you will consider this offer of an assignment with Sky Masters and Scion very seriously," he replied. "For Poland and for the whole free world, space represents the future." He studied her face. "Ultimately, though, considering the dangers involved, this must be your own decision, Major."

Nadia glanced back at Brad. "Dangers?"

"Oh, yeah," he said, with a lopsided grin. "I guess I should warn you that training for space operations will be tough . . . and dangerous as hell. Just for example, when you light the candle on an S-19 Midnight or an S-29 Shadow spaceplane, you're riding on top of thousands of pounds of highly explosive fuel. If there's even a tiny glitch, just one small malfunction . . ."

"Bad things happen?" she guessed, with the faintest hint of a wry smile of her own.

"Let's just say you could easily end up right in the middle of the biggest fireworks show anyone on the ground is ever likely to see," Brad agreed. "The man who developed the engines for the spaceplane, Hunter Noble, is nicknamed 'Boomer' for a reason."

"Good Lord," Nadia breathed.

"Then we can move on to explosive decompression, radiation hazards, micrometeorites, and a bunch of other perils. It's sort of a long list."

"So essentially you are asking me to join you . . . and risk being killed in any number of interesting new ways?" Nadia said.

"Pretty much," he admitted.

Smiling broadly now, she slipped her arm through his and laughed. "Very well, I accept. You really do know the way to a girl's heart, Brad McLanahan."

CHAPTER 3

FEDERAL SECURITY SERVICE HEADQUARTERS, THE LUBYANKA, MOSCOW, RUSSIA
That same time

From the outside, the Lubyanka hid its sordid history of terror and brutality behind the six stories of a beautiful neo-Baroque façade of yellow brick set above two lower levels layered in dark gray stone. For more than a century, the building had served as a headquarters for Russia's secret police—whether they were known as the Cheka, the GPU, the OGPU, the NKVD, or the KGB. Year after year and decade after decade, terrified political prisoners were hustled through its doors and thrown into the cruel hands of the torturers and executioners who lurked in the Lubyanka's dank and bloodstained basement.

Some Russians liked to pretend that had changed with the fall of the Soviet Union, that the excesses of the past were over, never to be repeated. See, they said in hushed voices, the old

KGB was gone, replaced by a newer and more professional intelligence and police organization, the *Federal'naya Sluzhba Bezopasnosti*, the Federal Security Service. Unlike its forerunners, the FSB was supposedly hedged in by law—answerable to both the *Duma*—the parliament—and the nation's elected president.

Looking up at the Lubyanka through the tinted windows of his black Cortege limousine, Colonel General Mikhail Leonov snorted in sour amusement. Too many of his countrymen preferred living among glittering illusions—of expanding national power and prosperity and reform—even though they still knew the darker truths in their own hearts. For Russia, the past was *never* another country. The Duma was currently nothing more than a rubber stamp for President Gennadiy Gryzlov's rule by decree. And while the old means of state terror and repression were now and then papered over with a veneer of civilized legality, they never fully disappeared.

True, the FSB's current head, Minister of State Security Viktor Kazyanov, was a weakling, more mouse than man. But Gryzlov was clever. He understood that he didn't need a stony-eyed killer like Lenin's Felix Dzerzhinsky or Stalin's Lavrentiy Beria to keep dissenters and potential rivals in line. So long as Kazyanov slavishly followed orders, the president's grip on power was secure. Gulags and mass executions were no longer necessary . . . not in an age in which social media could spread fear at the speed of light. All one needed were carefully planted rumors, a few stage-managed public arrests and show trials, and the occasional "mysterious" disappearance.

His driver pulled into the curb at the Lubyanka's main entrance.

Leonov leaned forward. "Find a parking spot around the back once I'm inside, Anatoly. I'll text you when I'm finished here."

Without waiting for a reply, he popped the rear passenger door open and climbed out. A few pedestrians scurrying past the infamous building glanced at him and then as quickly looked away, obviously seeing nothing of any interest. And why should they, after all? Who would waste time staring at yet another dull-looking Russian bureaucrat in a plain dark suit and subdued blue tie? Such men were as thick as fleas on Moscow's streets this close to the end of the workday.

Leonov knew he would have made more of a splash in his service uniform, shoulder boards, and high, peaked general's cap. But FSB officers, though nominally members of the military, preferred wearing civilian clothes while at work. Anonymity was a useful trait for spies and secret policemen. Imitating them suited his own purposes this afternoon.

Inside the Lubyanka, he was greeted by a younger officer whose own jacket and tie were considerably more stylish and expensive-looking. "My name is Popov, sir. If you will follow me? General Koshkin is waiting for you in his personal office."

Leonov raised an eyebrow at the other man's air of studied elegance. "Tell me you're not really one of Koshkin's *komp'utershchiks*."

Smiling, Popov shook his head. "One of the tech

geeks? Not me. I bathe more than once a week."
He shrugged his perfectly tailored shoulders. "No,
sir, I'm merely an errand boy for the general."

Which translates to bodyguard, Leonov thought
dryly, noting the slight bulge of a concealed pistol beneath the younger man's suit. Major General
Arkady Koshkin was evidently a careful man these
days. That was wise. Few officers reached the
higher echelons of Russia's spy services. Fewer still
could say they had survived Gryzlov's fury when a
crucial operation went sour. Fortunately for Koshkin, it appeared that even the president realized
how difficult it would be to replace him. Men with
the eclectic mix of arcane technical skills, leadership ability, and cyberwar operations experience
needed to manage the FSB's Q Directorate were
a rare breed.

Originally, the directorate's skilled programmers had been tasked with organizing and conducting Russia's covert cyberwar and computer-hacking
operations. Now, by direct presidential order, they
were also expected to protect critical defense in-
dustries and computer systems against foreign
intrusion and sabotage. Gryzlov's decree left no
doubt that this new cybersecurity role was their
primary mission.

It was a change in focus Leonov wholeheart-
edly welcomed.

He had witnessed the terrible damage an enemy
could inflict by hacking into computer programs
used to control sophisticated weapons. Three
years ago, Scion agents in Polish pay had somehow corrupted software upgrades for Russia's

S-300 and S-400 surface-to-air missiles—causing their target identification and acquisition subroutines to go haywire. The ensuing catastrophe had cost Russia many of its best Su-27, Su-30, and Su-35 fighter jets, shot down by their own air defenses. It had also cost Colonel General Valentin Maksimov, the former commander of the aerospace forces, his job . . . and, in the end, his life.

As the man who'd stepped into Maksimov's shoes, Leonov knew only too well how much depended on Q Directorate's competence. Besides the new Thunderbolt plasma rail gun, the other cutting-edge weapons, compact power-generation systems, and heavy-lift rockets needed to launch the Mars Project were nearing operational status. Gryzlov had invested a substantial portion of the nation's defense budget—and much of his political prestige—in these advanced technologies. He was convinced they would ensure Russia's dominion over the world for generations to come. With so much at stake, the president would never forgive even the slightest failure. And nothing short of complete success would satisfy him.

Leonov pondered these unpleasant truths while he followed Popov deeper into the massive building. Within five minutes, he felt lost in a maze of identical corridors with the same elegant parquet floors, pale green walls, and door after door marked only with cryptic numbers and letters. Obviously, the spies who worked here put a high value on their own secrets and privacy. Without a human guide or a map, a stranger entering the deeper recesses of the Lubyanka wouldn't have the slightest idea of which directorate was where or whose office was behind any given door.

Set in the dead center of the complex, Q Directorate was an exception to the sea of sameness.

Beyond a manned checkpoint, the parquet floors ended, replaced by sound-deadening mats. All the interior walls and ceilings were thicker, with interwoven layers of metal paneling, gypsum wallboard, wire mesh, and acoustic fill. Windows that had once looked out onto inner courtyards were gone—closed off behind new walls. In effect, the directorate's section had been converted into a highly secure facility that was virtually sealed off from the rest of the FSB headquarters.

That much at least was reassuring.

So was his first look at Arkady Koshkin himself. The head of Q Directorate was short and slight, with a high, wrinkled forehead. Eyes bright with intelligence and ambition gleamed behind thick spectacles. On the other hand, those same eyes were also wary, full of caution. They were the eyes of a man who understood that those close to Gennadiy Gryzlov necessarily danced along a razor's edge—poised between power and oblivion.

Politely, Koshkin ushered him to a chair in front of his desk and then nodded toward a small silver samovar on a sideboard. "Tea?"

Leonov shook his head. "Thank you, but no. Unfortunately, I find caffeine this late in the day is too hard on my stomach."

"Ulcers?"

"The doctors say no," Leonov said with a shrug. "Merely stress and worry."

Koshkin smiled sympathetically. "An occupational hazard of our respective professions, I fear." He looked over at Popov. "You may go, Dmitry. Colonel General Leonov and I can look after ourselves." Silently, the elegant young aide left, firmly closing the door behind him.

"Now, General," Koshkin said carefully. "What brings you to the Lubyanka?"

"First, how tight is your security?" Leonov asked, with equal care.

"In this office itself? Airtight," Koshkin assured him. "Nothing we say can be overheard or recorded in any way by foreign agents."

"Or by your colleagues in the FSB's counterintelligence department?"

Caught off guard, Koshkin blinked in surprise. Plainly buying time to think, he took off his glasses and swiped distractedly at them with a handkerchief. Then he put them back on and cleared his throat. "Is there some reason you are worried about possible surveillance by loyal forces of the state?"

Leonov's thin, answering smile didn't reach his eyes. "Only because none of your service's spy hunters hold high-level Mars Project clearances, Arkady," he said coolly. "So before you panic about being implicated as a possible traitor, get it through your head that my sole focus is safeguarding our Motherland's most vital secrets."

Relieved, Koshkin nodded his understanding. Information about the full scope of Gryzlov's new plan was restricted to a tight inner circle within the Russian government. Besides the president, Leonov, and Koshkin himself, no more than a tiny handful of others were cleared for full briefings on the project. Otherwise, individual government departments, research labs, and production facilities were told only what they needed to know to complete their own particular assignments.

"The antibugging measures I employ are effective against all forms of surveillance, whether by foreign spies or our own counterintelligence agents," he admitted.

"Good," Leonov said quietly. "Because we must be able to speak frankly to each other. To share ideas without the slightest constraint or reservation."

Koshkin looked on edge again. "Ideas about what?"

Here we go, Leonov told himself. This was where he found out if the other man understood the difference between sensible caution and crippling passivity. Or if he grasped that taking personal initiative was sometimes necessary—and might even be safer than clinging rigidly to set procedure and regulation. Careful to sound calm, almost bored, he shrugged. "About the possibility of making certain modifications to command and control programs for some of the Mars Project's components."

Koshkin stared back at him for several long seconds. "What kind of modifications?" he asked at last.

Leonov held up a hand. "First, let me make sure that I have a clear sense of how the system works, eh?" It was important not to rush this. He leaned forward. "As I understand it, your Q Directorate experts aren't actually writing any of the project's operational software themselves. Correct?"

Slowly, Koshkin nodded. "The research and development teams working on different weapons, power generation, maneuvering, and life-support systems are responsible for writing and validating their own code."

"And when they're finished?"

"My people go through each piece of software line by line—checking for anything suspicious or out of place. Once the programs have been thoroughly scrubbed, we subject them to stringent testing to make sure they work as promised—both on their own and in tandem with other crucial systems."

Leonov cocked his head. "And after that, your team embeds every piece of software in layer upon layer of high-grade cybersecurity protocols? So that no further alterations can be made . . . except by your directorate?"

Koshkin frowned, obviously not quite happy with this crude summary of a complex process. "More or less."

"In effect, then, no one else has access to the inner working elements of Mars Project software once your work is finished," Leonov continued, with a confident smile. "That's perfect. Exactly what we need."

"But I don't see what—"

"It's quite simple," Leonov explained. "Your directorate's procedures make it possible for us to do what *must* be done, without tipping our hand to our enemies—or unnecessarily worrying those here at home who might otherwise misinterpret our actions."

Tiny droplets of sweat suddenly beaded the other man's high forehead. "I will not do anything to compromise the integrity of the computer programs created for the Mars Project," he stammered.

"Don't be a fool, Arkady." Leonov shook his head impatiently. "That's the last thing I would expect." He looked Koshkin straight in the eye, choosing his words with care and precision. "I only want your programmers to create buried subroutines that will strengthen our security . . . and protect the Motherland in a worst-case scenario. Secret programs we can activate, in an emergency, to regain control over critical systems. To stop the enemy from turning our own new weapons against *us*."

"Fail-safe protocols, you mean?" Koshkin wondered.

"Exactly. I want a series of fail-safe protocols inserted into the project's operating software," Leonov agreed.

"On whose authority? Yours?"

Leonov nodded. "Yes."

"Not the president's?" Koshkin asked softly.

Leonov shrugged. "Gennadiy always expects his plans to unfold perfectly, without a hitch or snag."

"But you are afraid that the Mars Project will fail?"

"On the contrary, *I* think the president's confidence is fully justified," Leonov said flatly. "If we proceed wisely, our powerful new weapons and other technologies should give us an overwhelming advantage against the Americans and their allies. Once our space platforms are in orbit and operational, we will be free to attack targets in orbit or even on the ground without fear of serious retaliation." Then, coolly, he met Koshkin's troubled gaze. "But you and I also know—and only too well—that even the best-laid plans don't always survive contact with the enemy. Victory is never assured. Defeat is always possible. And sometimes it carries terrible consequences. Both for Russia itself . . . and for those who can be blamed for any failure."

Koshkin swallowed hard, clearly remembering the dreary procession of fellow officers, scientists, and other government officials who'd suffered the consequences of Gryzlov's wrath over the past several years. "You want an insurance policy," he realized.

"It is our duty to strive for complete success. But it is also our duty to prepare for the worst," Leonov said pointedly. "We've just spent considerably more than a trillion rubles developing some of the world's most advanced weapons and space hardware. So tell me, Arkady, are *you* willing to take even the slightest chance of letting the Americans waltz in and snatch them away from under our noses?"

"My God, no," Koshkin murmured, turning pale at the thought of what Gennadiy Gryzlov would do to anyone he held responsible for such a catastrophe. Tight-lipped now, he looked back across his desk at Leonov. "Very well, General. My programmers will do as you request. We'll create the fail-safe protocols you require."

CHAPTER 4

Brad McLanahan let the security door swing shut behind him. Then he slid his sunglasses into the pocket of his Sky Masters flight suit and stood still for a few seconds, waiting for his eyes to adjust. After the brilliant sunshine and typical scorching high-desert summer temperatures outside, something about entering the enormous hangar reminded him of the time Nadia had showed him Kraków's beautiful, centuries-old Gothic cathedral. Standing here in this equally vast, cool, and dimly lit space, he felt a touch of the same awe that had overwhelmed him then.

No surprise there, I guess, he thought. In its own way, Hangar Three was also a sacred space— though one dedicated to space-age aviation rather than to the deity. Come to think of it, he realized, maybe that impression wasn't as sacrilegious as it first sounded. To the despair of his English teachers in school, he'd never been much of a poetry fan, but some of "High Flight," written by a pilot who'd been killed during the Second World War, had stuck with him . . . especially the last couple of lines, where the poem talked about putting out your hand in space and touching the face of God.

Now that he could see more clearly, Brad focused on the big, black, blended-wing craft parked in the middle of the hangar. To a layman's untutored eye, it would look a lot like a larger version of the SR-71 Blackbird, only with four massive engines mounted under its highly swept delta wing instead of two. But to someone like him, who'd flown this model before, the distinctive shape was instantly recognizable.

That was a Sky Masters S-19 Midnight spaceplane—equipped with revolutionary LPDRS (Laser Pulse Detonation Rocket System) triple-hybrid engines. Those "leopard" engines, able to transform from air-breathing supersonic turbofans to hypersonic scramjets to pure, reusable rockets, were powerful enough to propel the spaceplane into Earth orbit. At the same time, the spaceplane, like its smaller counterpart, the S-9 Black Stallion, and its larger cousin, the S-29 Shadow, could take off and land on ordinary runways built for commercial airliners.

"Hey, kid, you planning to do any real work

this afternoon?" a tall, lanky man called from the foot of a high rolling ladder pushed up against the S-19's open twin cockpit canopies. "Or are you just here sightseeing?"

"Hey, Boomer!" With a cheerful grin, Brad waved back at Hunter "Boomer" Noble, the chief of aerospace engineering for Sky Masters and its lead test pilot for the reactivated S-series spaceplanes. "Sorry I'm late, but we had a slight problem on the last simulator run that I had to sort out."

"Shit," Boomer growled. "Tell me a newbie *didn't* just break one of the company's incredibly expensive machines?" Sky Masters Aerospace ran some of the world's most advanced flight simulators out of a converted hangar at the other end of the airport. Mounted on massive Hexapod-system hydraulic jacks, the full-motion simulators could be configured to mimic the flight characteristics and capabilities of virtually any aircraft—everything from single-engine turboprops to fifth-generation fighters like the F-35 Lightning II on up to the S-series spaceplanes. Between the company's immersive, virtual-reality simulator programs and its expert instructor pilots, Sky Masters made a tidy profit training fliers for airlines and even the armed forces of several smaller U.S. allies.

"'Break' is a harsh word," Brad said judiciously. "But I guess our trainee did bend it a little."

Boomer winced, probably imagining the outraged memos from corporate accounting that were likely to land on his desk. "Bent it how, exactly?"

"Well, it looks like a couple of the Hexapod actuators froze up when the simulator pod tried to spin end over end."

"No fucking way," Boomer said in disbelief. He pinched the bridge of his nose hard and closed his eyes for just a second. "Which one of our merry band of aspiring astronauts managed to mess up a simulator like that?"

"Constable."

"The Brit?"

Brad nodded. Peter Charles "Constable" Vasey had flown Harrier jump jets and other high-performance aircraft for the Fleet Air Arm. Several years before, bored out of his skull by peacetime service, the former Royal Navy flier had signed up with Scion. Since then, he'd flown a wide range of different aircraft for the private military company, taking part in a number of dangerous covert missions around the world. When offered a shot at flying spaceplanes for the new Sky Masters–Scion joint venture, the Englishman had naturally jumped at the chance.

From everything Brad could see so far, Vasey was a gifted pilot whose only weakness might be a tendency to push his luck and his aircraft to the limit. *Kind of like me*, he admitted to himself.

"What the hell did he do?" Boomer demanded.

"He tried to roll the S-29 in hypersonic flight," Brad said, not bothering now to hide his amusement.

Boomer stared back at him. "You're bullshit-ting me."

"Nope," Brad said virtuously. "Scout's honor. That's what he did."

"And, pray tell, what was Comrade Vasey's airspeed when he decided to commit virtual sui-cide?" Boomer asked, with yet another deep sigh.

"Mach eight."

"Jesus Christ." Boomer shook his head in sheer astonishment. At one hundred thousand feet above sea level, Mach 8 meant the space-plane was traveling at nearly forty-eight hundred knots. "What made that lunatic Brit think it was a good idea to try rolling a freaking spaceplane at Mach-fricking-eight—right in the middle of God's own little turbulent hell of skin friction and shock-wave heating?"

Brad laughed. "Constable told me he just wanted to find out what would happen in a ma-neuver at that speed. Plus, he was kind of curious to see how the simulation would handle some-thing so crazy."

"And?"

"Apparently, he and his copilot got one heck of a ride before the system went down and they lost power." Brad's grin grew even wider. "I believe it, too. When we overrode the locks and pried the simulator door open, they were hanging almost upside down in their harnesses."

Boomer eyed him suspiciously. "Who was fly-ing in the other seat during this little jaunt?"

"Nadia," Brad said simply.

"Nadia? Nadia Rozek? *Your* Nadia?" Boomer

whistled. "Oh, man. Please, *please*, tell me she killed that goofball Vasey with her bare hands when you got them unstrapped."

"Nope, I'm afraid not." Brad shook his head in mock sadness. "She was too busy whooping it up. She said it was more fun than all the thrill rides at Disneyland and Universal Studios combined."

"Swell," Boomer said wryly. "Look, Brad, I need you to ride herd on Vasey. Rein him in a little, okay? At least enough to satisfy the suits like Kaddiri and Martindale that we aren't running a total lunatic asylum here."

Brad nodded his agreement. Dr. Helen Kaddiri was the president and chairman of Sky Masters. Her Scion counterpart was former U.S. president Kevin Martindale. Neither was especially noted for having much of a sense of humor—at least not when it came to paying unexpected repair bills for expensive equipment.

Since he was one of the few surviving people with real-world spaceplane experience, Brad had been named second in command of the reactivated S-series flight program, which meant maintaining day-to-day discipline among the eager, hard-charging men and women they were training as crews was mostly his job. He couldn't pretend it was a task he enjoyed, but if that was the price of getting into space again, it was a price he was completely willing to pay. "Maybe I'll have Constable write 'I will not break my spaceplane without permission' on a whiteboard a couple of thousand times," he suggested.

Boomer snorted. "Think that'll work?"

"Probably not," Brad conceded. Mulling it over, he looked up at the sleek silhouette of the S-19 Midnight parked next to them. "Then I guess I read him the riot act. Warn him to cool his jets, or Mr. Vasey's Wild Simulator Ride will be the closest he'll ever get to actually flying one of these babies. That should settle him down a little."

"Harsh, but *seriously* motivating," Boomer agreed. "You do that."

"Speaking of actually flying . . ." Brad continued, deliberately changing the subject to something a lot nearer and dearer to his heart. He waved a hand at the spaceplane towering over them. "What's the latest word on when we can take this crate and the others out of mothballs and back into the sky?"

Boomer grinned at him. "Why? Getting itchy feet here on the ground, McLanahan?"

"Maybe a little."

The other man nodded. "Yeah, me too." He shrugged. "Not long now, I hope. Most of the birds look like they're in pretty good condition, but my crew chiefs are still checking every component from nose to tail fins. Anything that looks dodgy gets pulled."

"That can't be cheap," Brad said slowly.

"It sure isn't," Boomer agreed. "But the higher-ups saw the point when I told them it was a choice between spending a couple of million dollars on needed maintenance *now* . . . or maybe watching a spacecraft worth a couple of hundred million dollars burn up on reentry or auger into some Iowa farmer's cornfield *later*."

Brad flashed a smile of his own. "Nicely argued, Dr. Noble. I'm betting the other little fact, that you'd be one of the guys riding in the cockpit of that doomed spaceplane, wouldn't have been nearly as persuasive."

"Maybe not," Boomer allowed. "The definition of 'acceptable risk' sure changes when you're the one taking the risks." He jerked a thumb toward the rolling ladder up to the S-19's open cockpit. "Speaking of which, I've got something new to show you."

Curious now, Brad followed him up the ladder to a platform overlooking the cockpit. From this vantage point, everything about the S-19 Midnight looked identical to the one he'd flown into orbit five years before. Or, for that matter, to the digitally simulated versions he'd trained on for the last several weeks. It had the same two side-by-side seats for the pilot and copilot, who was called the mission commander—with all the usual consoles and panels crowded with touch-screen multifunction displays and other controls.

Boomer tapped him on the shoulder and pointed to a patch of metal deck visible between the seats. "See there?"

Brad squinted, and this time he spotted a small pull handle set almost flush with the deck itself. Thin, dark lines in the deck plating outlined what looked like a new hatch or compartment. That was weird. Unlike NASA's larger space shuttle, the S-19 only had one deck. Everything below the spaceplane's cockpit should be just sensor instrumentation, avionics, and heat shielding. He glanced back at the other man. "Okay, I'm officially baffled. What gives?"

For an answer, Boomer lowered himself into the open cockpit and settled into the right-hand mission commander's seat. He patted the other. "Take a seat, kid, and I'll show you."

Still puzzled, Brad climbed down into the left-hand pilot's seat. In his lightweight Nomex flight suit, it felt a lot wider and less cramped than it did when wearing a standard full-pressure space suit. "All right. Now what?"

Boomer reached down to the pull handle set between them. In one easy motion, he tugged it up and to the right. A section of the deck plating rose smoothly and pivoted away behind his seat, revealing a deep compartment extending below the cockpit. "We had to reroute some cabling and sacrifice a small amount of fuel tankage to make room for this," he explained.

Brad shot him a crooked grin. "So what's inside? A built-in bar?"

"In your dreams," Boomer said dryly. Still bent over, he caught hold of a piece of gear stored inside the compartment. Grunting with effort, he yanked a bulky, white backpack up into view. "This would be a heck of a lot easier in zero-G," he said through gritted teeth as he set it down carefully on the deck. "Here on Earth, this damned thing still weighs about fifty pounds."

Brad leaned over himself, taking a closer look at the backpack. It was about twenty inches high, eighteen inches wide, and eight inches deep. A number of ports, connectors, and valves dotted its outer surface. "That's a PLSS," he realized. "But it looks significantly smaller than the other models I've seen." A PLSS, or Primary Life Support System, contained oxygen, power, carbon-dioxide scrubbers, environmental controls, communications gear, and a small emergency maneuvering system. Astronauts wore them during EVAs.

Boomer nodded. "Yep. Our Sky Masters engineers took the advanced version of the PLSS that NASA's been working on at the Johnson Space Center and slimmed it down quite a bit. They had to, since everything has to fit into this one tight compartment." Straining, he pulled out a second life-support pack and rested it on top of the first.

"What's the trade-off involved in the reduced size?"

"These life-support packs only provide three hours of air and power, not the eight-plus hours of the bigger models," Boomer replied.

Brad frowned. "That's one hell of a negative trade-off."

"This new equipment isn't intended for routine use," Boomer said patiently. "It's all strictly for emergencies."

"Emergencies as in 'oh, shit, this spacecraft is kaput and we've gotta get out'?" Brad guessed.

"Yeah. Those kinds of emergencies."

"Three hours of life support doesn't seem like

nearly enough time for anyone to mount a rescue operation," Brad said dubiously.

"It's not," Boomer agreed. He reached down inside the compartment and retrieved another piece of gear. "Which is why we developed this little Rube Goldberg–looking device."

Brad felt his eyebrows rise. The other man was holding up a clear case packed full of smaller pieces of equipment, including what looked oddly like a large, deflated white balloon, a parachute pack, and what appeared to be a small, twin-nozzle, handheld rocket motor. "What is *that*?"

"The high-tech version of a 'Hail Mary' pass," Boomer said matter-of-factly. "More officially known as an ERO kit."

"ERO?"

"Emergency Return from Orbit." Boomer tapped the side of the clear case. "If everything works as intended, all this hardware assembles into a disposable one-man reentry vehicle." His expression was completely serious. "Way back in the 1960s, General Electric engineers designed a system they hoped would allow Gemini astronauts stranded in orbit to return safely to Earth . . . without using another spacecraft to retrieve them. They called the concept MOOSE, for Manned Orbital Operations Safety Equipment."

"But the system was never actually deployed?" Brad guessed.

"Canceled after early ground testing," Boomer acknowledged. "The ERO kit is our own up-dated version, using more advanced materials." He tapped the case. "For example, that weird balloon-like thing is actually a disk-shaped, six-foot-diameter aerogel bag with a thin Nomex cloth heat shield attached to one side and a parachute pack and retrorocket combo on the other."

"Aerogel? That's the super-lightweight stuff they call 'solid smoke,' isn't it?" Brad said slowly. At Boomer's nod, he frowned again. "But aerogel is made out of silica, basically beach sand. It's incredibly brittle."

"This is a new form of aerogel developed by NASA's Glenn Research Center out in Ohio," Boomer reassured him. "They make it out of polyimide, a really strong, amazingly heat-resistant polymer. It's hundreds of times sturdier than the traditional aerogels—so much so that you can actually support the weight of a car on a thick enough piece."

"Sounds pretty cool," Brad conceded. Then he shrugged. "But I still don't see how you turn this stuff into an honest-to-God reentry vehicle."

"ERO is really a fairly simple concept," Boomer said. "Once you're outside the spacecraft, you inflate the aerogel disk around you, filling it with a special, highly expandable polyurethane foam. That creates a conical dish shape that should remain stable at high speed when it hits the atmosphere. Then, when you're ready, you fire off those handheld retrorockets . . . and away you go—falling toward the ground at seventeen thousand miles per hour."

Brad felt his mouth fall open slightly in stunned disbelief. "You're serious?"

"Dead serious," Boomer told him quietly. "We

lost a lot of good people in orbit five years ago. I'm not willing to pass up anything that could save lives in the future."

"But has anyone actually tested this thing yet?"

"Oh, hell no, Brad," Boomer admitted with a laugh. "No one's *that* crazy!"

CHAPTER 5

Cued by the roar of four powerful turbofan engines, the crowd of reporters and aviation enthusiasts clustered outside the fence swung round in unison, like marionettes pulled by the same string. There, silhouetted against the rugged brown slopes of the Shoshone Range, a large blended-wing aircraft finished its turn toward the airport—clearly lining up for a final approach to Runway Three-Zero.

Cell-phone cameras clicked away at high speed, snapping pictures as the S-19 Midnight came in low and touched down just past the threshold. Clouds of white-gray smoke billowed away from the spaceplane's landing gear. Shimmering in the roiling heat haze, the S-19 rolled past the crowd with its massive underwing engines shrilly spooling down. Late-afternoon sunlight glinted off its twin-canopied cockpit.

Slowly, the big craft swung off the long runway onto a taxiway and headed toward a distant apron, already occupied by several other parked spaceplanes—ranging in size from the relatively tiny S-9 Black Stallion to the even larger S-29 Shadow. Gradually, once it was clear that nothing more exciting would be happening today, the crowd of onlookers started to dissipate.

Slipping easily through the chattering throng, Lieutenant Colonel Vasily Dragomirov headed toward the dark blue Buick SUV he had rented in Reno a few days ago. This was familiar ground to the veteran operative for Russia's military intelligence service, the GRU. Last year, posing as an FBI agent, he had deceived one of Sky Master's chief cybernetics engineers into handing over priceless secrets about the control interfaces used by the combat robots it built for the Iron Wolf Squadron—secrets that gave Russia the last pieces of the puzzle it needed to field its own *Kibernetischeskiye Voyennyye Mashiny*, cybernetic war machines.

For this espionage mission, he was posing as a journalist, with legitimate press credentials issued by *Zukünftige Flugzeugberichte*, a German digital magazine that specialized in aviation and space technology news. Most of its tiny staff and much larger group of freelance contributors remained blissfully unaware that the publication's funding ultimately came from Moscow.

Major Eduard Naumov looked up from his laptop when Dragomirov climbed behind the wheel of the SUV. The heavyset, gray-haired man was a technical officer with the GRU's Ninth Directorate—a specialist group tasked with analyzing advanced foreign military technology. "That was only an in-atmosphere supersonic test flight," he declared. "My working hypothesis is that this was a shakedown flight designed to identify any unexpected problems with the spaceplane's hybrid engines. That would be a sensible precaution for any complex machine after so long in cold storage."

"The S-19 did not go into space?" Dragomirov asked, surprised.

Naumov shook his head. "Not this time, Vasily." He turned his laptop so that the other man could see the map it displayed. Red dots blossomed like measles across a swath of the western and central United States. "I have gathered social media reports of sudden sonic booms— all of them occurring in the past hour. Plotting them out shows the S-19 flying a wide loop out as far as Kansas and then back here. To reach the speeds I estimate, between Mach six and Mach seven, it was undoubtedly flying at very high altitude, but definitely not above the atmosphere itself."

"Which means the Americans have not yet succeeded in restoring any of their spaceplanes to full operational status," Dragomirov realized.

Naumov nodded. "But I do not believe it will take them much longer. This successful test flight proves that."

"Then we have information worth relaying to Moscow," Dragomirov decided. He peered through the tinted windshield at the distant row of parked spaceplanes. His mouth tightened. "Somehow I doubt the news will be welcome."

THE KREMLIN, MOSCOW
The next day

With a quick, irritable gesture, Gennadiy Gryzlov swept his hand over the slick surface of the computer built into his desk. In response, new images scrolled across the large LED monitor set into the same desk. The photographs sent by the GRU team at Battle Mountain were crisp and clear. They showed a row of Sky Masters spaceplanes parked out in the open, surrounded by fuel tankers and other vehicles. Glowering, he turned to Colonel General Mikhail Leonov. "It appears the Americans are waking up from their torpor."

Calmly, Leonov nodded. "Dragomirov's report confirms what their own trade press has been saying for some time. Their new president is determined to restart his nation's manned space program. But he wants to send astronauts up in those reusable vehicles instead of NASA's expendable rockets." He shrugged. "The choice is sensible. When it comes to putting humans in orbit, the spaceplanes are much cheaper than any conventional space launch system. And their ability to fly from virtually any airfield also confers a significant operational advantage."

Still scowling, Gryzlov stared back at the photographs on his monitor. "How many of those damned things do the Americans have?"

"Based on our intelligence, those six spaceplanes are effectively their entire inventory," Leonov replied. "I count two of the older S-9 Black Stallions. Plus, the two surviving S-19 Midnights, and a pair of larger, considerably more capable S-29 Shadows." He pulled at his chin. "There *were* some reports that Sky Masters considered building a third S-29 spaceplane some years ago . . . but our agents were never able to confirm its existence."

"Why not?"

"Because even if those initial reports were accurate, I do not believe the spacecraft's construction was ever completed," Leonov said. "We know the Barbeau administration viewed the company as a political enemy and canceled all of its existing government contracts. Without federal appropriations, I doubt a private corporation like Sky Masters could afford the costs involved. Anyway, since the Americans abandoned manned spaceflight on President Barbeau's direct orders, building another spaceplane would have been nothing but wasted effort."

"Well, that's all changed now," Gryzlov growled.

Wisely, Leonov refrained from pointing out that Gryzlov himself was largely responsible for the recent shift in American space policy. The covert attacks he'd ordered against military and civilian targets inside the United States itself—culminating with an outright attempt to assassinate Stacy Anne Barbeau's presidential election opponent—had tipped the outcome against her. Now they faced a very different American president, one with every intention of reversing her earthbound policies of drift, indecision, and isolationism.

Impatiently, Gryzlov waved his hand again. The disturbing images from Battle Mountain's airport vanished from the screen. Then he shoved back his chair and stalked over to stare out across the Kremlin's rooftops and onion-domed towers. Without looking away, he demanded, "What do we know of Farrell's goals, Mikhail? What is this American really up to? Is he reactivating these spaceplanes to regain military superiority in orbit?"

"I do not believe so," Leonov said cautiously. "So far, the evidence indicates the new U.S. space program will be primarily scientific and commercial in nature."

Gryzlov turned his head. "In what way?"

"Besides a series of routine test flights to make sure the spaceplanes are safe for operational use, the Americans have only announced plans to practice orbital rendezvous with payloads lofted by heavy-lift cargo rockets like the SpaceX Falcon Heavy and its competitors," Leonov explained. "This tells me they view these spaceplanes largely as crew transports—ferrying astronauts and scientists to a talked-about new civilian space station or to spacecraft assembled in orbit for possible exploratory missions to the moon or even Mars."

"Only idiots would consider turning a revolutionary technology into a glorified bus service," Gryzlov scoffed. Then his gaze sharpened. "Which is why you should remember that Sky Masters has a long history of providing deadly weapons to our enemies around the world. And now you want me to believe its intentions are purely peaceful?" He shook his head. "I do not believe the leopard has changed its spots so completely."

"There is speculation that Sky Masters is seeking funding to develop an even more advanced follow-on spaceplane, tentatively dubbed the XS 39," Leonov admitted. "Rumors suggest it might be designed to carry weapons for use against targets on the ground . . . and in space."

"You see?" Gryzlov said cynically. His mouth tightened into a hard, thin line. "Which is all the more reason to press our advantage now— before the Americans realize what is happening. Correct?" Slowly, Leonov nodded. "Then you do your damnedest to make sure the Mars Project moves ahead as planned, Colonel General Leonov," Gryzlov told him coldly. "I don't want any excuses. I don't want to hear any bullshit about unavoidable technical delays. You tell your scientists and engineers and production chiefs that their lives are on the line this time. Understand?"

"Yes, sir," Leonov agreed. He rose to go.

"And one more thing, Mikhail," Gryzlov continued, more quietly now.

"Gennadiy?"

"Friend and old comrade-in-arms or not, your own life is on the line, too," Gryzlov said.

Leonov nodded somberly. "*That* is something I have never doubted for one moment, Mr. President."

CHAPTER 6

OVER THE PACIFIC OCEAN
Several days later

At nearly sixty thousand feet above the surface of the ocean, the view through the S-29 Shadow's forward cockpit canopy was spectacular. Seen from this altitude, the earth's curvature was obvious. The horizon fell away visibly on either side of the spaceplane's direction of flight. And while the sky was still a deep, rich blue along the edge of that distant horizon, higher up it thinned to paler and paler shades of the same color before fading away entirely into the infinite blackness of space.

"Coming up on Mach three," Peter "Constable" Vasey said, speaking through the open visor of his pressure helmet. The Englishman's gloved left hand held the sidestick controller, while his right rested on the bank of engine throttles set in the center console between the spaceplane's two forward seats. "Stand by for transition to scramjet mode."

"Affirmative. Standing by," Major Nadia Rozek replied from the right-hand mission commander's seat. "All engine readouts are nominal." Like the pilot, she wore an orange Advanced Crew Escape Suit, or ACES—a full-pressure suit similar to those once used by space shuttle astronauts and SR-71 Blackbird crews. Even after all these weeks of training, she was still astonished at how casually she now accepted the ease with which this marvelous machine attained these kinds of speeds. Their S-29 was already racing east toward the distant Pacific coast at nearly two thousand miles per hour and still accelerating rapidly.

"Mach three." Vasey had his light blue eyes fixed on his heads-up display. "Go for scramjet transition." His gloved right hand slowly advanced the throttles.

The pitch of the roar from their five powerful engines—two under each wing and one atop the aft fuselage—audibly changed.

Nadia saw the curves on her engine displays changing. "Spiking initiated," she reported. The large cone or "spike" in each engine's inlet was moving forward—diverting the air entering at supersonic speeds away from their turbine fans and into ducts where it could be compressed, mixed with jet fuel, and then ignited. Freed from the need to rely on any moving parts, their transformed engines could now push them up to around Mach 15, nearly ten thousand miles per hour.

Gently, Vasey pulled back on the stick. The S-29's nose pitched up at around twelve degrees and they soared skyward. Their angle of ascent grew steeper as their speed climbed. "Mach four. Approaching Mach five."

Pressed back into her seat, Nadia saw the sky ahead of them grow blacker. They were heading toward space, she thought exultantly—on their way into low Earth orbit for the first time.

Suddenly the S-29 Shadow lurched sharply, falling off to the right. They were thrown hard against their seat harnesses.

In that same moment, one of the readouts on Nadia's multifunction display flashed red. "Emergency shutdown on number four engine," she said tersely. Without waiting, she tapped an icon. "Shutting down number one engine to compensate." At these speeds, there was no way any control surface could possibly cope with the imbalanced thrust generated by having only one working engine under their starboard wing.

"Roger that." Gritting his teeth, Vasey tweaked his stick just a hair back to the left, struggling to keep their nearly hypersonic spaceplane out of a catastrophic spin. When flying at nearly three thousand knots, overcorrecting was almost as dangerous as undercorrecting. Responding to his slight touch, the S-29 rolled a few degrees back to the left, straightening out.

He risked a sidelong glance at Nadia. "Wake the lazy buggers for me, will you, Major?"

"Going for simultaneous engine restart," she acknowledged. Quick control inputs reconfigured the two idled engines so that neither could fire up without the other. Satisfied by what she saw,

Nadia tapped another icon. Nothing. The system function lights for both engines remained obstinately red. *"Gówno,"* she muttered in frustration. "Crap. No joy on the restart, Constable."

"Understood." Vasey spoke more formally. "Sky Masters Control, this is Shadow Two. Declaring a mission abort. Returning to Battle Mountain."

"Shadow Two, this is Control. Abort declaration acknowledged," Nadia heard Brad's voice say. For this flight, he was acting as CAPCOM, their intermediary with the Sky Masters engineers and other specialists monitoring this spaceplane flight from the ground. She sighed inside. With only three working engines, there was no way they could reach orbit—even after transitioning to full rocket power.

Gradually, Vasey lowered the S-29's nose, leveling off at a hundred and twenty thousand feet while he eased back on the throttles. The big spaceplane slowly decelerated. After a couple of minutes, he announced, "Dropping below Mach three."

The low, rumbling roar reaching them from outside the cockpit altered a bit, becoming slightly higher-pitched.

"Engine spikes reversing," Nadia confirmed. "Turbofans spooling up."

No sooner had she said that than two muffled bangs rattled through the spaceplane's fuselage. This time, the Shadow rolled sharply left. More red warning lights blossomed across her multifunction display. "Engine failure on numbers two and five," she snapped, tasting blood from where she'd bitten the inside of her lip. As she strained against her safety harness, her fingers danced across the screen, hurrying to shut off their last operational engine before it could drag them into a dizzying spiral down toward the waters of the Pacific Ocean far, far below.

The comforting roar of their engines died—replaced by the keening noise of thin air rushing past.

With great difficulty, Vasey regained control, bringing the S-29 back onto an easterly heading and slightly nose down. "APU status?" he asked coolly.

"The APU generator is on," Nadia confirmed. With all five engines dead or shut down, the S-29's auxiliary power unit was crucial. It was now the only source of the power needed to operate their computers and flight controls.

"Engine status."

She paged through diagnostic screens, rapidly evaluating the data provided by the spaceplane's internal and external sensors. "It looks like we lost multiple fan blades in both numbers two and five," she reported. "But the fan cases themselves held. The damage seems to have been contained inside the engines themselves. I show no fire or fuel-leak warnings."

Vasey nodded slightly. That was a small blessing. Using technology developed under a NASA grant, the turbofan casings for the S-29's massive LPDRS engines were manufactured out of tri-axial carbon braid. That made the casings both stronger and lighter than if they had been made out of a more conventional metal, like aluminum. "Let's try for a restart on numbers one and three."

Nadia tapped in a series of commands. If they could power up the two engines that hadn't actually failed, one under each wing, they should still be able to limp back to Battle Mountain. But when she hit the restart icon, a new row of red caution and warning lights lit up. "*Psiakrew!* Hell! Both of them show fuel-pump failures. They will not restart."

"Well, that tears it," Vasey muttered. He called the control center again. "Sky Masters Control, this is Shadow Two. We are negative return to Battle Mountain. I say again, we are negative return to Nevada. I'm afraid that we've just become a rather oversized and somewhat clumsy glider."

"*Copy that, Two,*" Brad radioed. "*Standing by for your emergency abort field decision.*"

Nadia switched her display to show the onboard computer's evaluation of their flight status and glide ratio. At their current supersonic speed and high altitude, the S-29's ratio was abysmal—something on the order of 3:1 . . . so for every thousand feet they descended, they'd cover just three thousand feet on the ground. But that would improve substantially when they got down into thicker air and slowed to subsonic speeds. In theory, they ought to be able to come close to the glide ratios achieved by modern jet airliners that had lost all their engines, somewhere between 15 and 17:1. By trading airspeed and elevation for distance, she estimated their probable maximum glide range at around one hundred and sixty nautical miles.

Given that, one quick glance at a digital navigation map showed their two best options for an emergency, engines-out landing. She flagged both in order of priority and sent them to Vasey's own display.

The Englishman's eyes narrowed for a split second in concentration as he ran through his own internal calculations. Then he nodded. "Sky Masters Control, this is Shadow Two. Submit we head for SFO, with OAK as the alternate field."

Both international airports, San Francisco and Oakland, had long runways that more than met their minimum parameters. Now that the spaceplane couldn't brake using reversed engine thrust, the flight manuals said they needed at least seventy-five hundred feet of smooth, hard-surfaced runway available for a safe landing.

"*Wait one, Shadow Two,*" Brad answered.

A minute passed, feeling like an eternity to Nadia.

"*Two, this is Sky Masters Control. Regret unable to approve requested abort to SFO or OAK,*" she heard Brad say. "*ATC says they can't clear the airspace in time.*"

"Bugger," Vasey said under his breath. With dozens of scheduled passenger and air cargo flights crisscrossing the skies above the Bay Area at any given moment, that wasn't especially surprising. But it was still very bad news.

"*Can you make Travis?*" Brad asked, sounding concerned now.

Vasey shot Nadia another glance. Frowning, she shook her head. Based on their projected rate of descent and airspeed, they would slam into the ground about eight miles short of Travis Air Force Base. Unfortunately, no other airport within their glide range had a runway that met the S-29's specified emergency requirements.

"Unable, insufficient range, Sky Masters Control," Vasey replied, sounding very cool, almost icily detached, now.

"*Copy that, Two,*" Brad said. "*Suggest you prepare to eject over the ocean. We've alerted the coast guard. They have two MH-65 Dolphin search-and-rescue helicopters on alert.*"

"Stand by on that, Sky Masters," Vasey said. He turned his head toward Nadia, with a single eyebrow arched in an eloquent, unspoken question.

Nadia shook her head. The thought of so casually abandoning this expensive and badly needed spaceplane was abhorrent to her. There must be another option, something else they could try. But what?

Through the forward canopy, a brownish haze now marked the far horizon. They were down to around sixty thousand feet and roughly one hundred nautical miles from the Northern California coast. Something about the word *nautical* tugged at her mind. Realizing what it was, she turned excitedly to Vasey. "You were a Royal Navy pilot, yes?"

He nodded with a slight, wry smile. "For my sins, I was."

"Then you have landed on aircraft carriers?"

Again, he nodded. "Hundreds of times." His smile grew wider. "But that's a nonstarter, Major.

Even a madman like me has *some* limits. I may be a damned fine pilot, but *no one* on God's good earth could put an ungainly beast like this one down on a patch of deck only a hundred and fifty meters long!"

Nadia shook her head impatiently, but with a grin of her own. "That is not enough, I agree." Swiftly, she scrolled through her computer's maps and satellite photos of different Bay Area regional and municipal airports. Settling on one, she flicked a hand across her display, sending it to Vasey's MFD. "But this one, you see?"

Intrigued, the Englishman studied her find. Sonoma County's Charles M. Schulz Airport, about fifty miles north of San Francisco, had a decent six-thousand-foot-long runway, with another six hundred feet or so of hard-packed dirt extending beyond it. Going strictly by the book, that was still too short, but flight safety manuals always built in a margin for pilot error. He whistled softly. "It's doable, by God." He flashed her a madcap grin. "So then, by God, we'll do it!"

While Vasey alerted Brad to their new plan, and secured both his reluctant approval and grudging clearance from the relevant air traffic controllers, Nadia locked the airport's Runway 32 into the S-29's flight computer. New steering cues blinked onto Vasey's HUD.

Following them, he banked the big spaceplane, turning a few degrees more to the east-northeast. They were descending rapidly now, slanting toward the ever-closer coast.

Nadia kept a close watch on their speed. After a

few more minutes, she announced, "We are subsonic again, slowing past five hundred knots." She pulled up another display, this one governing the S-29's twin fuel tanks. "I suggest we begin dumping fuel to reduce our landing weight."

"Roger," Vasey agreed. "Inert and dump our 'bomb' first." *Bomb* was Sky Masters slang for "borohydrogen metaoxide" or "BOHM." Essentially refined hydrogen peroxide, BOHM was the liquid oxidizer their engines would have needed for combustion after transitioning to pure rocket mode. While not quite as efficient as supercooled liquid oxygen, it was considerably less costly. BOHM could also be transferred by tanker aircraft—which was not yet possible for cryogenic oxygen.

Nadia typed in new orders, instructing the computers to flush the BOHM tank with helium to render the compound safe before she dumped it into the air high over the ocean. Green lights blinked, indicating the job was done. Quickly, she tapped the fuel-dump icon.

"*Bombs* away," she said with a slight, twisted smile.

Vasey blinked. "My God, really? That was terrible, Major. You should be ashamed of yourself."

"Sorry, Constable. But I've always wanted to say that," she admitted.

She waited another sixty seconds to begin dumping their conventional JP-8 jet fuel. No one in their right mind wanted to risk inadvertently mixing BOHM with jet fuel outside a "leopard" engine operating in rocket mode. Ordinarily, it took a pulsed laser igniter to set off the combination . . . but sometimes any source of friction or even just a vibration at the wrong frequency could trigger a massive explosion.

The S-29 was down to a little over six thousand feet by the time they crossed the coastline—gliding silently above a shore marked by jagged rocks and rolling, whitecapped breakers. Off to their right, Nadia could see a little town her computer identified as Bodega Bay. Ahead lay a jumble of hills and ridges. The slopes swept by winds coming off the Pacific were mostly scrub brush and tall grass. The hills and narrow valleys farther inland were either thickly wooded or a mix of terraced vineyards and fenced cattle-grazing land.

Buffeted by updrafts swirling above those slopes, the spaceplane juddered briefly. Their airspeed dropped further. Control surfaces whirred open, providing a little more lift as they flew lower across Sonoma County.

Beyond the range of coastal hills, housing developments and vineyards sprawled across flatter, more open country. Santa Rosa's more crowded streets and denser network of buildings lay ahead and to the right. The county's regional airport was off to the left, about six nautical miles northwest of the city. Live oaks lined both sides of a creek that meandered across the valley floor.

Nadia checked her navigation display. "Two nautical miles out."

"Copy that," Vasey said. He turned his attention to the airport tower controller monitoring for their approach. "Santa Rosa Tower, this is Shadow Two, descending through one thousand feet, airspeed one-nine-zero knots, full stop."

"Shadow Two, Santa Rosa Tower, winds light and from the west, cleared to land Runway Three-Two. Emergency has been declared. Rescue crews standing by," the controller responded.

The steering cues on Vasey's HUD slid sharply to the left, indicating this was the point selected for his final turn to line up on the runway. Concentrating fiercely, he tweaked the stick to follow them—rolling toward the northwest and then leveling out.

"One nautical mile out," Nadia told him.

Vasey nodded. He tapped the landing-gear icon on his own multifunction display. "Descending through five hundred feet. Gear down."

Hydraulics under their feet whined. The S-29's center fuselage gear and wing-mounted bogies were coming down. Robbed of its perfect streamlining, the big spaceplane shuddered and rattled.

An indicator on Vasey's HUD flashed solid green. "Gear down and locked."

The runway loomed ahead through the S-29's thick, heat-resistant windscreen, growing larger with every passing second. He peered ahead, blinking away a droplet of sweat. The gloved fingers of his left hand curled around the stick, making tiny movements as he fought to stay on the precisely computed glide path.

Now.

The spaceplane dropped the last few feet and touched down with a sharp jolt—right at the start of the angled yellow chevrons that marked the runway's overrun area. Braking hard, it rolled fast along the asphalt strip, slashing past the fire trucks and other emergency vehicles parked off to the side.

Looking ahead, Nadia clenched her teeth. *Święta Matka Boża*, Holy Mother of God, she realized. They weren't going to stop in time to stay on the runway's paved surface.

With another sharp jolt, the S-29 skidded off the far end of the runway. It bounced and bucked almost all the way across a furrowed dirt field before shuddering to a halt in a swirling cloud of dust . . . barely one hundred feet short of slamming nose first into a rusting metal viewing platform.

For a long, unbelieving moment, there was only silence in the cockpit. Finally, both Nadia and Vasey exhaled sharply, amazed to find themselves in one piece. Then, with wildly exuberant grins, they turned and exchanged high fives.

"Well . . . that was fun," Nadia said slowly, trying to control the tiny quaver in her voice. "But let's *not* do it again."

"Definitely not," Vasey agreed. "My mother always claimed I had a cat's nine lives. If so, that little exploit might easily have used up number seven."

Suddenly the view outside their cockpit windows went black. *"Mission complete,"* the Sky Masters computer said smoothly. Lights flickered on, outlining the door on the side of the S-29 flight simulator. *"Emergency landing successful."*

* * *

When they unstrapped and climbed out of the simulator, Brad McLanahan met them at the foot of the ladder. The tall, blond-haired young man had a grin of his own plastered across his face. "Nice job, guys!"

"We are not in trouble?" Nadia asked, surprised. "Despite choosing such a risky option?"

Surprised, Brad shook his head. "Heck no." He turned serious. "This was your graduation exercise. Losing all five engines? At hypersonic and supersonic speeds? Man, that's called a *really* bad day on the way into space. And yet you *still* figured out a way to save the spaceplane? Amazing. Believe it or not, you even managed to impress Boomer. Most trainee crews would have taken the easy way out and just ejected."

"And if we had?" Vasey wanted to know.

"You'd start over again in the simulator tomorrow morning," Brad told him. He shrugged. "Of course, the same thing would have happened if you crashed on landing. Boomer's not screwing around here. And I don't blame him. Tough, realistic training is the only real way to turn out a solid cadre of space-ready crews for these S-planes."

"So, what comes next?" Nadia asked quietly.

"Both of you already have decent experience handling high-Gs," Brad said. "So we can skip that part of the program."

"Which means we move on to zero-gravity?" Vasey guessed. "Riding the Vomit Comet?" Short of actual spaceflight, the best method of re-creating the sensation of weightlessness involved repeated high-angle parabolic maneuvers in an aircraft. During each stomach-churning climb and dive, passengers experienced short periods of zero-G. Airsickness was common, which explained the nickname.

Brad nodded. "And then you head to Houston for EVA training at NASA's Neutral Buoyancy Lab."

"It sounds . . . busy," Nadia observed.

"Too true," Brad admitted. Then his smile returned, lighting up his whole face. "But before that, we all get a whole day off for some much-needed R&R."

"You're going to show Major Rozek the cultural highlights of Battle Mountain, Nevada?" Vasey guessed, with a dry grin. "But what will you do for the next twenty-three hours and fifty-five minutes?"

Nadia laughed. "Oh, we will think of *some* way to occupy our time, Constable." Over Brad's sudden blush, she offered the Englishman a pitying smile. "We may even spare a moment to wonder what you are doing to entertain yourself."

"A hit, Major Rozek," Vasey declared grandly, putting his hand on his heart. "A palpable hit."

CHAPTER 7

VOSTOCHNY COSMODROME, AMUR OBLAST, EASTERN RUSSIA
A week later

Monitors in the launch observation bunker showed the enormous rocket waiting on Pad 3, five kilometers away. Securely nestled in a ring of retractable gantries, the three-stage Energia-5VR heavy-lift launch vehicle stood ninety meters tall and weighed more than twenty-five hundred tons. Digital readouts blinked rapidly, counting down the moments to the launch. Speakers carried audio patched in from Vostochny's control center.

"Guidance systems are configured."

"Energia flight computer is online and in control. The launch program is running."

"RD-171MV engines on standby."

"All stages look good, ready for flight."

Gennadiy Gryzlov kept his eyes fixed on the monitors while he listened to the litany of unhurried reports. For all of the confidence they displayed, he could still sense the tension in those voices—and in the shorter, barrel-chested man standing beside him. Like his subordinates, Colonel General Mikhail Leonov knew the risks involved in testing a new rocket. Much could go wrong, even though the Energia-5VR's main engines and many of its other components were based on tried-and-true systems that had flown successfully dozens, even hundreds, of times on other rocket designs.

No doubt, Gryzlov thought with amused contempt, his presence at this test launch made Leonov and the rest even more nervous. Watching their prized heavy-lift rocket explode on lift-off or disintegrate in midflight would be bad enough. But a disaster under the very eyes of Russia's mercurial, notoriously short-tempered leader would be infinitely worse . . . perhaps even fatal.

"Energia-5VR is go for launch."

Both Gryzlov and Leonov leaned forward, peering intently at the screens.

"*Zapusk*," the voice of Vostochny's flight director said crisply. "Launching."

Suddenly brownish smoke lit from within by orange-white flames billowed around the base of the huge rocket—accompanied by a low, crackling roar. "*Zazhiganiye*. Ignition."

Out the corner of his eye, Gryzlov saw the muscles around Leonov's strong, square jaw tighten suddenly. This was a rare moment, he realized: almost the first sign of an ordinary human reaction to stress. Usually, the burly commander of Russia's aerospace forces prided himself on exhibiting rigid self-control under pressure.

"*Predvaritel'naya tyaga*. Preliminary thrust," the director reported. "Booster and core engines at twenty percent. Throttling up."

Rapidly, the roar deepened, growing ever louder and more deafening. The clouds of smoke and flame grew denser and brighter. Through the shimmering heat waves curling off the launchpad, Gryzlov saw the rocket vibrate, almost as though it were a bird of prey straining to be set free.

"*Polnaya moshchnost'*. Full power." Abruptly, the blue-painted gantries that had locked the Energia-5VR in place pivoted up and away. Freed, the rocket surged upward—with what seemed surprising slowness at first and then with ever-increasing speed. "*Podnyat'!* Lift-off!"

Subdued cheers rolled through the observation bunker, echoed more loudly over the audio feed from the control center. Caught up in the excitement, several of the military officers and high-ranking civilian officials who'd accompanied Gryzlov from Moscow clapped each other on the back.

He ignored them. His whole being was focused on watching the mammoth heavy-lift rocket as it soared higher—arrowing skyward on a dazzling pillar of fire. Together, the five kerosene-fueled engines in the Energia-5VR's four strap-on boosters and second-stage central core were generating more than eight million pounds of thrust as they hurled it toward space. That was comparable to the Saturn V rockets used in America's vaunted Apollo program.

Long-range tracking cameras followed the swiftly ascending rocket as it climbed higher and higher through the atmosphere. One hundred and sixty-one seconds after launch, with the Energia-5VR already seventy kilometers above the earth and hundreds of kilometers downrange, the bright glow winked out abruptly. Four puffs of white vapor blossomed briefly around the speeding spacecraft.

"All four strap-on boosters have separated," the flight director announced, to more cheers in the control center. "Core engine cutoff was on schedule. Preparing for second-stage separation and third-stage ignition."

Gryzlov noticed Leonov's jaw clench again. This was another danger point, he knew. The Energia's third stage was powered by two brandnew, liquid-hydrogen RD-0150 engines. While more powerful and efficient than their kerosenefueled counterparts, these engines were also significantly more complex—which was one of the reasons the old Soviet-era space program had avoided using them until long after their American rivals had mastered the technology.

On-screen, the wavering, blurry shape of the rocket altered suddenly—apparently splitting in two. The larger of the two halves fell away, tumbling toward the waters of the Sea of Okhotsk. Between the four strap-on boosters and now its core second stage, the Energia had already shed more than 90 percent of its original mass. Seconds later, a bright flare appeared at the base of the much smaller section as it climbed onward.

"Good separation," the flight director reported. "Third-stage engine ignition confirmed. The burn looks good."

Gryzlov heard Leonov breathe out quietly as he relaxed.

Ten minutes later, the Energia-5VR entered a stable circular orbit six hundred and forty-four kilometers above the surface of the earth. There, over the next forty-eight hours, its payload would carry out a further set of tests and maneuvers. But for now, one thing was clear to Gennadiy Gryzlov. After decades of failure and many false starts, Russia at last had the heavy-lift rocket capability it had long desired. And it was the final piece of technology he needed to turn the Mars Project from a cherished dream into a solid reality—a reality the Americans and their allies would find nightmarish.

Openly delighted, he glanced at Leonov. "Well done, Mikhail! This was a complete success, despite all the risks." He snorted. "So much for the staid old fools who said it would take ten more years to develop the Energia-5VR." With a thin, pleased smile of his own, Leonov nodded.

Gryzlov turned back to study the monitors. They showed the projected ground track of the rocket's third stage as it circled the globe. Moving at more than twenty-seven thousand kilometers per hour, it was already well out over the Pacific Ocean. "How many of these big Energia rockets are currently under construction?"

"A dozen," Leonov told him.

"And how many of those are close to completion?"

"Four heavy-lift rockets should be available for launch in a matter of weeks, with two more not far behind," Leonov said, obviously glad to be able to report even more good news. "So we'll be able to conduct a rigorous flight-test program while still shaving months off the time needed to certify the Energia-5VR as fully operational."

"More flight tests? After this picture-perfect launch?" Gryzlov shook his head. "A waste of resources, Mikhail."

Leonov's face froze. "What?"

Gryzlov eyed him closely. "You heard me." He nodded toward the monitor. "The Americans are not fools. Not all of them, anyway. And now we've just revealed a space launch capability they never dreamed we could develop so quickly. Some of the brighter people in Washington, D.C., are going to start wondering what else we have up our sleeves." The corners of his mouth turned down. "No, we don't have any more time to throw away. Not when the Americans are already rushing to make those damned spaceplanes of theirs operational again. We need to move fast . . . even faster than we first planned."

For a long moment, Leonov stared back at him in stunned silence. "What are you proposing, Gennadiy?" he asked finally.

"*Proposing?* I'm not proposing anything. I think you mistake your place, Mikhail," Gryzlov snapped with biting sarcasm. "What I am doing is issuing *orders*." His voice grew colder. "So listen closely. You will *not* waste those expensive new Energia rockets conducting additional test flights. Instead, you will proceed immediately to the next phase of the Mars Project—the operational phase. When our next heavy-lift rockets launch, I expect them to carry the weapons and other equipment necessary to construct Mars One in orbit. Is that clear?"

Leonov's face might have been carved from stone. "With respect, Mr. President," he said, stressing every word. "I cannot guarantee the reliability of the Energia-5VR system on the basis of a single successful test flight. We were very lucky today. Tomorrow, we might not be so fortunate. Each rocket is an incredibly complex machine, with hundreds of thousands of separate parts. Even the smallest production fault or a single software glitch could be disastrous."

"You will make them work, Colonel General," Gryzlov interrupted curtly. His eyes held all the warmth of a Siberian winter. "I'm counting on you."

CHAPTER 8

THE WHITE HOUSE, WASHINGTON, D.C.
Two days later

Beyond the looming spire of the Washington Monument, the sky had turned a dark gray. Towering masses of clouds were rolling in from the south, bringing rain and predicted high winds. In the fading light, even the green, tree-covered South Lawn looked gloomy.

With a thoughtful frown, U.S. president John Dalton Farrell turned away from the Oval Office windows. After nearly six months in office, he still missed the wide-open horizons of his native Texas—especially those of the vast plains and plateaus of West Texas, where he'd made his fortune as a wildcatter in the energy industry. In the east, he felt more confined, more hemmed in, especially in crowded, bustling Washington, D.C. People here moved and talked faster, but somehow their words carried less meaning . . . and their dreams were narrower. The capital's political power brokers and federal bureaucrats had long ago mastered the art of drowning new and unconventional ideas in a morass of regulatory red tape and dreary, pompous, never-ending argument.

Then he shrugged. *Quit your bitching, J.D., pull on your britches and your boots, and get back to work*, he told himself firmly. He'd worked his butt off to beat Stacy Anne Barbeau and park himself behind the big Oval Office desk, hadn't he? Nobody'd ever promised him the job was going to be easy.

Besides, the American people had elected him for good reasons of their own. For one thing, they were sick of watching buttoned-down Washington insiders cozy up to favored interest groups, corporations, and government unions. Too many folks were getting rich playing inside baseball in this town. His commission from the voters was to break up the incestuous triangle of big business, big labor, and big government.

Outside of domestic politics, Farrell knew he faced challenges that were just as demanding. For four long years, Barbeau and her foreign policy team had sat idle, watching from the sidelines while the Russians ran roughshod over U.S. allies and U.S. interests abroad. She'd claimed she was saving American lives by avoiding unnecessary battles over insignificant places and peoples. Well, that had sure as shit come back to bite her in the ass when the Russians, masquerading as terrorist mercenaries, blew the hell out of civilian and military targets inside the U.S. itself last year.

The American people were sick of having sand kicked in their faces by Gennadiy Gryzlov. No one who was sane wanted to risk all-out war, but it was high time Moscow learned the rules had changed. Further aggressive moves by the Russians were going to be challenged, not ignored.

Which was why the two men who were being ushered discreetly into his office were here.

Neither former U.S. president Kevin Martindale nor retired Air Force Lieutenant General Patrick McLanahan was officially part of his administration. Both had made too many political enemies—inside the United States and overseas—for that to be practical. Besides, Farrell thought, naming either of them to an official intelligence agency or Defense Department slot would be a criminal waste of talent. In recent years, both men had proved they were far more effective when operating outside regular channels. Together with the Poles and the other courageous peoples of Eastern and Central Europe, their Iron Wolf Squadron and Scion weapons and intelligence specialists had held Gennadiy Gryzlov at bay—buying time for the United States to regain its senses.

Martindale's stylish, open-necked suit, long gray hair, and neatly trimmed gray beard gave him something of the air of an aging hipster playboy. While his shrewd, observant gaze dispelled that false impression, it was an image he often cultivated as a form of public-relations camouflage.

Unlike the former president, Patrick McLanahan could not conceal his own extraordinary nature. Critically injured years ago during a combat mission against the People's Republic of China, he was only alive now thanks to a remarkable piece of advanced medical hardware, the LEAF, or Life Enhancing Assistive Facility. Its motor-driven, carbon-fiber-and-metal exoskeleton, life-support backpack, and clear helmet kept him alive, despite wounds that were beyond the power of modern medicine to heal.

Farrell knew he owed both men his own life. Together with Brad McLanahan, who was Patrick's son, Nadia Rozek, and Whack Macomber, they had smashed Gryzlov's mercenary force when the Russians came storming onto his Texas Hill Country ranch to kill him. In a just world, their heroism and self-sacrifice would have earned a long period of rest and recovery. As it was, the country needed them too much for that to happen. With Russia still on the prowl probing for weaknesses, the high-tech weapons systems, intelligence assets, and combat experience Martindale, the McLanahans, and their people brought to the table were vital to the defense of the United States. It wasn't really fair, the president thought grimly, but then again, nobody ever said life was fair.

Getting back to business, he shook hands with the two men and waved them into chairs across from his desk. "I'm real glad you could fly all the way out here on such short notice. I surely do appreciate it."

"Invitations to the White House aren't exactly easy to refuse," Martindale told him wryly.

Farrell chuckled. "No, I suppose not." He shrugged. "I figure y'all probably realize this isn't a social call."

"That's too bad, Mr. President," Patrick said with a crooked, self-deprecating grin of his own, plainly visible through the clear visor of his LEAF helmet. His exoskeleton whirred softly as he leaned back in his chair. "Think of the tabloid headlines you could trigger: 'President Hosts Space Alien at State Dinner.'" His expression turned more serious. "But since this little get-together is about business, what can we do for you?"

"Well, for starters, I need your take on this big-ass new rocket the Russians fired off," Farrell said bluntly. "The one that's ruffled so many feathers in the Pentagon and the commercial space industry. To hear some of those folks squawk, this is the second coming of Sputnik."

"Seeing Moscow succeed at something most experts thought was outside its reach for at least another decade is naturally somewhat disconcerting," Martindale answered, a bit stiffly now.

"Experts that included you?" Farrell guessed, with a fleeting, sidelong grin.

Reluctantly, Martindale nodded. The head of Scion prided himself on his often uncanny ability to identify threats and trends that other, lesser analysts and defense experts had missed. Finding himself roped in with the common herd was never a very welcome development. "But what worries me even more is that the Russians pulled off this space launch without any of us getting a whiff of what they were planning."

"Our recon satellites snapped pictures of their new rocket out on the pad days before it took off," Farrell commented. "So we did get *some* warning."

"Months late," Patrick countered. "More probably, years late." He shook his head. "Moving this new heavy-lift Energia-5VR design from the drawing board to the launchpad must have required years of research and development, millions of man-hours, and tens of billions of dollars—involving aerospace engineering teams and factories all over the Russian Federation. With all that going on, we should have picked up solid intelligence about this program a long time ago. Instead, all we heard were a bunch of unsubstantiated rumors . . . none of which made it seem like the Russians were anywhere close to building a real working spacecraft."

"Gennadiy Gryzlov is proving entirely too adept at hiding his intentions and capabilities from us," Martindale agreed grimly. "And that is dangerous. Very dangerous."

Privately, Farrell shared that assessment. He didn't expect much yet from the CIA or the alphabet soup of other U.S. intelligence agencies. Under Stacy Anne Barbeau, the CIA and the rest had been thoroughly politicized. Analysts and agency heads who parroted the administration's preferred slant on global events had been praised and promoted. Those who stubbornly insisted on seeing the world as it really was had been muzzled and shunted aside into dead-end assignments. Fixing the damage would take months, maybe even years. But learning that Martindale's Scion intelligence-gathering teams—with their hard-earned reputation for competence—had also been caught off guard was seriously alarming.

Frowning, he looked over at Patrick. "NASA claims this new rocket is in roughly the same class as SpaceX's Falcon Heavy. Does that line up with what your own analysts at Sky Masters and Scion see?"

"Yes, sir," the other man said. "In fact, we believe the Energia-5VR could be even more capable than the Falcon Heavy. Preliminary data suggest the Russian rocket may be able to put close to a hundred tons of payload into low Earth orbit, compared to around seventy tons for the Falcon."

"A thirty percent payload advantage?" Farrell mused. "That's a big deal." He looked across his desk. "Sounds like SpaceX and our other commercial space companies could have some serious competition on their hands."

Patrick disagreed. "The Energia's boosters aren't reusable. Gryzlov's new space vehicle is damned big, but otherwise it's a pretty conventional design—with significantly higher launch costs. He can't hope to compete effectively in the commercial market . . . not unless Moscow is willing to dole out huge government subsidies for every launch."

"Subsidies that friend Gennadiy won't be able to afford for very long, even if he wanted to," Martindale chimed in. "The fracking and oil exploration boom your market-based energy policies have unleashed is putting serious downward pressure on world oil prices. Russia's economy is heavily dependent on oil and gas revenues, so Gryzlov must know he's going to be facing tight budgetary constraints in the not-so-distant future."

"And yet somehow he found the money to develop this new heavy-lift rocket of theirs, right under our noses," Farrell pointed out.

Martindale shrugged. "In my experience, Russian leaders will gladly beggar their people to build weapons or gain a strategic advantage. But politically speaking, I don't think even Gryzlov can risk doing the same thing just to benefit a bunch of rich Western businessmen who want to launch satellites and other cargo into space."

Farrell nodded slowly, working through Martindale's analysis in the light of his own experience. Gryzlov was popular with ordinary Russians because they believed he was a strong leader dedicated to national greatness. His people would make sacrifices for the sake of pride or patriotism. But if they started believing their sacrifices were only made to enrich others, especially foreigners, all bets were off. His jaw tightened. "Okay, if the Russians aren't making a play for the commercial space launch business, then why in God's name build a monster like this Energia rocket?"

"There are three possibilities," Patrick offered. "First, this was just a one-off flight, a Potemkin village–like exercise to demonstrate Russia's greatness."

"That's a lot of money to blow for a few television pictures and headlines," Farrell said dubiously.

"Yes, sir," Patrick agreed. "And I can't see Gryzlov wasting resources that way."

"So if this wasn't a PR stunt—?" Farrell prompted.

"Developing a heavy-lift launch system could

be a first step toward restarting Russia's deep-space exploration program. With an added fourth stage, my best guess right now is that an Energia-5VR-class rocket could send a spacecraft with a mass of up to twenty tons into lunar orbit . . . or maybe even beyond."

"Beyond lunar orbit?" Farrell said, surprised.

Patrick nodded. "Remember, those rumors we picked up earlier? The ones we couldn't confirm? Well, a lot of them talked about something called *Proyekt Marsa*, the Mars Project."

"Mars?" Farrell stared at him. "You think the Russians could be planning a manned mission to Mars?"

"Possibly," Patrick said, with a slight shrug. "When we beat them to the moon in 1969, the Soviets took a serious propaganda hit. Gryzlov might be hoping to do the same thing to us. If the Russians send cosmonauts all the way to Mars while we're still dicking around in low Earth orbit—"

"The U.S. would look like it couldn't organize a pissing contest in a goddamned brewery," Farrell finished with a grimace. Then he shook his head. "But even so, a Mars landing would still be just a PR exercise. And a hellaciously expensive one at that."

"Not if it marked the beginning of a more permanent program of exploration and colonization," Patrick said quietly. "One way or another, whoever controls outer space is going to end up controlling the earth." He spread his hands. "But you're right about the expense, sir. And I don't see how Russia could hope to fund the kind of massive effort that would be necessary—not with its current resources."

Martindale leaned forward. "Which brings us to the third possible interpretation of this so-called Mars Project, Mr. President. One that's frankly much more probable, given Gennadiy Gryzlov's track record."

"Y'all think this could be a secret military space program," Farrell realized.

Martindale nodded. "Mars *is* the god of war, after all."

"With what objective?"

"We don't know yet," Patrick admitted reluctantly. "Further study of the Energia launch and, most likely, the unusual deployment of the rocket's third stage before it deorbited and burned up over the Pacific Ocean earlier today could yield some answers. But right now we're still working the problem."

"Seems like the bright boys and girls who put together my daily intelligence briefings missed a few things," Farrell muttered, jotting down a reminder to himself to light a small fire under his national security staff about that. He looked up again. "Okay, shoot. What was so odd about the behavior of the Energia's third stage?"

"First, that third-stage burn put it into a circular orbit tilted, or inclined, at roughly fifty-one point six degrees," Patrick told him. "That's virtually the same orbit used by the old International Space Station and by our own Armstrong Station before the Russians destroyed it. With one big difference."

"Which is?"

"The Energia's third stage climbed to four hundred miles above the surface before going into orbit," Patrick explained. "That's approximately one hundred and fifty miles higher than the normal operating altitude for either the ISS or Armstrong." Armstrong Space Station was America's military space station that was attacked and brought down by Russian spaceplanes a few years earlier.

"Got it." Farrell nodded. "So then what?"

"Based on observations from our ground-based telescopes and from satellites, the stage—which must have been basically just a big empty fuel tank by then—spent the next several orbits using thrusters to carry out a set of complex maneuvers . . . a wide range of different pitches, yaws, and rolls . . . and all of them in rapid succession." Patrick frowned while he worked through the probabilities. "I'm confident that what we witnessed were tests of the flight control software and maneuvering thrusters needed for computer-controlled orbital rendezvous and docking with other spacecraft."

Martindale tossed in his own two cents. "That would be my bet, too. The Russians relied pretty heavily on automated systems to fly their old Soyuz and Progress capsules to the International Space Station. The odds are they're planning to do the same thing with a new generation of spacecraft."

Farrell looked from one man to the other with a puzzled frown of his own. "Okay, I must be missing something here, because none of this sounds off-kilter to me. What's so all-fired strange about the Russians testing out their spacecraft maneuvering systems?"

"Nothing in and of itself. It's the orbital altitude for those tests that bothers me," Patrick explained. "Reaching a four-hundred-mile-high orbit requires a longer engine burn and consumes significantly more fuel. And every pound of fuel a rocket burns is a pound less of useful payload it can take into space. Why develop a powerful new space launch system like the Energia and then essentially end up devoting a sizable fraction of its payload capacity to extra fuel?"

"It sure sounds mighty inefficient," Farrell said.

Patrick nodded. "It *is* inefficient. Which means the Russians have some compelling reason for practicing routine spacecraft maneuvers that far above the surface." His exoskeleton whirred softly as he shrugged his shoulders again, in frustration this time. "But I just can't put my finger on it. At least not yet."

"This could be a defensive move," Martindale reasoned out slowly. "Four hundred miles is beyond the effective range of our mobile Standard SM-3 antiballistic and antisatellite missiles, right? And while our ground-based missile defense interceptors at Vandenberg Air Force Base in California and Fort Drum in New York can boost that high, they're optimized to engage targets coming in at suborbital speeds and on very different trajectories. Maybe Gryzlov wants to be sure we can't easily shoot down whatever spacecraft he's planning to send up."

"Maybe so," Patrick agreed. His mouth twisted in anger. "But by the same token, that orbit is also safe from Russia's own S-500 SAMs and those MiG-31-lofted Wasp missiles he used to knock Armstrong Station out of the sky five years ago." He exhaled sharply. "Considering what we owe him, that son of a bitch is probably right to be running scared."

"What about the spaceplanes Sky Masters is re-activating on my orders?" Farrell asked suddenly. "Could the Russians see them as a threat? What's their effective operational ceiling?"

Patrick stared at him for a long moment. Through the clear LEAF helmet, his face showed first stunned realization and then chagrin. "I think you just scored a bull's-eye, Mr. President," he said slowly. "Four hundred miles up is right on the outer edge of the orbits we can maneuver into with our S-planes . . . at least in their current configuration." Looking even more concerned now, he shook his head. "I don't believe that's an accident. Whatever Gryzlov has planned, he's making sure we can't interfere."

CHAPTER 9

**EVOLUTION TOWER, INTERNATIONAL
BUSINESS CENTER, MOSCOW, RUSSIA**
Several days later

Tekhwerk, GmbH—a jointly owned German and Russian import-export company—ran its Moscow operations out of a large suite of offices on the forty-second floor of the ultra-modern Evolution Tower. Its corporate owners viewed the skyscraper's unique architecture, a DNA-like spiral created by a slight offset of each floor from the one below, as a valuable symbol of Tekhwerk's business focus on advanced industrial equipment. Those who knew how much of its profit came from surreptitiously helping the Kremlin obtain sanctions-limited high technology saw the building's twisting, corkscrew shape as an equally apt visual metaphor.

Crooked they might be, but it was just as clear that the import-export company's senior managers worked long hours. Even this late in the evening, its offices were still brightly lit.

When his secretary came in, the big beefy man who called himself Klaus Wernicke looked up from the thick dossier he'd been studying. He peered at her over the edge of his reading glasses. "Yes, Oksana?"

"Fräulein Roth is here, Herr Wernicke," the plump, middle-aged Russian woman said primly, with a hint of disapproval in her voice. In her view, corporate executives, especially those in accounting, should definitely not turn out to be young, good-looking redheads like this woman Erika Roth.

With a nod, Wernicke flipped the file closed. "Show her in, please." He glanced at his watch. "And then you may as well go home. It's very late already, and I expect it will take some hours for Fräulein Roth and me to finish going through the financial reports she's brought from Berlin."

"Very well, Herr Wernicke," she said tightly. From the rigid set of her shoulders, it was clear that she suspected paperwork was the last thing on her employer's mind. Turning on her heel, she pulled his office door open wider. "Herr Wernicke will see you now . . . Fräulein," she snapped.

Wernicke hid a smile when his guest came in. Though the young woman was dressed demurely in dark gray wool slacks, a white-collared cotton shirt, and a dark blue double-button blazer, there was no denying that she was remarkably attractive. No doubt many men would have been tempted into sin and vice by her beauty just as his secretary prudishly imagined he was.

He waited impassively until the door closed behind her and then got up from behind his desk. For a big man, he moved with surprising ease. "Welcome back to Moscow, Sam."

Amusement sparkled in Samantha Kerr's bright blue eyes. "I don't think the dragon guarding your gate likes me much, Marcus. Should I bring her chocolates next time?"

"It couldn't hurt," Marcus Cartwright said, with a thin smile of his own. "How was Berlin?"

"Damp, dreary, and cool when I passed through." Sam shrugged. "Which was still better than my time in D.C. By the way, Mr. Martindale said to give you his regards."

"I'm touched," Cartwright said dryly. "I had no idea our mutual employer was such a people person."

Ultimately, Tekhwerk was owned by Kevin Martindale and his private military corporation, Scion—though that fact was hidden from the Kremlin by a byzantine chain of holding companies and investment firms. Revenues earned by the company's day-to-day business deals paid for intelligence-gathering and covert-action operations inside Russia itself. Better yet, the need for frequent travel between its scattered offices and associated enterprises provided convenient cover for Scion operatives disguised as Tekhwerk executives and employees . . .

. . . such as Scion field agents Samantha Kerr and Marcus Cartwright.

At Cartwright's invitation, Sam dropped gratefully onto a leather couch with a spectacular view of the Moscow skyline. She'd been on the move for what seemed like days—ever since Martindale briefed her on this new assignment. Almost from the moment the Energia heavy-lift rocket launched, Cartwright and his small team of operatives had been working around the clock to collect intelligence on Moscow's new space program. Sam's orders were to assist them, by any means necessary.

Cartwright took a seat across from her. "Quite frankly, I'm very glad you're here. We desperately need a fresh pair of eyes." Now that he was off his feet, the big man looked almost as tired as Sam felt. "So far, the best thing I can say about this operation is that none of my people are dead or in an FSB interrogation cell. Not yet, anyway."

"That sounds ominous," Sam said lightly.

"Hyperbole and I are not old friends," Cartwright said grimly. "We've hit roadblocks at every turn. Both the Plesetsk and Vostochny launch sites are completely locked down, totally off-limits to anyone without special high-level security clearances. The same goes for Star City, where rumor says there's a very hush-hush cosmonaut training program going on."

Sam leaned forward with a frown. "Locked down in what way, exactly? Roving police patrols and checkpoints?"

Wearily, Cartwright shook his head. "More like minefields, barbed wire and bunkers, searchlights, mechanized infantry units, T-72 and T-90 tanks, helicopter gunships, and antiaircraft batteries. There's no way I can sneak a black-bag clandestine team past that kind of security. Nothing bigger than a butterfly has the slightest chance of getting within ten kilometers of any of those places without being detected, intercepted, and killed." He looked her right in the eye. "I've seen nuclear-weapons storage depots and ICBM bases with weaker perimeter defenses."

"So forced entry isn't an option either," she realized.

"Not unless Mr. Martindale can whistle up a team of those Iron Wolf combat robots for us," Cartwright agreed dourly.

Sam sighed. "That might be considered just a tad unsubtle."

Almost against his will, the big man smiled. "I suppose so."

"You said entry to Plesetsk, Vostochny, and Star City required special security clearances," she said slowly.

"Correct."

"Can we forge the necessary IDs?" Sam asked. It was a tactic the two of them had relied on in the past, all the way up to masquerading as officers on Russia's general staff. Scion's false document section had a justly earned reputation for working miracles.

"No," Cartwright said bluntly.

Now there was a surprise, Sam thought. She stared at him. "Why not?"

"Because we don't even know what the damned things look like," the big man told her. "Security clearances for what we *think* is called 'the Mars Project' are issued only to those on a special list tightly controlled by Gryzlov himself."

She frowned. "Tricky."

"That's not all," he said gloomily. "From what little we've been able to confirm, there's yet another layer of security—beyond those special ID cards. Even with the right documents, no one gets past the perimeter of any of those sites without positive biometric confirmation of their identity."

"Do tell," Sam murmured. "Well, that certainly suggests the Russians have something worth hiding. Something very big and very nasty."

Cartwright nodded. "No question there."

She leaned back against the couch, pondering the problem further. As a first step, they needed to focus their efforts. The Vostochny and Plesetsk launch sites were remote and difficult to reach from Moscow. They were also tight-knit technical communities devoted to a common purpose, firing off rockets into space. Strangers would stand out, no matter how good their forged documents. More importantly, U.S. reconnaissance satellites could easily monitor any new Russian spacecraft rolling out for launch. That was the sort of data-driven espionage America's official intelligence agencies had mastered long ago, from the earliest days of the Cold War.

The trouble was that this was primarily a human intelligence problem, Sam decided. Learning that Moscow had developed more powerful rockets meant little unless they could also figure out how the Russians planned to use them. All of which led her back to Star City and its rumored top secret cosmonaut training program. Finding out what these brand-new cosmonauts were being trained to *do* would answer a lot of questions. So figuring out how to penetrate the security around Star City was where the Scion team should devote its time, energy, and resources.

Cartwright nodded when she explained her reasoning. Then his broad face darkened. "But there's the rub, Sam," he pointed out with regret. "The equation's damnably simple: no special ID card and biometric confirmation, no access. So we're right back where we started: stuck outside the Star City security perimeter without a way in."

"So we take this one careful step at a time," Sam said dispassionately, concealing her own doubts. Seeing a veteran operative like Marcus Cartwright so spooked by Gryzlov's new security measures was not a confidence builder. "And the first step is taking a closer look at one of those new Mars Project identity cards."

The big man frowned. "Easier said than done, I'm afraid. As far as we can determine from distant surveillance, nobody with Mars-level clearance goes anywhere without an armed escort. Pulling a snatch job to grab one of those IDs would be messy as hell—"

"And end up triggering Russian security service red alerts from here to Vladivostok," she finished in disgust.

Cartwright nodded gloomily.

Now what, genius? Sam asked herself silently. Scion didn't recruit field agents who froze at the first hurdle. Obstacles, Martindale often said coldly during debriefings, were there to be overcome—not used as an excuse for failure. Sure, it was the kind of rear-echelon motivational bullshit that tempted a lot of people to strangle him . . . but that didn't make it any less true.

Thinking hard, she stared out toward the twinkling lights that marked Moscow's crowded city center, distantly noting her own reflected image superimposed on the darkened glass. During the last half hour the summer sun had slipped below the horizon. Somehow, she knew, they needed to lay their hands on a Mars Project ID. Which was manifestly impossible. So how was she supposed to untangle this particular Gordian knot?

Something about the way her own face stared back at her from the window tugged at her mind. And then, quite suddenly, Sam saw a path forward, or at least its first tentative, faltering steps. She looked back at Cartwright. "Okay, we don't try to steal a Mars Project ID card itself," she said cheerfully. "We just steal its soul."

Seeing the puzzled look on her colleague's broad face, she laughed. "Remember what some cultures think will happen to them if someone takes their picture with a camera? We don't need a physical copy of the identity card. We just need a good, solid image. At least as a start."

CHAPTER 10

SKY MASTERS AEROSPACE, INC.,
BATTLE MOUNTAIN, NEVADA
The next day

Brad McLanahan rapped on the open door of Hunter Noble's office and then poked his head around the doorjamb. "You called, O mighty wizard of aerospace engineering?"

With a tired nod, Boomer waved him inside. He was on the phone, listening to someone talking fast while he scrawled notes on a crumpled piece of scrap paper. "Yeah, I got it," he said briskly. Sighing, he hung up and rubbed hard at his eyes. "Man, I feel like a dog that actually caught the car it was chasing."

"Busy?" Brad asked in sympathy.

"With a capital *B*," Boomer said. "We're landing new contracts with the Pentagon, Poland, and other U.S. allies so fast that it seems like the ink isn't even dry on the paperwork before the next one hits my damned desk."

Brad nodded. Barbeau's administration, always eager to funnel federal defense dollars to favored campaign contributors and equally determined to punish companies it distrusted, had virtually blacklisted Sky Masters for four long years. Now free to compete fairly, without a hostile White House tipping the scales against it, Sky Masters was on a roll—beating out defense industry competitors with new aircraft, weapons, and sensor designs that were astonishingly innovative, cost-effective, and close to operational readiness.

"Anyway, I'd better stop bitching about all our good luck," Boomer said, ostentatiously crossing his fingers. "Dame Fortune is a fickle lady, after all. No sense in making her mad. The table will go cold soon enough."

Brad nodded seriously, hiding a smile. In his off-hours, the other man was an avid and successful amateur gambler, with a reputation for winning more than he lost at the big-name casinos in Reno, Lake Tahoe, and Las Vegas. But even the professionals knew there were moments when you caught a winning streak . . . and times when no amount of skill, intuition, and mathematical genius could affect the outcome. "I sort of figured you called me over here to work through that little flight-planning problem my dad and Martindale dumped in our laps."

"You figured right." Boomer shook his head. "But increasing the orbital maneuvering capability of our S-19s and S-29s at four hundred miles above the surface? 'Little' isn't exactly the word I'd choose to describe that kind of challenge."

"How about . . . difficult?" Brad suggested.

Boomer snorted. "More like totally freaking impossible." He leaned over and tapped a few keys on his computer. On the far wall of his office, the large LED screen he used for conferences with his widely scattered engineering teams lit up. "Unfortunately, figuring out how to match the orbital reach of that new Russian heavy-lift launcher is only part of the problem we face if Moscow starts screwing around in space again. Check this out, young Jedi."

Obediently, Brad swiveled in his chair to study the digital map of the earth the big screen now showed. A series of bright yellow lines across the face of the planet in a sine wave pattern showed the ground track of an orbit inclined at 51.6 degrees. They rose as high as southern Canada and Russia and as low as the southernmost tip of South America.

Boomer pressed another key. Red circles lit up across the territory of both the Russian Federation and the People's Republic of China, intersecting the projected orbital tracks at several points. Brad narrowed his eyes. "Those are the estimated engagement zones for deployed Russian and Chinese antisatellite weapons, right?"

"You got it in one, Brad," Boomer said with approval. "Of course, that's pretty much what I'd expect from General McLanahan's fair-haired boy." He nodded at the circles. "Thanks to our friends in Scion, you're looking at the best available intelligence on where Moscow and Beijing have stationed their S-500 surface-to-air missile regiments. Martindale's spooks didn't tell me where this information came from. And since I'm allergic to federal maximum-security prisons, I sure as hell didn't ask."

Brad nodded. Over the years, Kevin Martindale's private military company had regularly obtained highly classified data from U.S. intelligence databases without being detected. Even with an ally in the White House these days, he had a sneaking hunch that Scion analysts still didn't waste much time making formal requests to their counterparts in the National Geospatial-Intelligence Agency, the CIA, or others. He looked at the map again. "What about Russia's MiG-31Ds? Do we have any intel on their current status?"

"Ask and you shall receive," Boomer said graciously. More red circles appeared across southern Russia. These were centered on a network of air bases ranging eastward from Vornezh in the west to Yelizovo Airport on Siberia's Kamchatka Peninsula in the east. The MiG-31D was a high-altitude, Mach 3–capable fighter. Used in an antisatellite role, MiG-31s could fire Wasp missiles, an air-launched variant of Russia's Iskander theater ballistic weapons. "See the problem?"

"Yeah, I do. All too damned clearly," Brad said slowly, staring at the map. Thanks to their S-500 SAMs and MiG-31-launched Wasp missiles, Moscow and Beijing were poised to interdict a huge portion of low Earth orbit, all the way up to two hundred and sixty miles. Any spacecraft or satellite flying through those missile engagement zones was in danger of being shot down—including the S-19 and S-29 spaceplanes their Sky Masters team was working so hard to restore to flight status.

Sure, Sky Masters could launch into equatorial and low-inclination orbits instead, avoiding the risk of interception. But accepting those restrictions would mean conceding a huge swath of the most militarily, scientifically, and economically useful space above the earth to Gennadiy Gryzlov or to China's almost equally dictatorial leader, President Zhou. That would be one hell of a big and bitter pill to swallow, he thought grimly. And if Moscow's heavy-lift rocket program was part of a space-based military move against America or its allies, as his father and Martindale suspected, that gauntlet of ground-based missiles and MiG-31s would stop any possible Sky Masters counterattack cold.

Brad looked back at Boomer. "There has to be a way a spaceplane can dodge those potential kill zones," he said stubbornly.

"Oh, there is," the other man agreed. "Say we light the candle and head for space out over the Pacific, right? Out where no missile can touch us?" Brad nodded. "Okay, so once the spaceplane is safely in orbit around the equator, we execute another series of burns using the LPDRS engines in rocket mode," Boomer went on. "Essentially, we combine a plane change maneuver to shift our orbital inclination with a couple of fast-transfer burns to increase altitude." He shrugged. "And hocus-pocus, *abracadabra*, all of a sudden we're coasting along in orbit over Russia well beyond the reach of Comrade Gryzlov's menacing missiles—"

"With nearly empty fuel tanks," Brad realized abruptly.

"Pretty much," Boomer said. "The delta-v requirement for that kind of stunt is huge. Yeah, we can do it, but only by spending most of the fuel needed for other significant on-orbit maneuvers or to make a powered reentry."

Brad winced. Carrying out the maneuvers Boomer described would foreclose a lot of options. Reaching its final orbit with dry main-engine fuel tanks would leave a spaceplane entirely dependent on its much smaller, much less powerful hydrazine thrusters. It would also mean reentering the earth's atmosphere like the old space shuttle—using atmospheric drag to slow down until the spaceplane could glide safely to a landing. And that kind of high-drag reentry always inflicted damage to thermal protection tiles on the fuselage and wings, adding to mission costs and turnaround time.

"Well, that sucks," he grumbled.

"Tell me about it," Boomer said, sounding discouraged. "But however much I hate running up against problems I can't solve, I just don't see a workable way forward here. In the short run, we can't squeeze any more efficiency out of the S-19 and S-29 engines and thrusters."

Brad frowned, thinking out loud. "Maybe we could add auxiliary fuel tanks—"

Boomer shrugged. "We could, but only at the cost of passengers or cargo or crew. Or defensive and offensive weapons, if the Russians are planning new military operations in orbit against us. Mass is mass."

Brad pointed at the shelves lining the wall behind Boomer's desk. They were crowded with detailed scale models of every aircraft and spacecraft the other man had ever flown or worked on. "There's the XS-39 you're designing," he pointed out. "It'll have spare payload capacity according to the specs I've seen."

With a weary smile, Boomer shook his head. "The XS-39 is a beaut," he agreed. "The trouble is, right now it's just a collection of design drawings and models. We're at least a couple of years away from getting a prototype into space, even with a crash R&D, flight-test, and manufacturing effort."

Feeling more frustrated than ever, Brad bounced to his feet and started pacing around Boomer's cluttered office. All his life, he'd had a hard time sitting still—especially when he was thinking hard. As far as he was concerned, Rodin's famous sculpture *The Thinker* just showed a guy who looked constipated. Maybe, he mused, anyone who honestly tried to capture the process of real thought in solid stone should finish up with the blurred, impressionistic shape of a man in motion.

The high-pitched sound of two powerful jet engines spooling up broke in on his distracted thoughts. Drawn to the sound like a moth to the flame, Brad turned around to stare out a window that overlooked McLanahan Industrial Airport's main runway. He froze for one brief instant, pinned in place by a sudden burst of inspiration as it flashed through his restless mind.

Then he swung back again, unable to control a wild, shit-eating grin. "What if I told you the solution to our problem is out there right now, just staring us in the face?"

Curious now, Boomer got up from behind his desk and came over. "Yeah? So what have I missed?"

Brad nodded toward the runway, where a twin-engine Boeing 767 airliner was preparing for takeoff. It was one of the modified aircraft Sky Masters used as aerial refueling tankers for the S-series spaceplanes after they took off and climbed to thirty-five thousand feet. To make sure the spaceplanes had enough fuel for the rest of the mission, it was standard practice to top off their tanks before they lit their scramjets and rocketed into orbit.

Impatiently, Boomer shook his head. "Nice try, Brad. But there's no way we can pump in more fuel from those 767s. Not without completely re-jiggering the cargo hold and fuel system to cram in additional tankage. And even then, we'd still be sacrificing payload capacity we need."

Brad's grin grew even wider. "You are being way too literal here, Dr. Noble." He tapped the window. "I'm not talking about that 767 in particular. I'm talking about the whole concept of in-flight refueling. Transferring fuel from one aircraft to another is an old game. So why not try the same thing in space?"

For a long moment, Boomer just stared at him.

Then he looked again at the big tanker aircraft taxiing past on the runway . . . and back to one of the cutaway scale models behind his desk, this one an S-29 Shadow. His eyes narrowed in concentration while he worked through rapid-fire mental estimates of payload mass and necessary equipment modifications. Slowly at first and then faster, an answering smile spread across his face. "You know, Brad," he said with growing excitement. "That could actually work!"

CHAPTER 11

NASA's Neutral Buoyancy Laboratory occupied the core of a large white warehouse like building, the Sonny Carter Training Facility, located about ten miles southeast of Houston and right on the edge of Ellington Airport. Essentially, the NBL was an enormous indoor swimming pool. More than two hundred feet long, a hundred feet wide, and four stories deep, the tank held over six million gallons of water. Full-scale mock-ups of old International Space Station modules and newer spacecraft were submerged at different points below the surface.

While it was not a perfect simulation of the microgravity experienced in Earth orbit, training in the giant pool had allowed NASA astronauts to practice complex EVA maneuvers and tasks before flying missions aboard its now-retired space shuttles or aboard the ISS. Now it was being leased by Sky Masters, both to train its own spaceplane crews and for what Jason Richter, the company's CEO and chief inventor, euphemistically called "special technology development research."

Today two of Sky Masters' best customers were here to view Richter's most recent invention.

Awkwardly, Patrick McLanahan climbed down from a black Cadillac Escalade and into the sweltering heat of a southeast Texas afternoon. With Kevin Martindale at his elbow, he headed into the large, air-conditioned building. Two of the former president's bodyguards trailed along close behind.

Patrick walked rather stiffly, like an elderly man afflicted with osteoarthritis. The motor-driven LEAF exoskeleton and attached life-support pack he wore could keep him alive, but they would never make him graceful. Not that he would ever have been mistaken for Gene Kelly before he'd been hurt, he thought wryly.

Inside the massive NASA facility, they climbed a staircase up to the main pool deck and stopped to get their bearings. All around them, the Neutral Buoyancy Lab was a hive of activity. Small groups of technicians in jeans and short-sleeved polo shirts were busy at various places throughout the huge building—working on different types of equipment or helping trainees into cumbersome EVA suits. Divers wearing wet suits bobbed at the water's edge, ready to submerge and assist them at a moment's notice. In skybox-like control rooms fixed above the pool, teams of scientists and engineers monitored each practice session.

"Where, oh where, is Dr. Richter?" Martindale said quietly in his ear. "I do hope he remembers that he asked us to come here today."

Patrick smiled. Jason Richter had a deserved reputation as both a brilliant cybernetics engineer and a superb high-technology project manager. He had an equally well-earned reputation for occasionally losing all track of time while ironing out the bugs in pieces of prototype hardware. Working with and, from all accounts, sleeping with the elegant, highly focused Helen Kaddiri, Sky Masters' president, had rubbed off some of his rougher edges . . . but there were still moments when Jason was more of the geeky tech wizard than the buttoned-down corporate executive.

"General McLanahan! Mr. President," he heard, and turned to see the tall, fit-looking Richter headed their way at a fast clip. The other man looked ready to burst with enthusiasm.

"Brace yourself," Patrick murmured to Martindale. "My guess is that we're about to be shown the world's Eighth Great Wonder."

"And offered the chance to buy it, no doubt," Martindale agreed dryly.

"Hey! Glad you guys could make it," Richter told them with a broad grin when he joined them. He looked Patrick up and down. "It looks like that LEAF we designed and built for you is ticking over okay."

"I'm still breathing," Patrick acknowledged

gratefully. He chuckled. "Even if I don't get asked to dance very often."

Richter nodded seriously. "Sorry about that. I know the software interface between the exoskeleton's servos and the other hardware is a little rough." He pulled at his chin. "You know, we might be able to tweak that some. If you could set aside just a day or two to come to the lab, we could run a few tests and—"

"Excuse me, Dr. Richter," Martindale interrupted politely, though with the faintest hint of an edge to his voice. "But I believe you wanted to demonstrate some sort of revolutionary new space hardware for us?"

The other man visibly dragged his mind away from the complex problem of improving the LEAF's mobility and back to the present. "That I do, Mr. President," he agreed, grinning again. He guided them over to the edge of the Neutral Buoyancy Lab tank. "You came at the perfect time. We're right in the middle of an operational systems test. And I'm betting a huge portion of the Sky Masters R&D budget that you'll be mightily impressed by what you see."

More curious than ever, Patrick peered down into the blue-tinted depths. There, near the bottom of the enormous pool, he saw three strange machines maneuvering slowly around what appeared to be a space station module. They were egg-shaped spheroids—about nine feet tall and a little under eight feet in diameter at their widest point. The spheroids were equipped with several mechanical limbs ending in flexible appendages that resembled large, articulated metal fingers. Dozens of tiny thruster nozzles studded surfaces covered in advanced composite materials.

"Dr. Richter?" Martindale asked slowly. "Just what the devil are those machines?"

"They're a newly developed variant of CIDs, our Cybernetic Infantry Devices," the other man said proudly.

Patrick raised an eyebrow in disbelief. CIDs were combat robots—twelve-foot-tall human-piloted machines with two arms, two legs, and a six-sided head equipped with a wide range of advanced sensors. Covered in highly resistant composite armor, their powered exoskeletons were faster and stronger than any ten men combined. Feedback from haptic interfaces translated their pilots' smallest gestures into exoskeleton motion, allowing them to move with extraordinary precision and agility. In battle, they employed a wide range of deadly weaponry, everything from 20mm autocannons to electromagnetic rail guns. In conflicts over the past several years, CIDs had shown themselves to be lethal killing machines—as had Russia's own marginally less capable war robots.

Frankly, though, the egg-shaped spheroids he saw leisurely gliding through the depths of the NBL tank bore about as much resemblance to one of the Iron Wolf Squadron's manned combat robots as an octopus did to a grizzly bear.

"We've optimized this new design for zero-G operations and orbital construction work," Richter explained. "When it comes to maneuver and combat, a CID's humanlike arms and legs make sense in Earth-normal gravity. Not so much in space. Those multipurpose limbs attached at various points all around each spheroid are a lot more practical in an environment where there's essentially no 'up' or 'down.' That's also why their thrusters are oriented to fire in all directions. Right now they're fighting a lot of drag from the water in that tank. But out in space, in a vacuum, they should be extraordinarily maneuverable."

Martindale nodded pensively. He looked up at Richter. "Do these marvelous new machines of yours have a name?"

The other man hesitated. Selecting equipment names and acronyms had never been his forte. No matter how hard he tried to come up with something that was both descriptive and memorable, people usually told him his choices were awful—like the CIDs themselves and that LEAF he'd built for General McLanahan. "Well," he said nervously, "I *was* going to call them Cybernetic Orbital Construction Systems—"

"Oh God, no," Patrick said hastily, knowing exactly how any red-blooded pilot and astronaut like Hunter Noble or his own son would pronounce COCS. "Please tell me you did *not* stick that label on those things."

Richter winced. "There was some pushback," he admitted.

"So what *are* they called?" Martindale wondered. From the pained look on his face, he was prepared for something even worse.

"Cybernetic Orbital Maneuvering Systems, or COMS for short."

Martindale relaxed. "Well, at least COMS has the virtue of being a relatively safe choice," he said carefully. "Which I suppose is a blessing in these troubled times."

Relieved, Richter turned back to Patrick. "If you're interested, General, I can transmit copies of the technical specs for the COMS to you."

Patrick nodded. "I'm definitely interested." He frowned. "But one thing bothers me right off the bat. Those machines are way too big to fit through any standard airlock. How are we supposed to deploy a COMS from one of our spaceplanes?"

Richter shrugged. "You could retrofit a larger airlock into the S-19 and S-29s."

"That sounds rather expensive . . . and time-consuming," Martindale said. His mouth creased in a thin, dry smile. "There are limits to our resources, even with access to the federal government's top secret black-ops budget."

"The trade-offs would be worth it," Richter said persuasively. "Our data show that a single COMS can do the EVA work of any five conventionally suited astronauts . . . and in half the time."

Patrick whistled. "Okay, that's pretty damned impressive." He turned to Martindale. "One of the things we learned in building the ISS and Armstrong Station is that EVAs are incredibly demanding—both physically and mentally. Mechanical tasks that require only minor exertion on Earth take a lot more effort and time in orbit. The simple becomes hard. And the hard is almost impossible. If these space-rated robots are as good as Dr. Richter claims, they could be a real game changer."

Martindale nodded. "Acquiring this capability is extremely tempting," he agreed. Then he frowned. "But I worry that we may not be able to afford the time we'd need to retrofit our spaceplanes. Further flight delays could put us fatally behind the Russians."

"You know, come to think of it, you might not even need to change out the airlocks in the first place," Richter said suddenly.

Both men turned to stare at him. "Come again?" Patrick said slowly.

"Each COMS is effectively a miniature spacecraft, with its own life support," Richter pointed out. "So their operators should be able to ride them safely to orbit inside the cargo bay of any Sky Masters spaceplane. All each COMS would need is some bracing against acceleration and hard maneuvering. Plus, the haptic interfaces we use to control each machine should be a fantastic cushion against G-forces." His eyes lit up. "Once the S-plane reaches orbit, it just opens its cargo bay docks, the robots unlatch, and out they fly—ready to perform their tasks."

"Are you sure about this, Dr. Richter?" Martindale asked seriously.

The other man nodded. "We'll run some more tests and simulations to confirm that it's feasible, but figuring out if this will work or not isn't really rocket science." He saw their pained expressions and hurried on. "Okay, yeah, it actually *is* rocket science. Trust me, though, it's not the complicated kind. We *can* do this."

Patrick nodded slightly to Martindale. From an engineering and flight safety perspective, Richter's proposal sounded plausible enough. Sending COMS operators to orbit inside a cargo bay was probably somewhat riskier than he made it sound, but there were always risks involved in any spaceflight. Space was an incredibly hostile environment. You could improve your odds of survival with careful planning, rigorous training, and reliable equipment—but you could never entirely guarantee it.

"Very well," Martindale told Richter. "I think we have a deal, assuming your numbers pan out."

"They will," the other man said confidently. "In the meantime, I've got a couple more things to show you." He signaled one of Sky Masters technicians monitoring the robots at the bottom of the tank. "Tell COMS One to cut it short and return to the surface, Mike."

Patrick and Martindale watched with interest while one of the robots broke off from its work on the space station module. The machine rose slowly—cloaked in a cloud of bubbles from its maneuvering thrusters. Once it bobbed to the surface, a crane carefully lifted the COMS out of the water and set it down gently in a specially constructed cradle that kept it upright.

"So Humpty-Dumpty is safely back in the nest," Martindale murmured irreverently.

Patrick grinned. Seen out of the water, the

spheroid-shaped robot did look a hell of a lot like a big metal egg. He leaned forward, watching closely as a tight-fitting hatch on one of its flanks unsealed and then whined open.

"Meet my star COMS pupil," Richter said smugly.

A figure wearing a helmet and a silvery carbon-fiber space suit wriggled out through the opening and dropped lithely to the ground. The suit, which used electronically controlled fibers to compress the skin instead of pressurized oxygen, showed off every one of her curves.

"I'll be damned," Patrick muttered, seeing Nadia Rozek's triumphant face beaming back at him through the visor of her helmet. "That woman certainly gets around."

"Major Rozek is wearing a space suit as protection against vacuum if the COMS' outer shell is breached," he heard Richter explaining to Martindale.

"So who are the other two guinea pigs running the robots down there in the pool today?" Patrick asked. "Brad and Boomer?"

"No." Richter laughed. "That's my last surprise, General. Nadia was the only astronaut inside a COMS today. Between data links, the power of each machine's haptic interface and computer, and the advanced autonomous systems we've built into these robots, a skilled operator can pilot up to three machines simultaneously—using one for intricate tasks while the others handle easier or more repetitive work."

Patrick stared at him. "You're not bullshitting me?"

"Not in the slightest," Richter replied.

Astounded, Patrick looked back at the strange-looking machine resting quietly on its cradle. Calling the Cybernetic Orbital Maneuvering System revolutionary was almost an understatement, he decided. Sooner or later, humans were bound to rebuild permanent structures in Earth orbit. And when they did, this new technology would give Sky Masters and the United States and all their other allies an enormous competitive advantage.

CHAPTER 12

Right on schedule, the orange-and-gray-painted commuter train from Moscow pulled into the Tsiolkovskaya station and squealed to a stop midway along an open platform. Seconds later, passenger car doors slid open and a handful of middle-aged men and women in civilian suits and military uniforms stepped off the train—scientists, engineers, and administrators returning to Star City from high-level meetings at the Kremlin and other government ministries. Each was accompanied by a pair of security officers, hard-faced men who were assigned to keep an eye on them whenever they left the heavily guarded confines of the Star City cosmonaut training complex.

A wire fence topped with cameras and other sensors sealed off the station platform. Soldiers stood guard at the only opening in the barrier, a security checkpoint controlling further access to the compound. One by one, the passengers and their escorts filtered through the checkpoint—handing over their special ID cards for close inspection and submitting to biometric scans.

Unnoticed by any of them, a tiny, brown, birdlike glider circled silently overhead. The ultralight, palm-sized spy drone contained only a miniaturized digital camera and a few cell-phone components creating a communications link.

On the top floor of a dingy apartment building a mile outside the Star City security perimeter, a short, whip-thin young man tweaked the stick on a small handheld controller. His eyes were fixed on the images scrolling across the screen of his laptop computer. "Good pictures coming in now, Sam," he said in a lilting Welsh voice. "And I've no trouble with the Wren Bravo. None at all. The winds are just right and she's responding beautifully."

Samantha Kerr nodded. "Thanks, Davey."

David Jones was one of the veteran Scion operatives assigned to Marcus Cartwright's Moscow-based intelligence team. The ultralight Wren glider he controlled was a more advanced version of the Cicada, a miniature reconnaissance drone first developed by the U.S. Naval Research Laboratory in Washington, D.C. Cicadas were designed for use in mass swarms after being dropped over targets by manned aircraft and larger drones. They were intended to gather intelligence on large-scale enemy troop movements using a range of lightweight, low-bandwidth sensors. In sharp contrast, the camera-equipped Wren Bravo, like its microphone-carrying cousin, the Wren Alpha, carried out much narrower and more focused missions—conducting photo reconnaissance and surveillance of individual human targets. Floating silently on the wind, riding thermals rising from the ground as it circled, it was almost impossible to detect.

Signals between Jones and the bird-sized Scion spy drone were being relayed through a portable dish antenna he'd set up on the apartment's balcony. Anyone who noticed the dish would only assume the tenants, an elderly pensioner and his equally aged wife, had decided to sign up with one of Russia's increasingly popular satellite television providers. Right now, though, the old couple was enjoying a rare vacation trip to the Black Sea—courtesy of the large sum of cash Sam had paid to rent their small, cramped flat.

Sam smiled to herself, remembering their delight and their hushed assurances that they would be "very discreet, very careful." It was obvious they assumed she was a high-class prostitute who wanted to use their flat as a rendezvous for clients who worked inside Star City. She'd been very careful not to disabuse them of the notion. After all, it was the best kind of cover story, one dreamed up by the very people she wanted to deceive. Hadn't someone once said the lies you told yourself were always more convincing than falsehoods told by others?

"There we go! I've got what you wanted, look now," Jones said suddenly. He tapped a key on his laptop, freezing some of the pictures on its screen. "See here?"

Sam leaned forward, peering over his shoulder. The Wren had managed to capture good, clear images of at least two of the special Mars Project identity cards. Running those pictures through digital enhancement software should improve them to the point where Scion's document forgery specialists could work their black magic. "Nicely done, Davey," she said with delight. "Pull the Wren back now and set it down someplace near the highway. We'll scoop it up on our way back to Moscow."

With another small tug at the controller, Jones obeyed—breaking the tiny glider out of its orbit over the Tsiolkovskaya station and sending it sliding away downwind. Once the Wren ran out of airspeed and altitude, it would simply fall into the tall grass beside the road. There wasn't much risk of discovery even if someone else stumbled across the little spy drone before they could retrieve it. Most people would assume they'd only found a child's toy.

From across the tiny apartment, Marcus Cartwright caught Sam's eye. "I still don't see the point of this exercise," the big man grumbled. "Even with perfectly forged Mars Project IDs, we won't be able to break into Star City, or the Plesetsk and Vostochny launch sites. Our names and genuine biometric data aren't on Gryzlov's tightly controlled list of approved personnel . . . and we have no way to add them."

Sam nodded. The special cybersecurity protocols created by the FSB's Q Directorate to shield the Mars Project were too strong. Any attempt to hack through them would only set off alarms. "I agree," she said evenly. "Which is why we're not going to try cracking the perimeter security at any of those sites. Fortunately, we don't need to."

"Then what the hell is the point of going to all this trouble to forge some of those damned IDs?" Cartwright ground out through gritted teeth.

"Come now, Marcus," she said with a smile. "You know my methods."

"Sexual allure and carefully controlled violence?" he retorted.

"Well, okay, maybe not *those* methods," Sam said with a low, throaty chuckle. Taking pity on him, she explained her thinking. They needed a work-around. If they couldn't get into Star City themselves, they needed the next best thing— the chance to interrogate someone with direct, personal knowledge of the cosmonaut training program.

"Think about it," she said. "Moscow's apparently working up an elite cadre of military cosmonauts, right? Well, how many candidates usually make it all the way through that type of rigorous training?"

"Ten percent?" Cartwright said slowly. "Maybe twenty percent? Tops."

"Exactly," Sam said in satisfaction. "So there's

bound to be a much larger number of guys who made it through some part of the training course before washing out. We just zero in on the right cosmonaut wannabe and ask him a few pointed questions—backed up by the appropriate credentials. We don't need Mars Project ID cards that can actually spoof Gryzlov's multiple layers of security. We just need fakes that'll convince someone who's seen them up close and personal before."

Cartwright frowned. "There are around five hundred thousand men and women serving in Russia's aerospace forces," he said dryly. "Not counting those who've recently left the service. How do we find the right needle in a haystack that big?"

"Only a handful of those five hundred thousand people have the necessary qualifications to make it as a cosmonaut," Sam pointed out. "So that haystack of yours is really more like a handful of straw." She smiled sweetly. "Besides, Russia's Ministry of Defense personnel files aren't nearly as tightly guarded as the rest of Gryzlov's top secret programs, are they?"

"No, they're not," Cartwright agreed slowly. The Russians devoted a lot of cybersecurity effort to securing databases with information on weapons systems performance, procurement, and deployment. They spent far less energy safeguarding more mundane service and pay records. Exploiting this blind spot had paid dividends for Scion in the past. He looked at her. "So once we find the man you're looking for, then what?"

"Ah, Marcus," Sam said with a knowing grin. "That's when the *real* fun starts."

SECURE CONFERENCE ROOM, VOSTOCHNY COSMODROME, EASTERN RUSSIA
A short time later

The large conference room adjoining Vostochny's control center was on lockdown. Stern-faced members of Gennadiy Gryzlov's plainclothes security detail stood on guard outside. For the duration of this top secret briefing on the Mars Project's launch status, no one would be allowed in or out.

Inside the room, Colonel General Mikhail Leonov occupied the chair next to Gryzlov. Vostochny's launch director, Yuri Klementiyev, sat across the table from them. No one else was present in person. Two secure video links connected them with the launch directors at Plesetsk and the Baikonur space complex in Kazakhstan. A third monitor showed Colonel Vadim Strelkov listening in from Star City's cosmonaut training center. Strelkov would command the Mars One station once it was in orbit and operational.

"Our preparations here at Vostochny are proceeding on schedule," Klementiyev said confidently. He touched a control, bringing up live feeds from cameras around the cosmodrome. One television picture showed a massive Energia-5VR heavy-lift rocket already in place on Pad 3, secure within the ring of retractable gantries. Another feed focused on a second, still-horizontal Energia space launch vehicle as it rolled slowly out of the main assembly building aboard a powerful freight train. "Barring unforeseen technical problems, both rockets will be fueled and ready for launch within forty-eight hours."

Leonov nodded in satisfaction. Forty-eight hours was well inside their planned window. Given the number of problems that could crop up before any scheduled lift-off—ranging from glitches with the spacecraft itself to unexpected bad weather—it was always best to have plenty of time in hand.

The news from Plesetsk, located more than eight hundred kilometers north of Moscow, was equally good. Once mainly used to test new ICBM designs, the sprawling cosmodrome's space launch facilities had been upgraded and expanded in recent years. Four rockets —two more big heavy-lift Energia-5VRs and two smaller medium-lift Angara-A5s—were either in position, ready for launch, or moving out to the pads.

Keeping his face impassive, Leonov listened carefully to the final site status report, this one from Baikonur's Russian launch chief, Alexei Gregorjev. If it weren't for Gryzlov's sudden decision to drastically accelerate their timetable, he would have entirely avoided using the old space complex they were now leasing from Kazakhstan. In his judgment, the need to hide their real purposes and plans from Kazakhstan's independent government represented a grave threat to the Mars Project's secrecy. Kazakhstan's leaders were too interested in developing closer economic ties with both the People's Republic of China and the United States to be wholly reliable allies. If Kazakhs grew suspicious and started investigating Russia's recent activity at Baikonur, they could cause serious trouble. But as it was, Leonov had no real choice. To meet the president's ambitious schedule, he needed both Baikonur's LC-1 launchpad and the two-stage, crew-rated Soyuz-5 rocket assembled in its production facility.

"The Soyuz-5 is ready for launch," Gregorjev told them. "All indications show that the Federation orbiter is also fully flight-ready."

"Is your cover story still holding?" Leonov asked.

Gregorjev nodded. "Yes, sir. As far as the Kazakhs and the international journalists here are aware, this spacecraft is only an unmanned test version." He hesitated a moment. "Then again, why should they think otherwise?"

Leonov nodded back grimly. The Federation orbiter was Russia's next-generation manned spacecraft, similar in shape and size to NASA's Orion and SpaceX's Dragon. In normal circumstances, no one would ever contemplate sending a crew into orbit using a wholly untested spacecraft design. During their Apollo moon landing program, the Americans had flown no fewer than eight flights with unmanned command modules—checking and rechecking the hardware and electronics to make sure everything worked as planned. Even during the opening, highly competitive days of the space race, Russia itself had conducted seven test launches of the first Vostok capsule designs without human cosmonauts on board. From a safety standpoint, what Gryzlov demanded—firing six men into space aboard a vehicle that had so far been proven reliable only in computer simulations—was sheer madness.

But when he'd pointed out the serious risks involved, Gryzlov had dismissed his concerns with a casual shrug. "Apollo and Vostok were peacetime space programs, Mikhail. You and I are embarked on a military operation, where risk and reward go hand in hand, do they not?" His gaze had turned cold. "Show me a commander unwilling to take chances and I will show you a coward."

Now Gryzlov leaned forward, taking a direct part in the video conference for the first time. "How do the most recent weather forecasts look?" he demanded, addressing himself to the three directors at Vostochny, Plesetsk, and Baikonur. "Is there the slightest chance of a serious delay in any of our launches?"

One by one, they assured him the current forecasts were good, with only the minor possibility of a mild storm front pushing through Plesetsk before their scheduled launch date. Leonov, listening closely to these seemingly enthusiastic reports, nevertheless caught the faint undercurrent of anxiety emanating from his subordinates. Like him, they understood the grave dangers involved in flying so much new equipment without adequate tests. But like him, they also understood that they no longer had an alternative.

By now, the Americans, alerted by pictures

taken by their spy satellites, would know that
something very strange was going on at Russia's
space complexes. Moving seven rockets simultaneously toward launch readiness represented an
unprecedented level of activity. Very soon, Moscow could expect a flood of pointed, suspicious
queries from Washington.

No, Leonov thought, there was no going back.
Russia was committed. And win or lose, they
stood on the brink of a new age.

However, it still came as something of a shock
when he heard Gryzlov issue the final necessary
and irrevocable order to the military cosmonauts
on standby at Star City. "Colonel Strelkov," he
said flatly. "You will proceed immediately to Baikonur with your first Mars One crew and prepare
for launch."

CHAPTER 13

**THE WHITE HOUSE SITUATION ROOM,
WASHINGTON, D.C.**
The next day

President John Dalton Farrell let the satellite imagery displayed on the Situation Room's large wall screen speak for itself. Hours ago, the pictures collected during routine passes over Plesetsk, Vostochny, and Baikonur had sent shock waves rippling through the federal government's intelligence, defense, and space agencies—first among the analysts who interpreted them and then upward through level upon level of management. Now, finally, those shock waves had reached Washington's top decision-making echelon, the president and his national security team.

He looked down the crowded table toward his secretary of state, Andrew Taliaferro. Shorter than Farrell by a head, the former congressman from North Carolina already had a good working knowledge of foreign affairs when he'd been tapped to run Foggy Bottom. Almost as important in the president's eyes was Taliaferro's reputation as a top-notch amateur poker player. The way Farrell saw it, anyone that skilled at reading other people under pressure ought to have a distinct advantage in diplomatic negotiations. "Well, Andy? Did you hear back from Moscow yet?"

"I spoke to Foreign Minister Titeneva an hour ago, Mr. President," Taliaferro said. He snorted. "While she denied any personal knowledge of specific space program plans, the foreign minister assured me that the Russian Federation remains committed to the peaceful exploitation of outer space."

"Basically, just the usual diplomatic boilerplate."

Taliaferro nodded. "But Titeneva also sounded somewhat nervous to me. More than I would have expected, considering the way she's backed all of Gryzlov's aggressive moves from the moment he took office."

Farrell raised an eyebrow. That was interesting . . . and worrying, too. As Russia's chief diplomat, Daria Titeneva was famous for her uncompromising willingness to defend her leader's actions—no matter how far they strayed outside diplomatic norms and the rule of international law. Her slashing verbal attacks on the United States, Poland, and other Western allies both in public forums like the UN Security Council and in private talks were equally notorious. So what did it mean if one of Gryzlov's closest political allies—a woman even rumored to be his mistress—was so obviously on edge about whatever he was doing?

Frowning, Farrell glanced at his White House science adviser, Dr. Lawrence Dawson. "Any luck with Roscosmos, Lawrence?" Roscosmos was the government megacorporation in charge of Russia's civilian space program.

"I reached out to Director Polikarpov," the tall, rail-thin astrophysicist said dryly. "He was not very helpful. When I asked him why they were prepping so many space vehicles at one time, he claimed it was nothing more than random chance—the result of their new Energia program ramping up to the next phase of flight testing earlier than expected at the same time as other, older rockets were scheduled to carry replacement communications satellites into orbit." He shook his head in disgust. "In my former academic life, I flunked many undergraduates who came to me with far more plausible excuses."

Farrell shared his science adviser's assessment. Polikarpov's explanation had the distinctive odor of "the dog ate my homework" about it. He looked around the table and focused on the pragmatic, gray-haired woman he'd named to head the CIA. Unlike the incompetent but telegenic nonentity Stacy Anne Barbeau had foisted on Langley, Elizabeth Hildebrand was a talented, hardworking intelligence service professional with decades of experience in both analysis and operations. "Anything to add here, Liz?"

Hildebrand shrugged. "Not as much as I would like, Mr. President," she admitted. "Our HUMINT networks inside Russia are virtually nonexistent at the moment. Until we can recruit new sources, which could take years, my analysts are largely dependent on what they can glean from satellites and signals intelligence—or even from trying to read between the lines in public news sources."

Farrell nodded sympathetically. Even under competent leadership, HUMINT, or "human intelligence"—the art of recruiting and running agents—had never been the strongest suit of America's different intelligence agencies. That was part of the reason he'd reached out to Kevin Martindale and Scion for help right after taking the oath of office. Nevertheless, he judged it would be useful to hear the CIA's views. After all, even a blind squirrel could find a nut once in a while. "Taking that as a given," he pressed her gently, "how do your people see this?"

"Their general view is that the Russians may be feeling pressured by the recent successes of our American private space enterprises—and also by your determination to bring the Sky Masters spaceplanes back into active service. The consensus is that Moscow is planning a space 'spectacular' of its own to capture the imagination of the world and the interest of potential commercial customers."

"A spectacular," Farrell repeated flatly. He nodded his chin at the satellite pictures still frozen on the Situation Room's big screen. "Like firing off those seven rockets from three different launch complexes?"

"Quite possibly," the CIA director agreed. "According to stories circulating in the trade press and on some of the more reliable space news blogs, the Russians hope to radically compress their historically slow development and test cycle for new space hardware—especially those Energia heavy-lift rockets and their advanced Federation crew capsule. Launching so many rockets in such a short time would also demonstrate their ability to outbuild and outfly NASA or any other potential Western competitor." She shrugged. "Those reports do seem to match up with what our satellites are seeing."

"Except that those stories are nothing but a combination of speculative bullshit and deliberate Russian disinformation," a cool, hard-edged voice broke in abruptly from the back of the room.

Around the table, startled faces turned toward the man who'd spoken out so bluntly.

Farrell hid a grin. He'd been warned that Patrick McLanahan had both a flair for the dramatic and a take-no-prisoners attitude when it came to shredding arguments with which he disagreed. "Go on, General," he said with a small nod. "What are we missing?"

His servos whining softly, Patrick stood up and stalked over to the screen. "You're all forgetting just who you're dealing with," he said forcefully. "Gennadiy Gryzlov doesn't give a damn about space commerce. He's focused on one thing and one thing *only:* achieving global domination through overwhelming military superiority."

"Relying so heavily on perceived motivations

can be a risky exercise, General," Elizabeth Hildebrand said carefully. "In the long run, it's usually wiser to assess an opponent's capabilities and go from there."

"Sure. And that's the other thing you're missing," Patrick said. He waved an exoskeleton-cradled hand at satellite photos on the screen. "Everyone's fixated on the rockets waiting out on those launchpads. But those rockets don't matter a damn. Not in the end. They're just transportation. Their primary purpose is moving payload from the earth's surface into orbit." His expression was bleak. "Payload is what counts. And right now it sure as hell looks like Gryzlov is poised and ready to put four-hundred-plus *tons* of payload into low Earth orbit . . . all in only days or maybe even just hours."

Farrell saw Lawrence Dawson's eyes widen in amazement. "Four hundred tons of payload capacity," the science adviser mused slowly. "That is extraordinary. It required roughly that much mass to build the old International Space Station."

His observation drew low whistles of dismay from around the long table. It had taken dozens of separate rocket and space shuttle launches over more than a decade to assemble the ISS. Learning that the Russians might be able to replicate that grueling feat in a matter of days was sobering, to say the least.

Farrell felt cold suddenly. He turned to Patrick. "Isn't that also about the same size as our old Armstrong military space station, the Silver Tower, General?"

Steadily, Patrick looked back at him. "Yes, sir. It is." He shook his head. "And that's what has me scared."

BAIKONUR COSMODROME, KAZAKHSTAN
That same time

For more than sixty years, the silence of the desert steppe around Baikonur had been broken periodically by the crackling roar of powerful rockets as they soared toward space—or by shattering explosions when launches failed. Built by the Soviet government at enormous expense and amid tight security, the huge Baikonur complex was a sprawling labyrinth of nine separate launch complexes, two airfields, and dozens of buildings dedicated to vehicle assembly and cryogenic fuels production. A network of five-foot-gauge industrial railroad tracks tied all these facilities together.

Seen from above, the soil around Baikonur was a colored patchwork of browns, off-whites, rusts, and pale ghostly blues. Toxic chemicals draining from thousands of spent rocket stages had stained them forever. Sunlight glittered off mounds of contaminated scrap metal.

Looking down from the twin-engine Mi-8 helicopter ferrying his six-man Mars One crew north from Krayniy Airport, Colonel Vadim Strelkov supposed he should see some bitter irony in the desolation wrought here by man's efforts to escape the very planet that had given birth to humanity. As it was, he only felt impatient to arrive at their destination. They were heading for Baikonur pad LC-1, called "Gagarin's Start" because Yuri Gagarin's historic first manned space flight had lifted off from there sixty years before.

Leave irony to the poets, he thought. They had time to waste on nonessentials. He had none.

Strelkov and his five crewmen were traveling under false identities. Their papers and passports identified them as "technical observers" from Roscosmos, Russia's civilian space agency. As far as the cosmodrome's Kazakh landlords were concerned, they were here solely to monitor the first test flight of the new Federation orbiter. By the time they learned otherwise, it would be too late. Strelkov and his cosmonauts would be safely in space, far beyond the reach of any earthbound authority.

Or dead, he reminded himself coldly.

True, the Federation spacecraft was a beautifully designed machine. But like any highly complex device, the orbiter depended on the perfect functioning of tens of thousands of interconnected mechanical parts and electronic systems. If too many of them failed under the stress of launch or on exposure to the hostile environment of space, what had been a working spacecraft would instead become one of humanity's most expensive coffins.

Following in Gagarin's footsteps, Russian cosmonauts had developed a host of elaborate superstitious traditions to allay their fears—doing everything from planting trees and signing hotel doors to taking a piss against the back tires of the bus that brought them to the launch site. Unfortunately, Strelkov and his crew could not take solace in those customary protections against accident or bad luck before their own lift-off. The need to keep their mission secret was paramount, outweighing everything else. They would have to fly naked before the Fates.

With effort, the colonel pushed aside these sudden gloomy thoughts. One side of his taut face twitched in a crooked smile. What would be would be. Perhaps not quite as the Allah of the Arabs willed, but just as certainly as decreed by Gennadiy Gryzlov of the Russians.

Where it counted, he knew Colonel General Leonov shared his private concerns about this sudden rush to make the Mars Project operational ahead of schedule. Ultimately, though, none of that mattered. Both of them were patriots and dedicated soldiers. So both of them would obey their orders—no matter what the cost.

Through his headphones Strelkov heard the copilot conversing with Baikonur ground security, exchanging code letters gleaned from a codebook that was updated daily. When the interchange ended, the copilot reported on intercom, "Pad LC-1 in sight, Colonel. We have been cleared for approach."

Intently, Strelkov peered forward through the cockpit windscreen. There, only a few kilometers off, he could see the Soyuz-5 rocket that would carry them into orbit—a slender, sixty-meter-high spire of gray, orange, and white gleaming brightly under the harsh desert sun. For now, it was restrained in a web of gantries, fueling towers, and other support structures.

Closing fast, the helicopter veered away from the launchpad itself. Instead, it headed toward a nearby collection of buildings and settled lower in a swirling cloud of rotor-blown dust and sand. Through the sudden haze, the colonel could make out several small trailers nestled in among a grove of scraggly trees. Those trailers would serve as their temporary quarters during the last remaining hours before launch, he realized. Their support team from Star City should already be inside, checking over both the Sokol pressure suits they would wear during the ride into orbit and the bulkier Orlan-MK suits they would use during EVAs outside Mars One.

Gratefully, Strelkov felt his nerves beginning to settle. Perhaps it was time to discard old superstitions and old ways of doing things, he realized. Like Yuri Gagarin, he and his men were pioneers. But unlike Gagarin, if they were successful, their mission would forever alter the balance of power between the United States and Russia.

CHAPTER 14

ST. PETERSBURG, RUSSIA
Later that night

"**P**oyekhali! Here goes!" Major Alexei Rykov downed his shot of vodka in one gulp and then rapped the empty glass on the scarred wooden surface of the bar. "Another, please."

The bartender chuckled. "Please? You say please?" He shook his head and poured another shot into Rykov's glass. "Man, you must not be drunk enough yet."

"Not yet," the Sukhoi-27 fighter pilot agreed with a short, sharp laugh of his own. "But I will get there." He turned to the younger man next to him. "Won't I, Sergei?"

His wingman, Captain Sergei Novitski, already well over the line between sobriety and inebriation himself, nodded vigorously, with an owlish, glassy-eyed stare. "That is affirmative, Lead."

With his fresh drink in hand, Rykov turned to survey the packed, smoke-filled bar. The place was a dive, just the kind he liked. With only two days of leave from the 159th Fighter Aviation Regiment at Petrozavodsk, he and Novitski didn't have time to waste. They were on the prowl for cheap booze and fast women, in no particular order.

His gaze flitted lightly across the crowd, evaluating and discarding possible companions in rapid succession. Too chubby. Too short. There was a redhead parked over in the far corner who wasn't horrible, but she had far too many piercings and tattoos for his taste. God only knew what kind of diseases he might catch. Maybe that skinny blonde? Privately, he dubbed this process "target selection," likening it to the way his Su-27's Phazotron Zhuk-MSE active electronically scanned array radar sorted through air contacts—identifying those worth a heat-seeking or radar-guided missile.

Rykov's gaze drifted across to a slender, attractive woman sitting alone at a tiny table near the door. Now there was a real looker, he thought with sudden interest. Jet-black hair, ice-blue eyes, and a leather bomber jacket unzipped far enough to give him a good look at her assets. She seemed a bit out of place in a seedy bar like this, a little too elegant and composed. But that should work to his advantage, considering the slovenly, ill-kempt civilian schlubs who were his only competition.

Noticing his attention, the woman smiled back at him. Her eyes gleamed brightly in the dim light.

Very promising, he decided. He straightened up to his full, middling-tall height and raised his glass in a silent toast.

With an exaggerated shrug of regret, she held up her own glass and turned it upside down, indicating that it was empty.

Rykov smiled to himself. *Target locked on*, he thought. Turning back to the bartender, he ordered two shots of vodka, the most expensive brand this time, and then clapped Novitski on the shoulder. "Don't wait up for me, Sergei," he said cheerfully. "I'm flying solo tonight."

His wingman blinked a few times in confusion and then shot him a sly, understanding grin. "Good hunting, Alexei!"

Humming under his breath, Rykov sauntered across the bar, holding both drinks up high to avoid being jostled by a new wave of thirsty patrons crowding in out of the warm St. Petersburg summer night. From the look of them, all torn jeans and spiky hair, some punk rock concert must have just ended.

The attractive woman smiled up at him when he arrived at her table.

"Hello," Rykov said pleasantly, holding out the drink he'd ordered for her. "My name's Alexei. And *you* look thirsty."

"Parched," she admitted, taking the glass with a half-sheepish, half-delighted laugh. "Was it so obvious?"

"Not at all," Rykov lied gallantly. "I have a sixth sense for recognizing beautiful women in distress." He sat down in the chair across from her and raised his own vodka in another toast. "*Vashe zdorov'ye!* Your health!"

With a dimpled smile, she echoed him, downing the contents of her glass with a quick, head-back gulp that widened his own eyes in surprised admiration. Then she leaned across the table. "So, Alexei, what is a nice man like you doing in a dump like this?"

"Isn't that supposed to be my line?" he asked in mock protest.

She shrugged. "It seemed appropriate."

Rykov glanced around at their surroundings— now even more crowded and noisy than ever. Clouds of acrid cigarette smoke coiled across the bar's low ceiling, settling like a fog across the sea of sweating, hard-drinking regulars packed in elbow to elbow. He turned back to her with a wry shrug of his own. "Maybe I'm looking for somewhere nicer?"

"Me too." She cocked her head to one side. "Interested in finding it together?"

Better and better, Rykov thought with secret glee. Not only was this woman sexy as hell, she wasn't bothering with the usual coy games. He hadn't even had to play his Hero of the Motherland and fighter-pilot cards yet. "Quite interested," he said warmly. "Where do you think we should start looking?"

"Well, my car is parked close by," she said with a demure look that didn't fool him at all. "And my apartment is only a short drive away."

Delighted at his good fortune, Rykov rose to

his feet and chivalrously offered her his hand. "You know, that sounds like an excellent plan."

Outside on the sidewalk, she guided him toward a big black Mercedes sedan. But when they drew near, the rear passenger door swung open and a big, grim-faced man in a dark business suit climbed out.

Startled, Rykov stopped dead in his tracks. "Hey, what the hell is going on here?" he demanded.

"Get in the car, Major Rykov," the woman said coolly. There was no trace of warmth left in her eyes or in her voice.

He scowled at her. "Why should I?"

"Because my name is Colonel Natalia Talanova and you are now in preventative state security custody." She fished an identity card out of her bomber jacket for his inspection. "You would be wise not to try my patience."

Rykov stared down at it in confusion. The woman he'd thought he was picking up for some fun, no-strings-attached sex was a senior officer in the FSB's counterintelligence service. Moistening his lips nervously, he looked up into her unsmiling, wholly unsympathetic face. "Look . . . Colonel . . . what is this all about?"

"You don't know?" Talanova raised a skeptical eyebrow. "It seems that someone has been a very, very naughty boy, Alexei. Maybe it was you. Maybe it was someone you know." She nodded toward the big man. "That is what my colleague over there and I intend to discover."

Rykov swallowed hard, suddenly feeling very, very sober indeed. There were many unpleasant stories about how the FSB treated suspects it considered uncooperative. He had no desire to find out if any of those whispered tales of beatings and torture were true. This time, when the colonel ordered him into the car, he obeyed without question.

An hour outside St. Petersburg, the black Mercedes turned off onto a long gravel road that ran deep into the forest. Two kilometers farther on, it parked in front of a small wooden cottage—probably once the country dacha of a mid-ranking Communist Party official. A small light glowed dimly behind one curtained window. Otherwise, the house looked as dark and forbidding as the wilderness all around it.

Silently, Colonel Talanova and her fellow FSB officer marched Rykov inside and into an empty room at the back of the house. Apart from a plain wooden chair set directly under a bare overhead bulb and a small table along one wall, there was no furniture or any other sign of human habitation.

Talanova nodded toward the chair. "Sit down, Major."

Numbly, Rykov did as he was told. She moved around to stand in front of him. Her face was mostly in shadow, almost wholly unreadable. Cat-quiet despite his size, the big man moved around to take up a position behind the chair, somewhere close by but out of Rykov's sight. The back of his neck itched.

"You do know why you are here, Alexei, don't you?" Talanova said calmly.

Desperately, he shook his head. "Honestly, Colonel," he insisted. "I have no idea of what all this is about. I'm just a pilot, that's all."

She snorted. "*Just* a pilot?" She shook her head. "Try again, Alexei. Ordinary combat aviation officers do not have military service records which contain otherwise unexplained eighteen-month-long periods of 'special detached duty.'"

Oh, shit, Rykov thought, feeling his heart rate accelerate sharply. What had been a bad situation was about to get much, much worse. Someone, somewhere, in either the Ministry of Defense or the FSB itself, had really fucked up—and now he might be about to pay in blood, bruises, and broken teeth for their mistake. Nevertheless, the special security oath he'd sworn was crystal clear, as was the prescribed penalty for violating that oath. He forced himself to sit up straighter in the chair. "I am very sorry, Colonel," he said firmly. "But I really am not at liberty to discuss that subject."

"You think not?" she said, sounding amused. Reaching into her leather jacket again, she tossed him yet another identity card.

Rykov looked it over in stunned disbelief. The card confirmed that Colonel Natalia Nikolaevna Talanova held a Level Two Mars Project clearance—a full level above the one he'd been issued as a cosmonaut candidate at Star City. Slowly, he breathed out. Why should he be surprised? The FSB, like the KGB before it, involved itself in everything. With a repressed sigh, he handed the card back to her.

"Right, then," she said briskly. "I don't want to hear any more noble bullshit about how you can't talk about the program, Major. You spent those eighteen months of 'detached duty' training to become a cosmonaut. You know it. And I know it."

Reluctantly, he nodded. She was right. Commended for his courage, superb technical and analytical abilities, and excellent flying skills, he'd been among those chosen for Colonel General Leonov's rigorous cosmonaut selection and training program. His class had started the course one hundred strong. In twos and threes over the next months, they'd been whittled away. He had only failed to make the final selection cut by the narrowest of margins. Most of the failed candidates, like him, were sent back to their regular military duties. Several had died in training accidents. Others were probable suicides, the victims of intense psychological pressure and their own undiscovered inner weaknesses.

Talanova smiled thinly. "Now we are getting somewhere, Alexei." Her humorless smile faded. "Which brings me to the point of tonight's little excursion to this rather dreary dacha."

Rykov swallowed again.

"Someone has been talking out of school," she went on coldly. "And as a result, the West's spies may be close to learning what were supposed to be our Motherland's most closely guarded secrets."

He stared at her. "What?"

"That surprises you?" Talanova countered.

"Of course it does." Rykov grimaced. "But whoever's blabbing, it is not me. I swear it."

She studied him for a long, uncomfortable moment. Then she shrugged. "Oaths can be broken, Alexei. I prefer proof."

"For God's sake, how am I supposed to prove a negative?" he asked desperately, instantly despising himself for sounding so weak.

"*You* cannot," Talanova said bluntly. "But perhaps I can."

He stared at her. "How?"

"That depends on you, Major Rykov." She moved forward, coming more fully into the circle of light cast by the bare bulb overhead. "Are you prepared to cooperate fully—without reservation?"

"Yes, I will. Absolutely," Rykov said, almost stumbling over his words in his hurry to grasp the lifeline the colonel seemed to be offering. "What must I do?"

"Tell us your life story," Talanova said. Her mouth twitched. "Or, to be more precise, your life story from the moment you arrived at the Anatoliy Gryzlov Military Cosmonaut Training Center."

He stared at her in surprise. "But why? You already have access to the records of my time there, don't you?"

"A dry list of classes, test results, and comments from your instructors?" she scoffed. "Of what use are they in determining whether or not you have betrayed your country? No, Alexei, you are going to talk us through your experiences at Star

City—fully, honestly, in your own words, and in your own way. *We* already know what has been illicitly revealed to Western agents. And if you are the one responsible for this treason, so do you."

Talanova looked down at him. "Now, a skilled liar may be able to conceal the truth for a time by carefully controlling how much he says. But the more anyone talks, the harder that becomes. Small inconsistencies begin to mount up. Hidden falsehoods emerge from what seems a jumble of otherwise irrelevant details. Eventually, the liar unmasks himself." Her voice slashed at him, as sharp as a razor's edge. "You see?"

Rykov nodded tightly. He said nothing.

"Very well. Let's get started." She glanced toward the big man looming behind him. "Wire him up, Dmitry."

Without speaking, the other FSB officer began attaching electrodes to Rykov's scalp, chest, neck, and wrists—pressing them firmly into place. The Su-27 pilot sat rigid in his chair, all too aware of the sense of helplessness and terror crawling up his spine.

"We don't just use our ears to listen," Talanova explained dryly. "Lies can be discerned in many different ways." She leaned closer. "So, then, Alexei. Tell me a story . . ."

It was well past dawn when they dropped the exhausted and shaken Rykov at a commuter rail station outside St. Petersburg and drove away.

"Do you think he'll tell anyone about what

just happened?" Marcus Cartwright asked. He glanced in the rearview mirror, checking automatically to see if they were being followed.

"That he's been under suspicion as a possible traitor?" Sam Kerr shook her head with a wry smile. "Our friend the fighter pilot wasn't at his best last night, but he's not really a fool. No, he'll keep his mouth shut." She shrugged. "Even if he doesn't—"

"Colonel Natalia Talanova will have vanished," the big man finished for her.

Sam nodded contentedly. "It is very hard to find someone who never actually existed in the first place."

"And all those wild stories he told us? About the kind of training the Russians are doing at Star City? Do you believe them?"

She pondered that. Under their questioning, Rykov had painted a picture of an incredibly intense training regimen. He claimed that Russia's cosmonauts were learning everything from on-orbit construction techniques to sensor data analysis and the combat use of both lasers and missiles. From what she knew, all of it sounded plausible. But what about his insistence that he and his fellow cosmonaut trainees had also been taught how to manage highly advanced nuclear fusion power systems? For decades, scientists and engineers had claimed that working fusion reactors were just around the corner. But their predictions never panned out. Could the Russians finally have made the technological breakthroughs that had eluded so many other researchers for so long?

At length, Sam shrugged. "Hell if I can say." She frowned. "We certainly know that poor bastard Rykov believed he was telling us the truth and nothing but the truth. So I guess the sooner we send what we've learned to Mr. Martindale the better. Because I'm pretty sure our report is going to scare the living crap out of a lot of people back in the States."

CHAPTER 15

U.S. STRATEGIC COMMAND MISSILE AND SPACE LAUNCH WARNING CENTER, CHEYENNE MOUNTAIN COMPLEX, COLORADO
A few hours later

Air Force Major General Amanda Hayes was the senior officer on duty in the Missile and Space Launch Warning Center, two thousand feet under Cheyenne Mountain, when the shit hit the proverbial fan. Her desk was on the highest of three stepped tiers facing several large screens. Consoles fitted with computers, displays, and secure communication links lined each tier. Since USSTRATCOM was a unified command, officers and enlisted men from the Air Force, Army, Navy, and Marine Corps manned these consoles around the clock.

Hayes, a former bomber wing commander, couldn't pretend she enjoyed this assignment very much. She'd originally joined the Air Force to fly and to lead other fliers—not to spend her days hunkered down in the bowels of a steel-and-concrete-encased bunker buried far below Cheyenne Mountain. Emerging blinking into the sunlight after a long night on watch in the warning center always made her feel more like a mole than a steely-eyed aviator.

She took a sip of her coffee and glanced again at the large center screen. It displayed a digital map of Russia and its central Asian neighbors. Suddenly blinking red icons flashed onto the screen.

"Ma'am! SBIRS has detected multiple launches from the Russian Federation and Kazakhstan!" one of her watch officers reported urgently.

Carefully, Hayes set her coffee cup back down. "Well, shit."

She pulled up the data download from SBIRS, the Space-Based Infrared System—a network of five missile launch and tracking satellites stationed more than twenty-two thousand miles up in geosynchronous orbit. Their sensors scanned the entire globe, looking for significant heat signatures. Sensitive enough to detect large-scale explosions, plane crashes, and major fires, the satellites were a key component in the U.S. early warning system. Right now, in virtually real time, they were observing five separate rocket launches, two from Vostochny, two from Plesetsk, and one from Baikonur.

Hayes immediately contacted her counterpart at the headquarters of the North American Aerospace Defense Command at nearby Peterson Air Force Base. "Charlie, SBIRS evaluates these launches as non-ICBM. Do you concur?"

Through her headset, she heard the gravelly

voice of Canadian Army Brigadier General Charles Costello, the duty controller of the joint U.S. and Canada forces command responsible for the air defense of North America. "That's affirmative, Amanda. Based on the signatures and current trajectories, we show two Energia-5VRs, two Angara-5s, and one Soyuz-5 heading for Earth orbit. Their trajectories are nonballistic. Repeat, nonballistic."

Hayes allowed herself to relax slightly. Whatever was going on, at least the Russians weren't firing nuclear-tipped missiles aimed at the United States. These were some of the several medium- and heavy-lift space rockets Moscow had been readying for launch over the past several weeks. There were standing orders to cover this development. She tapped a series of key codes into her computer, activating another secure link—this one to the White House.

It beeped once and then was answered. "Commander Nishiyama here. Authentication Zulu-Bravo-Five-Tango."

Quickly, she checked the classified duty roster shown on her computer. Commander Thomas Nishiyama, USN, was the presidential military aide currently assigned to carry the "nuclear football," the briefcase containing launch codes, retaliatory options, and other emergency procedures. And ZB5T was the personalized authentication code he'd been issued for this shift. Satisfied that she was speaking to the right person, she said, "This is Major General Hayes at USSTRATCOM. We have a multiple non-ICBM launch event occurring in Russia and Kazakhstan. I need to speak to the president."

"Wait one," Nishiyama said.

Hayes saw another red icon blink onto the map.

"New launch from Plesetsk," one of her subordinates reported after studying the tracking data supplied by their satellites. "We evaluate it as a third Energia-5VR, on roughly the same trajectory as those first two Angara-5s."

Moments later, a familiar voice with a distinct Texas twang sounded in her headset. "General Hayes, this is J. D. Farrell. I understand those Russian sons of bitches are raising a ruckus?"

"Yes, Mr. President," she said, finding herself smiling despite the gravity of the situation. *Jesus*, she thought, what everyone said was true. You could take the boy out of Texas, but you could *not* take Texas out of the boy. "We have six confirmed launches so far—three from Plesetsk, two from Vostochny, and one from Baikonur. And all within the past ten minutes."

She heard Farrell inhale sharply. "Well, goddamn," he said. "Have you ever seen a rocket launch tempo like that before, General?"

"No, sir," Hayes said simply. "To my knowledge, no one has ever tried anything remotely resembling this."

Abruptly, a seventh icon blinked into existence on the map.

"SBIRS is confirming another launch, Mr. President. A fourth heavy-lift Energia just lifted off from Plesetsk," she reported.

"Any idea on where all of these spacecraft are headed?" Farrell asked.

Hayes checked the data scrolling across one

of her displays. "Most of the Russian rockets are still climbing toward orbit, sir. Until they finish maneuvering, we won't have a solid lock on their final track. But the first launch, an Energia-5VR from Vostochny, seems to have completed its third-stage burn. Our calculations show it inserting into a circular orbit—"

"Four hundred miles high, inclined at fifty-one point six degrees," Farrell guessed.

Hayes couldn't keep the surprise she felt out of her voice. "Yes, sir, that's correct. How did you know?"

"Chalk it up to my manly intuition," he said with a short, humorless laugh. "Which is why I have a bad feeling the rest of those Russian rockets are headed pretty much the same damned way."

And then, with breathtaking suddenness, the projected track of the seventh rocket—designated as Energia Four by the warning center's computers—disappeared from the screen. In its place, Major General Amanda Hayes saw a confused swirl of smaller scarlet trajectories bloom across a large portion of northern Russia. "Well," she heard herself say slowly. "Maybe not all of them, Mr. President."

OVER NORTHERN RUSSIA
That same time

One hundred and forty-five seconds after launch, Energia Four was climbing through an altitude of fifty-four kilometers at a speed of more than six thousand kilometers per hour. The five RD-171MV kerosene-fueled engines in its strap-on boosters and core stage were firing perfectly. Just sixteen seconds away from shutdown and booster separation, they were steadily burning through the remains of the nearly two thousand tons of original propellant mass.

Secure within the payload module that made up the upper portion of the rocket's third stage, the Energia's primary flight control computer went about its preprogrammed business—evaluating thousands of pieces of data from navigation sensors, engine subsystems, fuel feeds, and other systems. Periodically, the computer gimbaled individual rocket nozzles, making small corrections in the direction of thrust to keep the spacecraft stable and on its planned trajectory. And then, only seconds from booster separation, a minor power surge tripped the computer off-line.

Reacting immediately, the Energia's backup computer picked up the reins, smoothly taking command over the flight. Unfortunately, during the frantic rush to prepare so many rockets for launch, one small glitch had gone unnoticed. The backup computer's internal clock was set twelve seconds fast.

Following its programming, the computer immediately commanded the third stage's two RD-0150 liquid-hydrogen-fueled engines to fire . . . while the strap-on boosters and core stage were still attached. Milliseconds later, their white-hot exhaust plumes ripped through the thin metal shell surrounding the core stage's liquid-oxygen fuel tank.

Instantly, Energia Four blew apart in a huge explosion that lit the sky over northern Russia. Hurled out of the enormous fireball, thousands of pieces of burning debris rained down. Within minutes, nearly a dozen wildfires were raging across a vast stretch of primeval coniferous forest.

OVER THE CENTRAL PACIFIC OCEAN
That same time

Energia One's third-stage fuel tank and payload module coasted silently through space, on course to its intended orbit. Explosive bolts fired in quick puffs of vapor. Their task complete, the two spent RD-0150 main engines spiraled away, drifting lower on a trajectory that would eventually cause them to burn up somewhere over the South Atlantic. More explosive bolts detonated, jettisoning fairings—thin sheets of metal—which had protected the module's special radar-absorbent coatings during launch.

Years ago, under Colonel General Leonov's direction, Russia's aerospace engineers had come up with several ingenious variations on the Energia-5VR's original third-stage design. Its two large internal tanks—one for liquid hydrogen, the other for liquid oxygen—had been drastically reduced in size, leaving room for just enough fuel to reach the right orbit. The remaining space was now allocated to compartments containing deployable solar power arrays, military-grade radars and infrared sensors, retractable weapons mounts, crew living quarters, and life-support systems.

Seconds later, small valves opened. Plumes of liquid hydrogen and oxygen vented into space, instantly becoming clouds of glittering frozen gas. Once sensors confirmed the module's internal fuel tanks were empty, the valves closed again. Now even those spaces could be used for additional consumables storage.

Hundreds of kilometers behind the Energia One module, five faint, moving specks of light glittered against the infinite blackness—rising slowly above the cloud-dappled curve of the earth. The surviving components of Russia's Mars One space station were closing steadily, using energy-efficient Hohmann transfer orbits.

FEDERATION ORBITER, OVER THE PEOPLE'S REPUBLIC OF CHINA
That same time

Bulky in his Sokol pressure suit, Colonel Vadim Strelkov reached up and tapped a glowing communications icon on the multifunction display fixed within inches of his helmet. "Moscow Control, this is Federation One. Posigrade transfer burn complete. The burn was nominal and the spacecraft is stable."

"*Copy that, Federation One,*" one of their flight controllers radioed back. "*Well done on the good burn.*" There was a long, static-filled pause. "*Ah, One, please switch your communications settings to Mode Six and then recontact us.*"

"Roger, Control." Frowning, Strelkov entered the necessary commands. Mode Six was the highest possible voice encryption setting. Routine radio transmissions between a spacecraft and its flight controllers were ordinarily broadcast in the clear. And to preserve the fiction that this was a civilian spacecraft for as long as possible, he had been ordered to follow regular peacetime procedures. Why was Moscow altering that plan now, so early in the mission?

He saw the communications icon change shape to that of a padlock. "Control, this is Federation One. Mode Six is enabled."

"*Copy that. Stand by for Colonel General Leonov.*"

Strelkov glanced sideways at Major Georgy Konnikov, crammed into the next seat over, and got a slight shrug. Leonov had always been a hands-on commander. Whatever was happening, it wasn't too surprising that he would involve himself early on.

Then Leonov's deep voice boomed through his headset. "*I congratulate you on a successful launch and insertion to orbit, Colonel. I hope the spacecraft is performing to expectations?*"

"Perfectly, sir," Strelkov assured him. In truth,

their lift-off and ride to space had been much smoother and more trouble-free than he had thought possible in an untested vehicle. Only a couple of very minor systems had failed under the initial stress of flight, and both of them were back up now. "We expect to rendezvous with the other Mars One station components within twenty-four hours." With a dry smile, he looked at Konnikov, who mimed closing his eyes. "In fact, things are going so well that some of my crew seem to be planning to catch up on their beauty sleep."

"*Unfortunately, you will have to disabuse them of this notion,*" Leonov said heavily. "*I'm afraid we are all going to be very busy over the next several days. Many of our existing Mars One construction and operations procedures must be significantly revised— literally, in this case, on the fly.*"

Strapped snugly into the capsule's command seat, Strelkov could not sit bolt upright in shock. That was probably just as well, since he would have only banged his helmet on a bulkhead. Compared to Russia's old Soyuz spacecraft, the Federation orbiter was a technological marvel. But with six cosmonauts on board, it was still incredibly cramped. "What?"

"*We've lost one of the Mars One modules,*" Leonov said bluntly. "*An Energia-5VR blew up in flight— approximately two and a half minutes after launch.*"

Strelkov bit down on an obscenity. He took a couple of short breaths, trying to compose himself. Not that he would be fooling anyone, he knew. The doctors monitoring the telemetry of their vital signs would just have seen his blood pressure and heart rate spike. "What did we lose?" he asked at last.

Leonov's voice was grim. *"Your fusion power reactor, Colonel,"* he said quietly.

CHAPTER 16

"**Y**our secure video link to the White House will go live in thirty seconds," a Sky Masters technician announced over the conference room speakers. "Stand by."

Brad McLanahan glanced at Nadia Rozek and Hunter "Boomer" Noble. "Everybody set?"

His voice sounded tighter than he liked. He had briefed senior government officials before, all the way up to Poland's president, Piotr Wilk. For some reason, though, the prospect of performing this same task for his own country's commander in chief, President John D. Farrell, had him even more on edge than he'd expected. Maybe it was because he'd just been getting used to focusing on flying again—gratefully leaving concerns about geopolitics and strategy to those at higher pay grades. Wrestling with technical aeronautical and astronautical problems and spaceplane crew training had been strangely restful. But now, suddenly, here he was back in the big leagues. With U.S. intelligence agencies still half crippled by years of neglect, the president wanted the joint Scion–Sky Masters team's analysis of Russia's surprise lunge back into outer space.

Coolly, Boomer nodded back.

"We are ready," Nadia said, with complete assurance. Under the table, out of sight of the camera focused in their direction, she took Brad's hand in hers.

For a second, he allowed himself to relax. As long as he had this amazing woman at his side, what was there to worry about? Naturally, the undisciplined little voice inside his mind started running through a litany: *Well, let's see . . . there are still the Russians out there and the inherent dangers of spaceflight and the chance that you'll screw up your briefing and . . .*

Mercifully, the video camera light blinked to red, indicating that it was live. In that same moment, the big LED screen on the conference room wall lit up. President Farrell, Kevin Martindale, and his own father looked back at them from the Oval Office. Instantly, Brad felt his twitchy nerves start to settle down. All the waiting was over. Now, finally, he had an important job to do and no more time to fret.

"Captain McLanahan and Major Rozek, it's real nice to see y'all again," Farrell drawled out around a warm, welcoming grin. It was a politician's practiced expression, but no less real for that. For any truly successful elected official, a sincere liking for people was a fundamental requirement. Most voters could spot a phony a mile off—no matter how much "spin" a candidate's PR team imparted. "And you too, Dr. Noble. We haven't met before, but I can assure you that your reputation precedes you."

Boomer laughed. "Only the good parts, I hope, Mr. President."

Farrell's grin grew wider. "Son," he said with an even more pronounced twang, "I was riding herd on wildcatter oil drilling crews before you were out of middle school. Trust me, there ain't nothing I haven't already heard about loose women, fast cars, and cardplaying."

Brad heard Nadia choke back on a sudden amused snort. The scuttlebutt around Sky Masters was that Boomer's idea of a long-term romantic commitment was dinner and a movie . . . with breakfast in bed to follow.

"Flattery won't get you anywhere now, Mr. President," Boomer shot back, not abashed in the slightest. "I already voted for you last November."

Brad saw a pained look cross Martindale's face. The former president occasionally regretted the easy informality with which some in the Iron Wolf Squadron and Sky Masters approached those in authority.

"Perhaps we can dispense with any further recitation of Dr. Noble's extracurricular exploits, impressive though they are?" Martindale said, mildly exasperated. "And move on instead to recent events in outer space?"

Boomer glanced at Brad, saw his tiny nod, and shrugged. "Sure thing, Mr. Martindale." His expression grew more serious. "For the past twenty-four hours or so, we've been closely monitoring the situation since the Russians launched those seven rockets. Several things are now clear. First, despite the loss of one of their big Energia-5VR vehicles, the Russians have successfully put an enormous amount of material in orbit—something close to four hundred tons of payload, maybe even more."

"But not just material," Farrell interjected.

"That's correct, sir," Boomer said. "Reports from Baikonur suggest the supposedly 'unmanned' Federation orbiter actually launched with up to six cosmonauts on board. Since then, we've picked up radio transmissions between the spacecraft and a control center in Moscow which confirm the presence of at least one cosmonaut."

"Could there be just one man flying that thing?" Farrell asked. "As a sort of test pilot?"

"I doubt it, Mr. President," Boomer said. "If it were up to me, I'd want a minimum of two crew for any test flight. Even on a mature spacecraft, too many things can go wrong too fast for one man to handle. And from my experience, the Russians tend to think in terms of three-man or larger crews for anything except their rocket-launched Elektron spaceplanes."

Patrick McLanahan frowned. "It's pretty clear that Gryzlov isn't just testing this new spacecraft. This is a full-on operational flight. I bet that Federation is fully crewed, with all six seats occupied."

Boomer nodded. "That's our bet, too, General."

Using the laptop computer in front of him, he brought up a series of computer-generated 3-D visuals to illustrate his next points as he spoke. The images were mirrored in a corner of their screens. "Approximately twelve hours ago, six separate Russian spacecraft—which appear to be three large Energia third-stage fuel tanks with smaller payload modules attached, two Progress-MS cargo ships, and the manned Federation orbiter—successfully rendezvoused in orbit." Half a dozen red icons spiraled around a digital representation of the earth, drawing closer to each other with each successive orbit until they merged into a single glowing dot.

"Rendezvoused? Do you mean all those spacecraft docked with each other?" Farrell asked.

Boomer shook his head. "Not quite, Mr. President. Or at least not yet. Instead, they entered a tight formation . . . tight by the standards of space travel, I mean. Not the kind of wing-tip-to-wing-tip flying you'd see in a jet-fighter air show." He zoomed way in until the icons representing the six Russian spacecraft were again visible as distinct and different shapes. They were all traveling in the same orbital plane, separated by no more than a few miles. "They held this formation over the next several orbits. At that altitude, it takes them a little more than ninety-seven minutes to circle the earth."

"But now those Russian spaceships are on the move again?" the president guessed.

"Yes, sir." Boomer tapped a key. Five of the vehicles began adjusting their positions and orientations, apparently slowly closing in on a common center point. "Four hours ago, our ground- and space-based radars and telescopes picked up the start of what appears to be an intricate series of automated maneuvers. Our analysis indicates these maneuvers are designed to create a single, multicomponent structure in orbit. For now, the cosmonauts in that Federation orbiter are holding position a few miles off to the side—probably preparing to dock when it's safe to do so."

Farrell rocked back in his chair. His expression was pensive. "So Gennadiy Gryzlov is building himself a brand-new space station. And in a mighty big hurry."

It was Brad's turn now. "Yes, sir," he agreed. "We think the Russians are pulling the same stunt we used to build Skylab back in the 1970s and then Armstrong Station after that. We strongly suspect they've converted those Energia third-stage fuel tanks into modules containing living quarters and all the other hardware needed for an operational orbital platform."

Farrell nodded his understanding. America's first space station, Skylab, had begun life as an empty Saturn V third-stage fuel tank before its conversion into an orbiting habitat and science outpost. "Do you have any evidence to back up your suspicions?"

"We do, sir," Brad said. "We spotted each of those tanks intentionally venting gases after they reached orbit. And spectroscopic analysis confirms those gases were liquid oxygen and liquid hydrogen."

"They were dumping unneeded fuel," Martindale said slowly.

Brad nodded. "Yep. But here's the kicker. Our guys at both Sky Masters and NASA say the amounts involved were way too low. So either those big-ass fuel Energia tanks are going to dock with tons of liquid hydrogen and oxygen still sloshing around—"

"Or there's no fuel left on board any of them . . . because the vast majority of that tankage space has already been reconfigured for other purposes," his father said.

"That's our assessment," Brad confirmed.

"What about the rocket the Russians lost on launch?" the president asked. "Do we know what its payload was?"

"Beyond the probability that it was another of those converted fuel-tank modules? Not really," Brad said doubtfully. He highlighted the graphic representation Boomer had created again. It showed the five surviving unmanned spacecraft still firing thrusters—slowly pirouetting through space as they maneuvered into docking positions. "Though we might be able to make some educated guesses once we have a clearer picture of the Russian station's design architecture."

For a long moment, Farrell watched the computer-generated imagery play out across their screens. Then he shook his head with a frown and turned his attention back to Brad. "Which leads straight to the big question, Captain McLanahan," he said bluntly. "What the hell is Moscow up to?"

Brad looked him straight in the eye. "Considering the intelligence Mr. Martindale's agents picked up on Gryzlov's cosmonaut training program, we think there is only one reasonable conclusion: the Russians are building an armed orbital platform."

"Can you prove that?" the president demanded.

"In a court of law? Or in the court of international public opinion? No, sir." Brad nodded toward Martindale. "Not without blowing Scion's intelligence operation in Russia sky-high."

"Even doing that won't achieve much," Martindale pointed out quietly. "My people couldn't penetrate Gryzlov's security directly. We don't have any written or other clear-cut technical evidence to confirm what this failed Russian cosmonaut candidate told them."

"Which makes their report nothing more than hearsay," Farrell said with a sigh. "So if we go public with this situation as things stand now, it's just going to end up being my word against Gryzlov's."

Martindale nodded. "I'm afraid so. And that's not enough to sway any of the nonaligned nations our way. Nor can I see many of our allies thanking us for provoking a new confrontation with Russia without better proof."

"Poland will stand with you, Mr. President," Nadia said fiercely. "As will the other countries of the Alliance of Free Nations. I am sure of it."

Somberly, Farrell inclined his head to her. "I do thank you for that, Major." Then he shrugged his big shoulders. "But I'm not ready yet to ask anyone to go all in with us. Not when we're holding such a weak hand." He looked them all over. "At the same time, I'm sure as hell *not* inclined to sit back passively and wait for Gryzlov's next move. Whatever it might be."

"No, sir," Brad agreed, a sentiment instantly echoed by Nadia, his father, and the others.

"So our top priority is getting solid data on this space station. And *muy pronto*," Farrell told them firmly.

Brad saw his father frown.

"That could be difficult," the older man said. "Ground-based telescopes and conventional reconnaissance satellites probably won't provide enough information. The Russians aren't stupid. It's likely that they're using a mix of external camouflage and antithermal and radar-absorbent materials to shield many of their systems and capabilities from distant snooping."

From his seat on the other side of Nadia, Boomer nodded. "That matches up with our observations so far, General. The radar and thermal signatures of those converted fuel tanks are significantly weaker than they should be, given their estimated size and mass."

"Which is why we need to take a closer look," Nadia said flatly. "Close enough to pierce through the Russian *maskirova*, their disguise."

Martindale raised an eyebrow. "And just how

on earth do you propose to arrange that, Major Rozek?"

"Not on Earth at all," she replied with the faint hint of a mischievous smile. "Naturally, we will use one of our spaceplanes for the mission."

At her nod, Boomer pulled up another piece of 3-D animation. This one showed a green icon marked as an S-19 Midnight spaceplane climbing steeply on an intercept course to the orbiting Russian space station. Shortly before it flew on by, a cloud of other, smaller icons detached from the S-19 and angled toward the station—passing it on all sides at very close range, a matter of mere miles.

"We began developing this plan for a close reconnaissance as soon as we concluded Moscow was building a military platform in orbit," Nadia said, quite seriously now. "During its flyby, the S-19 will deploy a constellation of tiny spy satellites around the Russian station. These satellites will collect the information we need."

Farrell leaned forward, openly curious now. "Tiny spy satellites?"

"After the destruction of Armstrong Station, Sky Masters did some crash R&D work on a new class of very small recon satellites," Boomer explained. From the enthusiasm in his voice, it was pretty clear who had been the project lead. "We designed them to be equipped with a range of sensors, including high-resolution cameras, infrared sensors, and even an experimental low-powered 35.75 gigahertz Ka-band radar."

"How small are these satellites of yours exactly, Dr. Noble?" Martindale asked. "Microsatellites in the fifty-to-one-hundred-kilogram range?"

"Much smaller," Boomer told him proudly. "The prototypes we built are classed as nano-satellites. Each weighs less than five kilograms, around ten pounds, and they're only about a foot in diameter."

"Like the CubeSats so many colleges and small companies launch as science experiments," the president realized.

Boomer nodded. "Yes, sir. But ours are shaped to reduce their radar cross section—which makes them much more suitable for covert intelligence-gathering and military missions." He shrugged. "We figured the Pentagon and other agencies might be interested. But no such luck."

"Let me guess," the president said dryly. "Stacy Anne Barbeau's administration slammed the door in your face."

"Hell, they'd have had to open the door first," Boomer said with a pained look. "None of her people ever even answered my e-mails."

Farrell nodded slowly. His predecessor had a lot to answer for. Her lack of vision and obsession with settling petty political scores had cost the U.S. government dearly. Then he frowned. "Okay, but one thing bothers me. Why not simply launch these spy satellites into orbit using a conventional unmanned rocket? Wouldn't that be safer than flying one of the spaceplanes so close to this Russian space station?"

"Safer for us, maybe," Brad said. "But sending

the nanosats up on an unmanned rocket would almost certainly guarantee a mission failure."

"Why?"

"Because Boomer's nanosatellites have very limited thruster power and communications capabilities. It's part of the trade-off between size and sensor power. Deploying them properly around the Russian platform is going to require some seriously intricate flying, well beyond the capability of any existing autonomous system." Brad shrugged. "Basically, trusting the nanosat's dinky onboard computers to handle the mission entirely on their own would be risky—possibly even leading to unintended near misses the Russians could mistake for a deliberate attack. No, sir, to pull this off, we *need* a man in the loop."

"Or a woman," Nadia said stubbornly.

Brad shook his head with a lopsided grin. "Not this time, O Queen of the Skies. Boomer and I won the toss, remember? Besides, you and Constable Vasey are going to have your hands full managing that beast of an S-29 Shadow while we gas up."

Seeing the puzzled look on the president's face, he went on. "We actually need to fly two spaceplanes to pull this off, sir—not just one. There's only one way to put an S-19 Midnight into an orbit four hundred miles up with enough fuel for maneuvers and a powered reentry. We need to do a preliminary in-space refueling from an S-29 Shadow we've converted to a tanker first."

Farrell stared at him first and then at Nadia. "Refueling one spaceplane from another? Is that something that's ever been done before?"

"Oh, yes, many times," Nadia assured him blithely. She smiled broadly. "Well, at least in simulations."

"And in real life?" the president asked quietly.

"This will be the first time."

"Sweet jumping Jesus," Farrell muttered in astonishment. He glanced at Patrick McLanahan. "Do I have any alternative here?"

Although his own worries about this proposed flyby were plain on his lined face, Brad's father doggedly shook his head. "I'm afraid not, Mr. President. Not unless you're willing to wait for Gryzlov to act first—in his own sweet time and according to his own plans."

"Hell no," Farrell said tightly. He sighed. "So there it is. I don't like it. I don't like it much at all." He looked out of the screen at Brad, Boomer, and Nadia. "All right. I'll give my blessing to this little jaunt of yours. But y'all just be damned careful up there, *comprende?*"

Brad and Boomer both nodded gravely.

"*Tak, Panie Prezydencie.* Yes, Mr. President," Nadia said with equal gravity.

CHAPTER 17

"**T**his is a complete fucking disaster, Leonov," Gennadiy Gryzlov said icily. His eyes narrowed. "As far as I can judge, you might as well have just heaped up the two trillion rubles I gave you and then set them on fire."

Holding his own temper in check with difficulty, Leonov calmly shook his head. "Losing the Mars One reactor on launch is a setback. Nothing more."

Gryzlov snorted. "Don't play semantics games with me! Without the energy needed to fire them, your precious Thunderbolt plasma weapon and the station's Hobnail self-defense lasers are useless."

"Thunderbolt still has its supercapacitors and the two lasers have their own battery storage systems," Leonov insisted.

The other man angrily waved that away. "So they can each fire a few shots using stored power. Wonderful. We can start your planned war in space. And then what? Do we hope the Americans panic and yield to all our demands before they tumble to the fact that your vaunted orbital station is virtually defenseless?"

Leonov refrained from reminding him that Mars One's armament load-out included a number of ground-attack and defensive missiles. Where it counted, Gryzlov wasn't wrong to see the orbital station's energy weapons as crucial. Ultimately, to achieve Russia's strategic and operational objectives, both the longer-range Thunderbolt plasma rail gun and shorter-range Hobnail lasers were essential.

"To recharge Thunderbolt and the lasers, we can divert electricity from the station's secondary solar arrays as needed," he argued. "My engineers and Strelkov's crew are working out the details and procedures now."

Gryzlov raised an eyebrow. "Tell me, Leonov," he said with deceptive calmness. "How much electricity will be generated by those solar panels?"

"Seventy-five kilowatts."

Gryzlov nodded. His eyes were hooded. "And how much power *would* have been generated by the fusion reactor that's now scattered in a million twisted pieces all the way from Plesetsk to the Urals?"

Leonov grimaced. The compact fusion reactor destroyed aboard Energia Four had been a technological marvel. Within the reactor, rotating, ring-shaped magnetic fields were used to confine the plasma created by heating deuterium and helium-3 with low-frequency radio waves. Like the Thunderbolt rail gun, it was the product both of daring Russian espionage and years of expensive research and development. A small American company affiliated with Princeton University had researched such reactors in the hopes of building direct-drive fusion-powered rockets for long-duration deep-space missions. While the Americans limped along, hobbled by a lack of sufficient funding, Leonov's teams of scientists and engineers had taken their stolen data and designs and made them work.

"The Mars One reactor was rated at ten megawatts," he admitted.

"More than a hundred times greater than the amount produced by those solar arrays," Gryzlov noted dryly. "That is rather a drastic reduction in the station's available power supply, is it not?"

"Using solar cells to recharge the batteries and supercapacitors will significantly reduce the rate of fire for our energy weapons," Leonov acknowledged reluctantly.

"Below the optimum level recommended for effective, full-scale military operations?" Gryzlov pressed.

"I am afraid so."

Impassively, Gryzlov nodded. "I see." He looked across his desk at Leonov. "So what course of action do you recommend now, Colonel General?"

"Once the station's surviving modules are

connected and fully operational, Colonel Strelkov and his crew should sit tight," Leonov suggested. "For the time being, Mars One can appear to be exactly what we say it is, simply a new manned orbital science platform. Our own replacement for the old International Space Station."

Gryzlov smiled thinly. "And you think the Americans will buy that story?"

Leonov shrugged. "They may be suspicious, but absent proof of our hostile intentions, what can they do?"

Without further warning, Gryzlov's temper flared. "And so we come full circle, Colonel General," he snarled. "Without a combat-ready station, your whole damned Mars Project is useless! What do you have to show for all the resources I've given you? Nothing. Just a few horrifically expensive pieces of metal aimlessly circling the earth." He scowled. "I warned you earlier about the consequences of failure. And I assure you, those were *not* idle threats."

"I never thought they were," Leonov said steadily, all too aware that his freedom and his very life now hung by a slender thread. It would do him no good to protest that he'd warned about the hazards involved in relying so heavily on an inadequately tested heavy-lift rocket design. Russia's leader lived by one overriding principle: Failures were never the consequence of his own mistakes or hasty, ill-considered decisions. They were always the fault of other, lesser men.

"I meant what I said earlier about this being

a temporary setback, Gennadiy," he continued. "We lost one reactor, yes. But it can be replaced."

Gryzlov eyed him thoughtfully. "With the fusion reactor module being built for Mars Two, you mean?"

Leonov nodded. Full implementation of the Mars Project plan had always called for launching a second station—to increase the reach of Russia's new space-based weapons. Meeting the rushed tempo Gryzlov demanded had forced him to send the first station's modules into orbit before those for its planned counterpart were ready. "Our second reactor is nearly finished. According to the TRINITY Institute generator construction unit at Akademgorodok, they are less than a week away from certifying it as flight-ready."

"Tell them to cut that time in half," Gryzlov snapped. "I don't care how they do it—whether it means working around the clock or cutting normal safety procedures."

Wordlessly, Leonov nodded. Then he warned, "Even when Akademgorodok's work is finished, it will take more time to transport the reactor to Vostochny and mate it with a new Energia-5VR."

Gryzlov leaned forward. His hands balled into fists. "Make it happen fast, Mikhail. If you have to liquidate a few of the lazier railway workers to encourage their comrades, don't hesitate." His expression was unpleasant. "You've already tested the limits of my patience today. So no more screwups, eh?"

"No, Mr. President," Leonov agreed.

STAR CITY, OUTSIDE MOSCOW
Later that day

Head down in apparent thought, Leonov strolled along a winding dirt path—heading deeper into the woods around the cosmonaut training center. The late-afternoon sun filtered down through a high canopy of leaves, lighting up some slender, white-trunked birch trees and leaving others in shadow.

Leonov kept on walking as a short, slight figure detached itself from one of those shadows and joined him. "Did you have any trouble?" he asked, with a quick, sidelong glance.

"None," Major General Arkady Koshkin replied. "My staff knows I had a long-scheduled Mars Project software conference here today. None of them, except Popov, is aware that it ended earlier than originally planned. And I left him waiting back at my staff car. He may suspect I'm meeting someone else privately, but he cannot be sure."

Leonov remembered the other man's elegantly tailored bodyguard. "You can trust him not to blab?"

Koshkin smiled thinly. "Young Dmitry may look like an overdressed popinjay, but he is also shrewd enough to calculate the odds. As long as it's safer for him to keep a few of my secrets than it is to spill them, he will remain loyal."

"That seems a rather tenuous form of loyalty," Leonov said wryly.

"When one's life is at stake, all loyalty is tenuous, is it not?" the head of the FSB's Q Directorate said with equal irony. He shrugged. "Perhaps more so now than in the recent past." Leonov let that pass.

They walked on in silence for a few more moments. At last, Leonov stopped and turned to face his smaller companion. "Arkady, I need your guarantee that the fail-safe protocols you've planted in various Mars One station operating systems have not been compromised."

"They remain undetected," Koshkin told him confidently. "Attempts to pry into those codes would trip a large number of cybersecurity alarms. We would be alerted within seconds."

Leonov stared at him. "Even with the station modules already in orbit?"

Koshkin nodded. "We've buried a secret and highly secure back channel of our own among the routine telemetry feeds from Mars One." Behind his thick spectacles, his dark brown eyes revealed a small measure of the smug self-satisfaction of a magician astonishing his audience by pulling a rabbit out of an apparently empty hat. "We can monitor the station systems in real time, Mikhail. And communicate with them, as needed."

"Is there any chance that the fail-safe protocols could be triggered accidentally?"

Koshkin shook his head authoritatively. "None whatsoever. The protocols can only be activated by deliberate command—through encrypted signals from the ground using the codes I've already given you." For a second, he hesitated. "Perhaps

I should secretly alert Colonel Strelkov to their existence . . . as a further precaution. Then, if the Americans successfully attack Mars One, he could input the necessary commands directly."

"No," Leonov said flatly. "In such a case, Strelkov and his men would already be either dead or taken prisoner." He turned his hard-eyed gaze fully on the shorter man. "The knowledge of these hidden safeguards must remain between ourselves, Arkady. Ourselves *only*. You understand?"

"Yes, of course," Koshkin said slowly. He cleared his throat nervously. "There are others in Moscow who, I believe, share our concerns about the risks the president is running. If we could just brief them—"

"That would be foolish beyond measure," Leonov interrupted. His voice was harsh. "You forget, Koshkin. Three men *can* keep a secret. But only if two of them are dead."

CHAPTER 18

MINISTRY OF FOREIGN AFFAIRS, MOSCOW
The next day

Russia's Ministry of Foreign Affairs building was one of the Seven Sisters dotting Moscow's skyline—seven large skyscrapers built around the city on the express orders of Joseph Stalin. Intended to glorify the Soviet state in the waning days of the dictator's brutal reign, they were also an unintentional monument to Soviet inefficiency, since each building was squatter, heavier, and costlier to construct than those erected in the West at the same period.

Foreign Minister Daria Titeneva saw another irony in this vast slab of concrete and steel. For all of the size and prominence of its Moscow headquarters, Russia's diplomatic service was the poor stepsister in Gennadiy Gryzlov's government, an afterthought in the president's mind compared to the armed forces. He viewed negotiations and the ordinary give-and-take of day-to-day diplomacy with scarcely concealed contempt. At best, as far as he was concerned, they were useful only as a means of deceiving foreign enemies about his true intentions until it was too late.

Like now.

Squaring her shoulders resolutely, she strode out onto the stage of the ministry's press briefing room. Compared to the cramped press quarters in America's White House, the large chamber was almost luxurious, with elegant wood paneling, a backdrop featuring Russia's double-headed-eagle coat of arms, and plush red seats for journalists. *Perhaps lies are easier to swallow in comfort*, she thought cynically.

The chamber was full of television news crews and reporters from around the world. They had been summoned here with the promise of an official statement on the incredible developments currently taking place in orbit around the earth.

With a gracious smile plastered across her still-attractive face, Titeneva stopped behind a polished wood lectern topped by microphones. "Ladies and gentlemen, thank you for coming." Her words were in thickly accented English, a not-so-subtle indication of the intended audience. "My remarks this afternoon will be brief and to the point." She looked out across the sea of faces and cameras. "By now you have all heard reports that Russia has successfully launched several large rockets and their payloads into space. You have also been told that one of those space vehicles may have carried a manned Federation orbiter with Russian cosmonauts aboard. And finally, you have heard claims from several other nations that these orbiting spacecraft are currently assembling a large structure far above the earth's atmosphere."

She paused there, letting the tension build awhile, before uttering a short, simple declarative sentence. "Those reports are all true."

That got their attention, Titeneva thought with inner amusement, listening to the sudden excited buzz from the assembled journalists. Again, she waited a second longer, letting the noise die down a bit before continuing. "The Russian Federation today announces the construction of a long-planned replacement for the abandoned International Space Station. This orbital facility has been named Mars One—symbolizing my country's fervent hope that it will serve as a stepping-stone in the peaceful exploration of our solar system."

She made a show of checking her watch. "And now I have time for questions, but only one or two. This, as you may imagine, is a very busy day."

The clamor rose higher as individual journalists rose in their places, waving and calling out to gain her attention.

Titeneva pointed to one, the correspondent for a large German newspaper with noted pro-Moscow leanings. "Yes, Erich?"

"Madam Foreign Minister, you have described this new space station as a replacement for the ISS," he said deferentially. "Will it then be open to scientists from many nations? As was the ISS?"

She nodded. "So I understand. Even though Mars One, unlike the ISS, is entirely the creation of advanced Russian engineering and space technology, we do not intend to be selfish. Once initial construction is complete, and the orbital facility is certified as safe for human occupation, I am sure Russia will invite scientists from friendly nations to make use of its extensive research capabilities."

"There's been a lot of speculation in some informed circles that this Mars One space station of yours might actually be a weapons platform," a voice called out from the middle of the press corps. Simon Turner, the BBC's veteran Moscow correspondent, never hid his deep skepticism about the official statements issued by any government—including his own. "What is your response to the rumors that Russia is building a military outpost in space?"

Titeneva smiled pityingly. "Ah, Mr. Turner," she said, with a playful tone. "I assume these rumormongering circles you speak of are *American*?"

"Some of them."

She shook her head in mock sorrow. "I am truly surprised that you give any credibility to this kind of outdated Cold War propaganda. Russia honors its treaty commitments." Her eyes flashed with sudden righteous anger. "*All* of its treaty commitments, including those which prohibit the deployment of offensive weapons in outer space. You would do well to remember that only one nation on Earth has ever established a permanent military presence in orbit. And that was the United States itself, not Russia!"

That little piece of theater drew a smattering of appreciative applause from the more sycophantic journalists present. *Well done, Daria*, Titeneva congratulated herself silently. Her riposte to Turner's insulting suggestion should make every newscast and front page around the world.

With a graceful wave, she turned on her heel and left the stage.

As ordered, she'd just bought Gennadiy a little more breathing room. She only hoped he and Colonel General Leonov would make good use of it.

FEDERATION ORBITER, CLOSING ON MARS ONE, OVER AFRICA
That same time

From the Federation orbiter's station-keeping position a short distance from Mars One, Colonel Vadim Strelkov had a good view of the large structure. Russia's new space station now consisted of a thirty-five-meter-long command module and two comparably sized weapons and sensors modules. Together they formed a shape that looked a little like a capital *I* turned on its side, with the command module in the middle. Strelkov had already heard some of the younger members of his crew jokingly comparing the station's basic silhouette to that of a TIE fighter from the American *Star Wars* movies.

Large rectangular solar panels extended off each of the three modules. Without the missing fusion reactor, they were now Mars One's sole source of electricity. The two Progress-MS cargo ships were docked at ports on the command module's upper side. Blinking green and red position lights in the center of the station indicated the docking port for their orbiter.

Looking at the station up close, at zero relative velocity, gave one the odd sensation of hanging motionless in space, Strelkov thought. Only turning one's gaze toward the sunlit world as it spun past below revealed that both spacecraft were speeding along in tandem at well over twenty-seven thousand kilometers per hour.

"Moscow Control, this is Federation One," Strelkov radioed. Their communications with the ground were being relayed through a network of Russian satellites—a vast improvement over the old Soyuz models, where contact was only possible while over Russia itself. They were once again broadcasting in the clear, under orders to maintain the charade that the station was designed as a civilian science outpost. "We are in position and ready to dock with Mars One."

"Acknowledged, Federation One," a controller answered. *"Your position and readiness are confirmed. Proceed with the maneuver at your discretion."*

"Docking now," Strelkov said. He tapped the proper icon on his multifunction display, initiating an automated docking sequence. His screen changed, now showing an aiming reticle centered on the station port. Numbers appeared, indicating their relative distance, orientation, and closing rate. He heard a succession of soft hisses as thrusters fired and saw the port grow larger. The orbiter's sophisticated flight computer was now in full control.

Nevertheless, as a precaution, he kept both hands on the two controllers fixed below his MFD—the left for translation maneuvers and the right to rotate their spacecraft as needed. If something went wrong with the computer, he would dock manually. It was a maneuver he and the other cosmonauts had practiced hundreds of times in their preflight training.

From the seat beside him, Major Georgy Konnikov kept up a running commentary on their progress. "Closing at twenty centimeters per second. Range one hundred meters. We are slightly low and to the left." New thrusters fired briefly. "Closure rate now eighteen centimeters per second. Range eighty meters. Good position and angle."

Minutes passed, slowly at first, and then all in a rush as they drew nearer to the space station.

"Closing at ten centimeters per second. Range four meters. In the groove," Konnikov intoned.

Less than a minute later, the Federation's docking probe slid perfectly into the Mars One port's cone-shaped receptacle.

"Contact!" Konnikov reported. A tiny vibration rippled through their spacecraft as latches closed around the probe and retracted—pulling the Federation orbiter tightly against Mars One's port. "And capture."

Suddenly aware that his hands ached from

tension, Strelkov let go of the manual controls and radioed. "Moscow Center, this is Federation One. We have arrived."

Through his headphones, he heard muted cheers from the mission control center. *"Acknowledged, Federation. This is a great day for Russia."* There was a brief pause before the controller remembered they were broadcasting to an as-yet-unsuspecting international audience. *"And, of course, a great day for all of humanity, too."*

One hour later, after completing a series of pressurization tests to make sure they had a good seal, Strelkov ordered the hatch opened. He was the first one through, floating nimbly through the airlock and into his new command. It was time to bring Russia's new military space station to life.

ABOARD MARS ONE
Several hours later

Colonel Vadim Strelkov hooked his feet beneath an electronics console to hold himself in place and looked around the crowded compartment. The five cosmonauts who made up his crew hovered nearby, clinging to footholds or handholds of their own. "Very well, gentlemen," he said briskly. "Now that you've had some time to check things over, I need your status reports."

Intense training had rendered every one of them a jack-of-all-trades, intimately familiar with every piece of hardware and electronics aboard Mars

One. But each cosmonaut still had a specialty—a weapons, station support, or sensor system on which he was the acknowledged expert.

"The environmental control and life-support systems in all three modules are functioning within the expected parameters," Lieutenant Colonel Pavel Anikeyev said crisply. Besides being the station's designated second in command, the short, round-faced cosmonaut knew more about the carbon-dioxide scrubbers, water-reclamation systems, and other life-support equipment than anyone else aboard. "The consumables stores aboard our Progress cargo ships appear intact. Off-loading those should be our next priority."

Strelkov nodded in agreement. Shifting and stowing several tons of rations, drinking water, and other supplies would be grueling, time-consuming work. Better to get to it while they were relatively fresh.

Georgy Konnikov was the next one to speak. "I've run diagnostics on our X-band and L-band radars," he reported. "They appear to be in excellent condition." The younger man's mobile mouth quirked upward in a wry smile. "Pursuant to our new orders from Moscow, I have refrained from carrying out full-power tests."

Strelkov nodded somberly. It would not yet do to reveal that Mars One was equipped with military-grade radar systems. "What of our other detection systems?"

"Our IR sensors are working perfectly," Konnikov said. "As a test, I was able to pick out the thermal signature of the American MENTOR 9 signals intelligence satellite at a range of thirty-six thousand kilometers."

Strelkov was impressed. The geostationary MENTOR-series satellites, used by the Americans to collect a wide range of electronic signals—everything from rocket and missile telemetry to cell-phone calls—were enormous, with main antennas well over one hundred meters in diameter. While that made them relatively easy to detect visually, zeroing in on their small thermal output at such a long range was still a remarkable feat.

"Our data links to other ground- and space-based sensors are also fully functional," Konnikov continued. "We are already receiving data from our Persona and Razdan electro-optical, EKS ballistic early warning, and Kondor radar imaging satellites."

Strelkov nodded. That was good news indeed. Even while they were orbiting at six hundred and forty kilometers above the earth's surface, their visual and radar detection ranges were limited to some thousands of kilometers. Data links to other space-based and ground-based radars, cameras, and infrared sensors significantly improved their situational awareness—making it virtually impossible for the Americans to sneak anything past them.

He turned his attention to two more of his officers. Major Viktor Filatyev, tall and burly for a cosmonaut, was the sole nonaviator aboard. Before joining the Mars Project, he had been assigned to one of Russia's experimental ground-based laser R&D programs. On the station, he was in charge of their primary offensive weapon, the Thunder-bolt coaxial plasma rail gun. Filatyev's shorter and leaner subordinate, Captain Leonid Revin, was chiefly responsible for their two upgraded Hob-nail lasers. Primarily intended for close-in de-fense, the lasers had a maximum effective range of around one hundred kilometers. But even at that range, they were powerful enough to cut through a centimeter of solid steel in seconds.

"Leonid and I have run systems checks on the three energy weapons," Filatyev said. "All indi-cators are green." The big man frowned deeply. "But without our reactor, power supply is a very serious problem."

"We'll dig into that in a moment, Viktor," Strel-kov said with more patience than he felt. It would not do for the crew to know the depth of his own concern about their situation without the lost fusion generator. "Let's finish running through what works before we focus on what doesn't, eh?"

Abashed, Filatyev shrugged, quickly tighten-ing his grip on a handhold when the instinctive reaction threatened to send him drifting into the compartment ceiling. "Sorry, sir."

Strelkov grinned. "Zero-G takes some getting used to, doesn't it?"

Heads nodded in response. Three of the other cosmonauts looked slightly green around the gills. Even with antinausea medications, completely adjusting to the absence of any defined "up" or "down" would take some of them a few days.

He looked back at Filatyev. "What is the status of our kinetic weapons?"

The big man relaxed slightly, obviously glad to be able to report some good news. "Fully functional, Colonel."

"Very good," Strelkov said. Besides its revolutionary directed-energy weapons, Mars One's armament included a retractable rotary launcher with twelve Scimitar short-range hypersonic missiles and several *Rapira* or Rapier ground-attack weapons. Like the Hobnail lasers, the Scimitars were part of the station's defenses—ready to engage enemy missiles or spacecraft that posed a direct threat.

In sharp contrast, the Rapiers were purely offensive weapons. They were kinetic-kill warheads made of high-temperature composite materials originally developed for Russia's failed Avangard hypersonic glide-boost bomb carrier. Each warhead was mated to a thruster with enough delta-v to change its orbital inclination by up to ten degrees and then make a controlled reentry burn. Slashing down from space, Rapiers could strike fixed ground targets like airfields, ICBM silos, and other military and civilian installations at up to Mach 20.

That left just one member of the Mars One crew to hear from. Fit and trim, Major Pyotr Romanenko looked every inch the tough, aggressive Su-35 fighter pilot he had been before being tapped for Russia's military cosmonaut program. Assigned to manage both the reactor and solar power arrays as needed, he also had a secondary role—defending Mars One in close combat, should the Americans somehow manage the almost unthinkable . . .

docking with and boarding the station. "Our so-lar panels are presently operating at maximum efficiency," he said gruffly. "Right now, in full sun-light, we're generating approximately seventy-five kilowatts of electricity."

Strelkov nodded. Romanenko's stress on the words *in full sunlight* was the root of one of their biggest problems. At this altitude and with the sun's current angle to their orbital plane, Mars One spent approximately thirty-four minutes of each orbit in darkness. During those periods in shadow, the solar arrays would not generate any electricity, forcing the station to rely entirely on backup battery power for routine operations.

Even during the daylight portion of each orbit, the power provided by their solar panels fluctuated, depending on the station's position relative to the sun. And some of that was needed to recharge their batteries. After figuring in the electricity needed to run their life-support systems, computers, and var-ious sensors, relatively little would be left over to recharge the two lasers and their plasma rail gun.

Strelkov shifted his foothold a tiny bit so that he could face Filatyev and Revin more fully. "If we have to fire Thunderbolt or the Hobnails be-fore the replacement reactor we've been promised arrives, what is our tactical situation?"

Revin spoke up first. "Each laser's battery pack provides about thirty seconds of total firing time, sir."

"That's what? Maybe six or seven separate shots sufficient to destroy larger targets like incoming missiles or enemy spacecraft?" Strelkov estimated.

"Yes, sir. But killing or deflecting smaller pieces of shrapnel or space debris requires much less energy," Revin said. "We could successfully engage targets of that type with short, single-second bursts."

Strelkov breathed a little easier. Even relying solely on battery power, the Hobnail lasers could still defend Mars One against anything but a sustained mass attack. They were orbiting well above the reach of the Standard SM-3 anti-satellite missiles employed by the U.S. Navy and Japan's Maritime Self-Defense Force. And while the larger, more powerful ballistic-missile interceptors that formed America's Ground-Based Midcourse Defense might be able to attack the station, there were relatively few of them—and they were only deployed in fixed silos at California's Vandenberg Air Force Base and New York's Fort Drum. Given Mars One's high relative velocity, there should be no way the Americans could hope to launch their interceptors rapidly enough to overwhelm his defenses.

But what about the unknown factor? his mind reminded him coldly. What about the Sky Masters spaceplanes? Current intelligence reports from the GRU suggested they were unarmed, but Russia's spies were never infallible. Defeating an attack by missile- or laser-armed spaceplanes might take a longer-range weapon.

He looked at Filatyev. "And your Thunderbolt rail gun, Major? How many times can you fire using the energy stored in its supercapacitors?"

"Only twice, Colonel," the big man replied.

"The gun requires a substantial amount of power to create plasma toroids and magnetically accelerate them up to ten thousand kilometers per second."

"You can fire only twice," Strelkov repeated flatly. He turned to Romanenko. "How much time do you need to recharge the lasers and rail gun using power diverted from our solar arrays?"

The engineering officer shrugged. "Of the two weapons systems, Thunderbolt is the easier to replenish. Its supercapacitors can be charged much faster than conventional batteries. Based on the numbers I've worked out in consultation with Moscow, we ought to be able to fully power the rail gun every five or six minutes. That's assuming, of course, that we shut down every other nonessential system aboard the station. And that's also assuming the solar panels are in full sunlight and at peak efficiency," he warned. "Anything less will greatly slow the process."

"And the Hobnail lasers?"

"Given our battery technology and other power constraints, it would take a miracle to recharge them in anything less than two or three full orbits."

Strelkov's jaw tightened. That was pretty much what he'd expected to hear, but it didn't make the news any more welcome.

Pavel Anikeyev, his second in command, cleared his throat apologetically. "I'm afraid we do have one more problem, sir."

Briefly, Strelkov closed his eyes in frustration. Then he reopened them with a crooked smile.

"Only one, Pavel? I should kiss you," he said sardonically. The other cosmonauts laughed.

"Without power from the lost fusion reactor, the station's advanced ion thrusters are useless," Anikeyev pointed out.

"Shit," Strelkov muttered. Somehow he'd missed that fact in the frantic rush to figure out work-arounds for their energy weapons and bring Mars One's systems online after they boarded. But his deputy was right. And without those ion thrusters, their four-hundred-ton station's ability to maneuver in orbit would be severely limited. Whether compensating for the recoil generated by the plasma rail gun or fighting atmospheric drag, they would be forced to rely solely on the conventional rocket engines and thrusters of the two docked cargo modules and their own Federation orbiter. Until the replacement fusion reactor promised by Colonel General Leonov was docked with Mars One and functioning, they were far more vulnerable to an American attack than originally anticipated.

CHAPTER 19

Through the spaceplane's forward cockpit windows, Brad McLanahan could see a black sky stretching above them toward infinity. Stars, visible as hard bright pinpoints of light, were strewn across the blackness in all directions. The sheer beauty of it would have robbed him of breath if the G-forces they were pulling hadn't already accomplished that.

"Passing through . . . sixty-four miles," Boomer grunted from the left-hand pilot's seat. "Good ignition on the Leopards in rocket mode . . . speed fourteen thousand miles per hour and increasing." As he followed the steering cues on his heads-up display, his gloved hand nudged the sidestick controller forward a tiny bit. The nozzles of the four LPDRS engines gimbaled slightly, adjusting the direction of thrust. The S-19's nose dipped in response, until the spaceplane had almost completely leveled off.

Now the rounded curve of the world was distinctly visible—with a sharp blue band along the horizon marking the division between sky and space. They were just above the Kármán line, past the point where the increasingly tenuous upper atmosphere could provide any aerodynamic lift. Staying aloft now required attaining orbital velocity, the speed at which their forward motion would equal the acceleration of gravity pulling them downward.

"Altitude seventy-two miles. Speed now . . . seventeen thousand miles per hour and still climbing," Boomer said, pushing the words out against the four Gs pressing them back into their seats. "Engine cutoff coming up in five seconds . . . four . . . two . . . one. Shutdown."

Brad felt the sensation of enormous, overwhelming pressure gripping his body suddenly disappear. Even with the straps holding him tight in the seat, he experienced an eerie floating sensation. With a mental effort, he focused on *not* feeling queasy. It always took him a little time to acclimate to zero-G.

"Good burn," Boomer reported.

Brad checked the navigation and velocity data shown on his own multifunction display and nodded. "I confirm that. We're in the planned parking orbit."

Their S-19 Midnight was far out over the South Pacific, flying northeast along the same relative orbital track as the slower-moving Russian space station still several hundred miles ahead of and above them. Since the velocities necessary to stay in orbit decreased with altitude, if nothing else changed they would catch up with and pass far below Mars One in approximately one hour.

With a grin, Brad turned his helmeted head toward Boomer. "Hey, are we there yet? Huh? Huh? Are we?"

Boomer chuckled. "Ask me that one more time, kid, and I swear to God, I'll stop this thing and dump you out into the cold hard vacuum of space."

This had already been a long mission. Since taking off from Battle Mountain more than five hours ago, they'd flown a little over five thousand miles south-southeast out over the Pacific at Mach 2—slowing down a couple of times along the way to top up with JP-8 from Sky Masters–owned 767 aerial tankers. When they arrived at a precisely calculated mid-ocean point between New Zealand to the west and central Chile to the east, Boomer had executed a sharp turn back to the northeast. Then the instant they were on a course mirroring the Russian orbital track, he'd punched it—sending the spaceplane streaking spaceward at full power.

"*Radar contact at twelve o'clock high. Range is three miles and closing,*" the S-19's computer reported. "*Contact is an S-29 Shadow.*"

"Right on schedule," Brad said with satisfaction. "Man, I love it when a crazy-ass plan actually comes together." Reaching out, he punched in commands on his display and locked the contact into their navigation program. Instantly, the necessary steering cues appeared on Boomer's HUD.

"We're a little off to port and a scooch low," Boomer remarked with a slight smile of his own. "Not too shabby after traveling practically a bazillion miles like a bat out of hell." He locked out the sidestick controller and throttles for their main engines, and then pulled down what looked like a video game controller with two small knobs. "Thruster controls online." Gingerly, he tweaked the knobs. In response, hydrazine maneuvering thrusters fired in sequence, pushing them to the right and higher.

As they closed in from below, they could see the other spaceplane grow from just a small black dot lit up by the sun to a blended-wing craft identical to their own, except larger and with a fifth engine mounted atop the fuselage. Relative to them, the S-29 was upside down and backward, flying tail first at more than seventeen thousand five hundred miles per hour. Its cargo bay doors were open, revealing two large silver-colored fuel tanks tightly slotted inside.

Brad keyed his mike. "Shadow Two-One, this is Midnight Zero-One. We have good visual contact. Welcome to space!"

Through his headset, he heard Nadia's amused-sounding voice. *"That was supposed to be my line, Midnight Zero-One. After all, we were here first!"*

Well, Brad thought, that was true, though only by a few minutes. The S-29 piloted by Peter Vasey, with Nadia as mission commander, had kept them company for most of the long trip to the South Pacific before flying on ahead to make its own climb to this extremely low orbit.

"Fair enough, Shadow Two-One," he allowed. "Stand by. We're moving into precontact position now."

Carefully, using tiny bursts from the S-19's maneuvering thrusters, Boomer brought their spaceplane into position slightly below and behind its larger companion. The indicators on his HUD flashed green. "In precontact position, Two-One," he radioed. He flipped a switch to open the slipway doors above and behind the cockpit. "Ready to proceed. 'Bomb' first, please."

"*Roger, Zero-One,*" Nadia replied. "*We show you stabilized precontact. We are ready with 'bomb.' You are cleared into contact position.*"

Boomer glanced at Brad with a quick smile. "Now we find out if this cockamamie idea of yours will work."

"Hey, you're the one who did the math," Brad retorted virtuously. "I'm just the big-picture guy here." Ostentatiously, he folded his arms. "If we blow up, it's not *my* fault."

"Well, that'll be a comfort, no doubt," Boomer said dryly. "Shadow Two-One, Midnight is moving into contact position now," he said into his mike. His hands made small, precise movements on the thruster controls. Slowly, with infinite care, the S-19 slid closer to the larger spaceplane . . . drifting higher to within a few yards of its open cargo bay doors.

A new set of green indicators flashed on his HUD. One careful tap activated thrusters arrayed around the S-19's nose. They fired—canceling out the additional forward motion he'd imparted earlier.

"Good position. Zero relative velocity," Brad confirmed after checking his own display.

Boomer breathed out. Unlike a regular air tanker, the S-29 Shadow they'd hastily converted for this mission didn't have any of the visual guides—flashing director lights or painted lines—pilots relied on when maneuvering into position. To assist him, Sky Masters techs had done some very rapid coding to create a variation of the computer program used for docking with other spacecraft and space stations. He radioed Nadia. "Midnight Zero-One is stabilized in contact position. Over to you."

"*Roger, Zero-One,*" Nadia replied. "*I am maneuvering the BOHM refueling boom now.*"

Brad peered up through the canopy into the S-29's cargo bay. Directed by Nadia, a long, flexible boom unlatched from one side of the bay and slowly extended toward them. Tiny thrusters attached to the end of the boom fired in microsecond bursts.

Seconds later, he and Boomer felt a gentle *CL-CLUNK* as the nozzle at the end of the boom slid into the slipway and seated itself in their spaceplane's refueling receptacle. "*I show contact,*" Nadia told them.

"Contact confirmed," Boomer said.

Aboard the S-29, pumps whirred, using helium to "push" the thick borohydrogen metaoxide into the S-19's fuel tanks in zero-G conditions. Brad watched the readings collected by sensors inside the tanks themselves. Steadily, their oxidizer reserves increased. For long minutes, the two spaceplanes flew in tandem above the blue, cloud-decked ocean far below.

"BOHM transfer complete," Nadia radioed. *"Detaching the first boom."*

With another *CL-CLUNK*, the boom's nozzle slid back out of the slipway. Guided by thrusters, it retracted back into the converted tanker spaceplane's cargo bay and latched.

Repeating the process with a second boom, this one pumping JP-8 jet fuel from a second tank, went faster. Even so, by the time the fuel transfer was finished, the linked spacecraft were approaching the solar terminator, the earth's ever-moving dividing line between day and night. Ahead, city lights along the South American coast shone brightly, like diamonds against a black velvet backdrop.

Once the JP-8 fuel boom was clear, Boomer fired the S-19's thrusters again. Aboard the bigger S-29 Shadow, Vasey did the same while Nadia closed their cargo bay doors. The two spaceplanes separated vertically and horizontally.

"Nice job, Shadow Two-One," Brad radioed. "Midnight Zero-One is gassed up and ready to go."

"Copy that," Nadia replied. There was a slight pause. *"We are beginning our powered reentry now. Good luck and stay safe!"*

Brad saw a brief glow light up the other space-plane as it fired its five LPDRS engines in rocket mode. Decelerating hard, it dropped lower on its way back down into the atmosphere and, ultimately, Battle Mountain. "Thank you, Two-One," he said. "We'll see you back at the barn in a few hours."

Beside him, Boomer tapped their thrusters again, pitching the S-19's nose up and away from the earth's curving horizon. He glanced at Brad. "You ready to chase down that Russian space station?"

Dry-mouthed suddenly, Brad nodded tightly. "Yeah. But let's make sure we don't get *too* close, okay?"

"Amen to that," Boomer said cheerfully. "Don't sweat it, Brad. We're just gonna mosey on up to within a hundred miles or so of our cosmonaut buddies and launch our nanosats . . . unobtrusive-like. Then we just kick back and wait while the little birds do all the hard work." He brought their main engine controls back online. "Stand by for engine relight."

"Affirmative. Standing by." Brad checked his own displays. "Everything looks solid. No red lights. We are go for the burn."

Cued by their flight computer, Boomer advanced the throttles. "Okay, here we go. Next stop, Mars One."

With a muffled *whummp*, the S-19's rocket motors relit. Instantly, G-forces slammed Brad and Boomer back into their seats. Accelerating fast, the spaceplane streaked higher—climbing almost vertically toward the still-distant Russian orbital platform.

ABOARD MARS ONE, OVER SOUTH AMERICA
That same time

Tethered comfortably in front of his sensor console, Major Georgy Konnikov fought to keep his eyes open. He yawned once and then again, even deeper. His jaw muscles ached with the strain. Between the hard labor involved in unloading supplies from the two Progress cargo modules and the frantic rush to bring their life-support, electronics, and weapons systems online, no one in the Mars One crew had gotten much sleep in the past twenty-four hours.

BEEP-BEEP-BEEP.

The shrill warning tone warbling through his headset yanked Konnikov's eyes wide open. Startled, he floated backward against the tether and then pulled himself hurriedly back within reach of the console.

He pulled up the alert on his display. Mars One's passive IR sensors had just detected a major heat source—either a missile or a rocket launch. But which was it? And where the hell was it headed? His fingers rattled across a keyboard as he interrogated the station's primary computer. Unnoticed, a droplet of sweat broke free from his furrowed brow and drifted off across the component-crowded compartment.

In response to Konnikov's frantic queries, lines of text scrolled across the display. They were superimposed on a map that showed Mars One's orbital track as a green line. Suddenly a red line appeared, arrowing across the map . . . on an intercept course with the station.

"My God," the major muttered. Without any further hesitation, he punched a button on his console. Alarms blared in every compartment. *"Action stations,"* he yelled into the intercom. "All personnel to action stations. This is not a drill. Repeat, this is *not* a drill! Colonel Strelkov to Command at *once!*"

Colonel Vadim Strelkov reacted instantly to the ear-piercing shriek of the "action stations" alarm. He'd been dozing, half asleep and half awake, in a sleeping bag anchored to the wall of his small cabin. Now, before he even fully regained consciousness, his hands tugged the zipper down far enough so that he could worm free of its comforting embrace.

For a brief moment, floating free in the tiny space, he shook his head in a desperate bid to clear out the last cobwebs of fatigue. Then, hearing Konnikov's urgent summons, he swept the curtain to his cabin aside and launched himself down a narrow, conduit- and storage-cabinet-lined corridor.

Seconds later, Strelkov glided through an open hatch into the command compartment. He could hear confused voices echoing through other hatches as the rest of the station's crew struggled to wake up, comprehend what was happening, and maneuver in zero-G to their allotted posts. He gritted his teeth in mingled fury and humiliation. Years of rigorous training and drills and *this* . . . this disgraceful disorder . . . *this* was the result of the first real crisis?

Angrily, he shoved aside the pathetic excuse offered by his unruly subconscious, that his cosmonauts were simply exhausted and in serious need of rest. What did fatigue matter if Mars One was truly under attack? Would an enemy missile refuse to detonate out of pity because those it sought to kill were *tired*?

Before he sailed entirely across the compartment, Strelkov grabbed a handhold and arrested his momentum. "Give me a situation report!" he demanded.

Still bleary eyed himself, Konnikov complied. "Our thermal sensors have a contact, sir! The computer evaluates it as one of the American spaceplanes. It is currently accelerating into orbit on a converging course. Based on its present trajectory, I estimate it will come within two hundred kilometers of the station, possibly even closer."

Strelkov scowled. The Americans were reacting faster than he had hoped. Whether this was an attack or something else entirely—maybe only a reconnaissance flight—he would have to take precautions. He let go, pushed off the compartment wall with his fingertips, and floated over to the younger man. "Attention, all crew. Begin donning your Sokol pressure suits immediately. Major Romanenko, prep your special-action armor," he ordered over the intercom. "Report when ready."

GRU intelligence reports or not, he thought coldly, if that American spaceplane was armed after all and attacked them, depressurizing Mars One would at least minimize the danger of fire and explosive decompression. And since each man's space suit was stored close to his assigned action station, it shouldn't take them more than a few minutes to obey.

Seeing Konnikov reach for the tether holding him to his sensor console, Strelkov stopped him with a gesture. "Before you suit up, Georgy, I need you to contact Moscow," he snapped. "Get me Colonel General Leonov . . . and the president!"

CHAPTER 20

NATIONAL DEFENSE CONTROL CENTER, MOSCOW

That same time

Russia's new military command center was a large complex of buildings on the northern bank of the Moskva River, about three kilometers from the Kremlin. It featured three auditorium-sized control rooms equipped with enormous, wraparound projection screens, tiered seating with dozens of individual computer stations, and secure connections to what was billed as the world's most powerful military supercomputer.

Privately, Colonel General Mikhail Leonov judged those vast, futuristic-looking control rooms to be mere theater—stage sets to impress the gullible Russian public with a display of their nation's military power and advanced technology. For all their glitz and glitter, no sensible commander would run an actual operation in one of those fishbowls. When you were making crucial, life-or-death decisions, who needed IMAX-sized screens or an audience of surplus junior officers all tapping away on their computers in an effort to look useful?

He had chosen, instead, to direct Mars Project operations from a much smaller control room buried deep beneath the ground and guarded by several layers of both human and automated security. Four workstations, one for him and three more for his principal deputies, were sufficient to manage operations—especially when coupled with secure video links to the Kremlin, the Mars One station, Vostochny, Plesetsk, and other key sites across Russia.

It had one other advantage: an adjoining bedroom suite. While they were not luxurious, these living quarters allowed Leonov to exercise direct operational command at any time of the day or night, with minimal delays. And during these first critical weeks, he believed it was vital to keep a firm hand on matters.

So when Strelkov's emergency signal from Mars One arrived shortly before five A.M., Moscow time, Leonov was able to reach his desk within a matter of minutes. The colonel's image, bounced through a network of military communications satellites, was up on one screen. His normally lean face looked puffy, a common hydrostatic effect of prolonged weightlessness where fluids normally drawn by gravity down toward the legs and lower torso accumulated instead in the face and upper body.

A second screen showed Gennadiy Gryzlov in his

private Kremlin office. He appeared to be wide-awake. Given the president's proclivity for keeping late hours, Leonov suspected he had not yet gone to bed.

"What is your status, Colonel?" Leonov asked.

"We have detected an American spaceplane, probably an S-19 Midnight from its thermal signature, climbing toward Mars One."

"*Ni pizdi!*" Gryzlov thundered over the secure video teleconference link. "Don't bullshit me! I thought you told me the American spaceplanes could not fly high enough to reach Mars One!"

"We have not yet positively identified the spacecraft, sir," Strelkov said. "It could be a new model of their single-stage-to-orbit spaceplanes."

"You had better get a positive identification, and get it now!"

"On its current course and velocity, we predict this spaceplane will very shortly enter a stable orbit offset from ours by less than two hundred kilometers." Strelkov looked off-camera toward one of his subordinates and nodded sharply. "Major Konnikov is relaying our sensor data to you now."

"Is this an attack?" Gryzlov snapped. "Could that thing be a missile or weaponized satellite?"

"It is possible," Strelkov admitted. "Our cameras will give us a positive identification soon. I find it troubling that the Americans have timed their approach with such precision."

Gryzlov stared at him. "How so?"

"We are still in darkness and thus unable to recharge our directed-energy weapons," Strelkov said, unable to hide the anxiety he felt. "If the

Americans are making an offensive move against us, this is the best possible moment for them— when our defenses are at their weakest."

"Calm down, Vadim," Leonov said coolly. He needed to reel Strelkov back from the edge before he overreacted. Tired men could make very bad decisions. And tired and frightened men were prone to jump at every shadow. "There is no evidence our enemies have breached the Mars Project's security, let alone learned anything about your station's temporary vulnerability."

He looked at Gryzlov. "This American spacecraft is almost certainly only flying a reconnaissance mission. This is a probe, nothing more. It poses no real threat." He shrugged. "From the outside, Mars One looks exactly like the peaceful, unarmed orbital facility we have proclaimed it to be. If we are careful, the Americans will learn nothing of value—certainly nothing that will contradict our cover story."

Gryzlov frowned. "You seem very confident, Mikhail."

"For good reason," Leonov assured him. "At two hundred kilometers, or even at one hundred kilometers, an S-19's limited onboard sensors should not be able to penetrate the station's disguise."

"And if the Americans come even closer?" Gryzlov wondered acidly. "If they poke the nose of that spaceplane right up Mars One's ass, how well will your much-hyped camouflage and stealth measures work?"

Leonov shook his head. "The crew of that

spaceplane isn't likely to be so foolish, Gennadiy. Without positive coordination between Mars One and the American spacecraft, a very close approach would only risk a collision that could destroy them both. Since our two nations are nominally at peace, there is no reason for the Americans to take such a risk."

"You think not?" Gryzlov said with undisguised scorn. "Where have you been for the past twenty years, Leonov? In a monastery? Have you forgotten all the other times the United States has launched unprovoked surprise attacks on Russia or on our interests abroad?"

"No, Mr. President." Leonov saw little point in debating the subject. Gryzlov's definition of *unprovoked* was much the same as any four-year-old's complaint that his younger sibling had "hit him *back* first."

"Exactly. And how many of those illegal aggressions were carried out by that madman McLanahan or his lunatic son?" Gryzlov went on. His handsome face contorted in anger. "You would do well to remember that they, along with their coconspirator Martindale, now have the ear of the new American president."

Leonov noticed that Strelkov looked even more perturbed now. Acutely aware as the colonel was that the S-19 was closing fast, the last thing he needed was seeing open friction between his two superiors.

Gryzlov turned his attention to the commander of Mars One. "If the Americans don't behave as rationally as Leonov here imagines, are your defenses ready to destroy them?"

"Yes, Mr. President," Strelkov said quickly. "Our Hobnail lasers have more than enough power to destroy the spaceplane if it approaches within one hundred kilometers." Hesitantly, he offered a compromise. "If the Americans do try a close approach and fail to shear off after being warned, we could activate and fire a single laser."

"Why rely on only one laser?" Gryzlov asked.

"Because then we could blame the incident on an unintentional malfunction of Mars One's automated defenses against dangerous space debris," Strelkov said. "The Americans would find it difficult to prove otherwise . . . and the rest of our station's weapons systems would remain hidden."

Gryzlov nodded his approval. "A good plan, Colonel."

"Thank you, sir."

"Any comments, Mikhail?" Gryzlov asked, almost offhandedly.

Silently, Leonov shook his head. Strelkov's proposal threaded the needle between common sense—sitting tight until the Americans grew weary of seeing nothing suspicious on Mars One and departed—and the president's obvious eagerness to test their new weapons on a real live target. In the circumstances, it was probably the best they could do.

"Very well, Strelkov, you may proceed," Gryzlov said. "But maintain this direct link to Moscow. And stand by for further orders as the situation warrants."

ABOARD THE S-19 MIDNIGHT SPACEPLANE
A short time later

Again, Brad McLanahan felt himself pressed back into his seat as the spaceplane's main engines fired in rocket mode for the third time on this mission. But this time, they shut down after only a few seconds. Numbers and graphics flowed across his display. "Good burn," he announced. "Our orbit is circularized and stable at three hundred and eighty miles up."

"Fuel status?" Boomer asked.

Brad paged through to another screen. "Plenty of hydrazine for the thrusters. And we've got more than enough JP-8 and 'bomb' remaining for additional on orbit maneuvers and a powered descent. But I'd recommend a rendezvous with another 767 aerial tanker once we're back in the atmosphere." He raised an eyebrow. "Unless you want to try making a dead-stick landing like the one Nadia and Constable pulled off in the simulator?"

"Not me," Boomer retorted, smiling. "A man's gotta know his limitations and I draw the line at trying to fly this sucker like it's a glider. Sims are one thing. Reality . . . well, that's a whole lot different." He poked at his own display, transmitting a text to Sky Masters requesting additional tanker support. "In the meantime, let's do what we came here to do. Can you give me a visual cue to the Russian station?"

"No problem, boss," Brad said. Their S-19 was

in an orbit whose inclination matched that of Mars One, though offset by roughly one hundred miles. Right now they were also trailing the station by twenty miles. On the other hand, their lower altitude gave the spaceplane a slightly higher orbital velocity—not much, just around forty miles per hour. Still, that meant they would pass Mars One in a little over thirty minutes.

Quickly, he instructed their computer to match their known position in orbit with the current estimated location of the Russian space station. Fractions of a second later, it sent a steering indicator to Boomer's HUD.

Maneuvering thrusters fired as the spaceplane yawed, swinging its nose around until they were pointing almost at right angles to their direction of travel. Bright green brackets appeared in the upper part of their individual heads-up displays—highlighting where Mars One *should* be. But at this distance and deep in the darkness of the earth's shadow, it was still effectively invisible to them.

"Any luck with the nav radar?" Boomer asked.

"Little blips and skips," Brad said. "But I can't lock the station up. That damned thing is definitely coated with some kind of radar-absorbent material."

Boomer snorted. "Yeah, that's just what you'd expect from a *peaceful* civilian orbital platform." He shook his head. "Well, let's see how much info we can shake loose up close and impersonal. You ready on the nanosats?"

Brad nodded. "I'm on it. Spinning them up

now." He began entering the commands that would bring their payload of eight tiny recon satellites to life. One by one, he activated their propulsion systems and electronics. Green lights blossomed on his display. "Good indicators on all eight," he reported. "Initializing guidance systems."

More taps on his MFD sent precise navigation fixes to each nanosat's tiny onboard computer. These computers were essentially derivatives of consumer-grade smartphone technology. Using them to control a spacecraft sounded crazy, except for the fact that the Apollo computers that made it to the moon and back were millions of times slower and less powerful than a modern smartphone.

This time, though, Brad saw only seven green lights. One remained stubbornly red. One of their satellites, one of three rigged to carry a sensitive infrared camera, was refusing to accept data from the S-19's computer. He tried again. No joy. Without up-to-date navigation data, that particular nanosat was as good as dead. Sure, it could still fly, but God alone knew where it was likely to go if they launched it.

"Well, crap," he muttered. "We've lost Sierra Four. It won't accept data." He glanced across the cockpit. "I bet a cable connector jarred loose during one of our burns."

Boomer nodded. That was a reasonable theory. The need for speed in readying this mission had forced shortcuts in normal procedures—including having Sky Masters technicians double- and triple-check the bracing used to secure their pay-load under acceleration. Considering the shake, rattle, and roll they'd put the S-19 Midnight through over the past hours, he and Brad were lucky only to have lost one of the eight miniature spacecraft they'd brought into orbit.

He checked the elapsed time since they'd reached this orbit. "We'll cross into sunlight in ten minutes," he reminded Brad. "So let's crank open the cargo bay doors and get these birds in flight while we've got some cover."

"On it," Brad said in agreement. He punched a control to open the cargo bay. Releasing their tiny recon satellites while they were still in dark-ness was a good move. True, compared to Mars One or even the S-19, the nanosats were about as big as fleas on an elephant. But they weren't invisible, and launching a flock of them in full sunlight would certainly catch somebody's unwel-come eye. Since the whole point of this trip was to recon the Russians' new space station without unduly spooking them, that was definitely some-thing to avoid.

Through the deck plating beneath his booted feet, he felt a soft rumble as the spaceplane's cargo doors unlatched and swung open. A light above the control he'd pushed flashed green and stayed lit. "The doors are fully open."

"Roger that," Boomer acknowledged. "Launch at your discretion."

"Launching now," Brad said. He tapped icons in sequence, releasing clamps that had secured each of the seven functioning satellites in place.

Small spring mechanisms ejected them into space one by one.

As they floated free out of the cargo bay, the nanosats' onboard computers took over. Short bursts from their chemical engines—which used highly efficient and nontoxic AF-M315E, hydroxylammonium nitrate, as a propellant—sent them outward on diverging courses aimed roughly at where Mars One would be in approximately twenty minutes. If all went well, their little flock of satellites would pass on all sides of the station at ranges between fifteen and twenty-five miles.

A red icon suddenly blinked above the image of one of the stylized nanosats on Brad's screen. "Shit," he growled.

"Problem?" Boomer asked.

"The burn on Sierra Six was a fraction of a second too long. She's heading off into deep space," Brad answered. His fingers flew across the display, sending a series of new commands to the errant satellite's computer through a secure data link.

In response, three small magnets aboard the nanosat—oriented along the x, y, and z axes—powered up in a precise sequence. Together, they generated a tiny local magnetic field oriented in a specific direction. When the field created by these magnetorquers brushed against Earth's far more powerful ambient magnetic field, the reaction altered the nanosat's facing—in much the same way a child could use a more powerful magnet to tug at a smaller one. Once the satellite was properly aligned, its chemical engine fired again, using just a quick pulse to push it back onto its preplanned flight path.

The red icon blinked off.

Brad breathed out in relief. "We're good. All seven birds are flying straight and true."

"And there you see the value of having a man in the loop," Boomer said in satisfaction. "Now all we have to do is sit tight out here in the dark and see what turns up."

CHAPTER 21

Colonel Vadim Strelkov saw the earth below them emerge from darkness as Mars One crossed the terminator line and came back into daylight. Swirls of brilliant white cloud covered much of the North Atlantic. Just ahead lay the rugged mass of Portugal and Spain, an undulating mix of arid brown mountains and plateaus and green, wooded ridges and valleys.

"Our solar arrays are back online at maximum efficiency," Pyotr Romanenko reported from his post in another compartment near the aft end of the command module. "And our backup batteries are recharging at the expected rate."

Strelkov felt some of his tension ease slightly. "Very good, Major," he said over the intercom. "Cut power to all nonessential systems. I want electricity available to recharge the Thunderbolt rail gun and our lasers if necessary."

"Yes, sir," Romanenko said. "Cutting power now."

In response, lights dimmed across the command compartment. The constant background noise of their air-recirculation fans faded. Indicators on various consoles went yellow as whole subsystems—oxygen generators, water recovery, waste management, and others—were put on standby.

Satisfied that his orders were being obeyed, Strelkov turned his attention back to the distant American spaceplane. Up to now, it had been visible only as a blotchy, glowing heat signature. But as it crossed the terminator, still behind them though slowly catching up, the black-winged S-19 took on shape and definition in Mars One's powerful telescopes.

He frowned. The spaceplane's nose was aimed straight at them. "Are the Americans closing on us, Georgy?" he demanded.

From his sensor console, Konnikov replied: "No, sir. Their spacecraft is continuing on the same slightly lower orbit, offset from ours by one hundred and sixty kilometers." He leaned closer to his display. "They've probably rotated toward us to increase the efficiency of their onboard radar."

"Has it locked on to us?"

Konnikov turned his helmeted head. Since they were still on station air, his visor was up. "No, Colonel." He shrugged. "The S-19's radar is far too weak to penetrate our stealth coating." He turned back at his screen. "One thing is odd, though," he commented. "The spaceplane's payload bay doors appear to be open."

Strelkov felt colder suddenly. What were the Americans up to?

From the forward weapons module, Leonid Revin suggested, "Maybe they need to radiate heat generated by their life-support system, like NASA's old space shuttle orbiters?"

"I do not think so, Captain," Strelkov said slowly. While training for duty aboard Mars One, he had studied every piece of information gained by observing Sky Masters spaceplanes during their flights to and from America's Armstrong military space station and the International Space Station. Everything indicated they usually opened their cargo doors only after they were docked . . . not during flight.

Gryzlov broke in abruptly over their link to Moscow. "Those open doors could be proof the Americans are planning to attack you!" he growled. "What if they brought missiles with them into orbit, hidden inside that cargo bay?"

Strelkov felt his pulse speed up. *My God*, he realized, the president might be right. Frantically, he pulled up what was known about the S-19's payload capacity on his command console. Current intelligence suggested it was a little under three thousand kilograms. At first, that didn't seem like much . . . not until he had the computer run that figure against different U.S. missile types.

His eyes widened. The American AIM-120D advanced medium-range air-to-air missile was the most likely match. The AMRAAM's solid-fuel rocket motor meant it could be fired in space. With a maximum range of more than one hundred and eighty kilometers, attack speed of nearly five thousand kilometers per hour, and twenty-three kilogram high-explosive blast-fragmentation warhead, a salvo of AIM-120s might pose a serious threat to the Mars One station. And that Sky Masters S-19 out there could be carrying up to sixteen such missiles in its bay . . .

ABOARD THE S-19 MIDNIGHT SPACEPLANE
That same time

Hunter "Boomer" Noble kept his eyes fixed on the brightly lit dot that was Mars One. They were almost level with it now, though still at a lower altitude. Even from one hundred miles away, that Russian space station gave him the creeps. Something about it made him imagine a huge shark silently gliding through the ocean depths in search of smaller prey.

"Getting anything yet?" he asked.

"Well, nothing obviously bad. At least not so far," Brad told him. He had his eyes fixed on his display while he scrolled through the thermal and visual imagery collected by nanosatellites as they flew closer to Mars One. "But our birds are still a little too far out to pick up much detail. Our guys on the ground ought to be able to get a lot more with computer-assisted image enhancement, though."

Boomer nodded. Every piece of data obtained by their constellation of spy satellites was being relayed to Battle Mountain in real time. The Scion and Sky Masters intelligence analysts stationed there should be having a field day sorting through all the information they were gathering.

Through the S-19's cockpit canopy, the glittering point of light that was the Russian space station slid slowly to the left. They were passing Mars One now. Thrusters fired, yawing the spaceplane to keep its nose centered on target.

Boomer frowned. "You know, those bastards over there are being awfully quiet."

"You think they're all asleep?" Brad suggested with a lopsided grin.

"Fuck no," Boomer grunted. "The Russians must have spotted us almost as soon as we boosted. On any half-decent IR sensor, we'd have stood out like a sore thumb."

He chewed that over for a few seconds. From an astronautical point of view, their S-19 and the space station were practically within spitting distance. So why the prolonged silence? At a minimum, Mars One should be querying them about their intentions and warning them to keep a safe distance.

Boomer came to a decision. If that big-ass space station out there *was* armed, he sure as hell did not want the cosmonauts on board it going off half-cocked. It was time to establish contact and ease the tension. He punched in a new radio frequency—143.625 MHz FM, one of the two commonly used by manned Russian spacecraft for voice communications. "*Dobroye utro, Mars Odin!* Good morning, Mars One! This is Midnight Zero-One. Sorry to pop up on you unannounced like this, but we just thought we'd swing by to pay our respects and welcome you folks to orbit."

Half listening while Boomer talked, Brad stiffened suddenly. What the hell? He tapped his display. It froze on one of the pictures transmitted by their recon satellites. This was a close-up of a station module, one of those that formed the vertical "bars" of what sort of looked like a sideways capital letter *I*.

His eyes narrowed as he studied the image closely. Now that the nanosats had a good angle on Mars One in full sunlight, their cameras were spotting odd discontinuities in its surface structures. What first appeared to be ordinary cabling and conduits girding a section of hull plating looked wrong somehow. He zoomed in on a narrow section of the image. There were definitely places where those cables and conduits didn't connect up the way they should—not if they were supposed to serve any useful purpose. *Yeah*, he thought coldly, *that's not my imagination*. They were fakes. Window dressing. But why would the Russians build a space station hull and then layer it with phony conduits?

Struck by what at first seemed a pretty wild theory, Brad pulled up more data from another of their nanosatellites. Sierra Two was one of those equipped with a sensitive thermographic camera. The images it had captured showed Mars One as a riot of psychedelic colors, revealing even tiny differences in the station's surface temperatures. In some ways, that wasn't surprising. Depending on whether a given section of hull was in sunlight or shadow, you could expect its temperature to range anywhere from plus 250 degrees to minus 250 degrees Fahrenheit. But even allowing for highly efficient insulation, some of the readings he saw were significantly outside the predicted norms.

And that matched up with his suspicions.

Excitedly, he turned toward Boomer. "Holy shit! Parts of that space station's hull are definitely fake!"

"Fake? Fake, how?"

Swiftly, Brad highlighted sections on several of the pictures sent back by their tiny satellites and copied them to Boomer's display. "See? These are supposedly solid sections of hull. But that's bullshit. They're actually camouflaged hatches or ports!"

Slowly, Boomer nodded. "Yeah, I think you're right." His mouth tightened. "Okay, let's do our damnedest *not* to find out what's behind those hidden doors the hard way."

ABOARD MARS ONE
That same time

". . . *thought we'd swing by to pay our respects and welcome you folks to orbit.*"

Strelkov was caught off guard by the American

spaceplane pilot's cheerful, friendly-sounding greeting. Why this sudden radio transmission from the spaceplane that had been trailing them in silence for more than half an hour?

Konnikov glanced over at him from his sensor console. "Should I reply, Colonel?"

Strelkov nodded tightly. "Be polite, Georgy. But instruct them to keep their distance."

"Yes, sir." Konnikov keyed his own mike. "Midnight Zero-One, this is Mars One. Thank you for the kind sentiments. However, for flight safety reasons, we must insist that you approach no closer."

Long seconds passed before Strelkov heard the American's elaborately casual reply crackle through his headset. *"Copy that, Mars One. Don't sweat it. We'll be sure not to crowd you. The sky up here is plenty big for both of us."*

Perplexed, Strelkov turned back to the com screens showing Gryzlov and Colonel General Leonov listening in from Moscow. "What kind of game are these people playing?" he wondered. "First, they creep up on us in the dark . . . and now they pretend we're all friends together?"

Gryzlov scowled abruptly. "They're distracting you, Colonel," he snapped. "Like a sleight-of-hand conjurer gesturing broadly with one hand while he palms a card with the other!"

Dismayed, Strelkov stared at the president's furious image. "Distracting us from what?" he asked. "We have not detected any overt hostile activity from the American spaceplane since we made visual contact."

"Don't be an idiot!" Gryzlov snarled. "Remember those open cargo doors? They could have launched their weapons much earlier, while you were both orbiting through darkness!"

Strelkov saw Leonov frown.

"Using some kind of new stealth missile?" the colonel general asked dubiously. "A missile we've never heard of before? That seems highly unlikely—"

With an imperious gesture, Gryzlov cut him off. "Strelkov!" he demanded. "Is your L-band radar active?"

Despite the hydrostatic effects of zero-G, Strelkov felt the blood drain from his face. Mars One's long-wavelength L-band radar was the best choice to detect stealth targets. Without it, they were effectively blind to any attack by weapons purposely shaped to reduce their radar cross section.

But Moscow's earlier orders had been clear. To preserve the fiction that Mars One was a civilian space platform, they had been directed to avoid using either of their military-grade radars if at all possible. Unfortunately, caught up in the press of events since that American spaceplane appeared seemingly out of nowhere, he had neglected to request a change in those instructions. And equally unfortunately, the station's L-band radar, with its substantial electricity requirements, was one of the systems he'd deliberately ordered kept off-line to free up power in case it was needed to recharge their directed-energy weapons.

He stabbed down at the intercom button.

"Major Romanenko! Restore power to our radar systems! Right away!" Then, without waiting for a reply, he swiveled toward Konnikov—holding tight to his console to avoid spinning off helplessly across the compartment. "Georgy! Bring your L-band and X-radars online! And for Christ's sake, hurry! We may already be under missile attack!"

CHAPTER 22

**ABOARD THE S-19 MIDNIGHT SPACEPLANE,
NOW OVER WESTERN EUROPE**
Moments later

Two bright red warning icons flared suddenly on Hunter Noble's cockpit display. He tapped each of them. In response, text boxes opened, conveying information gathered by the S-19's radar warning receivers: *Unidentified L-band search radar detected at twelve o'clock, range one hundred miles. Unidentified X-band target search radar, same bearing, same range.*

"Well, shit, that tears it," Boomer muttered. The Russians aboard Mars One were lighting up powerful, military-grade radars—radars that no genuine civilian space station would need. Worse yet, the combination of radar types they'd activated indicated the Russians were definitely looking for stealth contacts like the Sky Masters recon nanosatellites. While that lower-frequency L-band system could detect stealth craft, it couldn't provide the weapons-quality tracking data needed to engage them. But what it *could* do was tell the station's X-band radar pretty much where it needed to look for potential targets to lock on to.

He glanced across the cockpit at Brad. The younger man was totally focused on his assigned task. The seven tiny satellites he'd launched were within seconds of their closest planned approach to Mars One. This was the point where any nano-sat engine or computer malfunction could prove catastrophic, creating the very real risk of an accidental collision with the Russian station. "They're onto us," he said. "Better grab all the information you can while we're still in data-link range of your birds . . . because I'm about to put some really *serious* distance between us and them."

"Roger that," Brad acknowledged.

Quickly, Boomer pulled up their orbital track. At this point, with the S-19 crossing fast over northern Italy, going for an immediate powered reentry would almost certainly take them down into firing range of Russia's S-500 surface-to-air missile batteries. Waiting a few minutes longer only added China's ground-based missiles to the mix of dangers they faced. In fact, along their current orbital path, it wouldn't be safe to descend for more than fifteen minutes. Which was about fourteen minutes and fifty-nine seconds too damned long in the present situation, he decided.

No, their best option was to shear off as rapidly as possible. He could fire the spaceplane's main engines to initiate a plane-change maneuver.

Increasing their orbit's inclination would separate them fast from Mars One. Unfortunately, it would also consume a hell of a lot of fuel. They might be forced to commit to a space-shuttle-like nose-first reentry after all. He shrugged. He'd rather risk some damage to their heat shielding than hang out here in range of whatever weapons that Russian space platform was carrying. Swiftly, he tapped the necessary icons on his display, instructing the S-19's flight computer to calculate the parameters of the engine burn required for his desired maneuver.

While the navigation program did its stuff, Boomer put his hands back on the thruster controls. He adjusted them gently, making small inputs. Tiny rockets fired in succession, spinning the spaceplane through almost one hundred and eighty degrees so that they were now tail first to the Russian space station. More thrusters popped, stabilizing their attitude.

He brought the sidestick controller and throttles for the S-19's four big engines back online. Readouts showed everything in the green. Numbers counted down across one corner of his HUD. They were ten seconds away from ignition. "Stand by for acceleration," he said tightly.

"Standing by," Brad replied. He leaned forward and sent an activation command to Sierra Six, their lone radar nanosat. Since active radar emissions were easily detected, the original mission plan had called for keeping this satellite's capabilities in reserve. But no plan survives contact with the enemy. And now that the Russians had tumbled to what

they were doing anyway, he figured they might as
well see what its Ka-band radar could pick up at
short range.

One second later, in obedience to his signal, Sierra
Six—presently crossing the orbital track of Mars
One only fifteen miles above the Russian station—
deployed its half-meter-wide radar antenna and
turned on.

ABOARD MARS ONE
That same time

"Our radars are powered up," Major Georgy Konnikov said. "Beginning search-mode sweeps now."

Across the command compartment, Colonel
Vadim Strelkov tensed. His rational mind told
him that Leonov's skepticism was warranted.
Why would the Americans conduct a stealth
weapons strike against Mars One now—without
warning or justification? From a diplomatic standpoint, such an unprovoked attack on what seemed
a peaceful orbital station would be madness. It
would only shatter American alliances already
damaged by the previous administration's foreign
policy blunders. His nerve endings and instincts,
though, were sending very different signals.

Nothing about the behavior of that Sky Masters spaceplane made sense. Its limited active and
passive sensors could not possibly penetrate his

station's camouflage, certainly not from so far away. If this unannounced space rendezvous was simply a reconnaissance mission, as Leonov asserted, why was the S-19 just sitting out there . . . apparently doing *nothing*?

And then, suddenly, the American spaceplane was in motion. The telescopes slaved to its distant image showed it yawing rapidly, spinning around on its axis.

In that same moment, across the compartment, Konnikov, who had been hunched over his radar displays, jerked upright in shock. "Colonel! L-band radar shows multiple small contacts on closing trajectories above and below our orbital track! Range close, less than fifty kilometers!" He grabbed the edges of the console to keep from drifting back against his tether and hammered at his keyboard, directing their X-band radar to lock on to the contacts detected by its lower-frequency counterpart. "The bogeys are very small! Less than a meter in diameter. Relative velocity is plus one hundred and forty meters per second!"

"Confirm that velocity!" Strelkov demanded. Everything in this orbit was traveling at well over twenty-seven thousand KPH. What mattered was relative velocity—how much faster or slower than Mars One these contacts were moving. But one hundred and forty meters per second worked out to less than five hundred kilometers per hour. What sort of missile traveled so slowly?

"Relative velocity is confirmed," Konnikov said tersely.

BEEP-BEEP-BEEP.

Abruptly, a new threat warning shrilled throughout the station.

"Unidentified Ka-band radar detected! Range very close. Frequency is 35.75 gigahertz!" Konnikov snapped.

On-screen, the silhouette of the American S-19 spaceplane glowed brightly for a fractional second. Its four rocket engines had just relit. As the Sky Masters spacecraft curved away, accelerating into a different orbit, its image shrank visibly.

Oh my God, Strelkov thought in horror. President Gryzlov had been right. Mars One *was* under assault by a salvo of stealthy, miniaturized weapons, devices that were probably more like mines than missiles, given their small size and comparatively slow speed. And now the Americans were fleeing the scene, leaving that newly active Ka-band radar to provide final guidance for their sneak attack.

Furiously, he stabbed the intercom control on his console. "All personnel! We are under attack! Close and seal your pressure suits at once!" Then, complying with his own order, Strelkov slammed down the visor of his helmet and plugged the suit's umbilical hose into a receptacle on his console. Instantly, he heard and felt the welcome hiss of oxygen as it flowed through the connection. He punched the intercom button again. "Captain Revin, this is Command. Deploy your Hobnail lasers and destroy those incoming enemy weapons before they reach us!"

"Affirmative, Colonel!" he heard Revin reply from the forward weapons module. "Tracking data handoff from our radar is complete. All targets are laid into my computer."

The station vibrated slightly as camouflaged hatches opened in both the forward and aft weapons modules. Smoothly, the mounts for Mars One's two one-hundred-kilowatt, carbon-dioxide, electric-discharge lasers elevated through the open hatches and locked in firing position.

Strelkov looked back at the screen on his console. Even in those few seconds, the American spaceplane had opened the range considerably. It was already well over two hundred kilometers away—outside the effective range of all but one of his space station's weapons. "Major Filatyev," he growled on the command circuit to the aft weapons module. "Activate Thunderbolt and engage that S-19 Midnight."

ABOARD THE S-19 MIDNIGHT SPACEPLANE
That same time

"Jesus, Boomer! Are you . . . seeing . . . what I'm . . . seeing?" Brad grunted. It took an effort of will to push each separate word out under the high-Gs they were pulling. This engine burn wouldn't last much longer, just long enough to kick them into a higher-inclination orbit—but it was intense.

"Yeah," the pilot said. "We figured Mars One . . . was . . . a military station . . . kinda sucks to be right, though."

No kidding, Brad thought. Straining against the

enormous forces pinning him to his seat, he tapped his display repeatedly, rapidly cycling through the video feeds coming from his flock of nanosatellites as they slid past the Russian space station. Three high-tech weapons of some kind had just popped up through previously concealed ports—one on each of the three connected modules.

Two of the Russian weapons looked oddly like long clear-glass tubes. They swiveled smoothly through different arcs. At short intervals, the tubes glowed brightly. Not for very long, no more than one or two seconds. But each time they did, one of his recon satellites died—going dark without so much as an electronic whimper, let alone a bang.

Those tubelike devices were combat lasers, Brad decided. Powerful ones, too, judging by how quickly they were knocking out his nanosats. He hoped the Sky Masters and Scion experts at Battle Mountain were picking up enough data to make some educated guesses about the Russian lasers' effective range and lethality.

What he couldn't make out was the nature of the space station's third weapons system. Much larger than the two lasers, this one had emerged through a camouflaged hatch in the central module. From what he could see, it consisted of a stubby cylinder surrounded by an array of other components mounted around it in a weird starfish pattern.

And then, as he stared at the image relayed by his last surviving nanosatellite, Brad saw the center of this strange weapon disappear in a dazzling pulse of light.

WHAAMMM.

Before he could even blink, he was hurled forward against his seat straps by a massive impact on the S-19's aft fuselage. A searing wave of heat rippled through the cockpit—painfully scorching even through his protective clothing, a skintight silvery carbon-fiber pressure suit layered with a lighter, unpressurized coverall containing additional radiation protection and a coolant system. Every display, control board, and instrument panel instantly short-circuited in a blinding cascade of sparks.

Utterly out of control, the crippled spaceplane tumbled away end over end through space—pitching, yawing, and rolling erratically as its thrusters and main engines fired at random.

CHAPTER 23

Colonel Vadim Strelkov stared at his displays in astonishment. Scarcely a minute after the battle began, it was over.

"Command, this is Revin. All targets engaged by our lasers have been destroyed. Hobnail battery power storage is at sixty percent."

"Excellent work, Leonid," Strelkov said gratefully. Not a single one of the stealth weapons launched by the Americans had gotten close enough to detonate. The only downside was that it would take hours to fully recharge the two lasers. He turned his attention to the S-19 Midnight. Their telescopes were having a hard time tracking it as it spun and jolted away from them. He opened a circuit to Filatyev. "Do you need to fire a second Thunderbolt shot at the enemy spaceplane, Viktor?"

"Negative, Colonel," Filatyev reported proudly. "We scored a direct hit. I evaluate the result as a mission kill. Their engines and electronics are crippled beyond any hope of repair."

Watching from the Kremlin, Gennadiy Gryzlov intervened. He rapped his desk sharply. "You should make sure of them, Strelkov. Launch one of your Scimitar missiles and blow that S-19 to hell!"

Strelkov hesitated. What the president demanded was impossible. With all the will in the world, he could not bend the laws of physics.

From his command post below the National Defense Control Center, Colonel General Leonov saw his dilemma. "What is the range to the enemy spaceplane, Colonel?" he asked.

"More than two hundred and fifty kilometers, sir . . . and opening very rapidly."

Leonov nodded. "That is well beyond the effective range of Mars One's missiles, Gennadiy," he told Gryzlov calmly. "Any Scimitar fired now would only end up going ballistic. The odds of scoring a hit are infinitesimal, especially against a target that is tumbling so wildly." He shrugged. "Besides, there's no need to waste any more weapons on them. The Americans inside that S-19 are already as good as dead."

The president scowled. "Are you sure of that?"

Strelkov saw one of his displays change. The station's computer had just updated the projected track of the enemy spacecraft. "Yes, Mr. President," he said with complete confidence. "The enemy spaceplane is falling out of orbit. It will re-enter the earth's atmosphere and burn up."

"When?"

"Within the next sixty minutes at most," Strel-kov said. "And quite probably, much sooner."

ABOARD THE WRECKED S-19 MIDNIGHT SPACEPLANE
That same time

As the crippled spaceplane spun end over end through space, the world's cloud-streaked blue, brown, and green surface unrolled across its cockpit windows, sank out of sight in a blaze of stars or the blinding glare of the sun, and then reappeared—never in quite the same place or for the same number of seconds . . . but always loom-ing ever closer, ever larger.

Pinned in his seat by sharp jolts as differ-ent engines or thrusters fired, Brad McLanahan fought to stay conscious. His vision was blurred by the dying spacecraft's wild, erratic motion. Awkwardly, he reached for the display in front of him. It was dark. Their computers, both the pri-mary and its backup, were down, knocked off-line or fried by whatever the hell it was that had just hit them. *C'mon, baby, wake up*, he thought as he punched buttons on the side of the display to try a hard reset. Out of the corner of his eye, he saw Hunter "Boomer" Noble doing the same thing from the pilot's seat.

Seconds passed. But nothing happened. The S-19's cockpit screens and instrument panels stayed obstinately black.

Brad scowled. *Swell. Just fucking swell.* Without those computers, they had absolutely no way to regain control over the spaceplane. Then he noticed the little row of red lights glowing on the right-sleeve control panel of his space suit . . . and realized he could not feel the comforting sensation of air flowing through the umbilical hose connected to his seat. Their life-support system was dead, too. So was the intercom that allowed them to talk to each other when suited up.

On the plus side, he guessed, was the fact that they hadn't blown up.

Yet.

Without waiting any longer, he reached out and grabbed Boomer's shoulder. With an effort, the other man turned his helmeted head to look back at him. One eyebrow strained upward in a silent question.

Brad jerked a thumb "up" toward the canopy over their heads. Every system in the cockpit was shot and they were pretty clearly dropping out of orbit. It was time to get out. Through the clear visor of his helmet, he saw Boomer nod and mouth back, "Gear up and grab your ERO kit."

Mercifully, the engines and thrusters that had been firing randomly began shutting down in ones and twos—either because they'd consumed all their fuel or because they'd burned out. At least that would make it slightly easier to move around inside the S-19's cramped cockpit. But only slightly. Between zero-G and the weird centrifugal and Coriolis effects induced by the spaceplane's tumbling motion, even getting out of the seat was going to be a bitch.

Brad swallowed, fighting the urge to throw up. He gritted his teeth. The longer he just sat here, the harder this would be. Carefully, he unbuckled his harness and pushed the straps out of the way. Then he bent at the waist and raised his thighs toward his chest, as though he were doing a stomach crunch. While his left hand gripped the edge of the seat, the fingertips of his right gently pushed off against the other side.

Still holding on, he pivoted slowly up and around to face the back of the cockpit. One of his knees slammed into Boomer's helmet. He tightened his hold on the seat as the reaction pushed him away. "Oops," he muttered, feeling his face redden slightly. He guessed no one would award him a prize for grace and style in zero-G anytime soon. *Or ever, McLanahan,* his mind scolded, *unless you stop screwing around.*

Cautiously, he reached out with his right hand, grabbed on to the back of his seat, pulled himself over it, and twisted around again. Then he reached down and grabbed the pull handle set almost flush with the deck between the cockpit seats. At his tug, a section of the deck plating rose smoothly and pivoted away—revealing the deep compartment containing their PLSS life-support gear and Emergency Return from Orbit kits.

Boomer had already unlatched his own harness and turned to face him. He reached out with a gloved hand and took the bulky white backpack Brad gave him. It took them both several minutes to struggle into the backpacks and connect up their umbilical hoses. Instantly, fresh oxygen started flowing to their suits. The red lights on their suit-sleeve environmental control panels turned green.

"Radio check."

Brad heard Boomer's voice clearly through his headset. The short-range radios in their backpacks were working. "Roger," he replied. "Loud and clear. How me?"

"I hear you, too, loud and clear," Boomer said back. He sighed. "Okay, McLanahan, are you ready to field-test those Rube Goldberg–style Emergency Return from Orbit kits I showed you way back when at Battle Mountain?"

Almost against his will, Brad shot him a crooked grin. "Do I have a choice?"

"Nope."

"I figured as much," Brad said. He pulled one of the ERO cases out from the storage compartment and passed it to the other man. Then he took the second kit for himself. Looking again at the weird assortment of gear it contained—the inflatable aerogel-Nomex shell, parachute pack, and twin-nozzle retro-rocket—didn't exactly inspire confidence. On the other hand, considering that his options boiled down to either rolling the dice with this untested piece of equipment or certain death aboard the crippled S-19 when it hit the atmosphere, maybe that wasn't such a tough choice after all. And Earth, as it slid across the spaceplane's cockpit windows, already looked a hell of a lot closer.

Boomer waited for him to float back across his seat and clip on. "Step one is to get these cockpit canopies open. Now, the motors are probably shot to shit. But even if they aren't, our control switches *are*, so—"

"We do this the old-fashioned way," Brad finished for him. He reached out to his side of the cockpit and pulled open a small panel. Inside was an emergency release lever and a manual crank handle to raise the starboard-side canopy. "Right?"

"I'll give you a gold star when we get down," Boomer said dryly. He opened an identical panel on his side of the S-19's cockpit. "Okay, let's get this done."

What would have been a comparatively simple task in Earth's gravity was much more difficult in zero-G. Brad found he had to wedge his booted feet under his seat to get enough traction just to turn the handle. With excruciating slowness, the twin canopies unlatched and cranked open— straining upward into the blackness of space.

"Who gets out first?" Brad grunted, struggling to turn the crank handle for his canopy.

"I already tossed that coin in my mind," Boomer said, sounding equally exhausted. "You won."

Brad forced a smile. "What's this? Noble by last name, noble by nature?"

"Hell no," Boomer retorted. "This is more like callow youth before crafty veteran. This way, I figure if you screw up somehow, I get a shot at seeing what went wrong in time to do better."

"Fair enough," Brad agreed. He tilted his helmet toward the open canopy, waiting as the earth, which now filled their whole view, twirled away out of sight, leaving only stars in its wake. The gap looked wide enough. There was no percentage in waiting any longer. He unclipped from the seat and triggered a short burst from his backpack's emergency maneuvering system. With the ERO clutched to his chest, he soared out into space—clearing the edge of the canopy with only inches to spare.

Another quick burst from the gas jets altered his trajectory, sending him corkscrewing away from the S-19's aft fuselage as it spun past on its descent toward the atmosphere. More finger taps on the maneuvering controls turned him around so that he could see the world below. He was so close now that its clouds and forests and mountains filled his whole field of view—growing larger and more defined with every passing second as he curved east and down at more than seventeen thousand miles per hour.

"Some view, huh?" he heard Boomer radio. The other man's space suit was visible only as a bright speck of reflected sunlight several miles away on their orbital track.

"I liked it a whole lot more from inside a working spacecraft," Brad admitted ruefully.

"Yeah, me too." Hissing static overlaid Boomer's words. They were already near the outside edge of the range of their low-powered radio gear and separating fast. "So we'll build our own. Now get to it, Brad . . . and good . . ." The static grew louder and louder until it drowned out every other sound.

"Good luck to you, too," Brad said softly, knowing the other man was already too far away to hear him. He switched the radio off. Since no other human being was within its limited range, there was no point in wasting battery power. For a brief, terrifying moment, he experienced the sudden, overwhelming sensation of being utterly and completely alone—totally cut off from everyone he knew and loved. If this emergency reentry went wrong, no one would ever really know what had happened to him. He'd simply vanish, like a shooting star that streaked across the night sky for one brief moment and then disappeared forever in a split-second flash of bright golden light.

Abruptly, he shook his head in self-reproach. *Whine when you're back on the ground, McLanahan*, he thought grimly, *not now*.

It took some doing to open and empty the clear ERO case without putting his suit into a spin. At last, though, Brad managed it.

Equally careful and precise movements allowed him to unfold the disk-shaped aerogel shell so that its thin Nomex cloth heat shield faced the earth below. Cautiously, he maneuvered into position inside the uninflated shell, strapped the parachute pack to his suit, and tightened his hold on the little handheld rocket motor. Then, satisfied that he was as close to the exact center as he could get, he activated a pair of pressurized containers. Instantly, expandable polyurethane foam spewed out of their nozzles—inflating the six-foot-diameter bag around him.

Within seconds, the foam had hardened, locking him snugly in place. And what had been a disk of ultrathin, ultrastrong material now had a conical dish shape.

Brad looked up at the star-speckled black depths above him and then took a deep breath. There was no sense in putting this off any longer. Sure, he was already on a course to deorbit anyway, but their derelict S-19 Midnight was on that same basic trajectory . . . and it was bound to break up on reentry, shredding into a massive fireball composed of thousands of burning fragments. It would be a whole lot better to drop out of orbit far, far away from where the spaceplane was doomed to meet its own fiery end.

Here goes, he thought. Next stop, Earth . . . or oblivion.

He squeezed the retro-rocket trigger.

At first, the ride was undramatic. When the rockets fired, he only saw two quick puffs of vapor and felt a tiny jolt . . . about the same as if someone had dropped a five-pound weight on his stomach. But the velocity decrease was just enough to steepen his descent, further tightening gravity's grip on his improvised reentry capsule. For long moments, though, nothing seemed to be happening. Since he couldn't see the world growing beneath his heat shield, Brad had no visible frame of reference and no way to judge his relative motion.

All that changed the moment he crossed the

Kármán line and hit the tenuous upper fringes of the atmosphere. As the aerogel-and-Nomex "sled" tore deeper and deeper into thicker and thicker air, it decelerated fast. G-forces slammed into Brad's chest, squeezing down harder and harder the farther he fell. Despite his training and pressure suit, the Gs kept piling up with crushing force. It grew more difficult to breathe. Desperately, he contracted his stomach, thigh, and shoulder muscles, fighting to keep enough blood in his brain to stay conscious. Colors started to leach out of the world at the far corners of his vision.

Superheated filaments of electrically charged plasma streamed past him in a dazzling light show. Gradually, the sky above him changed color, shading from the black of space to a rich blue hue. Rivulets of sweat stung his eyes. It was getting hotter now . . . much, much hotter.

Down and down Brad plunged—blazing across the sky like a meteor . . . or a fallen angel cast out of the heavens.

CHAPTER 24

President John Dalton Farrell watched the last few seconds of nanosatellite imagery through narrowed eyes. His jaw tightened angrily when the screen froze on a blinding flash from one of the Russian space station's weapons and then went black. "Those sons of bitches," he growled. "So much for Foreign Minister Titeneva's public-relations horseshit about the peaceful uses of outer space."

He turned his head toward the two other men in the room, Kevin Martindale and Patrick McLanahan. "What type of weapon was that?"

"It was definitely a directed-energy weapon . . . and a remarkably powerful one," Patrick said tiredly. He seemed to have aged at least ten more years in the last few minutes. "Brad and Boomer's spaceplane was more than one hundred and fifty miles from Mars One when it was hit. But we lost all telemetry from the S-19 within milliseconds of that flash. No conventional missile or projectile could possibly have covered that kind of distance so rapidly."

Farrell nodded. "Was it a laser? Like the ones we saw knock out our recon nanosatellites?"

"I don't believe so," Patrick replied. "A laser weapon of sufficient power could definitely destroy one of our spaceplanes, but not so quickly. At a minimum, we should have received telemetry from Midnight Zero-One indicating a rapidly rising hull temperature. But that is *not* what we observed." Using a small, palm-sized computer linked to the White House network, he sent more images to one of the Situation Room's large screens. "This is tracking data collected by the Globus II space surveillance radar at Vardø, Norway, right on the Russian border."

The radar images showed the S-19 as it started to move away from Mars One. A green line depicted its projected orbital track curving northward to enter an even more inclined orbit. "Seconds before they were fired on, Boomer had initiated a significant plane-change maneuver."

"To open the range fast," Farrell said.

Patrick nodded. "Yes, sir. By lighting up those undeclared military-grade radars, the Russians were demonstrating potential hostile intent. Boomer's reaction was exactly correct." He looked down for a moment, obviously trying to control his emotions. "I would have made the same move if I'd been in the pilot's seat."

"But they didn't get far," Farrell said carefully.

"No, sir." Patrick tapped an icon on his computer, advancing the radar footage. "This shows the precise moment of the attack."

On the screen, the blip representing the S-19 suddenly veered off its projected track—"falling" away from the Russian space station on a wildly eccentric trajectory.

"Everything we know now suggests the spaceplane sustained significant impact damage, probably coupled with intense electromagnetic pulse effects," the older McLanahan said bluntly. "That would explain why we immediately lost contact with both the crew *and* the S-19's computers . . . and why they haven't been able to regain control over the spacecraft yet."

"Assuming they're even still alive," Martindale said delicately, plainly aware that he was treading on painful ground.

Patrick nodded without speaking. He brought up a new map. This one showed the current trajectory of the crippled Sky Masters spaceplane. If nothing changed, it was on course to hit the earth's atmosphere somewhere over the Western Pacific. A digital readout showed the estimated time remaining before catastrophic reentry. It was down to less than twenty minutes. His lined face showed little emotion, but his eyes were full of sorrow. "If Brad and Boomer *are* still alive, one thing's certain . . . they're running out of time fast."

Farrell winced. What could he possibly say to a father about to watch his son die? Nothing useful, he supposed. Horrible though it was, however, he *needed* the other man's experience and knowledge right now. Expressions of shared grief and sympathy would have to wait. "Okay, so the S-19 wasn't hit by a laser," he said slowly. "Then what could have caused this impact and EMP damage you mentioned?"

"Probably a plasma cannon," Martindale said.

Farrell stared at him in surprise. "You're joking."

Martindale shook his head. "Unfortunately, I'm not." He nodded toward the screen. "It's the only thing I can think of that would explain what we just saw."

"You actually believe the Russians have built themselves an honest-to-God real live plasma weapon?" Farrell said dubiously. "Like something out of *Star Wars*?"

"Yes, but not *Star Wars* the movie," Martindale told him. "More likely, one of the advanced weapons concepts we explored decades ago as part of President Reagan's original Strategic Defense Initiative."

"Which were never developed," Farrell said. "Right?"

Martindale nodded. "True. But we learned enough to know plasma weapons were probably technologically feasible—at least given a huge investment of time, scientific and engineering resources, and money."

"And you think Gennadiy Gryzlov has gone ahead and done just that," Farrell said slowly.

"I do." Martindale's mouth turned downward.

"Though, I admit, much to my deep regret. Because if the Russians really have managed to put a working high-powered plasma weapons system in orbit, this country is in a great deal of danger."

Patrick's computer pinged suddenly. He read the alert and then looked up at them. His eyes now showed a tiny flicker of hope. "That was Mission Control at Battle Mountain. Several minutes ago, one of our space surveillance satellites detected two small objects separating from the S-19 Midnight."

Martindale looked wary. "That might just be debris breaking loose from the wreck," he cautioned.

"It could also be the crew bailing out," the older McLanahan countered sharply.

"Bailing out?" Farrell didn't bother hiding his confusion. "How the holy hell can anyone bail out in space, for Christ's sake? I mean, even ignoring the fact that there's no air . . . how could anyone hope to survive reentering the atmosphere wearing just a space suit?" His perplexity cleared slightly. "Or do you mean Brad and Boomer are clear of the S-19 and can stay in orbit long enough for us to send up another one of the spaceplanes to rescue them?"

Patrick shook his head. "I'm afraid not, Mr. President. Given the trajectory the spaceplane is on, their emergency backpack thrusters can't possibly boost the crew back into a stable orbit. They don't have the power or fuel required to do the job. And even if they could, by the time we can sortie another S-plane and achieve rendez-vous, Brad and Boomer would already be out of oxygen."

Farrell stared at him in honest bewilderment. "Then how—?" he began. Quickly, Patrick gave him a rundown on the Emergency Return from Orbit gear now carried by every Sky Masters spaceplane. When he finished, Farrell let out a low whistle. "Hell, General, that's like betting your whole stake without seeing a single god-damned card."

"It's not quite that bad," Martindale said evenly. "While I admit that no one has ever used the ERO system in real life, we have run a substantial number of computer simulations to pin down the odds of a successful reentry."

Farrell looked straight at him. "Which are?"

"Somewhere around fifty percent," Martindale admitted. "If everything goes perfectly."

Patrick's computer pinged again. He grabbed for it eagerly, read the new message, and looked up with the faint beginnings of a smile. "Brad and Boomer both made it out of the S-19 alive! That satellite spotted both contacts outside the spaceplane executing controlled burns . . . with a five-minute separation between the first and the second."

He tapped quickly on the tiny screen, sending a short text message. Seeing Martindale and Farrell's quizzical looks, he explained. "I've ordered Battle Mountain to send us estimates of the crew's probable landing zones. Between what we know about their known angles of descent, velocity, and the reported atmospheric conditions along their reentry tracks, our computers should be able to narrow those down pretty well."

Less than a minute later, Battle Mountain's updated estimates blinked onto the Situation Room's main screen. Red ovals centered on the most probable landing sites for each ERO were displayed on a large digital map of Asia and the Pacific. For a long moment, the three men stared at the map in horrified silence.

Recovering fast, Farrell grabbed the secure phone next to him. "Get me the commander of the Pacific Fleet," he snapped. "And then patch me through to the Japanese prime minister!"

NATIONAL DEFENSE CONTROL CENTER, MOSCOW
That same time

Leonov waited patiently for Gennadiy Gryzlov to run through the telescopic imagery collected during Mars One's first engagement yet another time. They were dramatic, he admitted to himself . . . more so than he would have predicted. Military-power laser beams, despite the way they were often depicted in films and popular entertainment, were not visible—especially in space. But their devastating effect on targets, especially small targets like the stealth mines or missiles the Americans had launched, was undeniable. Short Hobnail laser bursts had torn them into clouds of glowing superheated debris. The resulting plasma bloom had the additional benefit of nudging those debris clouds safely away from the space station. Eventually, they would drop out of orbit and burn up in the atmosphere.

The most incredible footage, though, showed the American spaceplane just as it was struck by Thunderbolt's plasma toroid. It disappeared momentarily in a dazzling flash . . . and when it reappeared the S-19 was already tumbling wildly away through space, obviously completely out of control.

"Beautiful," Gryzlov murmured. "Absolutely beautiful." On the secure video link from his Kremlin office, he looked up at Leonov with a cruel, wolfish smile. "Now *that* was a successful demonstration of Mars One's firepower, Mikhail. By now, the Americans must be shitting in their pants with fear."

Leonov nodded in agreement. While he would have preferred not to reveal the space station's armament so soon, the wholly one-sided battle ought to deter further American attacks for a time—with luck long enough for them to launch Mars One's replacement fusion reactor into orbit and bring it online.

"It seems we have been far too cautious," Gryzlov said, still smiling. "We worried too much about what the Americans could do to our space station before it was fully operational. But now we see the truth. They are impotent. With our new weapons, Mars One is safe from anything the Americans can throw at it."

"Nothing made by man is invulnerable,"

Leonov cautioned. "Without power from a reactor, Strelkov's defenses might still be overwhelmed by a sufficiently large attack."

Gryzlov dismissed his warning with a wave of his hand. "You sound like an old hen, Mikhail. Cluck, cluck, cluck."

"But, sir—"

"Enough." Gryzlov slapped his hand down on his desk. "I will no longer take counsel from your fears. It's time to move ahead with the next phase of the Mars Project. You will direct Colonel Strelkov to open offensive operations at once!"

Leonov set his jaw stubbornly. "Such a move would be premature. The scientists and engineers at Akademgorodok are very close to finishing their work on the replacement fusion reactor module. Even so, it will take several more days to transport the reactor to Vostochny and mate it with the Energia-5VR rocket that will carry it into space." He spread his hands. "True, we've won the opening skirmish. But that does not change the basic facts: right now the combat readiness of Mars One's weapons and sensors is still very limited. Opening full-scale military operations in space remains unnecessarily risky."

Gryzlov snorted. "How can you be so blind, Leonov? I thought you were a strategist." He shook his head in reproof. "The station's potential weaknesses are precisely *why* we should push ahead fast. Why give the Americans time to analyze their defeat and come up with some new plan to use against us? Now that they know we've deployed a military outpost in Earth orbit, it's more vital than ever to knock them off balance and blind them!"

He leaned closer to the camera. "My new orders stand, Colonel General Leonov. You will hit your targets as originally planned," he said fiercely. "You will *not* allow our enemies to regain their footing."

CHAPTER 25

IN THE NORTH PACIFIC
A short time later

Nearly six hundred nautical miles due east of Hokkaido, the northernmost of Japan's main islands, a scorched and seared ERO shell bobbed up and down—rising and falling as it crested waves rolling ever onward toward distant shores. Some yards off, its large red-and-white parachute, now cut loose and already waterlogged, drifted slowly away on the current.

Clumsily, a tall, lanky man wearing a space suit wriggled his head and shoulders out through the opening left by the detached parachute. Still shaken up by the rough, high-G ride through the atmosphere and hard splashdown, he cracked open the visor of his helmet and dragged in a few shuddering breaths of fresh air. The wind shifted slightly, bringing with it the acrid, charred smell of Nomex cloth and polyimide-based aerogels.

Gagging, he leaned over the edge of the shell and vomited into the choppy sea.

"Geez, Hunter, stick to the kiddie rides from now on," Boomer muttered to himself. He coughed, winced at the taste in his mouth, and threw up again. "Leave the roller coasters to the grown-ups."

For several minutes, he lay half folded up across the rocking ERO shell—feeling drained, sick to his stomach, and yet amazed and grateful to be alive. By rights, he should be dead, killed by any one of a thousand things that could have gone wrong during his wild ride down from orbit. Whenever a larger wave slapped into the half-submerged shell, the impact sent pain shooting through every part of his body. All his muscles and joints ached. He felt like he'd just run a marathon . . . while spectators bashed him with clubs and baseball bats. Considered rationally, he figured that wasn't too surprising, since he'd probably pulled around seven and maybe even eight Gs during some parts of the descent.

The clatter of a helicopter drawing closer broke into Boomer's dazed thoughts. Blearily, he raised his head to look up. A white-and-yellow UH-60J Seahawk swept across the waves at low altitude— undoubtedly homing in on the emergency radio beacon he'd activated the moment he splashed down. Beyond the helicopter, he could make out the long, sleek shape of a warship as it steamed toward his position at high speed. The Rising Sun ensign of Japan's Maritime Self-Defense Force streamed proudly from its mast.

* * *

Later, safely aboard the Atago-class destroyer *Ashigara*, Boomer took the headset offered by the ship's communications officer. Unsure of the formalities, he bowed slightly. "*Dōmo* . . . er, *arigatōgozaimashita*. Thank you very much."

The Japanese naval lieutenant grinned back at him. "No sweat," he answered in flawless, colloquial English. He spoke into his own mike. "Wait one, Washington. I have Dr. Noble standing by."

Feeling sheepish, Boomer donned the headset. "This is Hunter Noble. Go ahead."

"*I'm really glad to hear your voice, Boomer,*" Patrick McLanahan said. They were on an encrypted satellite radio link between the *Ashigara* and the White House. "*Are you okay?*"

Boomer shrugged. And then winced as his battered muscles protested. "I'm fine, General," he said. "Just a little banged up and bruised is all. My hosts gave me a head-to-toe exam almost as soon as they hoisted me on board. And I've got a clean bill of health from the ship's medical officer."

"*Good,*" the older McLanahan replied after a short pause. "*Because we've asked the Japanese to fly you to shore ASAP. We'll have a jet standing by to bring you back to the States for a mission debrief.*"

"Yes, sir." Boomer nodded tightly. It made sense for him to walk them through his side of this disaster while it was still relatively fresh in his mind. But that wouldn't make the process any more pleasant. He'd better try to grab some decent shut-eye on the flight home, because that might be his last real chance for a long time. He frowned. "Look, do you guys know yet what the hell hit us up there?"

"*We have a working hypothesis,*" Patrick said quietly. "*That's part of what we want to go over with you.*"

"Well, Brad got a closer look at that Russian space station and its armament than I did." Boomer grinned wryly. "And knowing your kid as well as I do, sir, I bet he's already worked up a few theories of his own. Some of them may even be in the right ballpark."

There was a long, uncomfortable silence on the other end.

Oh, shit, Boomer thought. He swallowed hard, suddenly feeling nauseous again. "Jesus, General. Brad *did* make it down okay, didn't he?"

"*We don't know,*" the older McLanahan said at last. "*His emergency radio beacon did activate. But then it went dead after just a couple of minutes.*" Now his voice openly betrayed the deep anxiety he felt. "*We are sure of one thing, though, Boomer. Even if Brad survived reentry, he is still in very grave danger.*"

ABOARD MARS ONE
A short time later

Colonel Vadim Strelkov listened intently to the instructions Leonov was issuing. Through the inevitable visual and audio distortions created when an encrypted signal bounced through a network of communications satellites, it was clear that the other man had misgivings about the president's command to commence full-scale offensive operations now—before they were fully ready. For what it was worth, he shared those reservations. But orders were orders, and neither of them was in any real position to disobey Gennadiy Gryzlov.

"I understand, sir," he said. "You can count on us to do our duty."

Leonov nodded gravely. "I am well aware of that, Vadim." He looked closely into the screen, obviously studying Strelkov's demeanor. "Maintain your station's defenses at the highest possible effectiveness, even when conducting an attack. I do not believe the Americans will give up so easily."

"Yes, sir. We will be watchful," Strelkov assured him.

"Then get to work, Colonel," Leonov said laconically. "Moscow Control out."

The screen blanked.

For a moment longer, Strelkov floated in front of his console, considering his options. Leonov's suggested precautions were justified. Without the massive amounts of electric power their lost fusion reactor would have provided, his most sensible course was to maintain a deliberate, carefully regulated tempo of attacks—conserving as much of their stored battery and supercapacitor energy as possible. Most obviously, that meant he and his cosmonauts should fire their Thunderbolt plasma rail gun offensively only when Mars One was in full sunlight and its solar arrays could recharge the weapon efficiently.

At last, he nodded to himself. The tactical situation might not be ideal, but any commander who dreamed that real war would match his picture-perfect plans was a simpleton. And when it mattered most, his crew and the station's weapons systems had passed the test of actual combat with flying colors.

Strelkov pushed the intercom control on his console. "Attention, all crew," he said calmly. "This is Command. Prepare for offensive operations. Repeat, prepare for offensive operations. Report when ready."

One by one, the other five cosmonauts confirmed their readiness. Except for Konnikov, their duty posts were in other compartments scattered throughout Mars One. That made it more difficult for him to judge their demeanor under pressure. Nevertheless, the cool professionalism he heard in their voices now was reassuring—a stark contrast to the undercurrent of panic he'd sensed during their frenetic, no-notice, short-range engagement against the American S-19 Midnight spaceplane and its stealth weapons.

Satisfied, Strelkov rotated toward Konnikov. "Time to the solar terminator, Georgy?"

The younger man checked his computer. "We will be in sunlight for another seventeen minutes, sir."

"Very well," Strelkov acknowledged. They had enough time to conduct at least one Thunderbolt attack before Mars One crossed back into darkness on its orbit around the earth. He opened a circuit to Major Pyotr Romanenko. "Solar array status?"

"We are currently generating seventy-two kilowatts," the engineering officer reported. "All surplus capacity is on standby to recharge Thunderbolt's supercapacitors."

Strelkov pulled up their targeting list on one of his console displays. It was a compilation of all known military and civilian satellites whose orbits lay within reach of Mars One's main armament. It took only seconds to winnow the list down to those currently in range. He highlighted one of them, already identified by the planners in Moscow as a top-priority target, and relayed it to Konnikov. "Georgy, designate Topaz-Four as target Alpha-One."

The sensor officer entered the necessary information with unruffled precision. "Target Alpha-One is designated, sir." He opened a new window. "Our secure data link to the Altai Optical-Laser Center is open. Confirming Alpha-One's current orbital parameters now."

Sited high in the Altai Mountains a few hundred kilometers south of Novosibirsk, the center's powerful one-hundred-ton telescope was a key component in Russia's optical space tracking network. Its constantly updated databases included observations of hundreds of satellites as their orbits brought them within view. Cross-checking them against computer predictions based on earlier observations would reveal if a given satellite had recently altered its orbit . . . and if so, what its new parameters were. Absolute accuracy was essential for a weapon firing on rapidly moving targets at very long ranges.

"Alpha-One's orbit confirmed," Konnikov reported. "Transferring tracking data to Thunderbolt's fire-control computer."

"Tracking data received," Major Viktor Filatyev said from his station in the aft weapons module. "I have a firing solution."

Strelkov nodded to himself. It seemed odd to open a new era in the history of warfare so prosaically, with so little fanfare or drama. Then again, perhaps that was fitting. After all, this would be a conflict fought by machines against other machines at vast ranges, with none of the carnage and chaos of close physical combat. "Weapons release granted," he said simply.

"Firing Thunderbolt . . . *now*," Filatyev announced.

Mars One shuddered slightly. Maneuvering thrusters aboard their docked Progress cargo ships and Federation orbiter had fired simultaneously to counteract the recoil from their plasma rail gun.

Two thousand kilometers away and two-tenths of a second later, Topaz-Four, one of America's most advanced radar reconnaissance satellites, glowed brightly—eerily wreathed in lightning. Shedding antennas, thruster cones, sections of fractured solar panels, and other fragments, the wrecked satellite spun away into space.

"Good hit. Altai Center confirms a kill on target Alpha-One," Konnikov said, with a grin. He checked their ground track again. "Time to solar terminator now twelve minutes and thirty seconds."

Strelkov felt himself relax. Despite his earlier show of confidence, and their destruction of the American spaceplane, he had never been completely sure Thunderbolt could actually engage and destroy targets at the ranges its creators promised. "Good shooting, Viktor," he told Filatyev. "Stand by for a new target."

Mars One was now officially at war.

ON THE GROUND
That same time

Clenching his teeth against stabs of pain from his much-abused muscles and joints, Brad McLanahan dumped a last armful of torn brush on top of a shallow mound of dirt, rocks, and clumps of moss. He'd spent the past half hour frantically burying his bright red-and-white parachute, silver carbon-fiber space suit, helmet, emergency radio beacon, and white life-support backpack, using just his left arm because it sure felt like his right shoulder might be dislocated.

Straightening up, he dusted off his hand and stepped back a few feet to survey his work with a critical eye. There was zero chance it would fool anyone up close, he decided. But his improvised cache should hide the gear he'd just ditched from anyone hunting him from the air . . . and that seemed the most immediate threat.

Brad swung around and checked the other side of the small woodland clearing he'd landed in. The most he'd been able to do over there was drag the blackened, six-foot-diameter aerogel ERO shell off into a thick stand of young spruce trees. Their overhanging branches ought to break up its silhouette. *Maybe*, he thought doubtfully. With some luck. Then again, he'd been pushing his luck pretty hard over the past several hours. How much further could it possibly carry him?

While chewing that over in his mind, he mopped at his sweaty forehead with a sleeve of his coverall. This outer garment he'd worn over his space suit wasn't exactly designed for hard manual labor on the ground. Or for trekking through what sure looked a lot like an uninhabited wilderness—a landscape of scattered woods, grassy meadows, boulder-strewn rises, and reed-choked bogs.

Brad shook his head in mild dismay. This was *not* going to be fun. Damn it, he'd signed on with Sky Masters and Scion to fly . . . not to go crawling around in swamps and forests like some U.S. Army grunt. Then he grinned wryly, imagining Nadia's reaction if she heard him whining like this. She'd probably kick his ass all the way from here—wherever *here* was—to Battle Mountain.

Besides, what was that old line? "If you can't take a joke, you shouldn't have joined up."

Well, at least his footgear, a pair of black leather zippered paratrooper boots, was appropriate for the task in front of him. Plus, Sky Masters had included a lightweight pouch with SERE—Survival, Evasion, Resistance, and Escape—supplies with the ERO kit. The water-purification tablets and protein bars it contained should keep him from dying of thirst or starving to death . . . at least for a few days.

Maybe even more important, the survival kit included a compact satellite phone with some additional capabilities—rudimentary language translation and digital map software—built in. Limited battery power meant he'd have to carefully ration its use . . . but at least he might be able to call for help.

But not right now. Like cell phones, satellite phones could be tracked through their GPS receivers. And if hostiles had monitored his flaming descent through the upper atmosphere or spotted the ERO's big parachute when it opened at thirty thousand feet, this whole area was likely to get unhealthy mighty fast. He'd do better to cover as much ground as he could before the light failed. "Phoning home" would have to wait until he could find someplace reasonably safe to hole up in.

Brad used a parachute riser cord he had collected before he buried the parachute to rig up a sling for his right arm. Some other injury was causing some intense pain in his right knee, but at least he could walk. Resolutely, he slung the

SERE pouch over his left shoulder and started hiking east—heading deeper into the cover offered by the forest. Behind him, the waters of a large lake glinted in the early-afternoon sun.

Half a mile from the clearing he'd crash-landed in, he struggled through a thicket of dwarf birch trees and unexpectedly emerged onto a narrow dirt road running north and south through the forest. The road's surface was deeply rutted, indicating that it was at least occasionally used by heavy wheeled vehicles. It was probably a logging trail, he thought.

Still, any road was a sign there might be people living or working close by. And stumbling into them could mean big trouble for him.

Careful to avoid making any sudden moves that might draw even more attention, Brad slowly backed a few feet into the thicket. Once he was in some cover, he squatted down. From this position, he spent several minutes studying the road and the woods on the other side. Nothing moved. At least nothing he could see. Everything seemed quiet.

About twenty yards up the road, he spotted what looked like a rusting metal sign nailed to a tree. Cautiously, he moved forward to examine it.

It was written in the Cyrillic alphabet: орджиканский государственный природный заповедник.

Dry-mouthed, Brad ran that through his satellite phone's software. It seemed worth the risk to get a fix on his location. A translation blinked onto the tiny screen, along with a digital map that highlighted "the Oldjikan State Nature Reserve."

"Yeah, that answers my question," Brad growled under his breath as he stared at the map. "I am so well and truly fucked."

The good news was that he'd survived the totally insane stunt of plunging four hundred miles down from orbit aboard a completely untested, foam-filled escape pod. The bad news was that he'd landed in Russia's far east region . . . just three hundred and fifty miles from the Vostochny Cosmodrome.

CHAPTER 26

It took a huge effort of will, but somehow President John D. Farrell restrained himself from giving Gennadiy Gryzlov a full broadside of all the masterful profanity he'd learned over the years he spent working side by side with Texas oil roughnecks—tough-minded men whose language could sometimes blister paint. Besides, he thought grimly, swearing at the Russian son of a bitch would only be a distant second best to physically kicking the shit out of his smug face.

"I make no apology whatsoever for destroying your spaceplane," Gryzlov said icily over the secure video link with Moscow. "The evidence is quite clear, despite your country's pitiful efforts to deny it. Your Sky Masters S-19 Midnight attacked Mars One without provocation, and my cosmonauts acted in self-defense."

Farrell snorted. "Using weapons your own foreign minister denied were even aboard that supposedly *peaceful* space station."

Gryzlov shrugged. "Foreign Minister Titeneva was . . . ill informed." His gaze sharpened. "Fortunately for Russia, others saw the probability of American aggression and took sensible precautions."

Farrell decided to let that piece of total bullshit slide, for now. It was just barely possible that the crew aboard Mars One had panicked, mistaking the recon nanosats launched by Brad McLanahan and Hunter Noble for weapons aimed at them. But one unintended clash in orbit could not justify the ongoing destruction of America's most vital reconnaissance satellites.

When he said as much, Gryzlov only sneered. "Why should I order my cosmonauts to stop now? For too long, your nation has arrogantly asserted its right to operate unchallenged in space with illegally armed spacecraft. You have spied on other countries, openly and without shame. You have destroyed Russian satellites and spacecraft. You have even conducted vicious attacks from space against civilian and military targets, both on the ground and at sea. Now I tell you plainly, those days are over."

"You'd better get one thing straight," Farrell warned flatly. There was a time for the polite circumlocutions of ordinary diplomacy and there was a time for plain talking. "There is no goddamned way my government will sit back and let y'all walk all over the United States. Stacy Anne

Barbeau's policies of appeasement and weakness are yesterday's news. Keep pushing us and you're liable to end up spitting teeth."

Gryzlov smiled thinly. "Do not make threats you cannot back up, Mr. President. It is unseemly, even embarrassing. Whether you understand it yet or not, the world has shifted beneath your feet. Now, thanks to the powerful weapons and revolutionary technologies aboard Mars One, Russia dominates space. And we will exercise this power as required to protect our people and our national interests from American aggression."

Seeing the fury rising on Farrell's broad, square-jawed face, Gryzlov held up a conciliatory hand. "Nevertheless, despite our overwhelming military superiority, I am willing to offer you certain guarantees. First, as an assurance Russia is not planning to conduct a nuclear first strike, we will refrain from destroying your early warning satellites in geosynchronous orbit. Nor will we eliminate your GPS navigation satellites, which are so crucial to both your military and civilian sectors. Nor, for the time being, will Mars One target your civilian space-based communications networks."

"How truly kind," Farrell said acidly.

"Yes, I think so," Gryzlov agreed, not even trying to hide his amused contempt. His expression hardened. "But I caution you not to mistake my restraint for weakness. From this moment forward, all other American or mercenary Sky Masters military spacecraft detected in orbit will be engaged and destroyed without further warning.

The same goes for all of your so-called civilian imaging satellites. Russia will no longer tolerate any further spying from space against its national territory, armed forces, or economic interests."

Farrell stared at him in outraged disbelief. "That sounds a hell of a lot like you're imposing a total blockade on low Earth orbit."

Gryzlov shrugged. "Call it what you will." He smiled. "In the future, certain peaceful civilian payloads *may* be allowed into space . . . but *only* after thorough inspection—either by my government or by trusted international authorities." He reached out a hand to the controls on his desk. "There is no basis for further discussion of these points, President Farrell. I have won . . . and you have lost. Accept this reality while the cost to you and your fellow countrymen is still so low."

The video link went dark.

For a moment, Farrell sat motionless, with his head bowed slightly. He felt like the whole weight of the world had just come crashing down on his shoulders. Intellectually, he'd known serving as America's president and commander in chief would be the most difficult challenge he had ever faced. But until now, he hadn't fully felt the burden of office—the realization that his decisions would directly affect the lives and freedoms of more than three hundred million of his fellow countrymen . . . and those of hundreds of millions more around the world. Especially when it was starting to look as though they might face a real no-win situation.

Not feeling so high-and-mighty now, eh, J.D., he

thought, *are you?* Then he gave himself a good swift mental kick in the pants. He'd asked the voters to dump Stacy Anne Barbeau out of the Oval Office on her ass, and they'd obliged. So it was time for him to man up and do his damnedest to fulfill the oath he'd sworn at his inauguration.

With a deep frown, Farrell looked up at the expectant faces around the room. He'd summoned his national security team to sit in on Gryzlov's call—figuring it made more sense for them to hear the volatile Russian leader in person than to rely on reading a sterile transcript later. "Well," he said heavily. "There you have it. Setting aside that bullcrap about us firing first, the Russians aren't bothering to hide their intentions. We're smackdab in the middle of a shooting war in space."

"Except right now the Russians are the only ones doing any shooting," Andrew Taliaferro, the secretary of state, commented dryly.

Grimly, Farrell nodded. "That's about the size of it." He looked down the table at Admiral Scott Firestone, the chairman of the Joint Chiefs. "What is the current military situation, Admiral?"

"It's bleak, Mr. President." The short, stocky man didn't pull any punches. "In just the past several hours, we've already lost three key reconnaissance spacecraft—a Topaz radar imaging satellite, a KH-11 optical imaging satellite, and one of the navy's Intruder SIGINT satellites. These satellites were destroyed by fire from that Russian orbital platform. All of them were at least a thousand miles from Mars One when they were hit, and in radically different orbits. This indicates we face a previously unknown Russian weapons system, one with enormous range and the ability to strike targets with astounding speed."

Farrell leaned forward. "How fast, exactly?"

"Based on the elapsed time between the instant we detect a light pulse, or flash, on the space station and the moment we lose contact with a satellite, we estimate something on the order of six thousand miles per second."

"Sweet Jesus," Farrell muttered. He turned to Lawrence Dawson, his science adviser. "What's your assessment?" he asked the astrophysicist.

"I concur with former president Martindale and retired general McLanahan," Dawson said. "This new weapon is most likely a plasma gun. In fact, based on the images collected by our spaceplane before it was destroyed, I believe its design is very similar to one we explored ourselves in the late 1980s and early 1990s—in the MARAUDER plasma-rail-gun program. If so, our satellites are being struck by toroids of superheated plasma moving at incredible speed. Such a strike would inflict lethal thermal, impact, and EMP damage."

Farrell swung back to the chairman of the Joint Chiefs. "Is there any way we can defend our spacecraft and satellites against this weapon?"

"No, sir," Firestone replied somberly. "Not with our existing technology."

"So the only way to stop the Russians is to blow that space station of theirs to kingdom come," Farrell said bluntly.

Slowly, the admiral nodded. "That's the way I see it, Mr. President."

"Using our missile defense interceptors?"

"Correct, sir." Firestone signaled an aide, who pulled up a map of the United States on one of the Situation Room's wall screens. Two red icons depicted the antiballistic-missile silos on the California coast at Vandenberg Air Force Base and at upstate New York's Fort Drum. A bright yellow line, showing the projected ground track of Mars One, arced across both places. "Approximately ten hours from now, the Russian space station's orbit will take it almost directly over both of our missile defense sites. This presents us with an opening to attack. The next such opportunity will not occur for another seventy-two hours."

Dawson cleared his throat. "Given Mars One's orbital velocity, those launch windows must be very small, Admiral."

Firestone nodded. "They are."

"How small?" Farrell asked.

"We would have time to launch two interceptors from each site," the admiral told him.

"But not simultaneously."

"No, sir," Firestone agreed. "The launch window at Fort Drum won't open until roughly nine minutes after the one at Vandenberg has closed."

Farrell studied the map in silence for a few moments. Then he looked carefully at the admiral. "Considering what we already know about that space station's armament—which includes at least two high-powered lasers and this plasma gun—what are the odds of success?"

"Slim," the other man said quietly.

Farrell nodded. "Let me think on this, Admiral," he said. "Make the necessary preparations, but y'all will not launch any of our interceptors against Mars One without my direct authorization. Is that clear?"

"Yes, Mr. President. Very clear."

"Now, do you have any other recommendations?" Farrell asked.

Firestone sat forward. "Yes, sir. I've spoken to the other members of the JCS. We unanimously recommend moving to DEFCON Two immediately."

Farrell frowned. DEFCON, or Defense Readiness Condition, was a graduated system for increasing the readiness of U.S. military forces for nuclear war. He had already ordered an increase to DEFCON Three shortly after the Russians attacked the Sky Masters S-19 spaceplane. Moving to DEFCON Two would mean bringing America's nuclear-armed and nuclear-capable air and naval forces to a much higher alert status—one that was just short of signaling an intention to wage all-out nuclear war.

"Are there any signs that the Russians have increased their own alert status?" he asked carefully.

"No, sir," Firestone admitted. "Not yet." He looked worried. "But that is precisely the problem, Mr. President. Right now Moscow seems determined to destroy our space-based reconnaissance capabilities. The Russians are systematically stripping away our ability to keep tabs on the deployment and readiness of their bombers, strategic rocket forces, naval units, and ground forces. Put simply, we are being blinded."

"We still have the SBIRS satellites," Dawson pointed out.

"Which can only alert us to a missile attack that is *already* under way," Firestone said tightly. "At which point, it will be too late to increase the readiness levels of our armed forces."

Farrell considered that. There was no doubt that the recommendation by the Joint Chiefs made a lot of military sense. On the other hand, openly ratcheting up to DEFCON Two would also spook many of America's European and Asian allies, especially if the Russians were holding tight everywhere but in space. According to Andrew Taliaferro, some of them weren't even sure whether they should believe Washington's story about the clash between the S-19 and Mars One . . . or Moscow's. He looked at Firestone. "We'll split the baby on this one, Admiral," he said firmly.

"Mr. President?"

"Officially, we're going to hold at DEFCON Three," Farrell told him. "But I want all of our ballistic-missile submarines to put out to sea as quickly as possible." Those submarines represented the bulk of the U.S. nuclear deterrent force anyway. He smiled wryly. "You can announce the move as a short-notice fleet-readiness exercise."

"That won't fool Gryzlov," Taliaferro warned.

Farrell shrugged. "No, I don't expect it will." His mouth was a hard, thin line. "Right now, though, that asshole thinks he can stomp all over us without any pushback. Well, I want him—and the generals and government officials around him—to know he's playing with fire."

As soon as the conference in the Situation Room broke up, Farrell headed back upstairs to the Oval Office. For what it was worth, he'd set the official forces of the U.S. military and government in motion. Now it was time to do the same with Scion and Sky Masters.

Kevin Martindale and Patrick McLanahan stood up when he entered. Impatiently, he waved them back down and sat at his desk. "Let's get to it. We're burning daylight while that bastard Gennadiy Gryzlov is burning satellites."

Martindale frowned. "I assume that is not simply a colorful Texanism."

"Hell no," Farrell said, with a sigh. They listened intently while he brought them up to speed on recent events in orbit. "We've lost two more satellites during just the last sixty minutes," he concluded. "A second Topaz radar sat and one of our Trumpet electronic intelligence satellites."

Patrick stared at him. "A Trumpet ELINT satellite? Those birds are in highly elliptical Molniya orbits to get maximum coverage over Russia and the northern hemisphere. Most of the time they're way up high, close to twenty-five thousand miles at apogee."

"The key phrase there being 'most of the time,'" Farrell said gloomily. "Mars One nailed this one on its way back down toward perigee. That plasma rail gun of theirs blew our Trumpeter satellite to pieces from three thousand miles away." Unable to sit still any longer, he kicked back his desk chair and got up to prowl around the room. "At this rate, we won't have a single working spy satellite in orbit by the end of the week."

Martindale pursed his lips. "There are a few hidden backup satellites, disguised as civilian platforms or even space junk."

"Sure," Patrick said with a shrug. "And as soon as we start maneuvering them into useful orbits, the Russians will knock them out."

"We could launch replacements while the space station is on the other side of its orbit," Martindale said slowly. "Its crew can't shoot what they can't see." Then his face darkened. "But by the same token, any new satellite would have to precisely mirror Mars One's orbit to stay safe—"

Patrick nodded. "And that particular orbit sucks for spying on Russia. Satellites inclined at fifty-one point six degrees can check out targets in the southern part of the country . . . but we'd have zero coverage over most of their ICBM fields, strategic bomber bases, and the Northern Fleet's ballistic-missile submarine pens." He shrugged. "And after Gryzlov launches his second armed space station, all bets are off."

Farrell swung around at that. "You really think he's planning to launch another Mars-class platform?"

"No question about it," Patrick said firmly. "I'm only surprised he sent the first one up on its own. There's no doubt Gryzlov is now determined to seize and hold the high ground. He's obviously figured out that dominating outer space will yield enormous military, commercial, and political advantages to Russia. And putting one or two more space stations armed with those plasma cannon into orbit would make it practically impossible for us to shake loose of Moscow's grip."

"I have absolutely *no* intention of ceding Earth orbit to Gennadiy Gryzlov's despicable regime," Farrell said through gritted teeth.

"I never thought you did," Martindale assured him. "Of course, that leaves open the question of what we can do to stop him."

Farrell nodded. He turned to Patrick. "What's your take on Admiral Firestone's proposal that we fire our missile defense interceptors against Mars One?"

"About the same as his," the other man replied. "There's almost no chance we could score a hit."

"Shit," Farrell muttered. His shoulders slumped slightly.

"But we should still try it."

Farrell stared at Patrick. "Why?"

"First, because if you're not even in the game, you can't possibly win," Patrick said simply. "There's always the chance—however improbable—that things may go wrong for those cosmonauts. Space is a harsh, unforgiving environment. And it's tough on hardware. If that plasma gun or those lasers break down at just the right moment, we might get lucky."

"That's one heck of a lot of maybes," Farrell commented sourly.

Patrick nodded. "Which is why I have a second reason for seeing those interceptors fly."

"Namely?" Martindale prompted.

"We're still operating in the dark," Patrick told him. "We need more information about how Mars One's weapons work and how effective its sensors are. Anything we can do to collect that kind of intelligence is worth trying. The more we know, the more likely we are to find a weak spot—some chink in its defenses we can exploit with the weapons and other hardware Sky Masters has developed."

He looked up at the president. "And you have my promise, sir. I will not rest until I find it." A wry grin sleeted across his face as he tapped the LEAF exoskeleton that kept him alive. "Fortunately, wearing all this hardware means I don't need quite as much sleep as the rest of you mere mortals."

Farrell studied him quietly for several long seconds. There was no doubting the other man's sincerity. "I appreciate your dedication, General McLanahan," he said gently. "But don't you think you should focus first on rescuing your son, if he's still alive?"

To his surprise, Patrick shook his head. "I know that Brad's fate is in good hands," he said confidently. "I can count on Nadia doing *whatever* it takes to bring him home in one piece."

"You trust her that much?" Farrell asked.

"I do."

Soberly, Martindale nodded. "Major Rozek is something of a force of nature." Then he warned,

"But any plan she comes up with is likely to get a bit messy. If any Russians get in her way, a lot of them are going to end up dead."

"I take your point," Farrell said with a thin smile. His eyes were cold. "Frankly, Mr. Martindale, right now that possibility suits me just fine."

CHAPTER 27

BATTLE MOUNTAIN, NEVADA
A few hours later

Conspicuously dry-eyed but nonetheless full of barely contained anger and apprehension, Nadia Rozek entered the secure conference room. She pulled the door firmly shut behind her. It locked with an audible click. The two men she'd chosen for her special-operations planning cell stood up to greet her.

She'd selected Peter "Constable" Vasey for his proven ability as a pilot and because of the experience he'd gained while flying secret Scion missions into hostile territory. Those were skill sets she knew would prove crucial to any rescue operation. The other man, Major Ian Schofield, was a veteran of Canada's Special Operations Regiment. Until recently, he'd commanded the Iron Wolf Squadron's deep penetration unit. Nadia and the lean, wiry Canadian had served together previously in two high-risk covert operations—the first to attack a fortified

Russian cyberwar complex deep in the Ural Mountains, and the second, just last year, to hunt down and destroy Gryzlov's war robots inside the United States itself. No one else knew more about how to survive and avoid capture behind enemy lines.

"Time is short. And we have much to do," Nadia said matter-of-factly. "So let us get started." She sat down at the table, opened her laptop, and synced it with the conference room's computer. "We have been tasked with a mission which, though simple enough in concept, will be difficult to plan . . . and even more challenging to carry out successfully."

"You have something of a gift for understatement, Major Rozek." Schofield's teeth gleamed white in a face tanned and weathered by years spent outdoors in harsh climates. He looked thoughtful. "All I've heard is that Captain McLanahan is missing somewhere inside Russian territory. Do we know any more than that?"

She nodded. "We do." She brought up a map. "This is the most recent computer analysis of Brad's reentry trajectory and probable landing zone."

Schofield and Vasey both whistled softly. If Brad had made it down from orbit alive, he'd landed squarely in the middle of the Khabarovsk federal region—in Russia's heavily defended far east. Northern Japan, the closest friendly territory, was more than five hundred miles away.

"Well, I suppose it could be worse," Schofield said slowly, after a few moments of silent study.

Vasey snorted. "Meaning, he could have come down right in the middle of Moscow?"

The Canadian shook his head. "Not quite." He nodded toward the map. "That part of the Khabarovsk region is lightly populated. Plus, the terrain there offers reasonable concealment, while still not being impassable for a man traveling on foot."

"Good," Nadia said firmly. "Anything that can help Brad evade capture while we organize a rescue operation is welcome news."

Vasey frowned. "I hate like hell to be the ghost at the feast, Major," he said gently. "But what actual evidence do we have that Brad even survived reentry? We both know the odds are not in his favor."

"His emergency beacon activated," she said forcefully. "And then it was switched off."

"We don't know if that was deliberate," Vasey pointed out. "The beacon might simply have been critically damaged when it hit the ground."

"Yes, that is possible," Nadia agreed. Her expression hardened. "But it is equally possible that Brad realized the beacon could give away his position to the Russians . . . and switched it off himself. At the very least, this shows that his ERO shell did not burn up when it hit the atmosphere."

Vasey's light blue eyes were full of sympathy. "That's rather a lot of ifs," he said.

"Yes," she said quietly. "I know this all too well." For an instant, the dark thoughts she'd suppressed threatened to break through into the open. *No*, she told herself fiercely, *you will not give in to your fears.* Weeping now would achieve nothing. She shrugged her shoulders. "We Poles have a saying, Constable. *Tonący brzytwy się chwyta.* The drowning man clutches at a razor blade. Until I *know* that Brad is gone, I will not abandon hope."

"Then neither will I," the Englishman assured her. "I've never especially enjoyed playing the devil's advocate." His eyes wrinkled. "On the other hand, raising hell is something I'm quite good at . . . and I rather suspect that's an attribute that will prove useful if we have to fly in to snatch our fair-haired boy out of Gryzlov's grip."

Nadia inclined her head, offering him her silent thanks. Then she turned to Schofield. "How likely is it that Brad can evade capture until we come up with a plan to extract him?"

Schofield frowned, thinking it over. "A lot would depend on how actively he's being hunted," he said carefully. "If the Russians are mounting a full-blown search operation—using helicopters in the air and troops and police on the ground—he's in serious trouble. Even worse if he's injured."

"So far, it does not seem that the Russians know any of the S-19's crew escaped," Nadia said. "Japan's signals intelligence ground stations and aircraft have not yet intercepted any military or police radio transmissions which indicate they are hunting for a downed American astronaut."

"Well, there's a bit of luck," Vasey said appreciatively. "Either no one spotted the fireball when Brad's ERO sled tore through the upper atmosphere. Or . . ."

"The authorities simply dismissed it as debris torn loose from the wrecked spaceplane burning up on reentry," Nadia said.

Schofield nodded. "In that case, the SERE

training Brad received as an Iron Wolf pilot will give him a fighting chance—as long as he wasn't seriously injured on landing. He'll be moving through unpopulated wilderness areas which should offer good cover and plenty of drinking water." He looked serious. "Dehydration is always the first and greatest enemy in a survival situation. Humans can go without food for a lot longer than they can go without water."

"And if he is badly hurt?" Vasey pressed. "Parachuting into a forest is always risky."

"In that case, Brad would have no chance at all," Schofield replied gravely. "If the Russians don't stumble across him and take him prisoner, he would die of exposure or thirst."

Nadia winced, suddenly picturing Brad trapped and helpless in the scorched wreckage of his ERO shell with broken bones or head injuries. Frowning, she shook the horrifying image away and rapped the table sharply. "There is no point in dwelling on worst-case scenarios," she said crisply, forcing herself to sound far more confident than she felt. "Our task is to plan a rescue operation— not a funeral." Suitably chastened, Vasey and Schofield both nodded. "Fortunately, we have the right aircraft available to extract Brad once he makes contact," Nadia continued.

She sent another picture to the conference room's big LED screen. It showed a batwing-configuration aircraft roughly the size of a Gulfstream G450 business jet, with four engines buried in the wing's upper surface. Built by Sky Masters as a prototype, the stealthy, short-takeoff-and-landing XCV-62 Ranger had proved its worth during the raid on Russia's Perun's Aerie cyberwar complex . . . and then again last year, when it allowed them to fly secretly into the United States. In the confused aftermath of the deadly battle against Gryzlov's war robots, the Ranger had been flown back to a hangar at Battle Mountain rather than returning to the Iron Wolf Squadron base in Poland.

She looked at Vasey. "With some simulator practice, you should not have much trouble flying the Ranger. I will be your copilot and systems officer."

The Englishman offered her a crooked grin. "You know, Major Rozek, I'm seriously beginning to regret telling you earlier about how good I am at raising hell. Because I had no idea you would take me so literally."

Seeing the puzzled look on Schofield's face, Vasey explained. "Using the XCV-62 to get Brad out means flying straight into a hornet's nest. Russia's air defenses in the far east are extremely powerful and they're backed by advanced radar systems."

"How powerful?"

In answer to Schofield's question, Nadia pulled up a map of the region between the Vostochny Cosmodrome in the west and Russia's Pacific coast in the east. Overlapping circles and icons revealed a layered web of S-400 long-range SAMs and medium-range SA-17 SAM, along with a network of airfields where Su-35, MiG-29, and MiG-31 fighter regiments were stationed.

Schofield stared at the map. "Good God."

"It is a difficult tactical problem," Nadia said evenly. "Compounded by the certainty that the Russians will be on the highest possible alert—ready to meet any American retaliatory air or missile attack on the Vostochny launch complex."

"'Difficult' isn't exactly the word I would choose," Schofield said. "Stealthy or not, there is absolutely no way a lone aircraft can make it through that kind of defensive net without being detected and engaged."

"Very true," Nadia agreed. A fierce, predatory look settled on her beautiful face. "That is precisely why we will *not* be going in alone." Speaking forcefully, she ran through the basics of what she contemplated. While it would take a lot more work to refine her rough sketch into a workable plan, the broad outlines were clear enough.

When she finished, Vasey shook his head in mingled disbelief and admiration. "By God, Major Rozek, I'll say one thing for you: when you decide to go for something, you certainly don't hold anything back."

DEEP IN THE OLDJIKAN STATE NATURE RESERVE, RUSSIA
Later that night

Brad McLanahan sat slumped with his back against the trunk of a large oak tree. The adrenaline rush sparked by surviving his fiery plunge through the earth's atmosphere, and then discovering that he'd landed in enemy territory, had kept him going during the first hours of his long afternoon trek. Eventually, though, it had faded, replaced by the throbbing pain in his shoulder and the increasing level of pain in his right leg. After that, his hike through the rugged landscape of low, forested hills and swampy lowlands had settled into a painful, exhausting slog. By the time the last light faded, making it too difficult and dangerous to keep going, he figured he'd walked about eight miles east from where he'd landed . . . though probably no more than four or five as the crow flew.

He stifled a ferocious yawn. Sound would carry farther at night than during the day. Not that there was much real risk that anyone would hear him, he thought. Since he'd crossed that dirt logging road with its telltale nature reserve sign, he hadn't seen any signs of human activity. No houses or buildings. No other roads. Not even any identifiable walking trails. He looked up through the canopy of oak leaves over his head. An infinity of stars, undimmed by any man-made light pollution, speckled the night sky. Apart from the soft rustle of leaves and small branches stirred by a gentle breeze, there wasn't a sound for miles around.

All things considered, Brad decided, this was about as good a time and place to try making contact with the outside world as he was likely to get. He unzipped the pouch holding his emergency supplies, took out the compact satellite phone, and switched it on. After a second or two, its small screen lit up with a soft hum. The GPS coordinates it displayed confirmed his position. *Hip-deep in shit*, he thought wryly.

A couple of quick icon presses configured the phone to hunt for the next available satellite that could route his signal. Almost immediately a quiet tone chimed. Relieved, he exhaled. One more hurdle down.

To tighten its control over mobile communications, Russia's government required the registration of all satellite phone SIM cards. Theoretically, this made it impossible for anyone to place a call inside Russian territory without positive identification. Fortunately, thanks to Scion's tech wizards, this phone had a special SIM card that could mimic those officially registered phones.

Mentally, Brad crossed his fingers and dialed a special number—one he'd had drummed into him during the intense SERE training Ian Schofield had run for all Iron Wolf combat pilots. After a series of soft clicks, the phone connected.

Someone on the other end picked up on the second ring. "Smallville Pizza Parlor," he heard a young man's voice say calmly. "This call may be monitored for quality-control purposes. Now, how can I help you, sir?"

A smile crossed Brad's face. He was in touch with a covert Scion communications center back in the States. But that bit about calls being monitored was a warning that there was a chance, however slim, of Russian eavesdropping. He would need to use a simple voice code suited to the cover identity chosen by the Scion operative. Fortunately, memorizing different key phrases had been another part of his SERE training. "I have an order for takeout."

In plain English, that was his request for an emergency extraction.

"Yes, sir," the other man said calmly. "And will you be paying by cash, check, or credit card?"

"Credit card," Brad told him. That was the code phrase for "the enemy appears unaware of my location." Saying he would pay with *cash* would have signaled that the Russians were in hot pursuit, while a *check* would have told the Scion agent that he was being hunted, but that the enemy was not close.

For the next couple of minutes, he ran through a litany of voice codes that reported his physical status and current situation—all disguised as an ordinary order for a pizza with different toppings. It occurred to him that one of the unintended benefits of speaking in code was that it forced him to concentrate and stay calm . . . when all the while he really wanted to yell, "For Christ's sake, hurry up and pull me out of here!"

When he finished, there was a brief pause. Then the Scion operative came back on the line. "I've placed your order, sir. It should be ready for pickup in thirty minutes, but you should call back just to be sure it's ready."

Brad nodded. "Got it." His message had been passed up the chain of command and he should recontact this number in thirty minutes to receive further instructions.

"Is there anything else I can get you?" the agent on the other end asked.

"Er, no . . . no, thanks," Brad said slowly. What he really wanted most of all was the chance to hear Nadia's voice again. Unfortunately, that wasn't a request covered in the covert communication codes he'd been taught.

"Then you have a nice night. And thank you for calling Smallville Pizza," the other man said. With a click, the line went dead.

Feeling very subdued suddenly, Brad shut down the phone to conserve its limited battery power. Its tiny screen blinked off, leaving him in darkness again. Ironically, now that he'd regained contact with the outside world, he felt more alone than ever.

CHAPTER 28

ABOARD MARS ONE
A short time later

Colonel Vadim Strelkov looked down at the Pacific Ocean as the station swung northeastward toward the coast of California. Masses of clouds, bright white in daylight, towered above the dark navy-blue waters of the deep sea. "Time to the first estimated American launch window?" he asked Konnikov.

"Two minutes, sir," the younger man replied from his sensor console.

Strelkov tapped the intercom button. "All personnel. Stand by for possible attack. Close and seal your suits." He closed his own helmet visor.

Readiness reports flowed smoothly from the rest of the crew. The lasers and Thunderbolt plasma rail gun were fully charged and ready to fire. The station's own sensors and data links to other satellites and ground-based radars were operational.

"Sixty seconds," Konnikov reported. A warning

tone pulsed through their headsets. "We are being painted by an X-band radar. My computer evaluates it as an AN/TPY-2 phased-array system."

Strelkov nodded. That was one of the bus-sized, long-range, very high-altitude surveillance radars the Americans used for a number of their missile and air defense systems, including the GMD interceptors based at Vandenberg Air Force Base. "Is that radar locked on to us?"

"Not reliably," Konnikov answered. "Our stealth coating is absorbing most of its energy." He glanced toward the colonel. "But they probably have enough tracking data to launch against us anyway."

"Understood, Major." By combining the bits and pieces of information gathered by their ground-based telescopes, radars, and geosynchronous SBIRS satellites, the Americans could certainly pin down their orbital track clearly enough to target Mars One. Briefly, he considered using the thrusters aboard the docked cargo spacecraft and orbiter to change their orbit slightly—in the hope of throwing off the enemy's firing solution. Then he rejected the idea. Such an evasive maneuver would consume too much of their precious fuel reserves with too little guarantee of success.

"Fifteen seconds."

Strelkov gripped the edges of his console. Yes, they had simulated this exact scenario dozens of times during training. But all those successes in computer-generated war games seemed less impressive when confronted by a real attack.

"Launch detection by EKS missile warning satellite!" Konnikov rapped out. "A missile has been fired from the silos at Vandenberg. Mars One is confirmed as the target." He leaned over his console. "Second launch detection! Same source. Same target."

"Time to impact for the first American interceptor?"

"Fifty seconds."

Strelkov spoke to Filatyev. "Engage those enemy missiles when ready, Viktor."

From his station, the burly major acknowledged with a terse, "Yes, sir."

Konnikov spoke up. "EKS data handoff to our X-band radar is complete. Time to impact for the first American missile is now thirty-five seconds. First-stage separation observed. Transferring data to Thunderbolt's fire-control computer."

"Data received," Filatyev confirmed. A second later, he said, "I have a firing solution. Firing now."

Mars One vibrated as the plasma rail gun pulsed.

"Good hit!" Konnikov reported excitedly. His radar display showed the image of the inbound American interceptor blossom into a cloud of separate fragments and veer off course. He shifted his attention to the second enemy missile still climbing toward them. Like its counterpart, it had already separated from its first stage and must be nearly ready to shed its second—which would leave only its payload, the much smaller EKV, or exoatmospheric kill vehicle, speeding aloft to home in on and strike the station. "Time to impact for the second interceptor is twenty-eight seconds."

"Firing Thunderbolt," Filatyev said.

Again, Mars One shuddered. And again, the plasma toroid fired by the rail gun slammed home. While it was still more than three hundred kilometers from the Russian space station, the second American missile swerved aside . . . shedding pieces of itself as it fell back toward Earth.

"Excellent shooting, Viktor!" Strelkov said with open delight. He let go of his console and drifted slightly into the middle of the compartment. He rotated to face Konnikov. "How long before we're in range of the interceptors based at Fort Drum, Georgy?"

"Just under eight minutes, Colonel."

Strelkov swiveled back to the intercom and spoke to Pyotr Romanenko. "What is the status of Thunderbolt's supercapacitors, Major?"

"They are recharging now," the engineering officer replied. "We should be able to fire two more shots in less than six minutes."

Strelkov allowed himself to relax. With the plasma rail gun operational, they were essentially safe from anything the Americans could throw at them. True, he thought, a sequenced attack like this would be more difficult to defeat if it were carried out while Mars One was in the earth's shadow. In those circumstances, using Thunderbolt to destroy a first wave of American missiles would drain their supercapacitors—leaving only their much-shorter-range Hobnail lasers to handle a second wave. Given the high closure rates in this kind of orbital engagement, Leonid Revin's lasers would have just seven seconds to hit and destroy the incoming interceptors. That was still feasible, but there was no denying that the odds that the Americans might score a crippling hit would increase dramatically.

Fortunately, given the orbital mechanics at work, the American missile defense sites could not conduct a coordinated attack in darkness for at least another nine days. And by that time, the replacement fusion reactor Colonel General Leonov had promised should be in orbit and mated with Mars One. Once that happened, nothing could touch them. Russia's total domination of low Earth orbit would be assured.

THE WHITE HOUSE, WASHINGTON, D.C.
Several hours later

President Farrell listened intently while Nadia Rozek outlined her proposed plan to snatch Brad McLanahan safely from Russian territory. Seen over the secure link to Battle Mountain, she looked exhausted, with dark shadows under her large blue-gray eyes. Despite her obvious fatigue, though, she sounded completely confident and fully in control of her faculties and emotions. He found that reassuring, because otherwise what she contemplated would have struck him as riding awfully close to the edge of crazy.

When she finished, he pursed his lips. "Let's assume I sign off on all of this, Major. Can you guarantee me that this rescue operation of yours will succeed?"

"No, I cannot, Mr. President," Nadia said frankly. "The challenges we face are enormous. And this plan is, of necessity, fairly complex—with many working parts. Should any of them go wrong . . . or if the Russians fail to react as I predict . . . we will fail."

Farrell nodded. That pretty much squared with his own assessment. He looked closely at her. "Basically, you're asking me to commit a substantial U.S. military force and run huge political and diplomatic risks—all in the hope of saving just one man. There's a lot of folks out there—especially in Congress and the media—who might not see that as real sensible."

"Yes, that is true," she agreed. She offered him a wan smile. "But remember, I will still be risking more than you."

He raised an eyebrow. "Oh? How's that?"

"I will be gambling with my own life, Mr. President," Nadia said quietly. "And that of the man I love."

Damn, J.D., this lady sure knows how to square up and throw a punch, Farrell thought with admiration. And the best of it was that he could tell she meant every single word. There was no artifice in Nadia Rozek. He sat quietly for a moment. Then he nodded decisively. "You've made your point, Major. If you're going all in, how can I do any less? I'll issue the necessary orders to the commander of the Pacific Fleet. No doubt there'll be some squawking from some of the Pentagon's wet hens, but you pay that no mind. I'll see to it that you get the help you need."

"Thank you," Nadia said simply. She looked down briefly, hiding her face from him.

She was probably concealing a few tears of relief, he judged. One thing he'd learned was that this young woman hated the thought of competing on anything but a level playing field. A lot of people would have gone straight for the emotional jugular—reminding him of how she'd lost her legs saving his miserable hide. Somehow, he doubted the idea of doing that had ever crossed her mind.

Farrell waited a few seconds, letting her recover, and then asked, "When do you figure you'll be ready to kick this thing off?"

"Approximately seventy-two hours from now," Nadia replied. "I wish it could be sooner, but I must contact my own government and request the use of some of its resources—those of the Iron Wolf Squadron. It will take time to assemble the necessary aircraft and munitions and transfer them here from Poland."

"Seventy-two hours," he said meditatively. "That's three days."

She nodded darkly. "Three days during which Brad must avoid detection and capture. Otherwise, *everything* we are doing will be in vain."

CHAPTER 29

THE KREMLIN
Later that day

Through narrowed eyes, Gennadiy Gryzlov studied the faces of his closest military, intelligence, and foreign policy advisers. As usual, he could sense the aura of unease emanating from most of them. *Cowards and do-nothing bureaucrats,* he thought contemptuously. Left on their own, without the lash of his own fierce will to drive them, they were useless, a pack of timid, time-serving drones whose fear of the Americans was only slightly outweighed by their fear of him. Only Mikhail Leonov and Daria Titeneva showed any real courage . . . and even those two were still far too prone to see the possible dangers of any action more clearly than its potential rewards.

His lip curled in disgust. It might be time soon to purge most of these incompetents. If so, the ensuing trials, imprisonments, and executions should teach a salutary lesson to their successors:

while he ruled this country, anyone who failed to act aggressively in Russia's interests was as much a traitor as anyone who actively conspired with enemies of the state.

Gryzlov shrugged inwardly. Winnowing the chaff from his national security team could wait a while longer—at least until the strategic situation in outer space and on Earth was more settled. Thus far, at least, the Americans were reacting with surprising meekness to the ongoing destruction of their military space infrastructure. Apart from a single failed attempt to shoot down Mars One with a handful of missile defense interceptors, the United States had done nothing. Honestly, he had expected a much stronger response from Farrell after all the man's superficial bluster and tough talk. Instead, the Texan appeared to be just as weak and ineffectual as his predecessor, Barbeau. In his own native idiom, he was "all hat and no cattle."

Still, there were some Americans who had proved themselves to be very dangerous enemies all too often in the past—Martindale, McLanahan, and their Scion and Sky Masters mercenaries. He was sure they were plotting something. It was for that reason he'd demanded such close GRU surveillance of their spaceplane base at Battle Mountain. Unfortunately, he thought icily, as usual, poor, bumbling Viktor Kazyanov had little light to shed on the subject.

"Our intelligence agents in Nevada have been forced to go to ground," the minister of state security admitted reluctantly. His face was pale. "Over the past forty-eight hours, security around Sky Masters facilities has been considerably strengthened. The Americans have established a strong cordon of armed corporate security guards, local and state police, and federal agents. According to the GRU, any further attempts to penetrate this cordon would only result in the exposure and capture of our officers."

Gryzlov scowled. In and of itself, this heightened security was revealing. McLanahan and Russia's other adversaries must be going crazy trying to come up with a way to attack Mars One with their remaining spaceplanes. He turned to Leonov. "Now that Kazyanov's spies have proved worthless, what about our own reconnaissance satellites? Have they spotted any unusual activity at this base?"

"Not thus far," Leonov said. "Our Razdan and Persona satellites have made several passes over the Battle Mountain area since we destroyed the S-19 Midnight. None of their pictures show any of the remaining spaceplanes. This suggests Sky Masters has moved them from the flight line back into hangars to hide them from our view."

"But you don't have continuous coverage of this area," Gryzlov pointed out sharply. "Those spaceplanes could be landing and taking off undetected whenever our spy satellites aren't within range."

Leonov nodded. "That is possible. But if so, they are *not* going into space. Our EKS ballistic-missile warning satellites will pick up any launch headed outside the earth's atmosphere."

"At which point, it might be too late!"

"So long as Colonel Strelkov and his cosmonauts remain vigilant, no space weapon in the current American arsenal poses a serious threat to Mars One," Leonov said. "This will be even more true once our new reactor is connected and running."

"No weapon that we know of now," Gryzlov said sourly. "We have been surprised before . . . and never pleasantly." His expression turned murderous. "It may be time to end any possible threat from Sky Masters once and for all."

Leonov looked surprised. "By what means?"

Gryzlov shrugged. "Two or three of our *Rapira* hypersonic missiles fired from orbit at Battle Mountain should do the job. Those spaceplanes won't be any threat if they're blown to smithereens."

He hid a smile at the looks of horror triggered by this seemingly offhand suggestion. From their expressions, he might as well have suggested bombing the White House or Buckingham Palace.

"I would strongly recommend against such a move," Daria Titeneva said carefully. "So far, our military operations have been confined to space, in a limited war that we are winning with ease. Suddenly attacking a crucial target inside the continental United States itself could easily provoke a massive escalation in this conflict—one that might lead to uncontrolled nuclear war."

Leonov nodded. "The foreign minister is right, Mr. President," he argued. "And with only one Mars-class station in orbit, we do not yet have the ability to intercept a significant retaliatory strike launched by their ballistic-missile submarines. Later, once we've put additional platforms into space, we will have more options. But for now, the game is not worth the candle."

Caution, caution, always caution, Gryzlov thought caustically. Though in this case, he realized, Leonov and Titeneva's advice was probably sensible. Tempting though it was, an orbital missile strike against Sky Masters now might frighten even Farrell into believing he faced the nightmare scenario of all nuclear war planners—the moment where you either had to launch your missiles or risk losing them to an unstoppable enemy attack.

No, he decided, it was better to stretch out the pretense that Russia had only limited aims in this conflict—control over low Earth orbit—for as long as possible. And if Sky Masters actually launched another attack on Mars One using its spaceplanes? Then all bets would be off . . . and destroying Battle Mountain from orbit would be a justifiable act of war.

"Very well," Gryzlov said curtly. "We'll hold off for the moment." He motioned for Leonov to continue. "What else do you have to report, Mikhail?"

"Our satellites have spotted increased activity at the U.S. Air Force space launch complex at Vandenberg," Leonov told him. "My analysts believe the Americans are preparing one of their Delta IV Heavy rockets for lift-off sometime soon. They might be planning to send up replacements for some of the satellites we've already destroyed."

Gryzlov smiled thinly. "Which would be futile."

Leonov nodded. "Sooner or later, the orbits of

those new satellites would bring them within firing range of Mars One. The Americans might regain some limited reconnaissance capability for a few days, but only at great cost."

That much was true, Gryzlov knew. By itself, launching a single Delta IV Heavy cost several hundred million dollars. Add in the cost of the satellites it carried, and the final price tag would soar into the billions. Not even the Americans could afford to be so profligate forever. Besides, even if they were prepared to throw away that much money for so little purpose, the simple reality was they would run out of replacement spy satellites very soon. Sophisticated spacecraft like the Topaz radar and KH-11 photoreconnaissance satellites could not be mass-produced. Building them required months and often years of painstaking precision work.

With Mars One already circling the world every ninety-seven minutes, poised to shoot down anything headed beyond the atmosphere, this was a space race the United States could not possibly win.

Already, the effects of Russia's surprise offensive actions in orbit were spreading fast, far beyond the purely military sphere. Previously scheduled commercial rocket launches from Kennedy Space Center and the European Space Agency's French Guiana launch site had been delayed indefinitely. There were signs of panic in Western stock exchanges as investors and economists tried frantically to calculate the possible repercussions of Russian control over outer space. The same thing was happening in the Asian markets—despite

Gryzlov's public promises to People's Republic of China president Zhou Qiang that Mars One's weapons were not a threat to the PRC's own spacecraft and satellites.

Gryzlov smiled cynically. It seemed that Chinese investors were a better judge of his own trustworthiness than their leaders. Then again, what could Beijing's rulers do, even if they suspected Moscow had no real intention of honoring its commitments in the long run? Once someone had a knife at your throat, it was already too late.

He looked across the table at Gregor Sokolov, the minister of defense. "Well, Gregor? Are the Americans making any threatening new military moves?"

"Their conventional and nuclear forces remain on a heightened state of alert, the one they call DEFCON Three," Sokolov said. "But this level has not increased significantly in the past forty-eight hours."

"Except that virtually all U.S. ballistic-missile submarines are now at sea," Leonov said dryly.

Gryzlov shrugged his shoulders. "That's merely a political move, a small gesture of defiance by Farrell. Ultimately, it changes nothing." He turned back to Sokolov. "Is that it?"

"Most American air, ground, and naval forces remain at their normal peacetime stations," Sokolov replied slowly. He hesitated for a moment—plainly reluctant to go on. "With one possible exception."

Gryzlov frowned. "Which is?"

"Approximately twenty-four hours ago, the U.S. Navy's *Ronald Reagan* carrier strike group, which had been conducting previously scheduled training exercises in the Western Pacific, off the Taiwanese coast, suddenly altered its course. It is now steaming north, toward Japan."

"Japan? Why head there?" Gryzlov demanded.

Leonov leaned forward, suddenly looking pensive. "Washington may be positioning military assets for a possible strike against the Vostochny Cosmodrome," he said. "If the Americans are planning a retaliatory attack against our space launch assets, it *is* the logical target."

Gryzlov stared at him. "Vostochny must be well over a thousand kilometers from Japan. That's beyond the range of a carrier strike force, isn't it?"

"Yes, sir," Leonov agreed. "Even using long-range cruise missiles, carrier-based aircraft would be hard-pressed to attack the complex."

"Then where is the threat?"

"The *Reagan*'s aircraft could be used to breach our outer defenses in the far east region," Leonov speculated. "That would open a path for a deep penetration raid by America's remaining heavy bombers."

"Six B-2 Spirit stealth bombers and a handful of refurbished B-1 Lancers?" Gryzlov scoffed. "What could they accomplish against Vostochny's defenses?"

"It would probably be a suicide mission," Leonov agreed carefully. "We have a full regiment of S-500 SAMs guarding the space center itself." His jaw tightened. "But I remind you that even a single bomb or missile hit scored against a spacecraft ready for launch would be catastrophic."

Gryzlov saw what he was driving at. The Energia-5VR heavy-lift rocket being assembled at Vostochny was the one slated to ferry Mars One's replacement reactor into orbit in just a few short days. If American bombers hit the launch complex and destroyed the Energia and its priceless payload on the pad, Russia's space station would remain dangerously vulnerable for months.

"Listen to me closely, Mikhail," he said coldly. "You *will* prevent such a disaster."

Leonov nodded. "I will put my forces on the highest possible alert. If the Americans do attack, their aircraft and missiles will be shot out of the sky."

"For your sake, I hope this show of confidence is justified," Gryzlov said bluntly. "Do not forget that others have failed to keep similar promises to me . . . and regretted it for the rest of their short and pain-filled lives."

KHABAROVSK REGION, RUSSIA
A short time later

With his boots held above his head in his left hand to keep them dry, Brad McLanahan waded cautiously across a shallow, muddy creek choked with reeds. Huge mosquitoes rose in swarms on all sides—buzzing noisily past his face. He grimaced. With his right arm in its improvised sling, he couldn't even swat at the ones that came swooping in, hungry for his blood.

"Wonderful, just wonderful. Join Sky Masters and see the festering armpits of the world," he spat out through clenched teeth. The air was thick with the stench of rotting vegetation.

On the other side of the creek, Brad grabbed at an overhanging branch and hauled himself back up onto drier land, his left arm shaking with fatigue and his right leg threatening to give out at any second. Despite the discomfort involved in walking barefoot through the tall grass and rocky soil, he resisted the temptation to put his boots back on right away. The last thing he needed right now was a case of trench foot, with its attendant blisters and painful skin infections.

Slowly, he toiled up a low rise and worked his way into the cover of a copse of trees. Time for a short breather, he decided. Once his feet dried off, he should be able to make better time.

When he drew near the top of the little ridge, Brad stopped and slumped down. He propped his back up against a tree trunk for support. Bone-weary as he was, lying down was a surefire recipe for falling asleep. Then, noticing that his mouth felt dry, he took out his canteen and swigged a quick drink.

He recapped the canteen and put it away. At least the purification tablets included in his SERE kit ensured he wasn't short of potable water. Food was another matter. His stomach growled softly. The need to ration his limited stock of protein bars meant he was already running a serious calorie deficit. Ideally, he would have been able to hunt, fish, and forage to supplement his emergency supplies. But that wasn't possible—not when he still had so much ground to cover before it grew too dark to travel safely.

Exhausted, Brad bent his head and focused on controlling his breathing. With every passing hour, he was growing more footsore and hungry. To avoid being spotted, he'd been forced to fight his way through the worst and most rugged sections of this seemingly empty countryside. The need to detour around clearings and patches of more open woodland added miles to his journey.

In some ways, the worst part was knowing that he was being deliberately kept in the dark about the details of any plans to rescue him. Intellectually, he understood the need for tight security. After all, what he didn't know he couldn't spill if the Russians caught him. Still, it was frustrating. And, as tired as he was, frustration felt dangerously close to despair.

The instructions Brad had been given were both clear as crystal and as murky as the bottom of that stream he'd just crossed. On first hearing, they'd seemed simple enough: Head southeast toward a set of map coordinates. And at all costs, reach those coordinates within seventy-two hours. But what he didn't know, and the Scion agents on the other end of his satellite phone connection would not tell him, was why this was so important. Did that X on the phone's digital map mark the end of this long trek, the place where someone would be waiting to help him out of this godforsaken country? Or was it only a waypoint on an even longer journey?

Well, Brad told himself grimly, there was only one sure way to find out. He would just have to get off his lazy ass and soldier on. Gritting his teeth against the pain, he tugged the paratrooper boots over his swollen feet, pushed himself back upright, and started walking again.

CHAPTER 30

SKY MASTERS AEROSPACE, INC.,
BATTLE MOUNTAIN, NEVADA
Some hours later

Patrick McLanahan knew he'd given in to sentiment by returning to Sky Masters to carry out his analysis of Russia's armed space station. The wireless links and limited neural interface built into his LEAF exoskeleton and its associated computer would have allowed him to carry out the work of combing through the accumulated intelligence from almost anywhere in the world. But Battle Mountain had been his adopted hometown—a home he'd shared with his son through much of Brad's childhood and teenage years. Coming back here now to search out ways to destroy the enemy orbital fortress that had knocked Brad and Boomer's S-19 out of the sky just felt right somehow.

It was a sentiment Jason Richter certainly understood. The Sky Masters CEO had set him up in an office just down the hall, with complete access to all of the company's secure computer systems . . . and to the accumulated knowledge and intuition of its top scientists and engineers.

Right now his eyes were closed. This shut out all outside distractions while he sorted through thousands of pieces of data collected about Mars One, both during Brad and Boomer's aborted reconnaissance and in the hours and days since then. While his LEAF's neural link was less capable than those used by the Iron Wolf Squadron's Cybernetic Infantry Devices, it still gave him the ability to assimilate and analyze information much faster than was possible for an unassisted human brain.

He was drawing on much more than just the material gathered by Sky Masters itself. Years before, while he was still president of the United States, Kevin Martindale had made sure carefully concealed back doors were secretly installed in the operating systems of most of the federal government's computer networks. Martindale had wanted to be able to bypass the sluggish federal bureaucracy during a national crisis. Now those same hidden back doors enabled Patrick to roam freely through the immense amounts of information collected by a vast array of different government agencies—ranging from the Pentagon to the National Reconnaissance Office to NASA.

Mentally, he dove headlong into this flow of raw intelligence, determined to tease out the significance of even the smallest scrap of data. Visual, radar, and infrared imagery, together with detailed reports prepared by various experts, scrolled through his mind at a rapid clip. Time in the sense used by the outside world ceased to have any real meaning for him.

Sorting through the pictures and other sensor readings amassed by Brad's nanosatellites during their close approach to the Russian station made several things clear. First, Mars One's three large modules had both inner and outer hulls. It was a construction technique similar to that used in Russian nuclear submarine designs, though never before for spacecraft. While this double-hulled design added mass and reduced the amount of usable interior space in each module, it also gave the station significant structural strength against damage from micrometeorites, shrapnel, and even weapons-grade lasers. And it provided the Russian station with good protection against radiation, something that was especially important since its relatively high orbit brushed against the lower fringes of the innermost Van Allen belt. Second, the spaces between its inner and outer hulls were occupied by retractable weapons and sensor mounts and stores of consumables—water, food, and oxygen. As another benefit, those stores added even more shielding against cosmic radiation.

Next, Patrick turned his efforts to analyzing Mars One's armament. Even what little was known left no doubt that the station had been designed and built for one purpose and one purpose only: to conduct sustained combat operations in space.

The two lasers Brad and Boomer had observed in action were plainly upgraded models of the Hobnail carbon-dioxide, electric-discharge weapons carried aboard Russia's rocket-launched Elektron spaceplanes. Their lethality at relatively short ranges had been demonstrated by the speed with which they engaged and destroyed the Sky Masters recon nanosats. By correlating the known thermal resistance of the materials used to build the nanosats and the time it took the lasers to kill them, he was able to develop a reasonable estimate of their energy output. And that, in turn, enabled him to pin down the Russian lasers' probable maximum effective range—which was somewhere between eighty-five and one hundred and twenty kilometers.

Patrick nodded to himself. The station's lasers were primarily defensive weapons. Against targets moving at orbital speeds, battles fought at one hundred kilometers or less were practically knife fights.

Mars One's offensive punch came from the plasma rail gun that had wrecked Brad and Boomer's spaceplane. Close study of images showing the starfish-shaped array of supercapacitors around the weapon's central tube confirmed Lawrence Dawson's speculation that it was a MARAUDER-type plasma gun. Somehow, Patrick doubted that was simply a coincidence. Over the years, the West's intelligence agencies had penetrated several of Russia's most closely held weapons research and development programs. But espionage was a door that opened both ways. He strongly suspected a thorough probe of the long-sealed MARAUDER research files would find Russian digital fingerprints all over them.

Still immersed in the data stream, he resisted the temptation to slide off target and waste time scanning through the U.S. Air Force Research Laboratory's computers to confirm his hunch. How the Russians originally got their hands on this technology was a question for another day and time. What mattered right now was that they'd turned it into a powerful and incredibly long-range weapon—one that had already destroyed most of America's reconnaissance satellites. Current observations suggested it could hit and kill targets at well over four thousand miles.

Patrick shook his head in astonishment. The Russian scientists and engineers who'd built that damned rail gun had evidently figured out how to create plasma toroids that remained stable for close to a second in a vacuum, far beyond anything yet achieved in any Western lab. Their success was a damning indictment of the shortsighted politicians and defense officials who'd abandoned similar U.S. efforts decades ago.

With an inward sigh at the folly and carelessness his countrymen had exhibited, he moved on.

During the nanosat flyby of Mars One, Brad had identified several other camouflaged hatches and ports. Knowing how the Russians, especially Gryzlov, thought, Patrick had little doubt those masked more weapons systems—probably a mix of missiles and conventional autocannons, like the 23mm gun the Soviets had test-fired aboard their old Salyut-3 space station back in the 1970s. But conventional missiles and cannons, powerful though they might be individually, could not begin to match the firepower produced by the station's plasma rail gun and its two shorter-range Hobnail lasers.

No, Patrick thought coldly, those directed-energy weapons were the chief threat posed by Mars One. Without them, the Russian station would be nothing more than an orbiting target—vulnerable to any number of missiles and lasers already in the U.S. and Sky Masters arsenals. With them, it circled the earth as a lethal, effectively impregnable fortress. Whatever Mars One's sensors could see, its plasma rail gun could kill . . . and at unprecedented distances.

He shifted slightly in his chair. The energy required to power those weapons must be significant, around a hundred kilowatts for each of the lasers and considerably more for the plasma gun. Where was it coming from? Certainly not from the space station's solar panels.

Images captured by ground-based telescopes and by the Sky Masters nanosatellites made it possible to calculate the size of those arrays. Even assuming the Russians had figured out how to increase their panel efficiency beyond the 30 to 40 percent range achieved by those aboard the old International Space Station, Mars One could not possibly generate more than one hundred kilowatts from solar power.

Patrick frowned. He'd read the reports from the Scion team in Russia. Alexei Rykov, the former

cosmonaut candidate they'd tricked into spill-
ing details about Gryzlov's top secret program,
had claimed Mars Project personnel were being
trained to operate and maintain small, high-
efficiency fusion power plants. Most analysts had
dismissed this otherwise unconfirmed claim as
dubious. They were skeptical that the Russians
could have developed compact fusion technology
ahead of the United States or other Western nations. And frankly, he'd shared that assessment . . .

But now?

Mars One had a working and deadly plasma
rail gun—a weapon that was beyond the current
technological reach of the United States and its
allies. That much was undeniable. Was it safe to
assume that was the *only* scientific and engineering breakthrough Moscow had achieved?

Hell no, Muck, Patrick told himself, using the
nickname his friends had given him long ago. Fusion reactor or not, it was obvious that the Russian
space station must have some kind of advanced
power generator aboard. How else could its crew
hope to fire their rail gun and lasers repeatedly in
combat? No amount of battery storage could keep
those weapons charged during a prolonged fight.

For a moment, he sat motionless, gripped by
a sudden fear that the Russians had gained an
insurmountable lead over the United States. In
seeking a way to defeat Mars One, he might only
be hunting a chimera, something that was impossible. How in Christ's name could they hope to
win a battle against this monstrosity? That space
station's plasma gun could kill any spacecraft

or missile long before it closed within striking range. And with the power generated by a working fusion reactor, the Russians had the ability to fire the damned thing as rapidly as they could recharge its supercapacitors.

Or could they?

Patrick suddenly opened his eyes, thinking hard. *Bring up all data collected during every observed attack on an American satellite and spacecraft,* he ordered his computer through the neural link. He closed his eyes again in intense concentration. Reams of information spooled through his mind. The intelligence gathered from more than thirty separate engagements was intriguing. Mars One's rail gun had killed targets over a wide variety of distances. Brad and Boomer's S-19 had been nailed at point-blank range, at least in astronautical terms. But the station's last kill, another Trumpeter ELINT satellite, had been fried at more than four thousand miles while on its way back up to apogee in an elliptical Molniya orbit. The intervals between Mars One's attacks were equally varied—varying from as short as several minutes to as long as an hour or more.

Images of the Russian space station cascaded past his closed eyes. In every case, there was the same dazzling pulse as the plasma gun fired—a flare of white light so intense that it obscured even the bright glare of the sun reflected off Mars One's solar arrays.

The sun . . .

Like a hunting dog suddenly catching a scent, Patrick leaned forward in his chair. The sun. *That* was the one constant amid all the variation. So far, Mars One had *never* fired its directed-energy weapons while the station itself was deep in Earth's shadow. Which could mean—

"General McLanahan?"

Startled by the sudden interruption, Patrick swam back up to full awareness of his surroundings. He disengaged his neural link. His racing thoughts abruptly decelerated, returning to the plodding, second-by-second routine of the nondigital world. Clumsily, he swiveled around in his chair. "Yes?"

Nadia Rozek stood framed in the open door. She wore a flight suit and cradled a helmet under one arm. Her expression was somber. "I have come to say good-bye," she told him. "And to give you my word that we will do our best."

He glanced at his watch and was shocked to see that several hours had passed while he'd been linked to his computer. Nadia and her team must be ready to depart for the distant airfield she'd chosen as a base for their planned rescue operation.

Quickly, Patrick levered himself up out of the chair, ignoring the whine of protest from his exoskeleton's servos. "Good hunting, Nadia," he said quietly. "Fly safe . . . and bring my son home with you."

"I will," she promised. For a brief second, unshed tears glistened in her eyes. Then, choked up by emotion, she threw her arms around him and buried her face against his chest.

Caught by surprise, Patrick stood motionless while Nadia hugged him. It had been many years since he'd felt the warm embrace of another human being, especially a woman. Even he and Brad were still trapped at that awkward father-son handshake stage. And he knew that most other people, Nadia among them, were viscerally un-settled by the sight of his LEAF exoskeleton, clear helmet, and life-support pack. They made him seem alien, a man set apart from his own species.

Awkwardly, he patted her shoulder.

After a moment more, Nadia let go and stepped back. She nodded to him in silence, still unable to speak, and then turned on her heel and left.

CHAPTER 31

Hunter Noble limped down the cargo ramp of the twin-tailed C-23C Sherpa turboprop and out into the blistering summer temperatures of southwest Utah. Heat waves shimmered across the concrete. He squinted against the brightness, looking out across a landscape of reddish rock. Mountains loomed in the west and to the north, with low ridges and hills in the east. This airport was just a mile north of the Arizona border and on the northeastern edge of the Mojave Desert.

He glanced back over his shoulder at the two hard-faced men following close on his heels. Both wore sunglasses, dark suits, and ties. Slight bulges marked the holstered pistols concealed under their jackets. "You know, guys, this isn't exactly what I had planned for my day off. I don't like making threats, but if things don't improve real soon, I may be forced to cut a couple of stars off your Yelp review."

"The casinos in Battle Mountain aren't going anywhere, Dr. Noble," one of them, a big bruiser with a blond crew cut, said coolly. Everything about the guy said former Marine to Boomer, who'd privately dubbed him Goon Number 1. "You can throw away your paycheck another time. This is more important."

"*This* being what exactly?" Boomer demanded.

The big man shrugged. "You'll see."

Boomer stopped at the foot of the ramp. He swung around and folded his arms. "Look, I've been toddling along like a good little soldier ever since you fellas came knocking on my town-house door a couple of hours ago. But now I think you owe me some straight answers."

"And you'll get them, Dr. Noble," Goon Number 1 said with exaggerated patience. He nodded toward the large aircraft hangar they were parked next to. "In there."

His partner, shorter and with close-cropped dark hair, said helpfully, "It's air-conditioned."

Boomer shot a finger at him. "Okay, *you*, I like. You've got solid motivational skills." He sighed and started ambling toward a small door visible on the side of the huge building. "Fine . . . I give up. I might as well get this over with."

As promised, the enormous hangar was air-conditioned. It was also occupied by a big, black, blended-wing aircraft with five large engines, four mounted beneath its highly swept delta wing and another atop the aft fuselage.

"What . . . the . . . hell?" Boomer said slowly, staring up in shock at what was unmistakably an S-29 Shadow spaceplane. He shook his head in sheer disbelief. "No fucking way."

"I *thought* you'd appreciate my little surprise," a smooth, resonant voice said from over his shoulder. Kevin Martindale came out of the shadows to stand next to Boomer.

"I knew we built most of the components for a third S-29 airframe and several extra LPDRS engines," Boomer said carefully. He turned toward the other man. "But I also know that we never finished the damned thing. Not after the feds shut down our manned spaceplane program."

"Sky Masters didn't finish it," Martindale agreed. He nodded toward the spaceplane. "I did." He shrugged. "Or more precisely, I contracted with Helen Kaddiri for the discreet services of certain Sky Masters aircraft production specialists and the necessary equipment. They've been flying to St. George off and on from California for the past several years."

Boomer stared at him. "You had our guys put the S-29 together here?" Martindale nodded, pleased that he had put one over on the cocky and sometimes arrogant astronaut-engineer. "In a hangar? Not in an aircraft factory?"

"It was . . . difficult," Martindale said with a slight frown. "Not to mention time-consuming and extremely expensive."

"Yeah, I bet." Boomer eyed him. "Mind telling me where you picked up the couple of hundred million dollars, minimum, building this bird must have cost?"

Martindale returned his gaze. "For the past four years, I've been funneling half the profits from Scion's international security, intelligence, and military contracts into this project."

Boomer raised an eyebrow. "Really? I kind of figured you needed all of that money to build a super-secret lair on a deserted volcanic island somewhere."

"There are only so many laser-armed sharks one can buy," Martindale said with a thin, dry smile. "After the first dozen or so, the excitement starts to fade."

"I'll take your word for that." Boomer looked back up at the huge spaceplane. "What I don't get is why you've gone to all this time and trouble, Mr. Martindale. We already have two S-29s ready to fly. Sure, a third one is nice to have . . . but it's not exactly a game changer."

The other man's smile widened. "You might want to look more closely, Dr. Noble," he said gently. "That isn't just a standard-model S-29 Shadow. We built this one to your own design specifications for the S-29B."

Boomer's eyes widened in amazement. In the aftermath of the destruction of Armstrong Station by Russian missile and Elektron spaceplanes, he'd worked up plans for armed versions of Sky Masters' spaceplanes—figuring the United States would need them in any future conflict in orbit. When President Barbeau abandoned all manned spaceflight, he'd reluctantly shoved the plans into a drawer, along with a lot of other innovative concepts that had never made it off the drawing board.

He'd designed the S-29B Shadow to mount a two-megawatt gas dynamic laser pod, along with a smaller targeting laser radar, in a retractable turret on top of its fuselage. The laser would be powerful enough to engage targets out to around three hundred miles—firing up to twenty times in five-second bursts before it needed to be refueled. Four microwave emitters in retractable pods—two near the wing tips, one atop the forward fuselage, and one on the underside of the aft fuselage—were intended to defend against incoming missiles, killer satellites, and enemy spacecraft. These defensive emitters operated automatically, either cued by the spaceplane's own sensors or by data-linked information from other platforms.

Boomer ran his gaze over the parked spaceplane. Now that he knew what he was looking for, he could see the subtle differences between it and its unarmed counterparts. He turned back to Martindale with a frown. "Who else in Sky Masters knows about this?"

"Apart from Helen Kaddiri? And the technicians who helped build it?" Martindale said. "No one."

"Not even General McLanahan?" Boomer asked in surprise.

The other man shrugged again. "Oh, I suspect Patrick may have guessed what I've been up to. But if so, he understood the importance of discretion. I've kept this project on a strict need-to-know basis."

"So why are you telling me all this?" Boomer wondered.

"Because, Dr. Noble," Martindale said, with another thin smile, "now *you* need to know."

Boomer snorted. "Yeah, well, it sure as hell would have been nice to find out about all this *before* Brad McLanahan and I got our tails singed facing off against Mars One. Maybe if we'd flown this spaceplane instead, things would have turned out differently."

Martindale shook his head. "The S-29B doesn't have any separate payload capacity, Dr. Noble . . . as you should remember. Every spare ounce is needed for its offensive and defensive weapons and sensors. So you wouldn't have been able to carry those reconnaissance nanosatellites of yours into orbit. Besides, it would have been viewed as somewhat impolitic to fly an armed spaceplane so close to what the Russians then asserted was merely a peaceful civilian space station."

"Maybe so," Boomer said with a sour tone. His mouth turned down. "Unfortunately, it's already too late for this S-29B you've spent so much money on to make one damned bit of difference. Before the Russians launched Mars One, this bird would have ruled Earth orbit." Angrily, he nodded toward the big spaceplane. "Sending that Shadow up to tangle with that plasma rail gun of Gryzlov's would be like throwing a Sopwith Camel into battle against an F-22 Raptor. It would be suicide, not any kind of fair fight."

Martindale nodded. "I agree. As matters stand, this spaceplane cannot engage in combat in orbit and hope to survive."

"Then why haul me all the way down here for this little dog and pony show?" Boomer asked cautiously.

Martindale looked at him in surprise. "Isn't that obvious? The S-29B may not be able to fly safely into orbit, but it can certainly fly elsewhere." Carefully, he laid out what he had in mind.

When he finished, Boomer stared at him for a few moments. Finally, he shook his head. "And you didn't see fit to mention any of this to Major Rozek?"

Now it was Martindale's turn to stare. "Do you really think I should have revealed the existence of a top secret armed spaceplane to a covert ops team preparing to fly deep into heavily defended Russian airspace?"

"Yeah, I guess I see your point." Boomer sighed. He nodded. "Okay, I'm in. But I'll need some time to rustle up a crew. My specs called for a crew of four plus the pilots. It'll take months to train them up."

Martindale shook his head. "That won't be necessary, Dr. Noble," he said with absolute assurance. "I've already selected a crew for this spaceplane. In fact, they've been training for missions for the past two years."

"*Two years?*" Boomer took a deep breath and

then let it out in a rush. "You know, you really are one spooky son of a bitch, Mr. Martindale," he said, half in disgust and half in sneaking admiration.

Martindale nodded serenely. "Yes," he agreed. "I suppose I am."

ATTU ISLAND, THE ALEUTIANS, IN THE BERING SEA
Several hours later

Attu, near the western end of the Aleutian island chain, lay only five hundred nautical miles from Russia's Kamchatka Peninsula. During the Second World War, the forty-mile-long island's rugged hills and mountains had been the scene of a horrific eighteen-day battle between occupying Japanese soldiers and the U.S. Army's 7th Infantry Division. More than four thousand men had died in the struggle over an otherwise unimportant speck in the middle of the Bering Sea. Now, though, the island was ordinarily entirely uninhabited, home only to the graves of the dead and dozens of rare bird species.

That was about to change.

Six hours after taking off from Battle Mountain, the Sky Masters XCV-62 Ranger piloted by Peter Vasey flew toward Attu, cruising at four hundred and fifty knots barely two thousand feet above the sea. Intently, he peered through the cockpit canopy into a dense gray wall of swirling fog. The Aleutians were known for horrible weather—fierce storms and squalls in winter and thick fog in summer.

"Bloody hell," he muttered. "My old grannie told me stories about the Great London Smog of 1952, where you couldn't see your hand in front of your face. But I never thought anyone would be daft enough to try flying through something almost as bad. Not even me."

Sitting in the copilot's seat, Major Nadia Rozek smiled wryly. "Your grandmother did not have the benefit of a DTF system, Constable."

"There is that," Vasey allowed. Between the detailed maps stored in their aircraft's computers and periodic, short bursts from its radar altimeter, the Ranger's digital terrain-following system was ordinarily used for prolonged, very low-altitude flight at high speeds. Together with its radar-absorbent stealth coating, DTF enabled the aircraft to avoid detection and dodge enemy SAMs. Today, the system's computerized maps and radars had another use—allowing them to fly, with reasonable confidence, in conditions where visibility was practically nil.

Nadia peered down at her display. "Eight nautical miles to our final turn to the airfield."

"Copy that." Vasey eased back on the throttles. The muted roar from the Ranger's four turbofan engines decreased. Their airspeed dropped fast.

They were heading for a runway on the southeastern side of the island, just inland from Massacre Bay. Closed more than a decade ago, Casco

Cove Coast Guard Station's airport was now officially reserved for emergency use only.

"Casco Station, this is Ranger Six-Two," Nadia said. "Two minutes to final approach fix. Descending through fifteen hundred feet. Airspeed two-five-zero knots, full stop."

"*Ranger Six-Two, Casco Station, roger,*" a crisp female voice replied. The airport was back in business, this time run by the men and women of a Scion advance team flown in the day before. "*Winds variable between one-eight-zero and two-four-zero degrees, twenty knots gusting to twenty-seven, ceiling indefinite, fog, haze, runway visual range variable between six hundred and zero, altimeter two-niner-four-zero. Runway braking action fair.*"

"Six-Two copies." Nadia brought the XCV-62's forward-looking passive thermal sensors online and activated its air-to-ground radar. In milliseconds, the aircraft's computer analyzed the information it was receiving from both sources and overlaid the resulting image across Vasey's HUD. "Lovely weather."

"*Fiat lux,*" the Englishman said appreciatively. "Let there be light." What had been a view of gray nothingness was now a green-tinted, three-dimensional picture of the rugged island ahead. The steering cues on his HUD slid right. He banked to follow them.

The mass of a steep, sixteen-hundred-foot volcanic mountain slid past off their left side. Snow still crowned its peak. Even in summer, temperatures on Attu never got much above fifty degrees

Fahrenheit. The runway loomed ahead, stretching across spongy tundra otherwise marked by old bomb craters, unused roads, and abandoned buildings.

"Casco Station, Six-Two," Nadia radioed. "Passing final approach fix. Descending through three hundred feet, airspeed two-zero-zero knots."

"Six-Two, roger. Winds two-five-zero at twenty-two gusting to thirty, RVR eight hundred."

Vasey entered a short command on one of his multifunction displays. "Configuring for landing." Control surfaces on the stealth aircraft's wing whirred open, providing more lift as their airspeed diminished. Their landing gear came down and locked in position.

They crossed over the threshold and slid lower. The Ranger was designed for short, rough-field landings, sometimes as short as a thousand feet. By comparison, landing on an asphalt runway that was over a mile long was child's play . . . even in dense fog that cut visibility to just a few yards.

Smoothly, Vasey came in to land, making small adjustments with his throttles and flight controls. They touched down with scarcely a bump. He braked gently, timing it so that the Ranger came to a complete stop not far from a small apron built adjacent to the runway.

Four other planes were visible as blurred shapes in the fog. One was the C-130 Hercules four-engine turboprop that had ferried in the Scion ground crew. The other three were stealthy flying-wing aircraft, each about the size of a small business jet with twin wing-buried turbofan engines. No windows or cockpit canopies broke their smooth lines. Designed for remote-control and autonomous, computer-directed flight, they did not require human pilots or crews.

Two of them were MQ-55 Coyotes, intended as pure weapons carriers. Their internal bays could hold up to ten AIM-120 AMRAAM air-to-air missiles. Built without radars of their own, they were low-cost platforms with one primary combat mission—dumping missiles out into the sky in a hurry for other friendly fighter pilots to control when engaged by superior numbers of enemy aircraft. The third stealth drone, built on the same airframe, was considerably more expensive and more capable. Designated as the EQ-55 Howler, it carried electronic jamming gear and was equipped with the same AN/APG-81 radar used by F-35 Lightning II stealth multi-role fighters.

Built by Sky Masters, the two Coyotes and the Howler had been in service with Poland's Iron Wolf Squadron. At Nadia's urgent request, they had been flown here, almost halfway around the world from their old operating base. The journey had taken close to forty hours. But because they were remotely piloted, the human controllers based in Poland had been able to swap in and out as needed during the marathon flight. All the Coyotes and the Howler had required were short periodic stops to refuel and undergo quick maintenance checks.

Nadia looked them over with a proprietary and predatory eye. Flown under her control using their built-in communications links, those three

Iron Wolf aircraft would give her mission force substantial air-to-air combat power. Reassured, she sat back in her seat. Now it was just a matter of waiting for the rest of the naval and air units committed to her plan to reach their jump-off positions.

CHAPTER 32

BATTLE MOUNTAIN, NEVADA
That same time

Using his neural link, Patrick McLanahan opened a secure channel to Martindale. The head of Scion was flying back to Washington aboard one of his private executive jets. He answered immediately. Thanks to a solid satellite connection, his image was only slightly distorted. "Yes, General?"

"Remember that Russian heavy-lift rocket that exploded in flight?" Patrick asked.

Martindale nodded. "Quite clearly." He frowned. "We've never been able to pin down what its payload could have been. Analysts for the Defense Intelligence have speculated it might have been another weapons module, or perhaps a refueling station and docking structure for Elektron spaceplanes."

Patrick shook his head. "They're wrong. Dead wrong." He looked intently at the older man.

"Because I'm pretty sure I've figured out what that Energia was really carrying. And if I'm right, Moscow must be sweating bullets to get a replacement into orbit ASAP."

"You have my attention, General," Martindale said dryly. "What was aboard that Russian spacecraft?"

"The station's main power generator."

Martindale stared at him. "How is that possible? The energy requirements for that Russian plasma rail gun alone must be—"

"I've run the numbers." Patrick pulled up his calculations and displayed them in an inset box. "Assuming they have reasonable battery and supercapacitor storage aboard Mars One, the Russians could divert electricity from those solar arrays to recharge their weapons. That would be incredibly inefficient . . . but it fits the tactical pattern I've observed."

Martindale listened closely while he explained his reasoning. When Patrick was finished, he asked, "Could there be some other reason the Russians don't fire the rail gun when their station is in Earth's shadow?"

"None," Patrick said decisively. "When the solar panels aren't producing electricity, Mars One has to rely on its backup batteries. And that's the only time when there isn't any surplus power available to recharge the rail gun or the lasers. So the station's crew tops them up in sunlight and then rides out the darkness without engaging any targets."

Slowly, Martindale nodded his understanding. Then he frowned. "If that's true, I don't understand Gryzlov's decision to start this war now. Why not wait until Mars One had a replacement generator online?"

Patrick shrugged. "Something about Brad and Boomer's reconnaissance flight spooked the cosmonauts aboard Mars One into opening fire. And after the balloon went up, Gryzlov must have figured it was better to hit us hard and fast."

"That he's certainly done," Martindale agreed grimly. There were no longer any functioning U.S. military reconnaissance satellites in low Earth orbit. Nor were there any non-Russian civilian imaging satellites left alive: Mars One had systematically destroyed them all. "How long do you think it would take the Russians to construct another generator from scratch?"

"Without knowing more about its type— whether it's truly a working fusion power plant or simply a more conventional fission reactor—I can't even make an educated guess," Patrick admitted. "But I doubt that's what Gryzlov has in mind." He looked Martindale straight in the eyes. "No, sir. My bet is that he'll cannibalize whatever components he can from those already built for a second Mars-class station. If so, a replacement reactor could already be on its way to the launchpad."

"Now *there's* a piece of intelligence we need rather badly, General," the older man told him.

Patrick nodded bleakly. "Unfortunately, without our satellites, we're operating in the dark.

We've got no way to see if Gryzlov's getting ready to launch more spacecraft from Plesetsk or Vostochny."

"Not entirely," Martindale mused. "While technological eyes in orbit are useful, so are human eyes on the ground. Remember, we still have a Scion team inside Russia."

Patrick frowned. "It would take a miracle for any of our people to penetrate the security barriers Gryzlov has wrapped around those launch sites," he argued.

"Indeed it would," Martindale agreed. "Fortunately, I don't believe miracles will be necessary. Our agents shouldn't need to go anywhere near Plesetsk or Vostochny." He smiled. "Even the tightest security net has a weak spot somewhere, General. And in this case, I think we'll find it's around five feet wide . . . and several thousand miles long."

KHABAROVSK REGION, RUSSIA
That evening

Panting, Brad McLanahan struggled to climb the slippery bank of yet another sluggish stream. Every step was agony. His right leg was almost completely useless now. He couldn't put more than a fraction of his weight on it, forcing him to rely almost entirely on his left. "I must look like a damned crab," he muttered. "Always moving at an angle."

Abruptly, a section of the muddy slope slid out

from under him and he toppled over. Desperately, he twisted sideways to avoid coming down on his right shoulder and damaging it further. With one hand immobilized in a sling and the other clinging to his boots, there was no way he could break the fall. Instead, he took the full brunt of the impact on his left side.

Pain flared through Brad's whole body—shooting through every nerve ending in a blaze of fire. He bit down on a scream. For a long moment, he lay dazed, half in and half out of the shallow stream . . . waiting for the pain to fade even a little. Finally, it eased off, not much, but enough so that he could breathe. "Okay, that *really fucking hurt*," he growled, tasting blood where he'd bitten his tongue.

Exhausted, he stayed down for a while longer. Maybe he'd gone far enough for the day, he thought tiredly. Maybe he should just rest here and try to recover some of his strength. *Yeah, that would be a smart move, McLanahan*, his mind sneered. Like falling asleep flat on his ass in a muddy, mosquito-infested quagmire would magically make him feel better . . .

"Fine," Brad groused. "I'm going."

Wearily, he tossed his boots higher up onto dry land, rolled over, and started crawling up the bank—digging the fingers of his left hand deep into the moist soil for leverage. It took several minutes of strenuous effort just to reach firmer ground.

Finally, he made it.

Determined now not to give in to the fatigue

and hunger and pain that threatened to overwhelm him, Brad scrubbed off some of the dried mud coating his feet and then hauled his boots back on. Steeling himself against another flash of agony from his injured shoulder and knee, he dragged himself back to his feet using the low-hanging branches of a small birch tree. He stood hunched over for several more minutes, breathing in shallow gasps.

At last, feeling a little better, Brad hobbled onward, holding on to branches and tree trunks to steady himself. The ground sloped upward through a tangle of trees and underbrush. After what seemed an eternity, he reached the top of the ridge and stopped dead in his tracks. He'd come right to the edge of the woods. Before him stretched a wide, grassy valley. Far off to the east, he could see the faint outline of another dirt road running north and south. In the west, the sun hung low on the horizon, casting long shadows across the open ground.

He stared out across the valley. Somewhere deep inside his drained mind, a tiny spark of hope flickered to life. Awkwardly, he tugged the satellite phone out of his survival pouch and turned it on. After a few seconds, the tiny screen lit up.

Brad stared down at the GPS coordinates it displayed. Slowly, a grin spread across his taut, pain-filled face. "I made it," he whispered, scarcely able to believe it could be true. "I damned well made it."

Gingerly, he slumped to the ground. A few

quick key presses sent a coded text reporting his arrival to the Scion communications center back in the States.

Their reply came back almost immediately. Stripped to its essentials, the message was clear: FIND A CONCEALED POSITION NEARBY. MAKE CONTACT AGAIN AT 2200 HOURS TOMORROW AND STAND BY.

TEKHWERK OFFICES, INTERNATIONAL BUSINESS CENTER, MOSCOW
That night

Scion field agent Samantha Kerr entered a security code on a door down the hall from the office Marcus Cartwright used in his Klaus Wernicke persona, waited for the lock to disengage, and went inside. Thanks to the racks of computer hardware stacked floor to ceiling, the windowless room beyond the door looked much smaller than it was. There was just enough space for a small desk, a chair, and a large wastebasket full to overflowing with crumpled disposable coffee cups and takeout containers.

A young man in a wrinkled, short-sleeved shirt and jeans looked up when she came in. "Hey, Sam."

She nodded toward his keyboard. "How's it going?"

"Good . . . and bad."

Sam waited patiently for him to explain further.

Zach Orlov sometimes found it difficult to communicate with people outside his highly specialized field, especially when he was deeply immersed in a complicated task. But his other skills more than made up for these occasional lapses. From his émigré parents, Orlov had picked up a fluent grasp of the Russian language in all its permutations. Highly intelligent and focused, he'd spent his teenage years hacking every computer network he could gain access to—though not with any serious criminal intent, more out of a perverse blend of insatiable curiosity and sheer boredom with regular school. In fact, if Scion hadn't recruited him, Sam was fairly certain he'd have ended up behind bars . . . or working for the National Security Agency.

"I can get inside the main Russian Railways network, no problem," he said. "Their basic security sucks."

Sam nodded. Russian Railways was a state-owned company set up to control both the infrastructure and the operation of the nation's freight and passenger rail services. "That sounds promising."

Orlov shrugged. "Sure, if we were interested in payroll data. Or corporate e-mails and financial reports." He jerked a thumb at his monitor. "But somebody's installed a whole new security firewall for anything to do with specific freight-train cargo manifests. And it's good. Really good. As in 'touch this and go straight to a Lubyanka basement interrogation cell' good."

"Do not pass Go. Do not collect two hundred

dollars. Do lose your fingernails and collect one bullet in the back of the skull," Sam murmured.

"You got it," he agreed sourly.

"Is that firewall Q Directorate work?" she asked.

"Probably," he agreed. His shoulders slumped slightly. "Anyway, I can't crack it. Not without blowing our whole operation here sky-high. And probably not even then."

Sam frowned. Their orders from Martindale were to look for signs of unusual freight traffic between the launch complexes at Vostochny and Plesetsk and the cities known to house Russian nuclear research institutes and production facilities—among them Moscow, Novosibirsk's Akademgorodok, Dubna, Podolsk, Sarov, Obninsk, and Dmitrovgrad. But how could they do that without access to the detailed records of what any particular train was carrying? Especially since the cargo they were hunting was supposed to be small enough to fit on just one or two freight cars.

Ordinarily, faced with this kind of roadblock, she'd have treated it as a human intelligence problem. Given enough time, it was usually possible to find the weak link in any security system. There was almost always someone on the inside who a resourceful agent could trick, bribe, or threaten into revealing the necessary passwords or codes. Unfortunately, time was exactly what she did not have in this case.

"What's behind this new firewall?" Sam asked curiously. "All freight operations?"

Orlov shook his head. "Just the manifests for anything even remotely considered national-security-related cargo." He looked up at her. "Russian Railways has around a million employees. Clearing everyone who handles any kind of freight for these new security measures would have been a total nightmare."

Sam tapped a finger against her chin, thinking hard. "So you can still pull up the company's signal and traffic logs, right?"

He nodded. "Sure."

Russian Railways prided itself on a centralized control system covering more than 70 percent of the nation's rail lines. Every train moving along those lines generated an automatic, computer-generated report whenever it rolled through a station or a control signal.

"Then take a look at traffic reports from the Northern Railway toward Plesetsk, and the Trans-Siberian Railway toward Vostochny," Sam said. "Over, say, the past week or ten days."

Orlov raised an eyebrow. "You realize those are two of the busiest rail lines in the whole country? Over that kind of time frame, we're talking about several hundred separate freight trains at a minimum. What am I supposed to look for?"

"Filter out everything carrying normal commercial freight," Sam suggested. "And look for a train that's moving through the system faster than normal. From what Mr. Martindale said, the Russians should be in a real hurry to get their replacement reactor to one of those two launch sites."

"Can do." The young man turned back to his computer and began entering commands—instructing his machine to conduct a search of Russian Railways' signal and traffic logs within her suggested parameters. Within moments, crowded lines of text started scrolling across his screen.

Watching Orlov work, Sam stayed quiet. When it came to zeroing in on useful bits of intelligence in an ocean of otherwise irrelevant data, he was a wizard.

Minutes passed. At last, he swung back to her with a frustrated look. "I've got nothing. I mean, yeah, there are trains with some kind of defense-related cargo aboard heading to both Plesetsk and Vostochny from several of the cities with nuclear facilities, but none of them seem to have any kind of special priority."

"Well, that's . . . interesting," Sam said slowly. Were they looking for a special reactor shipment that simply did not exist? Martindale's guesses had seemed reasonable to her, but no one in the intelligence game could count on every stab in the dark striking home.

She had already started considering the wording of what she knew would be a very unwelcome negative report when another possibility struck her. What if the FSB was playing a double game here? There were two ways to hide something important from prying eyes. The first, represented by the added layer of cybersecurity for military-related freight, was to conceal it behind a screen of armed guards and traps. But there was another way, she realized. If you were bold enough, you could also hide a secret in plain sight—like planting a stolen diamond in a crystal chandelier.

Suddenly excited, Sam put a hand on Orlov's shoulder. "Hold on a minute, Zach. Run that search again. Only this time, drop the filter for commercial freight."

"Playing a hunch?"

She nodded.

While he worked his way through the much larger pool of railroad signals and traffic reports turned up by this new search, Sam mentally crossed her fingers. Her nerves felt stretched to the breaking point. Given the tight security Gryzlov had thrown around the whole Mars Project, this was their only possible way in. She and the rest of Cartwright's Scion team had no other way to find out if the Russians really had lost the reactor slated for their Mars One space station . . . and if so, when its replacement might be launched.

"I'll be damned," Orlov said abruptly.

Startled, she leaned closer. "You found something?"

"Yeah," he told her. "A coal train headed east out of Novosibirsk on the Trans-Siberian Railway."

In and of itself, there was nothing mysterious about a coal train, Sam knew. There were several major mines in the Novosibirsk region. "So?"

Orlov grinned up at her. "Ever hear of a coal train that seems to have been awarded the highest possible priority—with all other traffic cleared out of its path? This thing hasn't hit a red light since it left Novosibirsk. I mean, not one. Every signal it comes to is green."

Got you, Sam thought triumphantly. Coal was a nonperishable bulk commodity. There was no reason to grant a genuine freight train loaded with coal any special traffic authorization. "Where is this train now?" she demanded.

"It just cleared the station at Ulan-Ude, south of Lake Baikal," Orlov said. "And based on its average speed since departing Novosibirsk, I figure it'll reach the Vostochny launch complex within the next forty-eight hours."

CHAPTER 33

ATTU ISLAND, THE ALEUTIANS
Late the next day

The sleek, jet-black, batwinged XCV-62 Ranger swung back onto the runway and rolled slowly toward its takeoff position. Three smaller stealth aircraft—the two MQ-55 Coyotes and the EQ-55 Howler—taxied off the apron and turned into line behind it. Spooked by the shrill noise of ten turbofan engines spooling up, flocks of birds swirled up from the tundra and nearby shore and vanished in seconds, swallowed up in the low-lying dense fog that still blanketed the island.

Peter Vasey glanced across the cockpit at Nadia Rozek. "We're ready for takeoff, on your order."

She nodded and opened a communications window on her left-hand multifunction display. Quickly, she typed in a short message: WOLF SIX-TWO TO ALL EXTRACTION FORCE UNITS. ATTU GROUP IS DEPARTING

NOW. The Ranger's computer automatically encrypted, compressed, and then transmitted her signal via satellite uplink. It would be routed to the White House, Battle Mountain, and the USS *Ronald Reagan* carrier strike group, currently one hundred and sixty nautical miles southeast of Hokkaido, Japan. From now on, radio voice transmissions, even if encrypted, would be held to a minimum to further reduce the odds of detection.

Nadia felt keyed up and fully alert. This was the moment toward which all their planning over the past several days had been directed. Their call-sign change, back to Wolf Six-Two, was another symbol of imminent action. It was the same call sign she and Brad McLanahan had used for this same aircraft on other risky missions. Using it again was a pledge of her fidelity and determination to bring him safely out of Russia. "*Z nim, albo wcale,*" she murmured under her breath. "With him, or not at all."

Leaving nothing to chance, she checked the flight status and navigation programs of the three Iron Wolf drones lined up on the runway behind them one last time. Rows of green indicators lit up across another of her displays. They were set.

"We are good to go," Nadia told Vasey.

In answer, his hand advanced the throttles. With a steadily rising roar, the Ranger's four jet engines ran up to full military power. Slowly at first and then with ever-increasing speed, the

XCV-62 thundered down the runway. The airspeed indicator on his HUD flashed and he pulled back on the stick. "Vr . . . rotating," he said calmly.

The Ranger soared off the ground and climbed into the fog. Its landing gear retracted and locked inside with a few muffled thumps.

Vasey tweaked his stick to the left, banking slightly to the southwest. The navigation cues on the HUD stabilized. They were on course. Satisfied, he throttled back a little and squeezed a paddle switch on the stick. "DTF engaged, set for two hundred feet, hard ride."

With the terrain-following system in control, their aircraft descended again. It leveled off only two hundred feet above the fogbound sea. From now on, occasional activations of its radar altimeter would measure the distance between its belly and the waves below, confirming the information in the digital database.

From her position in the right-hand seat, Nadia focused on the three waiting Iron Wolf drones. In sequence, she activated their autonomous programs. One by one, they sped down the runway, lifted off, and turned southwest to join up with the Ranger. One of the Coyotes took station off the XCV-62's starboard wing. The second slid into place off their port wing. The EQ-55 Howler, with its radars and jammers still inactive, brought up the rear.

Staying low, the whole formation flew on out over the Bering Sea at four hundred and fifty knots.

CVN-76 USS *RONALD REAGAN*, SOUTHEAST OF HOKKAIDO, JAPAN
Ninety minutes later

Surrounded by six Arleigh Burke–class guided missile destroyers and two Ticonderoga-class cruisers, the huge Nimitz-class aircraft carrier *Ronald Reagan* turned smoothly into the wind. Under a cloudless sky, it was almost pitch-black. The waning quarter moon would not rise for another half hour or so. Despite the darkness, none of the nine American warships were lit up. They were operating under strict wartime conditions.

Suddenly several tiny points of light appeared, then immediately shot down along the carrier's deck and screamed into the sky. It was an F/A-18E Super Hornet launched by one of the *Reagan*'s steam catapults. Seconds later, another Super Hornet streaked aloft, visible only by its position lights. Launch after launch followed at regular intervals, using three of the carrier's four catapults. As soon as each aircraft cleared the deck and configured for cruise, its regular position lights went out, replaced by night-vision-friendly position lights.

Within fifteen minutes, twenty-four Super Hornets and two EA-18G Growler electronic warfare aircraft were airborne. Those launched earlier in the cycle orbited some miles ahead of the carrier group, waiting for the rest to form up. With that accomplished, all twenty-six planes of the navy strike force turned and flew northwest toward Hokkaido.

POLICE STATION, IMENI POLINY OSIPENKO, KHABAROVSK REGION, RUSSIA
That same time

Imeni Poliny Osipenko was a rural village on the left bank of the Amgun River, about eighteen kilometers north of the boundary of the Oldjikan State Nature Reserve. On either side of a two-lane paved highway, red- and blue-roofed houses, barns, and sheds lined dirt roads. Behind each little cluster of buildings lay fields sown in barley and wheat.

Tired after a ten-hour drive from Komsomolsk-on-Amur's Dzemgi Air Base, Russian Air Force Lieutenant Nikolay Khryukin parked his mud-spattered UAZ Hunter jeep and climbed out from behind the steering wheel. He looked around in bored disdain. Until now, the isolated hamlet's only connection to the Russian Air Force was the fact that in 1939 it had been renamed after Major Polina Osipenko, holder of a women's flight record and a Hero of the Soviet Union. *What an honor,* he thought cynically. It was probably just as well Osipenko had been killed in a plane crash before the politicians made her pay a visit to this one-tractor dump.

Although the sun had only gone down a couple of hours before, most of the locals already seemed to be in bed, with all their lights off. *Peasant farmers need to be up early to care for their crops, I suppose,* Khryukin decided. He stretched his sore back and neck muscles and wished with all his heart that the local yokels had stuck closer to their dull labors—instead of scaring themselves half to death with nonsense and then screaming for help from the military authorities.

Khryukin scowled. Apparently, a couple of days ago, some students and their teacher had stumbled back into town from a nature hike in the Oldjikan reserve with some lunatic story about finding evidence of a secret space alien landing. Their shrill request for an official investigation had been bucked up the chain to land on his commanding officer's desk this morning. So naturally, Colonel Federov had picked his least favorite subordinate for this wild-goose chase . . . one Nikolay Khryukin. He was the 23rd Fighter Aviation Regiment's meteorology officer, not an Su-35S combat pilot, and Federov harbored an instinctive dislike for those he considered "pencil pushers in uniform."

"Go up there and settle their nerves, Lieutenant," the colonel had ordered offhandedly. "These so-called UFO objects are probably just the remains of a weather balloon, so you're the expert. Besides, it won't hurt the air force to build a little goodwill with the locals . . . and it won't hurt you to get out and see more of this beautiful Motherland of ours."

Well, from what Khryukin had seen on his long, tedious drive to Imeni Poliny Osipenko along crappy roads, this part of the beautiful Motherland was trees, a lot more trees, swamp, and even more damned trees. With an audible sigh, he settled his high-peaked officer's cap more firmly on his head and strode toward the police station.

The sergeant on duty, a thickset man whose uniform was about a size too small for him, was only too happy to see him. "I know you think we're probably crazy," he confided eagerly as he led Khryukin down a narrow hall to a locked storage room. "I thought so, too, until I clapped my own eyes on what those kids found out in the middle of the forest." He fumbled for his keys, opened the door, flipped on the overhead light, and then stepped aside. "But check it out for yourself, Lieutenant."

For a long moment, Khryukin just stood and stared at the strange artifacts the students had dug up. The most easily recognizable was the bundled remains of a large red-and-white parachute. *No mystery there*, he thought slowly. But what should he make of the other odd items, which included a man-sized suit of some peculiar shiny metal fabric and a helmet with a clear visor? Or that even weirder conical two-meter-wide shell covered in scorched and seared cloth on one side and some elastic substance on the other?

And then the understanding of what he saw hit him with full force. He whirled on the police sergeant. "I need a phone connection to Dzemgi Air Base! Right now!"

"See?" the policeman said, sounding pleased. "I told you it was aliens."

"It's not aliens, you idiot!" Khryukin snarled at him. "Those things belong to an American astronaut!"

WOLF SIX-TWO, OVER THE NORTH PACIFIC
A short time later

Nadia Rozek glanced out the right side of the Ranger's cockpit. The quarter moon hung there, just above the horizon. Its pale silvery light danced across the undulating surface of the ocean. She frowned. The moonlight was beautiful. But it was also dangerous, since that faint glow made it a bit easier for the enemy to spot her small group of jet-black aircraft as they darted in low over the water. It would have been marginally safer to make this flight into Russian territory on a moonless night. Unfortunately, the next such period was still several days away . . . and Brad was running out of time.

A warning tone sounded in her headset. *"Monolit-B surface search radar detected at one o'clock,"* her computer reported. *"Estimated range is one hundred miles and closing."*

She punched up a menu on her threat-warning display and read through it quickly. "Nothing for us to worry about," she assured Vasey. "This radar is assigned to the Russian K-300P Bastion coastal antiship missile battery on Matua."

Vasey nodded his understanding. The lethal, long-range supersonic ship-killing missiles of the Bastion battery they'd detected were intended for use against the U.S. Navy's aircraft carriers and surface warships. They could not engage aircraft.

Still, picking up that active Russian radar was a sign that they were standing into danger. Twenty minutes ago, already seven hundred nautical miles from Attu, they had altered their heading by ninety degrees. Now they were flying northwest, on a course that would cross the volcanic Kuril island chain right at the midpoint between northern Japan and Russia's Kamchatka Peninsula.

For the past several years, Gryzlov had been strengthening his garrisons scattered among the Kuril chain's fifty-six mountainous islands—installing antiship batteries and antiaircraft missiles and radars at various places. His strategic goal was to seal off the Sea of Okhotsk and most of the far east region's coast against intrusion by America's naval forces. Fortunately, there were still a few weak spots in this island fortress barrier, at least for a small handful of stealth aircraft. The most powerful air search radars and long-range SAM units were based on the northernmost and southernmost islands, where they could protect Russia's twin Pacific Fleet bases at Petropavlovsk-Kamchatsky and Vladivostok respectively. With a bit of luck and some help, the XCV-62 and its little flock of accompanying drones should be able to slide through where the enemy's radar coverage was weakest, trusting to their stealth characteristics and nap-of-the-earth flight to avoid detection.

An icon flashed on Nadia's left-hand multifunction display. She tapped it. A message opened up on the screen: REAGAN AIR GROUP AT POINT DELTA. "Our American friends are ready to make their move," she reported.

Vasey smiled in satisfaction. "Well, God bless the U.S. Navy," he said. He glanced at her. "Now to see if Gryzlov and his lads react the way you've hoped."

"They will," she said confidently. "Who pays attention to the little flea when confronted by a snarling mastiff?"

CHAPTER 34

That same time

Colonel Vladimir Titov pondered the intelligence report just flashed from Moscow. A short time ago, one of Russia's Kondor radar reconnaissance satellites orbiting high over the Pacific Ocean had spotted the U.S. Navy's *Ronald Reagan* carrier strike group executing a sudden course change toward the south. Until then, the American ships had been steaming generally north at high speed. Why the abrupt U-turn?

Struck by an unnerving possibility, he swung around to face one of the junior officers crowded with him into the mobile command center vehicle, a heavy-duty 8×8 Ural off-road truck. "Yvgeny! What is the current wind direction southeast of Hokkaido?"

"A moment, sir!" The young lieutenant's fingers darted across his keyboard. His fresh, unlined face wrinkled in concentration.

Titov nodded in approval. Many of his peers despised younger officers for their fixation on computers and the Internet. In his view, they were foolish. The wiser course was to use this obsession for the benefit of the forces under their command.

The lieutenant looked away from his screen. "Weather reports from Kushiro indicate the wind is from the south, sir."

Titov's unnerving "possibility" crystallized into a certainty. That big American aircraft carrier had suddenly turned *into* the direction of the wind—which meant it had launched aircraft. He looked at another of his subordinates. "Alert all missile battalions, Major. The Americans may be coming our way—"

"Sir! Early warning radar on Iturup, in the Kuril Islands, reports a large formation of high-speed aircraft bearing two-five-zero, relative," his communications officer reported. "Direction of flight is three-zero-zero, absolute. Range four hundred kilometers. Speed eleven hundred kilometers per hour. Altitude unknown."

"Plot that contact!" Titov demanded.

Titov leaned over the man's shoulder and saw a set of blinking red icons flash onto the map almost dead center in the Japanese island of Hokkaido. *Thank God for our new radar station in the southern Kurils,* he thought. Any part of Hokkaido was far outside the effective range of his regiment's own air surveillance radars. Based on their speed and observed direction of flight, this was almost certainly a formation of F/A-18E Super Hornet strike aircraft . . . and they were currently headed straight toward the city of Khabarovsk . . .

Or more likely, his own surface-to-air missile battalions, he realized coldly, if Colonel General Leonov's suspicion that the Americans were plotting an attack against the Vostochny Cosmodrome was correct. To have any hope of flying a bomber group far enough into Russia's far east region to hit the launch complex, they would have to cripple its outlying surface-to-air missile defenses. He blessed the recent decision to reequip his regiment with the newer, longer-range, and more capable S-400 *Triumf* system, in place of its old, shorter-range S-300PS units.

"Sound air-raid alert," Titov ordered, forcing himself to sound calm and completely in control. If those F/A-18s were carrying standoff land attack missiles, such as the AGM-158B joint air-to-surface standoff missile, they would be in range to launch within twenty-five minutes. And any missiles they fired would strike home less than twenty minutes later. True, his new S-400 SAMs could theoretically reach out and destroy enemy aircraft, or even their air-launched weapons, much farther out. But that was only true for targets they could "see" on radar. Long before those American strike aircraft came within his reach, they were sure to drop back down to very low altitude . . . which would drastically decrease the distance at which the regiment's search and fire-control radar systems could pick them up.

No, he decided, this battle would almost certainly be fought at much closer ranges than the theoretical maximums for either side's weapons. As it was, he was extremely fortunate that the enemy aircraft carrier had launched its attack planes so soon. By the time those Super Hornets were close enough to fire their standoff missiles, they should be very near the outside edge of their own effective combat range. They would be short on fuel, significantly reducing their ability to maneuver defensively against his S-400s, which ought to greatly increase his odds of scoring kills.

Now that his subordinates were in action, Titov realized he had one further duty. He grabbed a secure phone and punched in the code for the National Defense Control Center in Moscow. "This is Colonel Titov with the 1529th Guards Air Defense Missile Regiment. I need to speak to Colonel General Leonov or his senior deputy immediately!"

F/A-18E DIAMONDBACK ONE-FIVE, *REAGAN* AIR GROUP, OVER HOKKAIDO
That same time

Seen from ten thousand feet, Hokkaido was ablaze with light. A huge warm yellow glow marked the major city of Sapporo. Smaller radiances signaled the locations of other cities and towns scattered across the island. Thinner lines of light traced out a dense network of highways, roads, and rail lines.

Commander Dane "Viking" Thorsen listened to the steady warble in his headset and checked his Super Hornet's threat display one more time. It identified the enemy radar as a Nebo-M VHF-band air search system. Its signal strength and azimuth marked it as the Russian set deployed on Iturup, one of the Kuril Islands stretching northeast off Hokkaido's coast. He smiled beneath his oxygen mask and keyed his mike. "D-Back One-Five to all D-Back, Talon, and Outlaw aircraft. We've baited the hook. Execute strike plan Delta."

Crisp acknowledgments returned.

Thorsen dropped the nose of his F/A-18E. The navy strike fighter slid lower, losing altitude as it accelerated to more than six hundred and seventy knots. The other twenty-five aircraft in *Reagan*'s attack force followed him down.

The warning tone in his headset cut off abruptly as they descended into the radar shadow cast by Hokkaido's mountains and volcanoes. The Russian radar station on Iturup had lost contact.

Four minutes later, flying at altitudes of less than five hundred feet, the swarm of navy planes streaked across the coast and out over the Sea of Japan. "Feet wet," Thorsen reported laconically.

They flew on for a while longer, closing fast on a predetermined point one hundred and sixty nautical miles from Russian territory. The masthead lights of fishing boats bobbed across the surface of the sea in front of them and then vanished astern.

Thorsen kept his eyes moving between his

fighter's nav display and its threat-warning system. Winning tonight's little game with the Russians would demand both absolute precision . . . and deception. He listened intently for the chirping sound that would indicate he was being painted by enemy radar. There was only silence. "Confirm naked," he radioed.

Affirmative replies flowed through his headset. No one else in the strike force showed any hostile radar warning receiver indications either. For the moment, they were effectively invisible. Seconds later, his F/A-18E reached the preset point. "Action Delta," Thorsen ordered.

He pulled back on the stick slightly, climbed a couple of hundred feet, and then toggled the weapons release. One after another, two small ADM-160B miniature air-launched decoys, or MALDs, fell away from under his Super Hornet's wings.

Immediately Thorsen broke hard left, clearing the way for the pilots in his wake to launch their own decoys. His wingman turned with him. Thirteen of the fighters in the two Super Hornet squadrons were carrying MALDs. The other eleven were armed for air-to-air combat—ready to engage only if the strike force was jumped by Russian aircraft, or if the enemy launched a retaliatory attack against the *Reagan* and its escorts.

In pairs, the rest of the F/A-18Es reached the launch point, fired their MALDs, and rolled back toward Hokkaido. They were accompanied by the pair of EA-18G Growler electronic warfare aircraft assigned to this mission.

Behind the departing navy strike force, a flock of twenty-six tiny decoys arrowed onward toward the Russian coastline. Ultralight turbojet engines propelled them at close to six hundred knots. Programs were running in their onboard computers, counting down the minutes to activation. Once that happened, the decoys would begin mimicking the radar signatures and flight profiles of the Super Hornets and Growlers. Two of them were more advanced ADM-160C MALD-Js, equipped to act both as decoys and as radar jammers.

NATIONAL DEFENSE CONTROL CENTER, MOSCOW

A short time later

Colonel General Leonov sat down at his workstation and snapped, "Brief me, Semyon!"

His deputy, Lieutenant General Semyon Tikhomirov, obeyed, offering a quick rundown of the most recent developments. "Our air defense missile regiments at Knyaze, Komsomolsk, Vladivostok, and Nakhodka are on full alert. So are all army and Pacific Fleet units in Kamchatka and on the Kurils."

"What about our fighter and bomber regiments?" Leonov asked.

"The alert Su-35S fighters from both the 23rd Fighter Aviation Regiment at Dzemgi near Komsomolsk and the 22nd Regiment at Tsentralnaya Uglovaya near Vladivostok have already scrambled. They are currently orbiting over both air bases, awaiting further orders. Both regiments are fueling and arming their remaining aircraft with all possible speed. The Su-24s and Su-34s of the 277th Bomber Aviation Regiment and the Su-25s of the 18th Guards Attack Aviation Regiment have also been alerted, but it will take considerably more time to ready their planes for operations."

"And the Americans? Where are they now?"

Tikhomirov brought up a map. A solid red line indicated the flight path followed by the carrier-based aircraft while they were being tracked on radar. It faded out over Hokkaido, replaced by a dotted red line extending out across the Sea of Japan . . . aimed straight at Khabarovsk and onward toward the Vostochny Cosmodrome much farther inland. A small blip just off the Russian coast pulsed slowly, moving steadily northwest with every separate pulse. "This is the air staff's projection of that enemy formation's most likely current position, based on its last known course and speed."

Leonov nodded. This estimate could be wrong, particularly if the enemy strike force had radically altered its heading after dropping off radar. But that was doubtful. If the Americans were serious about hitting Vostochny, they first had to knock out the S-400 SAMs sited just east of Khabarovsk. Given the distances involved and the need to fly in heavily loaded with air-to-ground ordnance, those U.S. Navy F/A-18s couldn't dick around. They wouldn't have the fuel to carry out elaborate maneuvers designed to spread Russia's defenses. No, he thought coldly, it was straight up the middle or nothing for those American pilots—trusting in their Super Hornets' defensive systems and jamming support from electronic warfare planes to break through and destroy his S-400 launchers and radars.

That wasn't a particularly good bet.

Then Leonov frowned. But it wasn't impossible either, especially if the Americans used some of the high-tech drones and radar-spoofing technology pioneered by the mercenary Iron Wolf Squadron in recent conflicts with Russia. If so, it would be wise to move a backup force into position. He looked at Tikhomirov. "Tell Colonel Federov at Dzemgi that I want every available fighter from his regiment in the air as soon as possible. Send them west of Khabarovsk, ready to intercept any enemy strike aircraft that slip through."

23RD FIGHTER AVIATION REGIMENT FLIGHT LINE, DZEMGI AIR BASE, KOMSOMOLSK-ON-AMUR, RUSSIA

Minutes later

Impatiently, Colonel Ivan Federov tugged on his flight helmet and hurried toward his waiting Su-35S fighter. From all across the airfield, the earsplitting howl of Saturn AL-41F1S turbofan engines spooling up shattered the night. A handful of his regiment's aircraft were already taxiing out of their revetments and hardened shelters. He scowled. Between planes that were down for routine maintenance and the inevitable delays involved in rousting sleeping pilots and ground crews out of their quarters, the 23rd would be fortunate to get half its strength into the air before this American raid had come and gone.

It was not the sort of result that would endear him to his superiors, especially Colonel General Leonov. The commander of Russia's aerospace forces was not a man who accepted excuses, even when they were reasonable.

Swearing under his breath, Federov started up the ladder to the Su-35's cockpit. With a bit of luck, he might get a chance to tangle with the enemy's F/A-18s Coming back to Dzemgi with a couple of kills should absolve a host of other perceived sins.

"Colonel!" a voice yelled up at him, pitched to carry over the shrill din of jet engines coming to life.

He turned around on the ladder, furious at the interruption. "What?"

It was Uvarov, his executive officer. He looked out of breath. "Lieutenant Khryukin just phoned in from that little town up north. He says—"

Federov's temper exploded. "Fuck that little shit!" he snarled. "For God's sake, Uvarov, we're in a combat situation here! I don't have time to deal with that moron right now. *You* handle whatever mess Khryukin has made." Then, dismissing the interruption from his mind, he swung himself into the Su-35's cockpit and started strapping in.

WOLF SIX-TWO, OVER THE SEA OF OKHOTSK
A short time later

"Multiple faint S-band, X-band, and VHF radar emissions detected from ten o'clock to eight o'clock. Some are ground-based. Others are airborne. Ranges indeterminate. Detection probabilities are all nil," the XCV-62's computer announced calmly.

Nadia Rozek studied her threat-warning display closely and then turned to Peter Vasey with a triumphant smile. "Something seems to have rattled the Russians, Constable. They appear to be activating every available radar set between Vladivostok and Komsomolsk."

"Do tell," the Englishman said dryly. He kept his eyes fixed firmly on his HUD and his hands poised carefully on the stick and throttles. Even with the help of the Ranger's digital terrain-following system, a night flight at low altitude over the sea was a dangerous business. A split-second loss of focus at the wrong moment could send them plowing nose first into the ocean.

His steering cues slid left and he gently banked the XCV-62 to the west. Off the port and starboard sides of their aircraft, the two MQ-55 Coyote drones followed suit. The EQ-55 Howler trailing them made the same wide, curving turn a few seconds later. Somewhere out ahead, still invisible even in the faint light cast by the still-rising quarter moon, loomed the mass of Sakhalin Island—stretching five hundred nautical miles from north to south, but only seventy-five miles from east to west. Beyond Sakhalin lay the Russian mainland. "Position check?" he asked.

Nadia tapped on a screen, opening a navigation display. "We are approximately fifty minutes out from the LZ."

Vasey nodded tightly. "Right. Next stop Oldjikan Circus. All change to the Nevada line." Then, aware that she was staring at him, he grinned wryly. "Never mind me, Major. Just a throwback to a misspent youth riding the Tube in London while skiving off school."

Before she could comment, her left-hand multifunction display pinged, signaling the arrival of an encrypted satellite transmission. Her fingers rattled across the virtual keyboard. "SBIRS satellites report multiple launches from the vicinity of Khabarovsk," she read off. "Launches evaluated as S-400 surface-to-air missiles."

"Well, that opens the ball," Vasey said quietly.

CHAPTER 35

1529TH GUARDS AIR DEFENSE MISSILE REGIMENT, KNYAZE-VOLKONSKOYE, RUSSIA
That same time

"Contact lost," a radar operator reported in frustration over the command circuit. "Heavy jamming and possible terrain masking."

"First salvos going ballistic," another officer said. "Our missiles' active homing seeker heads were never able to lock on independently."

Colonel Vladimir Titov fought down the urge to swear out loud. It would do no good and it might further unnerve his subordinates. He'd known the odds were against scoring hits with such long-range shots, especially since the enemy attack force was coming at them across a wide band of rugged coastal hills and ridges. Staying low allowed the American strike aircraft to use this terrain to hide their approach. "Estimated range to the enemy formation at last solid contact?"

"Two hundred kilometers," the radar operator said.

"Have you detected any new, smaller contacts?" Titov demanded.

"No, sir."

He frowned. The twenty-plus F/A-18s headed his way were already near enough to fire any standoff air-to-ground missiles they were carrying. So why hadn't they done so? Were they so confident they could evade his SAMs that they had decided to keep coming . . . hoping to overwhelm his defenses with a massed missile salvo at close range?

"Contact regained!" he heard the radar operator say suddenly. "Formation of high-speed aircraft bearing one-three-five. Direction of flight now three-one five degrees."

Those American strike fighters are barreling right down our throats, Titov thought grimly. What had happened to their fuel constraints? Were they treating this as a one-way mission, like the Japanese kamikaze pilots of the Second World War?

"Range one hundred and seventy kilometers. Speed eleven hundred kilometers per hour. Altitude one hundred and fifty meters!"

"Handoff to 92N2E missile-guidance radars complete!" one of Titov's fire-control officers reported eagerly. "Twenty-six hostiles confirmed. Signatures correlated to F/A-18s. Solid lock on multiple targets. Ready to attack!"

"Release all batteries," Titov ordered. "Commence firing." Unable to resist seeing what was going on with his own eyes, he hurried over to the door of the mobile command center and peered out into the night.

Missile after missile thundered aloft from launchers deployed in the surrounding fields—slashing upward through the darkness on pillars of fire as they accelerated toward Mach 6. Within seconds, they arced high over and vanished downrange.

"New jamming!" the radar operator said suddenly. "Our radars are hopping frequencies to compensate. But we've lost the lock to some targets."

Titov yanked his head back inside, angry with himself for playing tourist in the middle of a battle. "Do you have an evaluation of the source of this jamming?"

"My computer evaluates it as originating from two, or possibly three, American EA-18G Growler electronic warfare aircraft."

The colonel nodded. That was in line with what they'd observed so far. The *Reagan* must have committed half her strike fighters to this attack, so it was no real surprise to see so many airborne jammers assigned in support.

"We've scored hits!" a fire-control officer crowed suddenly. "I count three kills from the salvo."

Titov refrained from pointing out that it left almost 90 percent of the attackers alive and closing fast. From the worried looks he could see on some of the faces around him in the command center, others were perfectly capable of drawing the same conclusions. Unless they got lucky and took out the American electronic warfare planes in the next couple of salvos, this engagement was going to get ugly fast.

"Damn," his radar operator muttered. "Contact lost again, sir. The enemy formation has dropped into a river valley. Our radars cannot see them."

Titov stared at the plot. If the Americans hugged that valley floor as far as they could, they would be less than one hundred and twenty kilometers away when his sensors regained contact . . . practically spitting distance for modern ground-attack weapons. His shoulders tightened involuntarily, almost as though he could already feel the searing heat of explosions and the hail of shrapnel. With an effort to stay calm, he turned to his communications officer. "What is the status of those Su-35 Super Flankers from Dzemgi?"

"Colonel Federov has twelve fighters en route to the air control point selected by Moscow," the younger man said. "They should arrive west of our position in the next ten minutes."

"Make sure they are tied into our target-tracking data uplink," Titov ordered. Crazy as it seemed, maybe this American strike force planned to blow right past his SAM regiment—driving onward to launch extended-range AGM-158B joint air-to-surface standoff missiles directly at Vostochny's launchpads, rocket assembly buildings, and cryogenic fuels storage tanks. If so, Federov's fighters would come into play. And the ability to use tracking and targeting data supplied by ground radars, rather than their own easily detected onboard radars, could give them a crucial edge . . . the ability to ambush those oncoming F/A-18s with air-to-air missiles fired from out of a clear night sky.

NATIONAL DEFENSE CONTROL CENTER, MOSCOW
A short time later

Leonov sat enthralled at his station, listening to the increasingly tense chatter between Titov's command post and his unit's outlying radar vehicles and missile launchers. Tracking and engagement data relayed from the S-400 SAM regiment were displayed in graphical form on screens around the room. They showed the American formation—now whittled down to just twelve aircraft—as it pressed steadily onward. The eleven F/A-18E Super Hornets and a single surviving Growler jammer plane were only eighty kilometers from Knyaze-Volkonskoye . . . well out over the broad, flat Amur River valley. There was no higher ground they could hide behind to break radar contact.

He shook his head in amazement. Those U.S. Navy pilots were brave men and women. But they were also being incredibly stupid. This was no longer a battle they could win.

"Next salvo, fire!" he heard Titov order.

Two dozen missile icons streaked across the

display. Moving at Mach 6, they closed the distance to the American planes in less than forty seconds. Aircraft winked off the screen as warheads found their targets and detonated. Leonov considered that an oddly antiseptic rendering for what was a supremely violent act. Out there, thousands of kilometers away in the real world, pilots were dying horribly—ripped apart by a lethal hail of fragments or burning to death in crippled aircraft spiraling down out of the sky.

"We hit the enemy EW aircraft!" one of Titov's fire-control officers announced gleefully.

With the destruction of their jammer aircraft, the radar images of the surviving seven American strike fighters sharpened considerably. Now they had no protection whatsoever against the next S-400 salvo.

It was all over in less than a minute.

Leonov pursed his lips as he listened to the whoops and cheers as Titov's relieved officers and missile battery crews celebrated their one-sided victory. *Something is wrong here*, he thought critically. This attack had been defeated too easily. Much too easily. They were all missing something.

He connected directly to Titov. "Were any of your sensor posts or missile launchers fired on by any of those American aircraft, Vladimir?"

The other man sounded equally puzzled. "No, sir. Not by so much as a single standoff attack missile or bomb."

An ugly realization dawned in Leonov's mind.

"Those were decoy drones, Colonel. There were no real U.S. Navy aircraft among them. This was a trick."

"But to what purpose?" Titov asked.

"How many of your surface-to-air missiles did you expend against this diversion?" Leonov asked in return.

There was a moment of stunned silence. "More than half," Titov admitted.

Leonov saw his deputy, Lieutenant General Tikhomirov, signaling frantically at him. He lowered the phone. "What is it, Semyon?"

Tikhomirov pointed toward one of their screens, which suddenly showed a new set of threat icons over Hokkaido. "The early warning radar on Iturup has just detected another large formation of enemy aircraft headed toward Knyaze-Volkonskoye."

Leonov's mouth tightened to a thin line. "Hell." He spoke into the phone again. "Get your men back in control and have your regiment stand to again, Titov. The Americans were drawing your fire earlier. Now they're sending in their real attack force."

REAGAN AIR GROUP, OVER HOKKAIDO
That same time

For the second time that night, Commander Dane "Viking" Thorsen listened to the continuous warble that showed the Russian radar on Iturup had spotted his strike force as it climbed higher, above the shelter of Hokkaido's mountains. *Now you see us*, he thought cheerfully, *but pretty soon you won't.*

He spoke into his radio. "This is D-Back One-Five. Nice wriggling, guys. We've definitely got their attention. Execute plan Echo as fragged."

Again, Thorsen took his F/A-18E Super Hornet back down, losing altitude fast to drop back into the radar shadow. The other strike fighters and electronic warfare aircraft under his command followed him.

But this time, as soon as the warning tone from that distant surveillance radar faded away, he banked southeast—turning toward a narrow pass that ran through the range of jagged volcanic peaks bisecting Hokkaido. His aircraft were headed back toward the *Reagan*. Only from now on, they would stay low all the way to avoid detection.

Thorsen grinned happily. Eventually, around thirty minutes from now, those Russian assholes were going to start figuring out that they'd been suckered . . . for the second time in the same night. While he wasn't sure exactly why he and the other *Reagan* pilots were putting on this show—that was information restricted to the CAG, the carrier air wing commander and his ultimate boss, the rear admiral in overall command of the carrier strike group—any chance to twist the bear's tail was always welcome.

WOLF SIX-TWO, OVER RUSSIA
A short time later

"We are ninety seconds out from the LZ," Nadia Rozek said. She knew that her voice sounded tight and strained, and she regretted this lapse in cool, calm professionalism. But there was no help for it. They were approaching the make-or-break moment in this attempt to rescue Brad McLanahan. If the wide stretch of clear ground they'd picked out from satellite photos and maps as a landing zone turned out to be unusable—either because it was too rough or too boggy—there was no second option.

Peter Vasey peered through his HUD. The XCV-62's forward-looking night-vision camera systems turned the darkness around them into a green-tinged version of daylight. Right now their planned landing area was a patch of brighter green against the darker green of the surrounding woods and low-lying marshes. "I have the LZ in sight," he confirmed.

Nadia tapped one of her MFDs, scanning the area through one of the Ranger's passive sensors. Her heart leaped when she saw the single human-sized thermal image crouched in good cover near the edge of the woods. "I see Brad!" she exclaimed. "He is alone. There are no other unidentified contacts around the LZ."

Quickly, she toggled a single pulse from their air-to-ground radar. A tone sounded in her headset as the Ranger's radar swept the valley ahead of them. The information it collected appeared as an image on her display. "No hidden obstructions," she reported. "And the ground looks firm."

"Right, then," Vasey said decisively. "We are go for landing." He entered a new command into his computer and throttled back. "We'd best let our passengers know."

Nadia tapped a key. "We are coming in to the LZ, Major Schofield. Stand by."

"Standing by," the Canadian's voice replied from the aft troop compartment. "My lads and I are ready to move out the moment you drop the ramp."

Beside her, Vasey scrolled a cursor across his HUD, selecting his planned touchdown point. Another quick series of movements lowered their landing gear and disengaged the Ranger's terrain-following system. He chopped the throttles back even farther. Control surfaces opened, providing more lift.

As its airspeed decreased, the XCV-62 descended toward the broad clearing ahead. The three Iron Wolf drones that had flown with them from Attu Island climbed slightly and banked away. Following the orders programmed in earlier by Nadia through their communications links, the two Coyotes and the Howler would circle low overhead while they were on the ground.

Alerted by the roar of several turbofan engines, Brad McLanahan looked up through overhanging branches in time to spot a distinctive batwinged aircraft slide across the sky, briefly silhouetted against the pale moon. For a moment, overcome with sheer relief, he blinked back sudden tears. *You are not going to start bawling like a baby, McLanahan*, he told himself fiercely. Not in front of Nadia. Or anyone else for that matter.

With his jaw clenched against an expected surge of discomfort from his injured right shoulder and leg, he forced himself back to his feet. And then the pain hit, more like a solid wall of white-hot flame than a passing wave. For a long moment, his whole world narrowed down to a single sensation.

"Jesus," Brad hissed through gritted teeth. He breathed out deeply in an effort to expel the sudden agony that otherwise threatened to overwhelm him. Slowly, the excruciating pain from his shoulder and leg eased up, becoming merely the usual sharp, throbbing aches that never really left him, even when he dozed.

At last, he lifted his head and saw the XCV-62 Ranger touch down on the clear ground beyond the woods. The aircraft bounced once and then slowed fast as its pilot reversed thrust. Trailing a cloud of torn grass and dust, it slowed to a stop no more than a couple of hundred yards from his position.

Without waiting any longer, Brad hobbled down the gentle slope and out into the open.

The Ranger's rear ramp whined down. Before it even settled into the tall grass, four men rushed out of the troop compartment and leaped to the ground. One went prone, sighting through the nightscope attached to a magazine-fed Remington sniper rifle. The other three Scion commandos sprinted toward him. They wore night-vision goggles, body armor, and carried HK416 carbines.

In the dim moonlight, Brad recognized the leader as soon as he came within a few yards. "Geez, Ian, you're a sight for sore eyes."

Ian Schofield pushed his night-vision goggles up his forehead and gave him a fast once-over. He shook his head with a quick, fleeting grin. "Whereas I'd have to call you more a sore sight to my eyes, Brad. No disrespect, but you look like hell."

"Yeah, well," Brad said, making an effort to match the other man's wry smile, "I kinda took a bad spill getting out of my spacecraft. The first few hundred miles went fine. But the last hundred thousand feet down were a little rough."

Schofield nodded sympathetically. He turned his head to his subordinates. "In the circumstances, gentlemen, I think we should offer Captain McLanahan a lift."

"You got it, Major," one of the two agreed. He slung his carbine over one shoulder, knelt down, and unfolded a collapsible field stretcher. He looked up at Brad. "Ready when you are, sir."

"I know being carried aboard isn't exactly dignified, Brad," Schofield murmured. "But we're in a bit of a hurry. The Russians aren't known for extending a friendly welcome to trespassers."

"Screw dignity," Brad said gratefully, easing himself down onto the stretcher. He closed his eyes, fighting against another wave of pain from his shoulder when they strapped him in. "The quicker we're out of here, the happier I'll be."

Within moments, the litter team was on its way back to the Ranger, moving at a rapid trot. The aircraft's engines were already spooling back up, preparing to take off the moment they were aboard with the ramp sealed.

CHAPTER 36

NATIONAL DEFENSE CONTROL CENTER, MOSCOW
That same time

"Still no radar contact with the second American strike group. All systems are operational. All launchers remain ready to fire."

Colonel General Leonov listened to the steady flow of reports from the 1529th Guards Air Defense Missile Regiment's headquarters with a growing sense of unease. He checked the digital clock on one of his screens and frowned. Where were those U.S. Navy strike fighters? Based on their observed track and speed over Hokkaido, the new attack group should have been picked up by Titov's 91N6E acquisition and battle management radar several minutes ago. The first raid, apparently composed entirely of decoy drones, had been conducted with flawless precision and timing. So why this unexplained delay now? What the hell were the Americans playing at? Every minute they loitered below the radar horizon over the Sea of Japan only burned more fuel and gave his defenses that much more time to recover from their earlier confusion.

He furrowed his brow, weighing different options. The 23rd Fighter Aviation Regiment had twelve of its Su-35S Super Flankers flying a fuel-conserving racetrack holding pattern west of Khabarovsk. Perhaps he should send them southeast to scout for the missing U.S. Navy planes, like beaters scaring up game in a hunt?

Just as quickly, Leonov dismissed the idea. If the Americans had more tricks up their sleeves, such a move might play into their hands. After all, to have any hope at all of striking the Vostochny launch complex, the enemy would need to wear down *all* of his outer defenses first . . . including his fighter regiments. So it was possible this was an effort to lure his best fighters into a trap of their own, somewhere outside the protection of Russia's S-400 SAM units.

No, he decided, it was better to hold tight and wait for the Americans to come to them. In any battle fought deep inside Russian airspace, his forces held all the advantages. Impatiently, he checked the clock again. Unfortunately, even knowing that time and distance were in his favor did not make this waiting any easier to bear.

At an adjacent workstation, Tikhomirov was on a secure phone, speaking softly and urgently with someone at Dzemgi Air Base. He looked perplexed. At last, he nodded. "Very well, Major.

Keep me posted if you get any more details." Then he hung up.

Leonov swiveled toward his deputy. "Trouble?"

"An anomaly, certainly," Tikhomirov said carefully. "That was Uvarov, the 23rd's executive officer. He wanted to relay a strange report from one of the regiment's junior officers, a Lieutenant Khryukin."

Leonov raised an eyebrow. The other man wasn't an idiot. Ordinarily, he wouldn't waste time with irrelevancies in the middle of a battle. There had to be more to this story than the babbling of some eccentric young lieutenant. "Go on."

"Khryukin was sent north from Komsomolsk to investigate reports of a UFO landing near a little village in the middle of nowhere." Tikhomirov opened a digital map at his station. "Here, at the Oldjikan State Nature Reserve."

Leonov estimated that was more than four hundred kilometers north of Knyaze-Volkonskoye. "So? What did he find on his ET hunt? A few scraps of weather balloon?"

Tikhomirov shook his head. "No . . . and that is what is odd. According to the lieutenant, the locals dug up what appears to be some kind of advanced space suit, along with what might be a disposable one-man reentry capsule." He looked apologetic. "It sounds like nonsense to me, of course, but Uvarov claims Khryukin is sure of his facts."

Leonov felt like he'd been punched in the stomach. His mouth fell open in shock. Suddenly the real reasons behind the events of the past couple of hours came into clear focus.

"Sir?" Tikhomirov sounded concerned. "Are you all right?"

"No, I am not all right!" Leonov snapped. He spun back to his own keyboard and brought up the recorded track of the crippled S-19 Midnight spaceplane as it fell out of orbit. It crossed high over the Oldjikan nature reserve. "Mother of God," he muttered. Scowling, he swiveled back to face his deputy. "Those American bastards have tricked us, Semyon! There is no real attack against the Vostochny Cosmodrome. Instead, everything we've seen so far is simply an element in an elaborate search-and-rescue mission."

Tikhomirov stared at him. "A rescue operation? For whom?"

Angrily, Leonov jabbed a finger at the map. "For one of their astronauts! One of the crewmen aboard the Sky Masters spaceplane we destroyed must have survived reentry!"

His deputy swallowed hard. "Then the decoy drone attack on Colonel Titov's regiment was—"

"Part of a much larger deception," Leonov finished grimly. He felt cold, imagining Gennadiy Gryzlov's likely reaction to this screwup. "We saw exactly what the Americans wanted us to see . . . and reacted precisely as they hoped we would."

His eyes narrowed in thought as he calculated distances and probable flight times. The start of this rescue operation must have been timed to coincide with that first detection of U.S. Navy aircraft over Hokkaido. From that moment on, Russia's air defenses and surveillance radars had been focused on what they thought was the developing threat against Vostochny and its outer defenses. There was no possibility that the Americans were using helicopters for their rescue operation. The Oldjikan wilderness area was more than a thousand kilometers inside Russia's defense perimeter—well outside the combat radius of any U.S. helicopter, or even their MV-22 Osprey tilt-rotor aircraft.

Leonov nodded to himself. There was really only one aircraft suited to this kind of mission, the stealthy short-takeoff-and-landing airlifter Poland's Iron Wolf mercenaries had used before against the Motherland. Little was known about its flight characteristics . . . *except* that it did not appear to be capable of achieving supersonic speeds. Which meant there was still a chance for his forces to intercept and destroy the American rescue plane before it escaped from Russia's airspace.

Reaching a decision, he looked up into Tikhomirov's troubled face. Clearly, the other man also understood the stakes involved. Allowing the Americans to retrieve a downed astronaut out from under their very noses would not win any accolades from their country's impulsive and often unforgiving leader. "Contact Colonel Federov! I want his Super Flankers headed back north at full speed!"

NORTH OF KHABAROVSK, OVER RUSSIA
Minutes later

With his force of twelve twin-tailed Su-35S Super Flankers spread in fighting pairs across a sixty-kilometer-wide front, Colonel Ivan Federov clicked his radio. "Sentry Flights, this is Sentry Lead. Let's not be subtle about this. Activate your radars and go to full military power! We'll climb to three thousand meters. There are *no* other friendly aircraft ahead of us. Repeat, no friendlies. You are cleared to engage any bogeys without positive IKS with every available missile."

IKS, or *identifikatsionnyy kod samolet*, was the Russian equivalent of the IFF, or identification friend or foe, system used by Western air forces. It was a transponder code used by aircraft to verify themselves as friendly to fighter interceptors and radar sites.

Federov called to his wingman. "Sentry Two, are you ready to go hunting?"

"*Two*," the other pilot confirmed.

"Then follow me." Federov advanced the throttles and pulled back on his stick. Accelerating fast, his Flanker soared higher into the night sky. Its dark and light blue "Shark" camouflage scheme rendered the fighter almost invisible to the naked eye. As it leveled off at three thousand meters, he thumbed a button on his stick to power up the Su-35's IRBIS-E hybrid phased-array radar. Instantly, one of the cockpit's two big multifunction displays lit up . . . showing a lot of empty sky ahead of them.

No great surprise there, he thought. They were still well south of the Oldjikan area. And against a stealthy target, the radar would be lucky to sniff out anything much farther than twenty or thirty kilometers away. In fact, his Flanker's passive infrared search-and-track system was more likely to spot the enemy stealth aircraft's heat signature first. Still, there was a value to coming in fast and loud, with all radars booming. Learning suddenly that a massive force of Su-35s was coming after them at high speed should scare the crap out of that American flight crew.

And frightened men were more likely to make mistakes, Federov knew. One of the keys to victory in any air-to-air fight was getting inside your opponent's decision cycle. If you could push another pilot into reacting to your moves . . . or better yet, to what he feared you *might* do . . . instead of carrying out his own plan, you were well on your way to scoring a kill.

WOLF SIX-TWO
That same time

Nestled between the two MQ-55 Coyotes, the XCV-62 Ranger streaked southeast over the pitch-black Russian countryside. The radar- and jammer-equipped Howler drone followed right behind. All four aircraft were flying so low that they almost brushed the treetops that flashed past below them in a blur.

"*S-band search radar and multiple I-band radars at two o'clock. Estimated range is seventy miles,*" the Ranger's computer said calmly. "*Detection probability at this altitude is nil.*"

"Those are the 'Big Bird' and 'Clam Shell' radars operating with the S-300PM regiment stationed near Komsomolsk," Nadia Rozek said, after checking the signal characteristics shown on her threat display. "We are not at risk on this course."

"Understood." Peter Vasey's voice was calm. Only the slight sheen of sweat on his forehead revealed the intense concentration required to avoid slamming them into the ground at more than four hundred knots.

Momentarily free to focus on her personal concerns, Nadia clicked the intercom, opening a channel to the troop compartment. "Major Schofield, how is Captain McLanahan?"

To her surprise, Brad answered for himself. "Captain McLanahan is just fine."

But Nadia could hear the pain and tension in his voice. "You do not sound . . . *fine*," she said cautiously.

"Okay, so my shoulder and leg hurt like hell . . . and we're probably going to have to dodge about a billion SAMs to get out of this mess alive," Brad acknowledged. Curiously enough, she could almost "hear" the crooked smile on his face. "But trust me, Nadia Rozek, I *am* fine. Because we're together now . . . and that's good enough for me."

"Oh," she said quietly. Her cheeks flamed red. "Well, I love y . . ."

"Warning, warning, multiple airborne X-band search radars detected from two o'clock to three o'clock," the computer interrupted. *"New radar contacts evaluated as IRBIS-E Su-35S Super Flanker systems. Range ninety miles and closing. Detection probability very low, but rising."*

"Bother," Vasey said softly. He risked a quick glance in Nadia's direction. "It seems the Russians have finally tumbled to our little game. Should we engage those fighter radars with SPEAR?" Like almost all Sky Masters–designed aircraft, the Ranger carried the ALQ-293 Self-Protection Electronically Agile Reaction system. When active, SPEAR transmitted precisely tailored signals intended to hoax enemy radars. By changing the timing of the pulses sent back to a hostile radar, it could fool an enemy set into "seeing" the XCV-62 somewhere else in the sky . . . or even render it essentially invisible.

Nadia shook her head. "Not yet." She paged through her threat displays. "I count ten-plus Su-35s flying northeast toward us at more than six hundred knots. SPEAR cannot successfully deceive so many radars."

"Then it's time to let our little friends off the leash?"

"It is," Nadia confirmed. Unless things changed, their tactical situation was going to go from bad to worse . . . and quickly. On their own, they could not outrun or outmaneuver the large force of Russian warplanes hunting them. Nor could they fight them, since the XCV-62 was completely unarmed. And there was no chance they could slip past that oncoming aerial wall of Su-35s unnoticed. Based on their current course and speed, at least six of those enemy fighters had a very high probability of picking up the Ranger either on radar or with their thermal detection systems. Turning back to the northeast to reduce the rate at which the Russians were closing on them would delay the inevitable . . . but not for long.

That left her with one viable option.

Quickly, she opened data links to the two Coyotes and the Howler electronic warfare drone. Her fingers flew across a virtual keyboard, programming new navigation waypoints and other instructions into their autonomous flight control systems. Lights blinked green, confirming that each unmanned aircraft had received her orders. "Stand by to execute breakaway maneuver," she told Vasey.

All three drones climbed a couple of hundred feet and flew on toward the southeast.

"Execute."

Below the three Iron Wolf drones now, Vasey inched his throttles back. Gradually, the XCV-62's airspeed dropped by fifty knots. The aircraft shuddered slightly, buffeted by turbulence as the trailing EQ-55 Howler passed low overhead. Gently, he nudged the stick slightly left, banking into a gentle turn toward the northeast. Then, rolling back out of the turn, he throttled back up to four hundred and fifty knots. They entered a valley that ran generally in the same direction and flew on, with rugged hills rising more than a thousand feet above them off the port side.

Out in the night sky far off on their starboard side, the two Coyotes dropped back down to two hundred feet. They separated, with one veering left and the other right. Once they were several miles apart, the two MQ-55s slowed and started circling—orbiting low over wooded slopes that marked the eastern edge of the high ground west of the Amur River. The Howler kept going straight southeast, apparently headed for the coast, Sakhalin Island, and then the Sea of Okhotsk.

Nadia checked the status of each drone through her data links and nodded. They were carrying out the plan she had devised. Now to see if it would work. She opened a com window and entered a brief situation report, including their current position, heading, and speed. It ended with a short declarative statement: HOUNDS UNLEASHED. ACTION IMMINENT. As soon as she finished, their computer took over. It encrypted and compressed her message to a quick millisecond-long burst sent via satellite uplink.

SHADOW TWO-NINE BRAVO,
OVER THE NORTH PACIFIC
That same time

Fifteen thousand feet above the ocean, a very large, black, blended-wing aircraft banked gently—

beginning yet another slow, lazy turn in the race-track holding pattern it had already been flying for more than an hour.

"Round and round we go, and when we stop only Martindale knows," Hunter "Boomer" Noble groused.

The S-29B's copilot, a petite redhead named Liz Gallagher, laughed. She was a former U.S. Air Force lieutenant colonel who had more than a thousand hours in B-2 stealth bombers before joining Scion. "C'mon, Boomer, toughen up," she teased. "This is a piece of cake. I used to fly forty-hour-plus round-trip missions all the time."

"Yeah, and I bet when you were a kid, you had to walk ten miles to school . . . going uphill both ways. In the snow."

"It was only six miles," she said with a sly grin. "And I had my older brother's hand-me-down bike."

Boomer had to admit he was beginning to find Liz Gallagher mighty attractive. Sure, she was a little older than the women he usually dated, but maybe that wasn't such a bad thing. Much as he hated to admit it, he might be getting a little long in the tooth for twentysomethings. Plus, she had a lot more in common with him than the ditzy cocktail waitresses he'd been spending so much of his time and money on over the past couple of years.

"Boomer, this is Reyes," a voice said over the intercom from the spaceplane's aft cabin. Javier Reyes was another former air-force officer, like

the rest of the crewmen Martindale had recruited
to fly and fight this S-29B Shadow. He was their
data-link officer, charged with monitoring their
communications and the information flow from
other sensor platforms—satellites, other aircraft,
ships, and ground installations. "We just received
a priority signal from Ghost One."

Boomer snorted. Ghost One was the call sign
Martindale had given himself for this mission.
He figured that was a perfect fit, given the former
president's penchant for operating in the shadows.
"Go ahead," he said. "What's the word from ol'
Spooky?"

"Sending it to you now," Reyes told him.

One of Boomer's MFDs pinged. He tapped
at it, opening the message from Martindale. He
whistled softly as he read it. Then he glanced
across the cockpit at Gallagher. "Okay, Liz, we
just got the go-code. Let's get this baby configured for supersonic flight."

"On it, Boomer," she said crisply, all business
now. She brought up their automated checklists
and set them in motion . . . double-checking the
computers at every step. Like many Sky Masters–
designed vehicles, the S-29 Shadow was fully
capable of autonomous operation, if necessary.
In fact, its advanced computers could handle all
routine flight tasks, up to and including air-to-air
refueling, supersonic flight, and orbital insertion.
The same went for its sensors, data links, and
defensive microwave emitters. The human crewmen assigned to each of those stations were there

primarily to monitor the automated systems, intervening manually only in case things went wrong.

Today, though, Boomer planned to make this a hands-on flight wherever possible. After all, complex computer programs sometimes crashed, especially when a number of different programs had to interact with one another in perfect sync. In his experience, anyone who relied too heavily on automated systems in a largely untested aircraft like this B-model S-29 was pushing the envelope way outside the edge of common sense.

"All checklists complete," Gallagher reported. "All engines and systems are go for supersonic flight."

"Roger that." Boomer spoke over the intercom to the aft cabin. "All right, boys and girls, it's showtime. Buckle up tight and stand by on all sensors and defenses."

He banked the big spaceplane again, bringing its nose back around to the northwest. Then his right hand pushed the throttles forward. The roar of their five powerful engines changed.

Instantly, the S-29 responded—streaking across the sky at an ever-increasing speed.

CHAPTER 37

OVER THE NORTHERN AMUR RIVER VALLEY, RUSSIA

A short time later

Six pairs of Su-35S Super Flanker fighters flew onward in a line abreast at three thousand meters above the undulating river valley. Lights twinkled at widely spaced intervals, identifying small towns and villages that lined both sides of the two-kilometer-wide river.

Colonel Ivan Federov scowled beneath his oxygen mask. They were well northeast of Komsomolsk now and very close to where he'd expected to intercept the American rescue aircraft as it fled Russian airspace. But neither he nor any of his pilots had spotted anything yet. The sky ahead still seemed utterly empty. Had he misjudged the situation? Were the Americans instead heading deeper into Russia to throw off his pursuit rather than bolting straight for the coast? Should he detach some of his fighters to cover that possibility?

Suddenly a sharp tone sounded in his headset, signaling a possible detection by his radar. A green diamond blinked onto the lower right corner of his HUD and then vanished almost immediately. Instantly, Federov glanced down at his radar display. That brief moment of contact had revealed a target out around forty kilometers ahead of his Su-35—moving southeast across his field of view at more than eight hundred kilometers per hour. And it was flying less than two hundred meters above the ground.

That was definitely a stealth aircraft, he thought.

Federov's scowl smoothed into a tight-lipped smile. He'd been fretting over nothing. The Americans were acting exactly as he'd predicted, running like frightened rabbits to escape out to sea. He keyed his radio. "Sentry Flights, this is Sentry Lead. Stealth target bearing two o'clock moving to three at low altitude. Range approximately forty kilometers. Intermittent radar contact only. I am turning to intercept!"

Reacting quickly, he rolled his fighter to the right and dove. Trading altitude for more speed would let him close on this elusive enemy that much faster. One finger pushed a switch on his stick. Two missile symbols appeared in the corner of his HUD. Two of his six R-77 radar-guided missiles were armed and set for a salvo launch. "Weapons hot."

Eager voices greeted his declaration of intent.

The other eleven Super Flankers were turning tightly with him—straining to be in at the kill.

Twenty-three nautical miles ahead of the Russian fighters, the EQ-55 Howler's threat-warning sensors recorded the first faint brush of Federov's IRBIS-E radar as it momentarily locked on. That triggered one of the commands Nadia had programmed in minutes before. Circuits closed within the business-jet-sized, flying-wing drone. Three things happened in quick succession. First, the Howler's electronic jamming gear activated—blasting out radio waves at frequencies designed to disrupt the active enemy radars it detected. Next, its own AN/APG-81 radar powered up. In seconds, this system had locked on to all twelve Su-35S Super Flankers. And last of all, the Howler allocated the targeting data it collected into separate packets and relayed them to the two MQ-55 Coyotes loitering forty nautical miles to the northwest.

Seconds later, the computers aboard those Coyotes finished feeding the targeting information they received into the AIM-120D missiles carried in their weapons bays. Both drones climbed higher, gaining altitude to clear the surrounding hills. Their bay doors whined open. One by one, twenty advanced medium-range air-to-air missiles dropped out into the night sky and ignited. Flashes lit the darkness.

Propelled by solid-fuel rocket motors, the missiles raced southeast at Mach 4. For the moment, their own radar-seeker heads were silent, standing by to energize only when the missiles reached close range.

Federov's radar display blanked out and then lit back up with a hash of greenish static slathered across its whole forward arc. He swore vehemently. He was being jammed. And based on the apparent signal strength, his radar-guided missiles were now useless. He pressed another switch on his stick, arming two of the K-74M heat-seekers his Super Flanker carried instead. Now he just had to get close enough to that American stealth aircraft somewhere out ahead of him to pick up its heat signature.

A new warning tone warbled through his earphones. "Christ," he muttered. "What now?" Checking his threat display showed that he was being painted by a powerful airborne radar aboard that fleeing enemy aircraft. It was radiating across an astonishing range of frequencies and altering them with incredible speed. Frantically, his computer sorted through a database of recorded signals characteristics, hunting for a match.

Grimly, Federov held his course. Jamming or no jamming, that damned American plane couldn't hide forever.

And then, suddenly, there it was. Another green diamond appeared almost in the center of his HUD, highlighting a small glowing dot. The

Super Flanker's infrared search-and-track system had detected a thermal signature. It was small, not much bigger than that created by a missile, but he had no doubt that this was the prey he was seeking.

Without waiting longer, Federov squeezed the trigger on his stick. At its heart, air-to-air combat was governed as much by instinctive reactions and intuition as it was by conscious thought. Two K-74 missiles released in sequence from under his fighter's wings and lit off. At two and a half times the speed of sound, they slashed ahead across the sky, trailing fire and smoke.

To the colonel's astonishment, the American stealth aircraft made no attempt to evade his attack. It didn't even launch flares in an effort to decoy his heat-seeking missiles. Instead, it flew on, straight and level—seemingly completely oblivious to its fast-approaching doom.

Triggered by its laser proximity fuse, the first K-74's warhead detonated within meters of the fleeing enemy plane. Ripped by dozens of pieces of razor-edged shrapnel, it spun out of control, slammed wing first into the Amur River, and disintegrated in a blinding ball of fire.

In that same instant, Federov's computer finally found the match it had been seeking. Its report flashed onto one of the Super Flanker's cockpit displays: *Enemy radar is an AN/APG-81 identical to that employed by F-35 Lightning fighters.*

"You mean it *was* an APG-81," the colonel corrected ironically. "*Now* it's burning wreckage." He shook his head in disbelief. Why would the

Americans waste a top-of-the-line fighter radar in a transport aircraft, especially one that hadn't even tried to fight back?

BEEP-BEEP-BEEP.

Federov went cold. *My God*, he realized in horror. A huge number of AIM-120D radar-seeker heads had just lit up . . . and they were close, practically right on top of his fighters . . . coming in from the rear at Mach 4. That aircraft he'd just shot down had been setting them up for an ambush! "All Sentry Flights! Break! Break *right now*!" he shouted. "We're under missile attack!"

Immediately he yanked his stick hard right, rolling away from the wave of AIM-120Ds in a high-G turn. He thumbed another switch desperately, setting off the Su-35's defensive systems. Automated chaff dispensers fired, hurling cartridges into the air behind his violently maneuvering fighter. They burst, strewing thousands of tiny Mylar strips across the sky. Simultaneously, his wing-tip ECM pods spewed energy into a wide band of radar frequencies, hoping to jam the seekers on missiles that might be homing in on his aircraft.

Explosions speckled the night sky all around him as American weapons slammed home with lethal force. Frantic voices flooded through his headset. Chaff blossoms and jamming turned the Su-35's radar display into a blur of static and false images.

Straining against seven times the force of gravity, Federov rolled inverted and dove toward the ground. With luck, he'd lose any missiles still homing in on him in the ground clutter. Something flashed past his canopy and impacted on the wooded slope of a hill below in a dazzling burst of light.

Too close, he thought grimly.

At five hundred meters, Federov rolled out of his dive and swung southwest. His threat-warning systems fell blessedly silent. Any enemy weapons that hadn't scored kills were gone—either decoyed away by chaff, blinded by jamming, or run out of energy as they tried to turn with their desperately evading targets. For a time, he flew grimly onward, trying to make sense out of the reports pouring through the data links connecting him with his surviving fighters.

What he saw was a catastrophe. Five of his twelve Su-35S Super Flankers were gone, blown to pieces by high-explosive blast-fragmentation warheads. In the chaos, only one pilot had ejected successfully. The other four were dead, including his own wingman. His seven surviving aircraft were scattered across a huge stretch of the Amur River valley, wherever their wild evasive maneuvers had taken them.

"*Sentry Lead, this is Warlord One,*" a deep voice said over the radio.

Federov stiffened. This was Leonov himself, calling from Moscow. "Go ahead, Warlord."

"*It seems we underestimated this enemy, Colonel,*" Leonov said. "*Instead of a single stealth aircraft, the Americans have penetrated our airspace with a significant armed force.*"

No shit, Federov thought bitterly. Aloud, he fought to sound coolly professional. "Yes, sir. What are your orders?"

"You will rally your fighters and continue the pursuit," Leonov radioed coldly. *"But this time I suggest you rely solely on IRST until you make positive contact."*

Federov gritted his teeth. In retrospect, his decision to conduct his fighter sweep with active radars had been a blunder—giving the Americans all the warning and time they needed to set their trap. He would not make the same mistake again. "Affirmative, Warlord One," he acknowledged. "Sentry Lead out."

Quickly, he selected a rally point on his digital map display and sent it to the rest of his pilots via data link. It was almost due south of where those missiles must have been launched at them. "We'll form up here," he ordered. "And then we hunt down and destroy those *Amerikanskiye* bastards!"

WOLF SIX-TWO
That same time

Nadia Rozek saw the seven remaining IRBIS-E radars wink off her threat display. The surviving Su-35s were about ninety nautical miles to their south-southwest. "The Russians have switched to thermal sights only," she told Vasey.

"Do you suppose they're calling it quits and returning to base?"

She glanced at him with a raised eyebrow. "Would you?"

The Englishman shook his head. "'Flee? And

leave my friends unavenged? Nay, rather I come, bristling with fury and hot for blood,'" he quoted sonorously.

"Shakespeare?" Nadia asked.

"God no." He grinned. "One Vasey, Peter Charles, from an unfinished play written during my school days."

"I see why you became a pilot instead," Nadia said dryly.

"It did seem a more promising career," Vasey allowed. He banked the XCV-62 gently to the right, turning back to the southeast. The valley they'd been flying through opened up ahead, widening into a flat plain riddled with streams, swamps, and rivers that ran almost all the way to the Russian coast. "Up to now, that is." He shrugged. "So what's our next move, Major?"

In answer, she opened data links to the two MQ-55 Coyote drones, which were still circling over the hills well south and west of their current position. Swiftly, she programmed new navigation waypoints and instructions into their computers. Green lights glowed again on her display as each unmanned aircraft signaled that it had received her orders and would obey. "If the Russians want revenge, we must give them what they desire," she told Vasey.

On her display, the two icons representing the MQ-55s broke out of their orbits, climbed to five hundred feet, and flew off in separate directions— one headed north, the other southwest.

"Alas, poor Coyotes, we knew them well," Vasey agreed.

NATIONAL DEFENSE CONTROL CENTER, MOSCOW

A short time later

"Sentry Lead, this is Five! I have a thermal contact! Stealth target bears ten o'clock moving to nine at low altitude. Range is twenty kilometers."

"Acknowledged, Five, you are cleared to engage!"

"Weapons hot, Lead. Turning to make my attack now. Good tone! Missiles away!"

"Lead, this is Nine! Separate contact! Second stealth aircraft bears one o'clock and is flying north at low altitude! Range is thirty kilometers! I am in pursuit and arming heat-seekers."

Leonov listened closely to the radio chatter from Federov's Super Flankers as they spotted, attacked, and destroyed the two American aircraft. Like most air-to-air missile engagements, the fighting ended with astonishing speed.

"Warlord One, this is Sentry Lead," Federov reported exultantly. *"Good kills on both targets. No parachutes observed. There are no enemy survivors."*

Leonov frowned. He'd expected the American stealth aircraft to put up more of a fight, especially considering the slaughter they'd inflicted on the colonel's fighter force in their first encounter. Instead, both engagements had been easy—more like target practice than real combat.

Perhaps too easy?

He leaned forward. "Sentry Lead, this is Warlord. Did either American aircraft attempt to evade your missiles? Or use flares to confuse them?"

"Negative on that, Warlord," Federov admitted.

Leonov's suspicions solidified into absolute certainty. "Those were more damned decoys, Colonel," he snapped. "You and your pilots just shot down a pair of unmanned drones."

There was a long moment of static-filled silence.

At last, Federov radioed. *"Request further instructions, Warlord."*

"Stand by, Sentry Lead," Leonov growled. Before tonight's clusterfuck, he would have rated the other man as one of his best regimental commanders. Now he was beginning to think the colonel would be much better suited to a considerably less challenging post . . . perhaps something like one of the remote weather stations far north of the Arctic Circle.

Aware of Tikhomirov's worried gaze, he studied the large map displayed on his screen. Tracks showed the last observed courses of all three downed American drones. His eyes narrowed. "Do you see the pattern, Semyon?"

Without waiting for an answer, Leonov continued. "Our line of Su-35s came northeast at high speed with their radars active. Nothing could have slipped past them, correct?"

Tikhomirov nodded.

"So . . . Federov picked up that first enemy stealth aircraft heading southeast—crossing his path like a hare running from the hounds. Naturally, he turned after it . . ."

"Into an ambush, probably conducted by those other two drones," Tikhomirov realized.

"Correct," Leonov agreed. He tapped the two remaining tracks. "Both of which then veered off, one to the southwest and the other to the north . . . only to be caught and killed by our fighters." He looked back at his deputy. "So what direction did the American stealth transport fly during all of this confusion?"

Tikhomirov sighed. "Northeast, to stay as far away from Federov's Super Flankers as possible."

"Exactly. And by now, it's headed back toward the open sea."

Leonov sat back, contemplating his next moves. It was unlikely the Americans would try to break straight east. Doing so would mean crossing the Kamchatka Peninsula, flying right into the teeth of more S-400 SAM battalions and the MiG-31 interceptors based at Yelizovo. No, he decided, the safest and most logical escape route ran through the Kuril Islands, where Russia's air surveillance and air defense were weakest. And if so, Federov's fighters still had a chance to catch up with, detect, and destroy the enemy rescue aircraft before it reached safety. He reopened the circuit to the Su-35s. "Sentry Lead, this is Warlord. Listen closely. Here are your new orders . . ."

CHAPTER 38

OVER THE SEA OF OKHOTSK
Thirty minutes later

A lone Su-35S Super Flanker raced low across the moonlit sea, weaving back and forth in an S-shaped pattern to cover as much of the sky as possible with its passive infrared search-and-track system. The fighter's IRST might have a very limited field of view compared to its nose-mounted phased-array radar, but at least it could be used without fear of detection by an enemy.

Resolutely, Colonel Ivan Federov pressed on, gloomily aware that his continued command of the 23rd Fighter Aviation Regiment hung by a single, slender thread. Stripped to their essentials, his orders from Leonov were simple: find and kill that American stealth transport before it escaped . . . or face a court-martial for incompetence. To have any hope at all of doing that, he'd been forced to spread his remaining Su-35s across a wide front—dispersing them as single aircraft rather than deploying them in fighting pairs. Though that was a clear breach of both doctrine and sound tactics, it was also the only way his weakened force could cover every likely escape route.

He'd chosen their most probable exit course for himself. These Americans had made him look like a fool at every turn. Only by personally shooting them down could he erase that stain.

Federov's head swiveled from side to side in the cockpit, checking every quadrant of the sky around his fighter for the slightest sign of movement. Besides the IRST, he could rely only on his own eyesight. And even a quick glimpse of stars occluded by the passage of another aircraft would be enough to set him on the right track.

He got lucky.

A tone sounded in his headset. The Su-35's infrared sensors had picked out the heat emanating from an aircraft flying very, very low over the water. A new green diamond blinked into the middle of Federov's HUD. Its range was still uncertain. Carefully, he tugged his stick to the right and then back to the left, initiating another quick, S-curved weave to triangulate on the contact. This maneuver gave his passive sensors enough information to determine that the American stealth aircraft was approximately forty kilometers ahead, still beyond the effective reach of his K-74M heat-seekers.

For a moment, one of his fingers hovered over the radio button. Should he report this contact to Moscow and to the rest of his fighter force before engaging? No, he decided, it would be better to wait and signal a confirmed kill instead. If it were detected, a sighting report would only alert the Americans prematurely. Besides, the other Su-35s were too far away to intervene anyway. This was his fight. And his alone.

Instead, Federov swung in behind the fleeing enemy aircraft. Propelled by its larger, more powerful engines, the Super Flanker closed the gap fast. His thumb moved to the control for the fighter's radar. Very soon now, he would light the IRBIS-E up and pop a couple of radar-guided missiles right up the unsuspecting ass of that American son of a bitch.

WOLF SIX-TWO
That same time

"*Warning, warning, IR detection. Hostile aircraft at six o'clock. Range twenty miles and closing,*" the Ranger's computer said calmly.

Reacting fast, Nadia cued one of her displays to their rear-facing thermal sensors. She checked the image it showed. "Hostile aircraft is an Su-35 Super Flanker," she said tightly.

"Well . . . bugger," Vasey said reflectively. His eyes flicked across his own displays and the HUD. The Russian fighter had caught them squarely in the middle of the Sea of Okhotsk, far from any masking terrain features they could use to break contact. "We've nowhere to run and nowhere to hide."

"It is unfortunate," Nadia agreed. Her fingers tapped rapidly across a virtual keyboard. "Preparing defensive systems. SPEAR is ready to engage. Flares are set for K-74M heat-seekers. Chaff is configured for R-77 radar-guided missiles. Spinning up inertial navigation systems for both MALDs. Their GPS receivers are initialized." Besides flares and chaff and SPEAR, the only other defenses carried by the XCV-62 were two miniature air-launched decoys slotted into an internal bay. In the circumstances, they were unlikely to be useful . . . since the Su-35 was almost close enough now to see them visually. Nevertheless, she was not prepared to give up without readying every possible option.

"*Warning, warning, X-band radar powering up,*" the computer said. And then, "*IRBIS-E is locked on.*"

"Engaging enemy radar," Nadia said. She tapped a display, commanding their SPEAR system to try to jam or spoof the Super Flanker's airborne radar.

"*Warning, warning, radar missile launch detection at six o'clock,*" the Ranger's computer announced. "*Two missiles inbound at Mach four.*"

"Time to impact, twenty-six seconds," Nadia said. She peered intently at her displays. "Countermeasures ready."

Beside her, Vasey blinked away a droplet of sweat that stung his eye. This was going to be . . . difficult. The Russian fighter pilot behind them was certainly an eager bastard. He'd fired at almost the first possible moment, before SPEAR could break his lock-on. And now those two missiles headed their way no longer needed any radar data supplied by the Su-35. They were on inertial guidance, ready to shift to their own active radar homing seekers at close range.

"Countermeasures!" he rapped out. Nadia's finger stabbed at her display. Instantly, Vasey yanked the Ranger into a hard right turn. G-forces slammed him back against his seat. The world started to gray out. His hand gripped the control stick, straining to keep them from rolling out of control and slamming into the sea.

Chaff cartridges tumbled behind them and exploded.

"*Seeker heads are active*," the computer said.

Seduced by a chaff bloom, one of the Russian missiles veered away and detonated well behind them. The second kept coming.

"*Time to impact eight seconds*," the computer said matter-of-factly.

Nadia strained against the G-forces to punch in a command on her display. "Engaging missile with SPEAR."

Precisely calculated radio waves lashed the incoming Russian missile's radar-seeker head, altering its perception of where it "saw" the Ranger. Not by much—just a small fraction of a degree horizontally and only a few yards vertically. But it was enough. The second R-77 slashed past the XCV-62's cockpit and corkscrewed away into the sea, vanishing in a brief plume of white foam.

"*New unidentified airborne thermal contact at eleven o'clock*," the Ranger's computer warned. "*Altitude three thousand feet. Range indefinite, but closing. Contact speed is high, sixteen hundred knots.*"

Vasey rolled the aircraft into another evasive
turn away from the Su-35 on their tail. "That's
probably a MiG-31 interceptor out of Yelizovo."
His face was an expressionless mask. "It seems
our cup runneth over with bloody enemies today,
Major."

SENTRY LEAD
That same time

Federov glanced down at his now-useless radar display and cursed in frustration. His Super
Flanker's system could not pierce the wall of
electronic noise broadcast by the enemy aircraft
ahead. And without the ability to lock on to a target, his remaining radar-guided missiles had suddenly become deadweight.

He turned with the American stealth plane as
it tried to evade, easily matching it maneuver for
maneuver. His Su-35 was now less than fifteen kilometers behind and catching up fast.

Federov toggled another switch on his control
stick, arming his last two heat-seekers. All the electronic jamming in the world wouldn't stop them
from homing in on the enemy's thermal signature.

More seconds passed as the range dropped
steadily. Fourteen kilometers. Thirteen. Twelve.

Now! He squeezed the trigger. The two K-74M
missiles flashed out from under the Super Flanker's wings and curved ahead trailing smoke and
fire—already guiding perfectly on their target.

Instantly, the American stealth aircraft broke hard left, spiraling upward in a tight, climbing turn. Dozens of white-hot flares streamed out behind it, each a tiny sunburst against the night.

Federov saw both of his missiles tear through the falling curtain of decoy flares, ignoring them completely in favor of their real prey. They streaked upward after the desperately turning enemy plane. *Any second now*, he thought, feeling the joyful anticipation of a kill rising fast. The Americans were out of cards to play.

And then his smile vanished.

Less than a hundred meters from the enemy aircraft, both K-74s went wild. They spun away in different directions and detonated harmlessly high over the surface of the sea.

"Damn it!" Federov growled, unable to believe what he'd just seen. Did those American bastards have yet another new defensive system—some black-magic means of killing even IR missiles?

Abruptly, his Super Flanker rocked wildly, hammered by the jet wash of another large, fast-moving aircraft as it streaked past overhead . . . appearing as nothing more than a darkened blur against the starlit sky before it vanished astern. His jaw tightened. One of the MiG-31s based on the Kamchatka Peninsula must have decided to join the party.

But this would all be over before that other Russian pilot could circle back around, Federov decided coldly. Nobody was stealing this kill from him. He switched his fire-control computer to guns mode and saw a glowing pipper appear on his HUD. Maybe the Americans could disable his missiles . . . but nothing in the world could stop a 30mm armor-piercing incendiary round from striking home.

He shoved the throttles for the Super Flanker's engines to afterburner and felt the jolt as his fighter accelerated. Gripping the stick, he focused entirely on staying with the fleeing stealth aircraft as it maneuvered desperately to shake him off its tail. *Nothing doing*, he thought. *You're mine.*

As Federov's speed climbed higher, the range decreased even more rapidly. He could see the gun computer estimates flickering down on his HUD. Four kilometers. Three kilometers. Two kilometers. One thousand meters.

He throttled back. Now that he was this close, there was no sense in risking an overshoot. His thumb moved to the guns switch on his stick. The maximum effective range for the GSh-301 cannon mounted in the Su-35's starboard wing root was around eight hundred meters. He planned to get in even closer—close enough to be sure he could score the hits needed to rip that American aircraft apart in midair and send its crew tumbling to hell.

ZZZAAATTT.

Federov's eyes widened in stunned horror as his instrument panels and cockpit displays suddenly erupted in a shower of sparks . . . and then went black. With its digital fly-by-wire system dead, the Super Flanker started to roll out of control. Frantically, he grabbed for the ejection handle.

Too late.

Still moving at more than six hundred knots, the Su-35S plowed into the sea and exploded.

SHADOW TWO-NINE BRAVO
That same time

"Ouch," Hunter Noble muttered, seeing the Russian fighter auger in and vanish in a huge ball of fire and foam. "Bet that hurt." He opened the intercom to the spaceplane's aft cabin. "Nice work, Jacobs!"

"Thanks, Boomer," Paul Jacobs replied. The former B-52 electronic warfare officer ran the S-29B's defensive systems. The microwave emitters under his control had just proved their effectiveness in real-world combat—first by frying the electronics in the two Russian heat-seeking missiles just before they hit the XCV-62 and then by shorting out every computer and digital control system aboard that Super Flanker.

Hunter eased back on the big spaceplane's throttles and curved away to avoid overflying the Ranger at supersonic speed a second time. One side of his mouth quirked upward. *I bet Constable Vasey and Nadia are already plenty spooked as it is*, he thought smugly. He keyed his mike. "Wolf Six-Two, this is Shadow Two-Nine Bravo. Sorry we cut things a little close there. But don't worry, we'll stick with you from here on out. Hold your course across the Kurils and we'll run interference if the Russians make another missile or fighter attack on you."

There was a moment's silence before Nadia Rozek replied. *"Boomer?"* Her voice sounded strained.

"Yep."

"Where did you get an armed spaceplane?" she demanded.

Boomer winked across the cockpit at Liz Gallagher. "Well, Major, that's sort of a long story. Tell you what, I promise you'll hear all about it once we're back on the ground."

"Yes," she said flatly. *"I will. Wolf Six-Two out."*

Liz Gallagher arched an eyebrow at him. "That was Major Nadia Rozek? The ex–Iron Wolf commando? The one I've heard so many stories about?" Boomer nodded. "She sounds kind of pissed off," his copilot said carefully. "Like maybe this was one surprise too many?"

"Well, she might be a little testy about that, I guess," Boomer allowed. "But Nadia'll get over it. After all, we just saved her life . . . and Brad McLanahan's, too. Plus, we're pretty good friends."

"Oh, Boomer," Gallagher said, shooting him a pitying smile. "That probably means she'll only beat you *half* to death." She shrugged. "But don't worry, I'll stick close to you."

"You will?"

"Sure," she said judiciously. "Somebody needs to supply the bandages."

CHAPTER 39

Colonel General Leonov sat alone on one side of the large conference table. His colleagues among Russia's national security and foreign policy elite were crowded practically elbow to elbow around the other three sides. *I have become a plague carrier,* he thought with morbid humor. No one wanted to risk even the slightest association with someone who had become a focus of Gennadiy Gryzlov's ire.

"You were an idiot, Leonov," the president said icily. "How could you let yourself be duped by so obvious a ploy?"

Leonov kept his voice level. "Without knowing that one of the American astronauts survived re-entry, we had no way to judge that their attack on our surface-to-air missile defenses was only a feint."

"Your ignorance of yet one more important fact is hardly a persuasive defense," Gryzlov snapped.

"For days, the world has trembled before Russia's power. But now you've allowed the Americans to rescue their downed astronaut and run rings around you." His eyes were coldly furious. "And your failure threatens to make the Motherland a laughingstock."

"This was a covert operation by the Americans," Leonov pointed out carefully. "They aren't likely to publicize its results."

Gryzlov snorted. "You think not? Then you're an even bigger fool than I believed. Washington will be only too happy to spread the news to its allies, if only to stiffen the backs of those who had been wavering. We just lost six of our best single-seat fighters and fired off more than a hundred sophisticated missiles . . . and for what? To kill a handful of cheap decoys!"

Angrily, he shoved back his chair, stood up, and began pacing around the table. He loomed over everyone else in the room like a bird of prey on the lookout for its next victim. "Of what value, *Colonel General*," he sneered, "is your expensive military space station if our enemies can still violate Russia's sovereignty with impunity?"

Leonov kept his mouth shut.

"Now you show some wisdom," Gryzlov commented acidly. He stopped pacing. "Despite the dominance we have achieved in near-Earth orbit, the Americans still apparently believe they can act freely against us here on Earth itself. They must be made to regret this error."

"In what way, Gennadiy?" Foreign Minister Daria Titeneva asked. Her eyes were watchful.

Gryzlov bared his teeth in a cold, cruel smile. "By the most logical means, Daria. We will carry out an immediate reprisal attack, employing one of Mars One's *Rapira* hypersonic warheads."

Leonov nodded to himself. That was the logical move. And it was one he had anticipated as soon as Gryzlov had summoned his senior officials to this emergency meeting.

Titeneva frowned. "Firing those space-based missiles still involves serious risk," she said slowly. "And it would not be in our interest to trigger an uncontrolled escalation of this conflict."

"Weapons that we are too afraid to use are not weapons at all," Gryzlov said with contempt.

"I understand that, Mr. President," the foreign minister said. She looked straight up at him. "Which is why I agree that we should launch one of the *Rapiras*—but only against an uninhabited area first. Doing so would demonstrate the power of this new weapons system quite convincingly, especially if we couple it with a clear warning that further attacks against us or our interests will be avenged with overwhelming force."

Gryzlov waved away her suggestion with obvious scorn. "That is the counsel of cowardice, Daria. I thought better of you." He shook his head. "Pulverizing a few hundred square meters of dirt and rock will not terrify anyone. Especially not the Americans." He looked around the table with a challenging stare. "Did the Americans 'demonstrate' the power of their first atomic bomb to the Japanese by dropping it on empty ocean?"

No one answered his rhetorical question.

"Of course not," he continued. "They set it off over an inhabited city—killing tens of thousands to make a point." He smiled thinly. "Why should we fear to tread the same ground?"

Titeneva looked horrified.

"Oh, relax," Gryzlov told her impatiently. "I am not contemplating an attack on a civilian city . . . yet." He turned back to Leonov. "Instead, your cosmonauts aboard Mars One will attack a legitimate *military* target . . . the USS *Ronald Reagan*. After all, aircraft from that carrier were instrumental in your recent humiliation. Sinking it from orbit should prove to President Farrell the folly of continued resistance."

Leonov felt his pulse speed up. Adrenaline flooded his system. This was the moment of maximum danger for him, and millions of years of evolution were now signaling the necessity of "fight or flight." "Unfortunately, Mr. President," he said quietly, "I must advise you that such an attack would almost certainly fail. Even at Mach twenty, a *Rapira* warhead falling from orbit takes around ninety-five seconds to reach its target."

"So?" Gryzlov demanded.

"The ships of the American carrier strike group zigzag at irregular intervals as a matter of routine," Leonov explained. "And under attack, they can maneuver even more violently and at higher speeds. A warhead aimed at the *Reagan*, or any of her escorts, could easily miss by a thousand meters or more."

For a long moment, Gryzlov stared at him in brooding silence.

Leonov sensed the others around the table recoiling even farther into their seats. None of them would meet his eyes. Plainly, they expected, and dreaded, a temper tantrum by their leader that would end in his arrest and probable execution.

At last, Gryzlov's thin, calculating smile returned. "You seem to have given this some thought, Leonov."

"Yes, sir, I have," he agreed calmly.

"Then do you have an alternative to offer me? Another military target whose destruction will make Farrell shit himself with fear?"

Leonov nodded. "I do." He sent a series of black-and-white images from his tablet computer to the conference room's large screen. "These pictures are being relayed from one of our reconnaissance satellites. The ship you see here is currently departing from the U.S. Navy base at Yokosuka, Japan."

Gryzlov frowned. "If you can't hit an aircraft carrier with a *Rapira*, how do you expect to succeed against another moving vessel?"

"Because *this* ship is steaming at a set speed and on a strictly prescribed course in one of the world's busiest and most crowded shipping lanes," Leonov said. "It cannot maneuver evasively without risking a fatal collision." He tapped his tablet again. In response, text scrolled across the screen, identifying the U.S. Navy ship and its cargo.

"Ah, I see," Gryzlov said in satisfaction. His

mouth twisted into an exultant, vicious grin. "Yes, that is perfect, Mikhail! Let it be done."

ABOARD MARS ONE, IN EARTH ORBIT
Several minutes later

Colonel Vadim Strelkov looked across the command compartment. "Are we receiving good data, Georgy?"

Konnikov nodded. "Yes, sir. Our link to the Kondor satellite is solid." He entered commands on his console. "Transferring tracking data to the *Rapira* fire-control computer now."

"Tracking data received," Major Viktor Filatyev announced over the intercom from his post in the space station's aft weapons module. "The computer is calculating a firing solution."

Seconds passed.

"I have a good solution," Filatyev said. "Feeding it to *Rapira* One." Moments later. "*Rapira* One has accepted the data. I am ready to launch the weapon."

Strelkov turned his gaze to his own console. One of his displays showed a feed from one of their outside cameras. It was focused on the underside of the station's central command module. "Very well, Major. Launch now."

"Launching."

On the colonel's display, an armored hatch slid open. With a puff of gas, an elongated shape— the *Rapira* warhead with its attached rocket motor—drifted out into space, separating from Mars One at ten meters per second.

One minute later, now safely away from the Russian space platform, the rocket motor attached to the *Rapira* fired. It was aimed against the direction of orbit. One short burn slowed the weapon just enough to send it slanting down toward the earth on a precisely calculated vector.

As it fell out of orbit, maneuvering thrusters puffed, flipping the *Rapira* end over end, so that the warhead was nose first. Small explosive bolts popped, separating the rocket motor from the rest of the assembly. With its task complete, the little rocket engine drifted away . . . on course to burn up in reentry.

On its own now, the sleek, carefully shaped warhead crossed into the upper atmosphere and plunged onward, trailing a plume of white-hot plasma. As it fell, it tore a blinding streak of light across the night sky above the Pacific.

Ninety seconds later, the *Rapira* warhead slammed into the USNS *Amelia Earhart* at more than thirteen thousand miles per hour. Torn apart by a kinetic impact akin to more than two thousand tons of high explosive, the forty-thousand-ton naval stores ship suddenly vanished in an enormous ball of fire—obliterated by the sympathetic detonation of the hundreds of missiles and bombs in its cargo holds.

The huge white flash turned the night into day across Tokyo, just twenty-five miles to the north.

Burning shards of metal rained down across the densely populated streets and crowded piers of Yokohama and Yokosuka—setting fires and damaging buildings and ships. More than one hundred American sailors on the *Amelia Earhart* and dozens of Japanese civilians on land were killed instantly. But the real death toll would rise for days, as those who were wounded by shrapnel or trapped amid the flames succumbed to their terrible injuries.

CHAPTER 40

THE WHITE HOUSE, WASHINGTON, D.C.
A short time later

President John D. Farrell watched the secure video to Moscow go live, revealing Gennadiy Gryzlov seated at his own desk. His jaw tightened when he saw the sly, self-satisfied smile on the Russian leader's chiseled face. "Now you listen here, you . . ."

"I do not have to listen to anything," Gryzlov said bluntly. "This is not a conversation, Farrell. We have nothing to *discuss*." He leaned forward. "I have been patient with you, but my patience is at an end. I will no longer tolerate foolishness."

"Meaning what, exactly?" Farrell asked coldly.

"Let me be very clear, so that no more lives will be lost through your idiocy. Further American attacks against my country—in the air, on the ground, at sea, or in space—will be met with overwhelming and unstoppable missile strikes from orbit. Nothing will be safe. No American military base. No vital infrastructure." Gryzlov's voice hardened. "Not even the White House itself." Then, before Farrell could reply, he reached out and cut the connection.

The screen went black.

"Well, that went well," Kevin Martindale said quietly. The head of Scion had been seated off-camera during the brief call.

Farrell snorted. "About as well as could be expected." He nodded toward the blank screen. "That Russian son of a bitch thinks he's sitting in the catbird seat."

"He's not far wrong."

"No, he's not," Farrell agreed bitterly. "Besides killing a bunch of our sailors and Japanese civilians and blowing the shit out of Carrier Strike Group Five's ammo resupply, sinking the *Amelia Earhart* just showed the whole world that no one's safe. The Russians can hit virtually any target they want from orbit . . . and we can't do a damned thing to stop them."

He steepled his hands. "As long as Gryzlov has that space station and its weapons hanging over our heads, we're screwed. The Pentagon's run the numbers. No antimissile system in our existing arsenal has a shot in hell at stopping that Rapier warhead of theirs. Not when we're likely to have less than two minutes warning of any attack."

Martindale frowned. "Sky Masters has certain weapons under development that might do the job—battlefield lasers, hypersonic interceptors, and the like. Unfortunately, they're not yet ready for deployment." He looked up. "Our Cybernetic

Infantry Devices might be able to shoot down one of those incoming warheads using their electromagnetic rail guns. While I imagine the odds of success would be very low, they'd still be better than nothing."

"And how many operational CIDs are there currently?" Farrell asked.

"Just six," Martindale admitted. "Three in Poland with the Iron Wolf Squadron and three more at Battle Mountain. We were able to repair one of the machines damaged during the fight with Gryzlov's KVMs last year. The other two are new construction."

Farrell nodded grimly. "That's about what I thought," he said. "Six CIDs divided among thousands of potential targets around the world isn't exactly going to cut it."

"Not really," Martindale said heavily. "Which leaves us . . . where?"

"In a world of hurt." Farrell got up from behind his desk and turned to look out the Oval Office windows. For once, the sky over Washington was a deep, rich blue, without a single cloud to break its perfection. "As a precaution, I've ordered the vice president to board one of our E-4B command posts and get airborne." He checked his watch. "By now, Tom and his national security team should be orbiting somewhere over the Midwest at forty thousand feet."

Martindale nodded. That was a sensible move. E-4Bs were Boeing 747-200s converted into strategic command and control aircraft. Constant air-to-air refueling enabled the large four-engine jets to remain aloft for a week or more. Putting the vice president out of harm's way aboard one of the National Airborne Operations Centers at least made sure that Gryzlov could not carry out a successful decapitation strike against the United States.

And if necessary, Vice President Thomas Knox and the battle staff aboard that U.S. Air Force mobile command post could pick up the reins and carry on. It helped that Farrell had picked his running mate for more reasons than just the votes he could help swing. Knox, a popular former senator and onetime chairman of both the Senate Armed Services and Intelligence Committees, brought a wealth of institutional knowledge and experience to the job. He was the slick, smooth insider to Farrell's rugged outsider . . . and they'd made a very effective team so far.

Farrell turned away from the windows. "One thing's sure. I'm damned tired of playing defense. That's a sucker's game in the long run." He looked toward Martindale. "We need a plan to take out Mars One. And we need it fast."

"Patrick's working up some ideas now," Martindale promised.

"Good." Farrell sat back down. "I'm convening an emergency national security meeting tomorrow afternoon. Admiral Firestone and the rest of the JCS have been crafting their own plans to attack that space station. I want you and General McLanahan—and anyone else from Battle Mountain you think necessary—in on that meeting."

Somberly, Martindale nodded. "We'll be there, Mr. President."

BATTLE MOUNTAIN GENERAL HOSPITAL, NEVADA
Early the next day

Hunter Noble knocked on the open door of Brad McLanahan's room and then cautiously poked his head inside. "Anyone conscious in here?"

"Maybe not bright-eyed, but definitely conscious," Brad said from a wheelchair parked by the bed. He looked thinner, still had his right arm in a sling, and wore a compress around his elevated right knee. He had a walking cane perched across his lap.

Nadia Rozek looked up from the travel bag she was packing. She nodded to the visitor with a slight smile. "Hello, Boomer."

"Does that mean I'm forgiven?"

"I negotiated a plea bargain for you on the flight home from Japan," Brad told him dryly. After crossing the Kuril island barrier safely, Peter Vasey and Nadia had flown the Ranger south to Chitose Air Base on Hokkaido. Martindale had one of his fastest private executive jets, a Gulfstream G500, waiting there to bring the XCV-62's flight crew and passengers back to the States. "You have her permission to save our lives again as necessary . . . but you've got to promise not to scare the crap out of her by showing up unannounced in some new super-secret armed spaceplane next time."

"It's a deal," Boomer said gratefully. He shrugged. "In my defense, I didn't learn Martindale actually built that S-29B until after everybody had already left for Attu."

"We figured as much," Brad assured him.

Boomer glanced back down the hall. "Speaking of secrets, what'd you tell the doctors here?"

"The official story is that I got hurt skydiving."

"That's close enough to the truth, I guess," Boomer acknowledged. "For a certain definition of 'sky,' anyway." He waved a hand at the wheelchair. "So what's the deal with that? Shouldn't you be resting comfortably in bed?"

Nadia zipped the bag shut. "We are busting Brad out of this Popsicle joint."

Boomer stared at the two of them. "Come again?"

She frowned. "Did I not use the proper idioms?"

"No, that's not it," Boomer said. He turned to Brad. "It's just that I thought you had a dislocated shoulder."

Brad's mouth twitched into a wry smile. "Yeah, I did, for probably about twenty minutes."

"Huh?"

"My best guess is the shock when my ERO parachute opened at thirty thousand feet yanked my right shoulder partially out of its socket." Brad winced, remembering the sudden, intense spasm of pain he'd felt. He'd definitely blacked out for some amount of time, coming to not far above the ground. "But then my hard landing must have slammed it back into place."

"Holy shit," Boomer muttered. "I bet that's not a medically recommended procedure."

"It is not," Nadia said quietly. "Fortunately, there were no serious complications. While it will take weeks of physical therapy for Brad to regain his full strength with that shoulder, no additional surgery is required."

"And the knee?" Boomer asked.

"It's badly sprained, but no ligaments are torn," Brad told him. He smiled crookedly again. "I got lucky. Though the nurses gave me hell for not following the whole RICE—rest, ice, compression, and elevation—protocol sooner."

Nadia sniffed. "That would have been somewhat difficult to arrange while on the run in enemy territory."

"Just a little," Brad agreed. He looked back at Boomer. "Anyway, the only reason for this wheelchair is to get me out of the hospital. After that, I should be able to hobble around okay using a cane."

"But why the hurry?" Boomer asked carefully, already suspecting he knew the answer.

"First, because I hate hospitals," Brad said quietly. "And second, because I've read through my dad's intelligence reports on Mars One . . . along with the attack plan he's worked up, with input from you and from Jason Richter. Banged up or not, you guys are going to need me."

Boomer sighed. "I figured as much." He shook his head. "Look, Brad, considering how close you came to getting killed on our last trip into orbit, don't you think maybe you should just sit this one out?"

"I can't do that," Brad said flatly. His mouth tightened angrily. "Not after seeing the footage of that missile strike on the *Amelia Earhart*. Gennadiy Gryzlov just murdered hundreds of people because of me. Because you, Nadia, Peter Vasey, and the others helped me escape. So that makes this my fight, now more than ever."

CHAPTER 41

**THE WHITE HOUSE SITUATION ROOM,
WASHINGTON, D.C.**
A few hours later

President Farrell entered the crowded Situation
Room at a rapid clip. He waved the men and
women who'd started to rise to greet him back
down into their seats and took his own place at
the head of the table. Besides his top national security advisers, Patrick McLanahan and Kevin
Martindale were physically present. A video link
to Battle Mountain showed other members of
the Scion and Sky Masters team listening in—
including Brad, looking much the worse for wear,
Nadia, Hunter Noble, and Peter Vasey.

"Okay, y'all," the president said briskly. "Time's
short, so we need to move along fast." He turned
to Admiral Scott Firestone, chairman of the Joint
Chiefs. "Let's start with what your folks at the
Pentagon and Space Command have come up
with, Admiral."

"Yes, sir," Firestone agreed. "At its core, the plan we propose is simple: We put a large fragmentation warhead aboard the Delta IV rocket being prepped out at Vandenberg. And then we launch this warhead into a four-hundred-mile-high retrograde orbit with an inclination of 128.4 degrees." He looked around the table. "If all goes well, that ought to place it on a collision course with Mars One, which is orbiting in the opposite direction."

"And then you plan to detonate the warhead," Farrell realized.

The admiral nodded. "Exactly, Mr. President. This explosion should create a large cloud of shrapnel, right in the path of Mars One. Any fragments that strike the Russian space station will do so with a combined velocity of close to thirty-four thousand miles per hour, inflicting lethal damage."

That created a pleased stir throughout the Situation Room. It was easy to imagine the devastation that would be caused even by a single shard of metal hitting at such speed, let alone by many.

Farrell noticed one man shaking his head. "You see a problem, General?"

"Oh, it's a great plan," Patrick McLanahan said forcefully. "Except for just one little thing: it won't work." He leaned forward. "We'd have to detonate that warhead far around the curve of the earth from the oncoming Russian station—thousands of miles away. Because otherwise, Mars One will simply destroy our Delta IV in flight with its long-range plasma rail gun."

Firestone shrugged. "So?"

"The Russians still have satellites up, Admiral," Patrick reminded him. "Even if we don't. So they'll detect our rocket launch and the detonation in real time. Mars One will have plenty of warning, which would allow the station to maneuver safely out of reach of most of our expanding and thinning shrapnel cloud. Once that's accomplished, their defensive lasers can easily deflect or vaporize any larger fragments that might pose a risk." Seen through the clear visor of his life-support helmet, his expression was grim. "Given all of that, the odds of scoring a genuinely damaging hit are far too low. We might as well toss a lit firecracker at a charging grizzly bear in the hope that pieces of the scorched wrapper will smack into both eyes and blind it."

"And earn a disemboweling swipe of its claws in return," Farrell said directly.

Patrick nodded. "All pain for no gain whatsoever."

Farrell looked closely at him. "I assume you're not arguing that we sit back and do nothing, General?"

"I am not, Mr. President," the older McLanahan answered. "Unless we take out that Russian space station, and damned soon, we might as well start negotiating the terms of our surrender."

"Surrender to a murderous thug like Gennadiy Gryzlov? Hell no. Not on my watch," Farrell growled.

"No, sir," Patrick agreed. "Fortunately, my analysis of the available intelligence suggests that

Mars One does have one weakness. A weakness we can turn to our own advantage."

"What kind of weakness?" Farrell demanded.

"A severe shortage of electrical power," Patrick told him. Speaking carefully, he talked them through the reasoning that led him to conclude that the Russians had lost their power generator—almost certainly a revolutionary compact fusion reactor—aboard the one Energia-5VR heavy-lift rocket they'd lost after launch.

Admiral Firestone looked thoughtful. "Assuming that's true, what are the tactical implications?"

"Without a working reactor, Mars One's ability to fire its energy weapons must be severely restricted," Patrick explained. "Once fired, its plasma rail gun and lasers can only be recharged with power diverted from the station's solar panels—and even then at a comparatively slow rate."

"So launching an attack when Mars One crosses into the earth's shadow—"

"Should significantly limit the amount of firepower the Russians can employ against our strike force," Patrick agreed.

"To what extent, exactly?" Andrew Taliaferro, the secretary of state, asked carefully.

Patrick shrugged, a gesture amplified by his motor-driven exoskeleton. "I can't give you exact figures. But my best guess is that Mars One can store enough energy in its supercapacitors and battery packs for roughly two or three shots from that plasma rail gun . . . and twelve to sixteen short bursts from each of the two Hobnail lasers."

His words were met first with stunned silence and then with open consternation.

"Good God, man," Taliaferro said in shock, speaking for the others. "Even if you're right, that's more than enough firepower to make any assault futile. Sending spacecraft, even Sky Masters spaceplanes, up against that station would still be a suicide run."

"Not quite," Patrick said, with quiet determination. "The trick will be to throw enough potential targets into orbit to drain those supercapacitors and batteries. If we can do that, some attackers should survive long enough to close with and board Mars One."

Farrell saw his advisers exchange appalled glances.

This time it was the CIA's director, Elizabeth Hildebrand, who spoke up. "With respect, General McLanahan," she said quietly. "Where are you going to find trained personnel crazy enough to try that kind of space banzai charge?"

On the large wall screen, Brad, Nadia, Boomer, and Vasey sheepishly raised their hands. "That would be us," Boomer said solemnly.

Farrell felt suddenly humbled. All four of those people were younger than anyone else involved in this debate. They came here today with most of their lives still ahead of them. Two of them weren't even American citizens. And yet there they were, ready and willing to risk all they had in the service of the United States and the world's other free nations. Nadia, especially, had already paid a high personal price for her dedication and courage. He felt a pressing urge to find some way for this deadly cup to pass them by.

He turned to Patrick. "I understand your plan, General. What I don't understand is why we should risk so many precious lives in what's bound to be a high-risk assault to capture this Russian space station. Wouldn't it be wiser to use the same tactics—multiple launches to run those enemy energy weapons out of power—but with unmanned weapons instead? Why not just blow Mars One to hell from a safe distance?"

From the carefully controlled anguish he read on the other man's face, he knew he'd struck a chord.

Martindale laid a hand on Patrick's metal-reinforced shoulder. "I'll take this one," he murmured. "Put bluntly, Mr. President," he said, "we need to seize and hold that Russian space platform because it's painfully obvious that Moscow has leapfrogged us in certain key technological areas—including sophisticated energy weapons and, probably, fusion power generation. Unless our scientists and engineers get a good solid look at some of these devices, we're likely to lag behind the enemy for years . . . with disastrous consequences."

Coolly, he swept his gaze around the crowded table, watching as his arguments hit home. Then he turned back to Farrell. "Gryzlov isn't likely to back off, no matter what happens to his first military station. Even if we destroy Mars One, we may face the beginning of a prolonged struggle in space, one that will be fought with ever-more-sophisticated weapons. To have any chance at all of winning this conflict, we simply must capture Mars One intact."

Farrell considered his words and nodded slowly. "You've made your point, Mr. Martindale." He frowned. "I don't like it one goddamned little bit, but I'm not going to make the same mistake as some of my predecessors by assuming I can ignore reality in favor of my own hopes and dreams."

He swung around to face Patrick squarely. "*If* I give the go-ahead, when can you set your operation in motion?"

"Speed is absolutely critical," the older McLanahan said. "But to have any chance at all, our assault has to be timed very precisely to meet certain key requirements."

"Which are?" Farrell asked.

"First, we've got to launch our spaceplanes at a moment when the enemy station's solar arrays aren't generating power."

Admiral Firestone shrugged. "Mars One passes through the earth's shadow on every orbit, doesn't it?"

Patrick nodded. "Yes, but we also need to select a period of darkness that won't expose our spaceplanes to salvos by Russia's S-500 SAMs and MiG-31-launched missiles during their boost phase. That narrows the range of suitable orbits considerably." He looked at Farrell. "Plus, if it's at all possible, I want to time our attack to minimize the number of important American and allied targets Mars One could strike with its ground-attack weapons before we capture or destroy it."

"So, not when that space station is passing right over Washington, D.C., for example?" Farrell suggested with a quick, wry smile.

"Or Warsaw. Or London. Or any number of other places," Patrick agreed. Then he motioned toward the screen showing Brad and the others watching intently. "And, maybe most important of all, it will take time to train our assault force in simulators . . . and to jury-rig the weapons and other equipment they'll use in this mission."

He brought his attention back to the president. "With all that in mind, our first window to go opens in less than two hundred hours." Impatiently, he overrode the sudden babble of protest from around the room. "I know that isn't much time," he said flatly. "But that's also likely to be our *only* window. The clock is ticking. Right now new intelligence from Scion strongly indicates the Russians are already prepping a replacement fusion reactor for launch from the Vostochny complex."

Patrick leaned forward, fixing his eyes on Farrell. "Either we go before that reactor is operational," he said grimly, "or we don't go at all."

VOSTOCHNY COSMODROME
Several hours later

Live feeds from around the complex were displayed on the control center's wall-sized screens. One showed the inside of the huge Energia assembly building. Technicians wearing red hard hats and blue-and-black uniforms clustered around the massive rocket's still-separate engine and payload stages. They were inspecting each with care—checking for even the slightest signs of any mechanical or electronic glitches. Only when those checks were complete would they begin the intricate task of mating each stage to its companions to form a finished space vehicle. No one at Vostochny wanted to see a repeat of the disastrous launch from Plesetsk.

Launch director Yuri Klementiyev checked the digital timer displayed above that screen. It was counting down the time toward the new Energia-5VR's planned lift-off. He glanced at his deputy, who was standing beside him. "Well, Sergei?"

"We'll make it," the other man said confidently. "Our assembly team is on schedule, maybe even a little ahead. Even if the preflight inspection turns up problems, we have a built-in margin."

"Not much of one." Klementiyev felt like his nerves were frayed. Moscow seemed to think he could run this launch complex as though it were a commuter railroad—firing off rockets into space on order, to a timetable dictated by the Kremlin.

To hide his worries, he turned his attention to the other two wall screens. They were focused on Pads 5 and 7, seven and nine kilometers respectively from the control center. Floodlights illuminated the Soyuz-5 rocket on each pad. They were already surrounded by gantries and fueling towers. The top stage of each Soyuz contained a single-seater Elektron spaceplane, with its wings and tail folded inside a protective shroud.

Gennadiy Gryzlov and Colonel General Leonov were not taking any chances this time. When the new fusion reactor reached orbit, it would be escorted by armed Russian spacecraft all the way to Mars One.

CHAPTER 42

MCLANAHAN INDUSTRIAL AIRPORT, SKY MASTERS AEROSPACE, INC., BATTLE MOUNTAIN, NEVADA
Forty-eight hours later

Brad McLanahan showed his ID to the group of armed security officers on duty. They checked it carefully against the list of approved personnel and then waved him on toward Hangar Three. Before going in, he turned back briefly to look across the empty airport runway. Anyone surveying the Sky Masters complex around the airport, whether through binoculars from the nearby mountains or from a satellite in space, would see no unusual activity. There were no aircraft lined up on the tarmac or parked outside any of the hangars. Everything seemed quiet.

This early in the morning, the sun rising over the mountains of the Shoshone Range sent long shadows stretching westward. He shivered slightly. Nights on the high deserts of Nevada were chilly, even in the summer, and it would be another couple of hours before temperatures would climb back to their usual searing midnineties.

Which meant that faint shimmer he saw drifting across the tarmac was not a heat mirage. It was one of the three Cybernetic Infantry Devices assigned to protect the Sky Masters facility against possible Russian attack. The patrolling war machine was using both of its advanced camouflage systems to full effect. Hundreds of hexagonal thermal adaptive tiles covered the robot's armor, made of a special material that could change temperature with astonishing speed. Computers could adjust them to mimic the heat signatures of the CID's surroundings, rendering it effectively invisible to enemy IR sensors. The machines also had thousands of paper-thin electrochromatic plates layered over those thermal tiles. Tiny voltage changes could alter the mix of colors displayed by each plate, giving the CIDs a chameleonlike ability to blend in with their environment. By using both systems in tandem, the robots could essentially hide in plain sight when they were stationary or moving slowly.

Their presence was a sign of just how seriously Martindale and Brad's father took the Russian threat and the need for tighter security around Battle Mountain—especially now that their handful of Sky Masters spaceplanes represented America's only real hope to conduct a counterattack against Mars One. If Gryzlov decided to carry out a preemptive strike against them, using one of his space-based hypersonic warheads, the three CIDs permanently on guard might be able to block the attack with a well-aimed rail-gun shot.

On a good day. With a lot of luck.

But then again, Brad realized, any chance was better than none at all.

He turned away and limped on toward the nearest hangar door. Even with a regular dose of painkillers, his shoulder and knee still hurt like hell . . . but at least he'd been able to ditch the sling. Walking with a cane took some getting used to, though. Sky Masters had offered him a golf cart and assigned driver to get around the facility, but he'd turned them down. He figured it was better to sweat a little than to risk his knee stiffening up on him again.

After the deceptive early-morning tranquility outside, entering the vast building was a shock to his system. The hangar was a sea of bright lights, rapid, purposeful activity, and ear-shattering noise. Sky Masters and Scion ground crews surrounded three spaceplanes, readying them for flight. One was a comparatively small twin-engine S-9 Black Stallion. The others were the two Sky Masters S-29 Shadows—one still rigged up as an in-space refueling tanker. Scion's armed S-29B spaceplane was back in its own secret Scion hangar in southwestern Utah, undergoing the same preparations, under Boomer's watchful eye.

Nadia Rozek stood near one of the S-29s, following along while a crew chief ran a maintenance check on one of the big LPDRS engines. Brad crossed the huge hangar floor to join her. When she turned her head to greet him, a smile crossed her tired face. "You look better." Then she reconsidered. "Or at least not quite so much like an old man tottering about in a daze."

"Gee, thanks," Brad said. "I think."

"*Nie ma za co*," she said with a slightly wider smile. "You're welcome."

Brad nodded up at the large spaceplane, which was the Shadow configured to carry cargo and passengers. Its bay doors were open and he could hear the shrill whine of drills and other power tools coming from inside. "How's it going?"

"Very well," Nadia told him. "The special payload modifications we require should be finished within the next few hours."

That was good news. When the S-29s were designed, no one had ever imagined anything quite like what they were about to attempt. Modifying a standard spaceplane cargo bay to hold the complicated array of supports, webbing, and auxiliary power and communication leads necessary for this mission—especially in such a short amount of time—had been a difficult job.

"So our spaceplanes will be ready. But will they have anything to carry into orbit?" Nadia asked.

"Definitely," Brad assured her. "I just checked in with Richter. His engineering and production crews are working around the clock. Whatever they can't pull off the shelves, they're fabricating on the fly. He's mastered the art and science of large-scale, super-precise 3-D printing and has his machines spitting out parts at the speed of light. I think they're actually enjoying the challenge."

He grinned, remembering the oddball collection of pieces and parts he'd seen strewn across lab benches and worktables. Crossing a high school robotics competition with a late-night party of drunken mad scientists might produce a similar jumble. "None of our new little birds are going to win awards for clean lines or elegant design . . . but they'll fly all right."

"On a one-way trip," Nadia pointed out quietly.

"There is that," Brad agreed. He shrugged. "It does simplify the design process."

"And the rest of our equipment? What is its status?"

"Loading on an air force C-17 in Houston now," he said. "Everything should be here by early afternoon."

"So until then, we wait and worry . . . and train," she said.

"Yep," Brad said. "Which is mostly why I'm here now. My dad just uploaded a new variation on our attack plan. Constable's configuring the simulators now. They should be ready for the three of us to try another run-through in about half an hour."

Nadia sighed. "I will be there." She put a gentle hand on his left arm. "But after that, I would like to spend some time with you. Only with you." Her blue-gray eyes were serious. "Because we both know this mission is likely to be a one-way trip for more than just our little satellites."

Brad suddenly wished with all his heart that he were a better liar . . . so that he could offer her a more optimistic assessment of their chances and be believed. But as it was, all he could do was give her a quick, silent nod.

VOSTOCHNY COSMODROME
Forty hours later

"Energia-5VR guidance systems are configured," one of the controllers reported.

From his station on the top tier of Vostochny's control center, Yuri Klementiyev followed the progress of the automated launch sequence with a certain fatalistic calm. At this point, the computers aboard the huge rocket out on Pad 3 were fully in control. Short of ordering an emergency abort, there was nothing more he could do. Success or failure was now wholly in the hands of the gods of probability, physics, and fortune. Despite that, he was keenly aware that both Gennadiy Gryzlov and Colonel General Leonov were closely monitoring this operation from Moscow. It had been made clear to him that he would not survive any launch accident that destroyed the new reactor intended for Mars One.

Vostochny's director closed his eyes. If he were a genuinely religious man, he could have passed the time with a litany of heartfelt, unspoken prayers. As it was, all he could do was await the outcome.

"All stages look good," another controller said through his headset. "We are ready for flight."

Klementiyev opened his eyes.

The base of Pad 3 disappeared in a cloud of brownish smoke and bright flames. "*Zazhiganiye.* Ignition," his deputy announced. And then, seconds later, "Engines throttling up. Full power!"

Through the thickening smoke, Klementiyev saw the gantries holding the massive, twenty-five-hundred-ton rocket in place swing up and away. Unrestrained now, the Energia-5VR rose on a column of fire, climbing toward the heavens with rapidly increasing speed. "*Podnyat'!* Lift-off!"

Unable to sit idle any longer, he stood up—mentally urging the rocket onward as it roared higher, pierced a layer of low-lying cloud, and kept going. Nearly three minutes later, long-range tracking cameras captured the welcome sight of a perfect third-stage ignition. Mars One's replacement fusion reactor was on its way safely into orbit.

Klementiyev breathed out, feeling as though an enormous weight had been lifted from his shoulders. Slowly, he took his seat again and turned his attention to the Soyuz-5 rockets waiting on Pads 7 and 9. "Status on the Elektrons?"

"Both are go for launch. Their flight computers and automated programs look solid. We are holding for ignition," his deputy reported.

He nodded. If something had gone wrong with the Energia heavy-lift rocket, there would have been no point in sending its escorts into orbit. Now it was time to send the two armed spaceplanes and their cosmonaut pilots aloft. "Light the fires, Sergei," he ordered. "Let's give that reactor some company."

A few short minutes later, both Soyuz-5 rockets blazed into the sky and headed toward space.

BATTLE MOUNTAIN
A short time later

Orbiting high above the earth in geosynchronous orbit, America's space-based infrared satellites detected all three launches from Vostochny. Within minutes, their reports were relayed to the White House and from there to the members of the Sky Masters–Scion assault force in Nevada and Utah.

The news triggered an immediate operational readiness conference.

Brad McLanahan looked around the table. Nadia and Peter Vasey were seated with him. His father, Martindale, and President Farrell were visible on one side of the conference room's large LED screen, present via secure link from the Oval Office. Boomer and the five members of his S-29B Shadow crew looked out from the other side of the screen. They were being broadcast from their hangar at St. George.

"The Russians have definitely put their reactor module into space," Brad told them. "The Space Surveillance Telescope in western Australia took this image as it passed overhead a few minutes ago." He used his laptop computer to pull up the picture he'd downloaded. It showed an unmistakable cylindrical shape, identical to the other three that already made up Mars One.

"Three rockets lifted off from Vostochny," Boomer pointed out. "So what sort of payloads were the other two carrying?"

Brad kept as much control over his voice and expression as he could. "These," he said, pulling up two more images captured by the powerful U.S. Air Force–operated telescope. Both showed winged spacecraft with their cargo bays open, revealing a fixed weapons mount inside.

"Elektron spaceplanes," Boomer muttered. "Armed with more of those fucking Hobnail lasers."

Brad nodded. "I'm afraid so."

"What's your evaluation?" his father asked.

"Both Russian spacecraft have entered the same orbit as the reactor module. One Elektron is on station about twenty miles ahead of the module. The second trails it by about the same distance," Brad told him. "Based on that, it's pretty clear that they're acting as escorts, with orders to protect that reactor until it's safely docked with Mars One."

"I concur," the older McLanahan said. He turned to Farrell. "If we needed any further confirmation that Gryzlov has launched a replacement fusion generator, there it is. There's no reason he would commit those two armed spacecraft to protect anything that he didn't consider absolutely vital."

The president nodded his understanding. He looked at Brad. "How much time do we have before this module is in a position to link up with the Russian space station?"

"Based on its current trajectory, our computers estimate it will be ready to dock with Mars One in five, or possibly six more orbits," Brad said. "That's approximately eight hours from now."

"And after it's docked? How long will it take the Mars One crew to bring their new reactor online?"

Patrick shrugged. "Without a clearer understanding of the technology the Russians have developed, there's no way to be sure, Mr. President. But we can't count on it taking them very long."

Privately, Brad agreed. The Russians were smart enough to design their systems so that all the necessary power connections from the reactor to the rest of their station ran through its docking port. And unlike a conventional power plant or even a fission-based reactor with its steam turbines, it was unlikely that any functioning small fusion generator had many moving parts. Spinning it up might be as simple as running a number of safety checks and then flipping a switch.

"So we must go and go soon," Nadia said decisively.

"Nadia's right," Brad said. He pulled up Mars One's projected orbital track. "A little under three orbits from now, in roughly four hours, the Russian station will cross into darkness over South America. That's our best chance to jump them while they can't recharge their plasma rail gun and lasers."

"But attacking then isn't ideal," Farrell guessed.

"No, sir," Brad admitted. "On that orbit, the

ground track for Mars One passes within striking range of a number of high-priority European targets."

"Including Warsaw," the president said flatly.

"Yes, sir."

Nadia shook her head impatiently. "Yes, the risk exists. We cannot avoid it. I will brief President Wilk, but I already know what he will say: better death than slavery. Is not that the lesson of the heroic defenders of your own Alamo?"

Beside her, Peter Vasey hid a sudden grin. Nadia had the duelist's gift, all right. Give her any opening, however small, and she would thrust home straight through it—striking straight to the heart.

"I take your point, Major," Farrell said quietly, with a wry smile. He looked at Brad. "Then I guess it comes down to whether or not y'all can be ready to go in time."

"We can," Brad said firmly. "I've run the flight times to the necessary jump-off point over Ecuador. All of the spaceplanes we're committing to this operation can make it with time to spare . . . but only if we take off within the next hour."

Martindale nodded. "Sky Masters has already staged the necessary refueling aircraft to airports in Mexico and Central America." He looked at Farrell. "As soon as you give the word, I can get those tankers airborne."

Farrell sat in silence for a moment. Then he turned to Patrick. "Do I have an alternative?"

"Short of eventual capitulation to anything Gryzlov demands?" the older McLanahan said.

He shook his head. "No, Mr. President, I'm afraid you really don't."

Farrell grimaced. He seemed to have aged several years in as many minutes. Finally, he looked up at Brad and the others. "All right. Y'all have my permission to go into orbit and kick some Russian ass."

"We will not let you down," Nadia promised.

"See that you don't," the president said gruffly. "And make damned sure you come back in one piece."

No one had anything much to say to that.

CHAPTER 43

ABOARD MARS ONE, OVER THE SOUTH PACIFIC
Several hours later

Colonel Vadim Strelkov looked ahead and saw a line of darkness curving across the surface of the earth. They were approaching the terminator, the point where Mars One would cross into darkness for thirty-four minutes on this orbit. He opened an intercom channel to Pyotr Romanenko. "Solar array status?"

"We are currently generating twenty-four kilowatts. But that is dropping fast," the engineering officer reported. "Shifting to station backup batteries now."

"Understood," Strelkov said. He switched channels. "Filatyev. Revin. Give me a report on your weapons."

Filatyev spoke first from his post in the aft weapons module. "Thunderbolt's supercapacitors are fully charged. The weapon is ready to fire."

"Both Hobnail battery packs are at maximum

capacity," Leonid Revin said from the forward weapons module. "All indicators are green on both lasers."

"Very well," Strelkov said. During most periods of darkness, he relied on those on duty to handle their own preparations. After so many orbits, this process was quickly becoming routine, but it never hurt to be fully ready for action when they were forced to rely completely on stored power. That was why he ran drills like this two or three times during any given "day." Soon, though, they would no longer be necessary. To keep from drifting off across the command compartment, he made sure his feet were hooked under the edge of his console and then carefully swiveled toward Georgy Konnikov. "Give me an update on the reactor module, Major."

Konnikov had the answer at his fingertips. "It is currently six hundred kilometers behind us, sir, and closing on an elliptical transfer orbit."

"Time to the final docking maneuver?"

"Currently estimated at three hours and thirty-five minutes," the sensor officer told him.

Strelkov nodded. In just two more orbits, once their fusion generator was online and providing massive amounts of power, this station would be invulnerable—safe against any conceivable American attack.

Abruptly, their lights and displays flickered for a fraction of a second and then stabilized.

"We've crossed the solar terminator," Romanenko reported. "Shift to battery power is complete."

BEEP-BEEP-BEEP.

Caught off guard by the loud warning echoing through the station, Strelkov grabbed for his console. "Identify this threat!" he demanded.

"One of our EKS warning satellites has detected a launch over Ecuador—almost directly below us!" Konnikov said urgently. He hammered at his keyboard, interrogating their primary computer. "The launch detection is confirmed by our own IR sensors."

Ecuador? Strelkov felt cold. Could the Americans have deployed some of their missile defense interceptors to South America to ambush Mars One as it crossed through the earth's shadow? All the intelligence reports he'd studied claimed those weapons weren't supposed to be mobile. Then again, spies were never infallible. "Is that a missile?"

"Negative, Colonel," Konnikov said. He turned his head. "The computer evaluates this contact as an American spaceplane. Based on its thermal signature, I believe it is an S-9 Black Stallion. It is boosting to orbit on a converging course with us."

"Time to intercept?"

Konnikov scrolled through his displays. "Fourteen minutes."

Strelkov frowned. The S-9 was the oldest, smallest, and least capable of the Sky Masters S-series spaceplanes, not much larger than a two-seater F-16D fighter. How much of a threat could it pose to his station? He considered waiting to engage it, hoping to see what else the Americans might have planned.

"*Sukin syn*," Konnikov muttered in shock. He spun around toward the colonel and was pulled up short by the tether connecting him to his sensor console. "EKS and IR data handoff to our X-band radar is complete. I have a more accurate trajectory for the enemy spacecraft!"

"And?"

"It's not attempting to simply match our orbit, sir," Konnikov said hurriedly. "That S-9 is on a direct collision course! It's coming right at us!"

Strelkov felt his mouth open in surprise. The Americans were using their spaceplane as a kamikaze—sacrificing the S-9 and its pilot to destroy Mars One on impact. He stabbed down at another intercom button. "Pavel! Fire the thrusters! Take us higher!"

"Activating thrusters," Lieutenant Colonel Pavel Anikeyev acknowledged. Strelkov's second in command was at his station in the aft compartment he shared with Romanenko. "Stand by for a five-second burn."

Strelkov held tight as Mars One shook briefly. The maneuvering thrusters of their docked Progress cargo ships and the Federation orbiter were pushing them higher in this orbit. A five-second burn wouldn't add much to their altitude, no more than a few kilometers, but that should be enough.

The station steadied again, back at zero-G.

"Burn complete. But our fuel reserves are now

critically low, Vadim," Anikeyev said tightly. "We have enough hydrazine left to counter the recoil of several more Thunderbolt shots and to conduct another short maneuvering burn . . . but nothing more."

"I understand," Strelkov replied. Once the reactor was docked and online, they would no longer have to rely on conventional fuels. They would have abundant electrical power to run the ion thrusters ringing the exterior of each station section.

Then, to his horror, he heard Konnikov report, "The American spaceplane has adjusted its trajectory! It has matched our maneuver and is still on a collision course!"

Enough, Strelkov decided. "Major Filatyev," he said over the command circuit. "Activate Thunderbolt and destroy that enemy spacecraft."

"Tracking data received," the weapons officer confirmed. "Firing now."

Mars One shook again as the rail gun pulsed— hurling a ring of superheated, ultradense plasma outward at ten thousand kilometers per second.

"Good kill!" Konnikov crowed. His radar showed the American S-9 Black Stallion spinning away off course, trailing debris and a cloud of frozen fuel. "The enemy spacecraft will hit the atmosphere and burn up in just a few minutes."

Strelkov nodded. "Very good, Major." He relaxed his grip on his console. "Connect me to Moscow. We need to report in."

NATIONAL DEFENSE CONTROL CENTER, MOSCOW
One minute later

Alerted by the emergency signal from Mars One, Leonov reached his workstation in time to hear the tail end of Strelkov's excited account. "Our sensors are monitoring the wreckage as it falls toward the atmosphere. So far, we've seen no sign of any attempt to bail out."

"Excellent work, Colonel!" Gennadiy Gryzlov said from another screen. The president was in his Kremlin office. He smiled coldly. "Now we'll show Farrell how stupid he has been. You will carry out an immediate *Rapira* retaliatory strike on the Sky Masters spaceplane base in Nevada."

Strelkov swallowed hard. "Unfortunately, Mr. President, we will not be in range of any targets in the continental United States during this orbit." He looked apologetic. "The Americans must have timed this new attack with that in mind."

Gryzlov's smile disappeared. He was plainly irked by the news that orbital mechanics would delay the execution of his desired counterstroke. But then he shrugged his shoulders irritably. "I suppose it won't matter that much if we strike now . . . or in two hours."

"No, sir," Strelkov agreed quickly.

"If anything, the delay will only increase the terror the Americans suffer as they realize how foolish it was to challenge us," Gryzlov commented, regaining his good humor.

Listening to the president's confident assessment, Leonov kept his own counsel. Nothing in his study of previous Scion, Sky Masters, and Iron Wolf operations suggested this single spaceplane sortie would be all they had planned. It was possible, he decided, that launching that small S-9 Black Stallion against Mars One was just another feint—one intended to mask a sudden American lunge against the fusion reactor module before it could dock.

Unnoticed by the other two men, he opened a new secure communications channel, this one to the two Elektron spaceplanes escorting the reactor. ACTIVATE ALL SENSORS AND COME TO FULL ALERT, he typed. ENEMY ATTACK MAY BE IMMINENT. LEONOV OUT.

MARS ONE
That same time

"We will be ready to attack the Sky Masters air base as soon as we come within range," Strelkov assured the president. "You can rely on . . ."

He broke off in midsentence, interrupted by another high-pitched warning tone that warbled through his headset.

"New launch detection!" Konnikov shouted. "Over Venezuela, this time!" Working with desperate speed, he sorted through the information pouring in from different sensors. "It appears to be another American spaceplane, much larger than the S-9 Black Stallion."

"Another S-19 Midnight?" Strelkov asked.

Konnikov matched the heat signature of this new contact against the sensor data he'd collected during their first space battle ten days before. Only ten days . . . and yet it felt like years had passed, he thought in amazement. He stared at the results for a moment and then turned toward Strelkov. "No, sir, the engine plume from this spacecraft is more intense. It's almost certainly an S-29 Shadow."

"On what trajectory?" the colonel snapped.

Again, Konnikov saw a red line intersect their own green orbital track on a map display. "Straight at us."

Strelkov nodded grimly. "Of course."

He could feel himself starting to sweat. Mars One would not emerge into full sunlight for another thirty minutes, and their plasma rail gun had only enough power left in its supercapacitors for one more shot. Had the Americans somehow deduced that he couldn't recharge his energy weapons without electricity from the solar panels? Were they trying to wear down his defenses with repeated attacks? If so, it might be wiser to keep the rail gun's last shot in reserve and risk a closer engagement against this second spaceplane using the station's Hobnail lasers and Scimitar missiles.

Gryzlov broke in over the still-open satellite communications link to Moscow. "What are you waiting for? Why haven't you already fired on this new target?"

When Strelkov hesitantly tried to explain his concerns, the president snapped, "Don't be a fool! The Americans have almost certainly armed at least one of their spaceplanes already. If you don't fire Thunderbolt now, you may never get a second chance."

Helplessly, the colonel looked toward Leonov. "Sir?"

"The president is right," the other man admitted. "We've analyzed radar data collected during the final stages of the successful American effort to rescue their downed astronaut. They seem to show the intervention of a large supersonic craft in the battle area shortly before the confirmed disappearance of one of our Su-35 fighters. If so, that S-29 Shadow headed your way may well be armed with weapons of its own."

"Very well," Strelkov said slowly. Unable to shake the premonition that he was making a tactical error, he looked across the command compartment at Konnikov. "Transfer your tracking data to Thunderbolt's fire-control computer, Major."

"Transfer complete," the younger man reported seconds later.

"My computer has a solution, Colonel," Filatyev announced over the intercom circuit. "Standing by to fire on your order."

"Weapons release granted," Strelkov said reluctantly.

"Firing."

The plasma rail gun pulsed a second time.

"Good hit!" Konnikov exulted. He slaved the station's powerful telescopes to its X-band radar and sent the light-intensified images they captured to Strelkov's console. They showed the dead Sky Masters S-29 Shadow curving away with a ragged hole torn in its aft fuselage. It was surrounded by a dense fog of frozen fuel, oxidizer, and debris.

Strelkov studied the pictures intently. He frowned, puzzled by what he observed. "There is a lot more fuel in that debris cloud than I would have expected," he noted.

On-screen, Gryzlov nodded sagely. "The spaceplane must have been carrying long-range missiles in its payload bay, Colonel. That would explain the extra fuel." He smiled. "So you see, you were wise not to let that S-29 get any closer to Mars One before killing it."

CHAPTER 44

SHADOW TWO-TWO, OVER THE NORTH ATLANTIC, OFF THE COAST OF GUYANA
That same time

Almost invisible from below against the night sky and from above against the darkened surface of the ocean fifty thousand feet below, a second S-29 Shadow streaked northeast at high speed. As the spaceplane's airspeed reached Mach 3, its five hybrid LPDRS engines finished their transition to scramjet mode. Immediately the S-29's nose pitched up and it climbed toward the upper edges of the atmosphere, accelerating at an ever-increasing rate.

The forward section of the spaceplane's cargo bay contained two dozen Sky Masters–built nanosatellites. Each tiny satellite sat nestled in metal bracing. Power and data cables connected them to the S-29's computers. None of the twenty-four nanosats were identical. Each carried a unique blend of antennas, other emitters, maneuvering thrusters, and power supplies.

In the aft cargo bay, seven large spheroid COMS—Cybernetic Orbital Maneuvering Systems—were packed in tight, held in place by a lattice of webbing. Three of the egg-shaped robots were occupied by human pilots. The other four were configured for a mix of autonomous and remote control. All seven one-man construction spacecraft had been hurriedly modified for combat use. Three of the unpiloted COMS were equipped with electromagnetic rail guns. The numerous mechanical limbs of the other four held a variety of tools repurposed for use as weapons—including drills, laser welders, explosive breaching devices, and powered cutting saws.

Secure inside the cockpit of his COMS, Brad McLanahan opened a channel to the other two pilots. "This is Wolf One, communications check," he said.

"Wolf Two copies," Nadia Rozek said calmly.

"Wolf Three has you loud and clear," Peter Vasey replied.

"Passing three hundred and sixty thousand feet, engines spiking," a calm female voice reported. *"Spiking complete. Scramjets indicate full shutdown. Shadow Two-Two is go for rocket transition."*

Brad sighed. So far at least, Shadow Two-Two's computer had performed perfectly, taking off from Battle Mountain and handling the required air-to-air refueling rendezvous without a hitch. But understanding that the S-29 they were riding in was capable of fully autonomous, computer-controlled flight was one thing. Being comfortable with that as a passenger was quite another. Still, he had to admit feeling relieved that those first two Russian plasma rail-gun shots hadn't killed anyone . . . since both the S-9 Black Stallion and the S-29 refueling tanker they'd sent into orbit first had been flown by computers, not human pilots.

"Good ignition on all five engines. Throttling up to full power," the computer announced.

Instantly, high G-forces slammed Brad deeper into the haptic interface gel around him. He gritted his teeth against a sudden wave of pain from his damaged shoulder and knee. *Hold it together, McLanahan,* he thought. He'd assured everyone that he could handle this mission. Well, he'd be damned if he made a liar out of himself by losing consciousness on the trip into space.

"Now we find out . . . if your father . . . was right . . . or if he was wrong," Nadia said. Beneath the clear physical effort required to speak under acceleration, she sounded completely calm.

"How's that?" Brad forced out past the pressure on his chest.

"Can the Russians fire that plasma weapon of theirs twice . . . or three times?" she replied.

Despite the G-forces acting on him, Brad felt a wry smile cross his contorted face. "We'll see, I guess. But I feel . . . lucky," he grunted. "Even if I am a . . . punk."

MARS ONE
That same time

"Sir!" Konnikov rapped out. "The enemy has launched a third spaceplane into orbit! It appears to be another S-29 Shadow and the time to intercept is twenty minutes."

Strelkov froze. *The Americans know about our missing reactor*, he thought bitterly. Somehow, the Mars Project's unprecedented security measures had been breached. The method of this attack was proof of that. They'd forced him to use up his long-range firepower first. Now, instead of killing his enemies while they were still hundreds or even thousands of kilometers away and unable to strike back, this battle would be fought out within tens of kilometers of the space station.

"Colonel?" Konnikov asked uncertainly. "What are your orders?"

Strelkov shook himself back to the present. He punched the intercom button, opening a general channel to everywhere on Mars One. "Attention, all crew, this is Command. Get into your pressure suits immediately! You have eight minutes before we vent atmosphere."

Wearing bulky space suits would make it more difficult for his cosmonauts to work their displays and controls, but if the Americans scored hits, depressurizing the station would at least avoid the twin dangers of explosive decompression and fire.

"Major Romanenko! Don your special-action armor and await further orders."

"Understood, sir," Romanenko replied. "I'm heading for the KVM bay now." As the station's engineering officer, he could do nothing more until they crossed back into sunlight and had electrical power to spare to recharge Thunderbolt's supercapacitors. So now it was time for him to prepare to defend Mars One in close combat.

MOSCOW
That same time

Leonov's eyes narrowed as he watched the unfolding tactical situation. The defensive measures Strelkov and his cosmonauts had initiated were sound—but they might not be sufficient. Too much depended on what the Americans intended, and that was still unclear. Mars One's twin lasers and Scimitar missiles were formidable against targets within one hundred kilometers . . . but what if that Sky Masters spaceplane rocketing into orbit carried longer-range weapons? If so, it would be able to stand off at a distance and pound the space station into scrap.

He opened a new window on his display, one that showed a wider view of Earth orbit around Mars One. Their recently launched reactor module was still nearly six hundred kilometers behind and sixty kilometers below the station. Green triangles showed the positions of its two armed escorts—one thirty kilometers ahead and the other the same distance behind. Their assigned mission was to protect the replacement fusion generator from American attack. Then again, he thought, of what use was that power plant if Mars One itself was destroyed?

Leonov made up his mind. He opened an encrypted voice link to the leading Russian spaceplane. A simple text message would not suffice, not for what he was about to order. "Elektron One, this is Warlord One."

"*Go ahead, Warlord One,*" the pilot, Lieutenant Colonel Ilya Alferov, said.

"You will execute an immediate emergency burn," Leonov told him calmly. "I want you to close the gap with Mars One and be in position to engage that enemy S-29 before it is too late."

"*Wait one, Warlord,*" Alferov radioed. There was a short pause while the cosmonaut, another of his carefully trained cadre for the Mars Project, ran the necessary calculations through his computer. When he spoke again, his voice held a strong undercurrent of concern. "*Warlord One, the only feasible burn will consume all of my available fuel. I will be unable to dock with the station . . . or deorbit and return to Earth.*"

"I understand that, Elektron One," Leonov said patiently.

This time there was an even longer pause. "*Sir, what you're asking is . . .*"

Leonov's patience cracked. "Follow your orders, Alferov!" he growled. "If necessary, we will retrieve you from orbit."

And if that proves impossible, at least you will die

a beloved hero of the Motherland, he thought with weary cynicism. That might be small consolation to the cosmonaut's young family, but war created many widows and fatherless children.

"Affirmative, Warlord One," he heard the other man say at last. *"I am maneuvering now. Elektron One out."*

On his display, Leonov saw the icon tagged ELEKTRON ONE break away from its position ahead of the reactor module. The armed spaceplane was accelerating hard to enter a new transfer orbit, one that would bring it within one hundred kilometers of Mars One around the same time as the American S-29 Shadow.

He sat back, still pondering the situation he saw developing high over the earth. All of his available forces were moving into play, far out of his direct control for the moment. Not quite all, he realized suddenly. There was still one more precaution he could take.

Carefully, Leonov entered a new series of commands into his computer and hit the button—transmitting them through a network of Russian satellites to a secondary communications antenna on Mars One. Ostensibly, he had just queried the status of a water storage tank in the central command module. In reality, this seemingly innocuous request triggered one of the hidden fail-safe protocols Arkady Koshkin's programmers had inserted into the station's operating software.

Seconds later, a response scrolled across his screen: *RAPIRA* SEVEN ON STANDBY. READY FOR TARGET SELECTION.

Leonov took his hands off the keyboard and sat back. Now, like everyone else on the ground, he would watch . . . and wait.

HIGH OVER THE NORTH ATLANTIC
A short time later

"Engine cutoff in five seconds . . . four . . . three . . . two . . . one. Shutdown," the S-29's flight computer announced.

All five rocket motors cut out.

Cocooned inside his COMS cockpit, Brad felt the G-forces that had pressed him deeper into the robot's haptic interface gel suddenly vanish. They were replaced by the floating sensation that marked the onset of weightlessness. Gingerly, he rolled his aching shoulder, being careful not to dislocate it a second time.

"Good burn," the computer's calm female voice said. *"No residuals."*

He checked the data for himself and confirmed that the S-29's autonomous programs were correct. The spaceplane had entered an elliptical orbit that would intercept Mars One eight minutes before the Russian space station crossed back into daylight. Now they were coasting upward at more than seventeen thousand miles per hour.

Aboard Mars One, Konnikov saw the heat signature of the American spaceplane's engines fade abruptly. Awkward in his thick Sokol pressure suit, he tugged on the tether connecting him to his sensor console, spinning slowly to face Strelkov. "The S-29 has completed its burn!"

From his own console, the colonel looked up. His expression was impossible to read through the visor of his helmet. "Are you sure of that, Georgy?"

Konnikov nodded. "Yes, sir. The enemy spacecraft is still on a trajectory to intercept us with a low relative velocity. My computer estimates it will be within the effective range of our Hobnail lasers in approximately ten minutes."

"Right," Strelkov said decisively. "Let's see if we can dodge this bastard now that he's committed." He opened an intercom channel to Anikeyev. "Take us into a higher orbit, Pavel," he ordered. "Burn every drop of fuel that we have!"

"The target is maneuvering," the S-29's computer said calmly. *"Calculating the parameters for a new burn. Engine relight . . . now."*

Brad felt himself shoved backward again as the spaceplane's five powerful rocket motors fired for a second time. The flight computer was using its last remaining stores of JP-8 and BOHM oxidizer to match Mars One's new orbit. From this moment on, the Shadow and its passengers were fully committed. There was no longer any way to abort this mission and reenter the earth's atmosphere before the Russian space station flew back into full sunlight and recharged its plasma rail gun.

CHAPTER 45

IN ORBIT
A short time later

Maneuvering thrusters fired in sequence, pitching the S-29 Shadow spaceplane "downward" so that it was now flying toward Mars One with its nose pointed to the earth below and its upper fuselage aimed straight at the Russian space station.

"Range to target now ninety miles. Closing velocity is eleven hundred feet per second," the S-29 reported. *"Opening cargo bay doors. Doors are unlatched."*

Through his COMS sensors, Brad saw a thin, almost impossibly black line appear down the length of the cargo bay's ceiling. Slowly, the twin clamshell doors opened wider, revealing the star-filled infinity of space. And suddenly the realization of what they were about to attempt hit him with full force. *We must be absolutely batshit crazy,* he thought in amazement. "Wolf One to Wolf

Two and Three," he said. "I suppose it's too late to come up with another plan?"

"I wondered that myself," Vasey replied dryly.

Nadia laughed quietly. "Come now, boys. This should be fun."

Almost against his will, Brad smiled. "Remind me to go over the precise American English definition of 'fun' with you when we're back home."

"It is a date," she said.

The voice of the S-29's computer intruded. *"Propulsion systems and electronics are go for all nanosatellites. Guidance systems initialized and final navigation data downloaded."* Moments later, it said, *"Range to target now eighty-two miles. Launching nanosatellites."*

Brad held his breath as spring mechanisms ejected the cloud of twenty-four tiny Sky Masters–built machines out into space—releasing them from separate points around the forward section of the bay at quarter-second intervals to avoid any collisions. Once the nanosats were clear of the doors, short bursts from their small chemical engines sent them flying on ahead of the spaceplane in a carefully calculated constellation.

"Good launches on all nanosatellites," the S-29 reported, sounding almost smug . . . for a collection of electronic circuits and computer chips.

Brad exhaled. That was one hurdle down. Now they would see how the ingenuity and hard work of Jason Richter's engineers and technicians stacked up against Mars One's array of high-powered radars, IR sensors, and telescopes.

"*Activating ECM constellation,*" the spaceplane's computer said.

Konnikov bent over his console, paging through displays from his different sensors at a rapid, controlled pace. "Our X-band radar has a solid lock on the enemy S-29 Shadow. Range is one hundred thirty kilometers and closing. I'm transferring the tracking data to the laser fire-control computers."

"Tracking data received," Revin confirmed from the station's forward weapons module. "Both Hobnail lasers are locked on and ready to fire. The target will be at maximum effective range in twenty-five seconds."

Konnikov stiffened suddenly. "New launch detection, centered on the American spacecraft! L-band radar shows many new contacts, twenty-plus, on closing trajectories." He locked their X-band radar on to the contacts picked up by the lower-frequency system. "The bogeys are small, not even one meter in diameter. Relative closing velocity is roughly three hundred and fifty meters per second."

This was definitely a saturation attack, Strelkov decided. The Americans were throwing large numbers of weapons at Mars One in an effort to overwhelm the defensive lasers and drain their battery packs. The comparatively slow speed of the devices the S-29 had just launched suggested their propulsion systems must be small . . . with a correspondingly larger fragmentation warhead. If just one or two of those mobile space mines made it past Revin's lasers and detonated, they might be able to inflict crippling damage on the station. "Shift targets, Leonid," he ordered quickly. "Destroy those newly launched weapons first!"

"Yes, Colonel," Revin replied. "All targets are laid into my computer. I am . . ."

"Jamming!" Konnikov shouted. "Both radars have lost all contact." He tapped frantically at his keyboard. "Initiating frequency-hopping to counter the jamming and regain contact."

Strelkov fought to stay calm. "What is the source of this jamming? The American spaceplane?"

Konnikov shook his head. "No, sir. It's coming from that cloud of small spacecraft the Americans launched at us." He swallowed hard. "Radar frequency hopping is ineffective. There are too many different jamming sources and they're changing frequencies to match my systems with incredible speed."

"Then shift to your IR sensors," Strelkov said tightly. "And send the information you obtain from them to the laser fire-control computers."

"Other enemy countermeasures make that impossible," Konnikov told him. "My thermal sensors now show well over one hundred potential targets!" There was a definite undercurrent of fear in the younger officer's voice now. "At this range, I cannot discriminate between the decoys and the genuine enemy contacts!"

Strelkov stared at him. "What the hell are you talking about?"

Konnikov twisted away from his console. "I think several of those small spacecraft are dispensing the equivalent of aircraft decoy flares, Colonel," he explained urgently. "Made of some kind of pyrotechnic mixture with its own oxidizer to allow combustion in a vacuum."

"Find a way to penetrate the enemy's counter-measures screen, Major," Strelkov said. "And *fast*."

He could sense his heart rate increasing in time with their deteriorating tactical situation. The mix of weapons and jammers launched by the Americans could be within lethal range of Mars One in minutes. And who knew what the S-29 Shadow itself was doing while it was hidden from their sight? With Konnikov's X-band radar jammed, they didn't have enough tracking infor-mation to zero in visually on the enemy space-plane using the station's powerful telescopes. For now, the colonel and his fellow cosmonauts were effectively blind.

"ECM constellation is fully operational," the S-29's computer reported. *"No lock by enemy X-band radar system."*

Through his COMS' IR sensors, Brad saw the space between their spaceplane and the Russian space station come alive with hundreds of new bright green heat signatures. Imagining the frus-tration aboard Mars One as its crew tried des-perately to sort out which of those were real and which were fakes made him smile, despite his own rapidly increasing tension.

He opened a channel to Nadia and Peter Vasey.

"Wolf One to all Wolves. Report status on Wolf cubs."

"Cubs Two and Three are ready," Nadia said. The two unpiloted COMS under her control were good to fly.

Vasey came in next. "Cub Four is in the green."

Through a data link, Brad checked Cub One, the robot spacecraft remotely tied to his own Wolf One. It was also ready.

"Estimated range to target now seventy-one miles. COMS release in five seconds."

Pulled by motors attached to the sides of the S-29's cargo bay, the webbing holding their egg-shaped robots in place retracted. Freed from restraint, the seven COMS deployed one by one, propelled "up" out of the spaceplane by short bursts from the tiny maneuvering thrusters that studded their outer surfaces.

Secure in his cockpit, Brad stared in wonder at the immensity all around him. Through his neural link, the visual and other sensors set around the robot's exterior gave him a three-hundred-and-sixty-degree view of his surroundings—creating the eerie illusion that he was flying through space without a helmet to obstruct his view. He had almost complete situational awareness of the darkened earth below, the other six COMS around him, and the winged Sky Masters spaceplane behind them.

The S-29 Shadow's thrusters popped briefly—altering its trajectory just enough so that it would pass beneath Mars One without risking a collision. The large spacecraft's cargo bay doors were already closing as it rolled to turn the thermal protection tiles on its undercarriage toward the still-invisible Russian space station.

"Predicted time to rendezvous with target now four minutes, thirty-five seconds," the COMS computer told him. *"Closing velocity is one thousand feet per second."*

Resolutely, Brad tamped down on the sudden queasy sensation in his gut. Knowing that they were all orbiting the world at more than seventeen thousand miles per hour was one thing. Realizing that he was headed straight for Mars One fast enough to slam into its metal surface at nearly seven hundred miles per hour was quite another. Braking safely was going to stress the COMS thrusters to the very edge of their rated capabilities—requiring a deceleration rate twelve times greater than would have been possible with the Manned Maneuvering Units used by NASA astronauts during EVAs.

They were still crossing high above the pitch-black Atlantic. There, in the distance, he could see the orangish glow of city lights along the fast-approaching coastline of Europe.

"Wolf One to Wolf Two and Three," Brad radioed. "Ready all weapons. This is going to happen awfully fast."

Listening to their affirmative replies, he fed power to the mechanical limbs attached to his robot and to the improvised weapons they held. Information flowing through his neural link confirmed that all of the limbs were online, ready to respond as though they were his own arms. Then he powered up the CID electromagnetic rail gun held by Cub One. Using the data link between the two robots allowed him to "see" through the remotely piloted COMS' sensors just as well as he could through those of his own. Carefully, he aimed the rail gun at the center of the bright green brackets that showed where the Russian station *should* be.

MARS ONE

A short time later

Keenly aware that their lives now depended entirely on him, Major Georgy Konnikov kept working to penetrate the enemy's jamming. His gloved fingers stabbed at different controls on his console, commanding both his X-band and L-band radars to change their operating frequencies as randomly as he could. For far too long, nothing worked. His displays still showed only a glowing splotch of green-tinged static across the projected track of the inbound American space weapons.

He blinked hard at a droplet of sweat that had somehow wormed its way out from under his communications cap. It floated away and clung to the visor of his helmet, slightly distorting his vision through that small section. *"Der'mo,"* he muttered. "Shit."

Suddenly the static cluttering his radar displays thinned and then rolled backward—revealing a large cluster of small distinct blips. They were within forty kilometers of Mars One. The area behind the oncoming formation was still hazed by jamming.

"Burn through!" Konnikov said loudly. The approaching cloud of American weapons had reached the point where the effective radiated power of his radars was sufficient to overwhelm that of their jamming systems. His hands swept across his controls, selecting different contacts and locking them up. "Transferring targeting information!"

"Data handoff complete," Revin reported from his post in the forward weapons module. "I have fire-control solutions."

"Open fire!" Strelkov ordered.

Immediately both of Mars One's Hobnail lasers went into action. One- and two-second bursts were sufficient to destroy individual American weapons, reducing them to clouds of half-melted scrap metal shoved onto trajectories that would not impact the space station.

"Ten targets destroyed. Battery packs down to sixty-eight percent," Revin reported. "Continuing to engage."

Konnikov kept his gaze fixed intently on his displays. Every laser hit tore another hole in the enemy's ECM "screen." Already, the hash of green static that had blinded his radars was much thinner. At any second now, he should be able to get a fix on that American spaceplane.

"Eighteen targets destroyed. Six remaining. Battery power down to forty-two percent."

Across the command compartment, Colonel Vadim Strelkov winced. Revin was doing his best, firing his lasers only long enough to confirm the destruction of each enemy weapon or jammer. But even so, this battle was consuming their energy supplies at an alarming rate. The supercapacitors for the station's Thunderbolt plasma rail gun were already drained, rendering the weapon useless. Soon the same would be true of the Hobnail lasers . . . which would leave only the short-range, hypersonic Scimitar missiles available to defend Mars One. He spoke over the intercom to Major Filatyev. "Viktor, activate your missile launcher."

"At once, sir," Filatyev replied.

Strelkov felt the deck of the command module vibrate as a hatch opened, allowing the Scimitar rotary missile launcher to elevate into firing position.

Only half listening to this exchange, Konnikov saw a new blip appear on his X-band radar display, emerging out of the now-faint haze of enemy jamming. "New contact at thirty-five kilometers!" he announced excitedly. "It's the S-29. The spaceplane has changed its trajectory to pass below us at a distance of approximately ten kilometers."

"Revin! Destroy that spaceplane!" Strelkov snapped.

As Revin obeyed his order, both Hobnail lasers swung round, locked on to the S-29 Shadow, and fired. Each burst was much longer this time, nearly five seconds. "Solid hits by both lasers," Revin reported. Then he warned, "My battery packs are below twenty percent. I have enough remaining energy to attack the S-29 again . . . or to destroy the surviving American space weapons. I cannot do both."

Strelkov stared down at his own display, which showed the American spaceplane continuing on without any observable deviation from its plotted course. Why wasn't their radar picking up traces of debris? Had the enemy spacecraft somehow survived those laser shots? He swiveled toward Konnikov. "Get me a visual on that target!"

Quickly, the other man tied one of the station's telescopes to the tracking data supplied by its X-band radar.

Strelkov frowned at the pictures as they appeared on his screen. The American pilot had maneuvered to present the S-29's underside to Mars One's lasers—evidently hoping the spaceplane's heat-resistant thermal tiles would offer some protection. The gamble had paid off, at least to the extent that neither Hobnail burst seemed to have penetrated the spaceplane's outer hull. On the other hand, he could see significant damage to those thermal tiles in two separate places, large areas where they had been deeply scored and cracked all the way through. Damaged as it was, there was no longer any possibility the S-29 Shadow could survive reentry.

"The six remaining American space weapons are now within twenty-five kilometers and still closing," Konnikov pointed out carefully.

Strelkov nodded. He made his decision. "Shift your fire back to those weapons, Captain," he told

Revin. "We'll finish that spaceplane off with a Scimitar missile instead."

The Hobnail lasers spun back to their first targets and opened fire again.

"All targets destroyed," Revin said with evident satisfaction several seconds later.

"What is your battery status?" Strelkov asked.

"Hobnail One has no stored power remaining. Hobnail Two has enough left for a single one-second shot."

Strelkov opened a channel to Filatyev. "Prepare to engage the S-29 with a single missile, Viktor." He smiled, feeling a wave of relief sweep over him. If the enemy spaceplane had mounted other weapons, it would already have used them. Now it was just a question of mopping up. The American attack had come closer to success than he would have thought possible, but in the end all of their cleverness and suicidal willingness to spend lives had fallen short. And by the time they could organize another assault on Mars One, the station's replacement fusion reactor would be operational.

"Sir! This isn't over," Konnikov blurted out. He looked down in dismay at his radar displays. "I've detected seven new bogeys on a direct trajectory to intercept us! They're within thirty kilometers and closing at three hundred meters per second!"

Strelkov felt the blood drain from his face. "Show me!"

Konnikov sent him the light-intensified images captured by their telescopes.

For a long moment, Strelkov stared at the pictures in horrified silence. They showed seven spheroids headed straight for Mars One, each bristling with several limbs and what appeared to be hand weapons. They looked eerily like some sort of ancient predatory sea creatures rising out of the abyss. He shivered. What kind of new Sky Masters devilry was this? He swallowed hard, fighting down the urge to vomit. "Major Filatyev," he rapped out. "Stand by to fire the Scimitar launcher. I want those . . . *things* . . . dead."

CHAPTER 46

Nadia Rozek shifted her point of view from her own Wolf Two COMS to Cub Two, one of her remotely piloted robots. They were within eighteen miles of the Russian space station, flying through the darkness of Earth's shadow at high speed. The images coming through Cub Two's light intensifiers were still fuzzy but sharpening up fast as the robot's computer enhanced them using information gathered during Brad and Boomer's first flyby and by ground telescopes in the following days.

Bright targeting reticles highlighted Mars One's known weapons—the two lasers, one each on the two vertically mounted station modules, and the starfish shape of its plasma rail gun on the connecting module. She shifted the aiming point for Cub Two's electromagnetic rail gun toward one of the lasers . . . and then stopped.

Some new device had popped up through a hatch in the Russian space station's central module, something they hadn't seen before. Since the computer didn't have any stored images to use for enhancement, its precise shape and function were still difficult to make out. It was bulky, though, with what could be a group of cannisters set around a central core.

Nadia reacted fast, trusting to instincts honed by hard-earned combat experience. Encountering something "new" in a battle situation was never good. And everything about that device screamed "missile launcher" to her. Through her neural link, she selected that section of Mars One as her active target. The instant the robot's rail gun centered on the newly deployed Russian weapon, she squeezed the trigger.

In a brief, blinding flash, a small super-dense metal projectile streaked toward the distant space station at nearly four thousand miles per hour.

Instantly, Nadia "felt" Cub Two start to tumble as it was shoved backward and slowed by the intense recoil generated by her shot. Knocked out of control, the spheroid-shaped robot whirled end over end through space—dropping into a new elliptical orbit that would eventually intersect with the earth's atmosphere . . . with fatal consequences. *"Power and thruster status?"* she queried the computer.

"Insufficient battery and fuel-cell power for another rail-gun shot," it replied. *"Insufficient thruster fuel*

remaining to achieve rendezvous with enemy station at survivable relative velocity."

Nadia sighed. Based on the attack profile they'd been forced to fly, their rail guns were essentially one-shot weapons. Since most of the COMS' battery and fuel-cell energy was needed to cool its electronics and other systems in the harsh environment of outer space, there was too little surplus power to charge an electromagnetic rail gun more than once. And the robot's maneuvering thrusters had either enough fuel to decelerate safely before slamming into Mars One, or to compensate for the gun's recoil . . . but not both. There was nothing more she could do. Cub Two was doomed to spin down out of orbit and burn up on reentry.

"*Launch detection,*" the robot's computer reported calmly.

Through its sensors, she saw a cylindrical shape ejected from one of the cannisters spaced around the Russian launcher. A bright glow lit the aft end of the enemy missile as it sped across the intervening miles at astonishing speed.

"*Target?*" Nadia asked sharply.

In reply, Cub Two's computer flashed a trajectory across her display.

Without hesitating, Nadia cut her data link to the remotely piloted robot and came back to full awareness inside her own COMS . . . just in time to see the Russian missile slam straight into Cub Two with enormous force. The impact vaporized both, leaving only a swirling fog of thousands of glowing fragments.

In that same moment, the Russian launcher disintegrated—ripped to pieces by the rail-gun round she'd fired seventeen seconds before. Jagged shards of metal and carbon-fiber composites spun away and tore through the large rectangular solar panels extended off Mars One's modules.

A second later, rail-gun rounds smashed both Hobnail lasers into splinters. Two more COMS robots, Brad's remotely piloted Cub One and Vasey's Cub Four, spiraled downward, knocked out of orbit by the recoil from their own fire.

"Wolf Two to all Wolves," Nadia said, elated. "The enemy's outer defenses are down! Let's go pay the Russians a very close and personal visit."

"Roger that, Wolf Two," Brad replied, echoed a moment later by Vasey. "Range to Mars One is now sixteen miles. Stand by to initiate braking maneuver in sixty seconds."

"Warning, warning, X-band fire-control radar lock-on," Nadia's COMS computer said abruptly. *"New radar is at five o'clock low. Evaluated as N036 Byelka–equivalent active electronically scanned array system."*

Startled, she focused her robot's rear-facing visual sensors along that bearing. There, sixty miles away, was the distinctive winged shape of a Russian Elektron spaceplane. It was closing on them fast, with its laser up and locked in attack position.

"Hell," Nadia said quietly. Caught without the long-range rail guns they'd just expended against Mars One, they had no way to fight back.

ELEKTRON ONE
That same time

Lieutenant Colonel Ilya Alferov checked his radar display with a fierce, satisfied smile. He had a solid lock on one of the four small, odd-looking American spacecraft still aimed at Mars One. Two others were no longer a threat, based on their current trajectories.

Very soon, he thought coldly, all of the attackers would be dead . . . but at his hands, rather than those of Strelkov and his so-called wonder weapons. Maybe now Colonel General Leonov would realize the mistake he'd made in abandoning further development of Russia's own spaceplanes in favor of that orbiting monstrosity. Speed and flexibility were the keys to space warfare. The American general Patton had been right when he'd said that fixed fortifications were a monument to man's stupidity. Cramming weapons into a platform like Mars One that was forced to follow a predictable orbit only made the enemy's job easier.

Alferov entered commands into his autopilot and waited while it took control over the Elektron—firing attitude thrusters to center the Hobnail laser precisely on his chosen target. His spaceplane rotated slightly and then stabilized. The laser targeting reticle on his display went solid green.

He reached out to activate the laser and then stopped. His smile disappeared. The reticle was blinking again. His Elektron had drifted off target for some reason. More thrusters popped, rotating the spaceplane back into position . . . and kept firing in an effort to keep the laser centered.

Alferov frowned. What the devil was going on? It was as though his Elektron was being pushed aside by some strange force.

And then a glistening blob of molten metal drifted past his helmet and splashed against the right side of the cockpit. Horrified, he turned his head to look left—just as the high-powered laser beam that had been focused on his spaceplane for the past several seconds finished cutting through its hull, sliced through the fabric of his suit, ignited his oxygen, and ripped him in half.

SHADOW TWO-NINE BRAVO
That same time

One hundred and fifty miles below the Elektron, Hunter Noble saw a sudden flare of light as the S-29B's two-megawatt laser pierced the Russian spaceplane's fuselage. It veered off its previous trajectory, pitching and yawing while its attitude thrusters fired randomly for a few seconds and then went dead.

"Enemy X-band fire-control radar is off-line," the computer reported.

For "off-line," *read* "fried to hell," Boomer thought grimly, *along with the pilot.*

"Good kill . . . Anderson," he forced out against

the G-forces squeezing him back into his seat. They were still boosting to orbit, having opted for a near-vertical ascent that took them up out of the atmosphere in less than a minute—long before any warning from Russia's EKS satellites could be relayed from Moscow to the Elektron they'd just wrecked. "Nice shooting . . . for . . . a squid."

"Thanks . . . Boomer." Jill Anderson was the S-29B's offensive weapons officer. Before joining Scion, the former U.S. Navy lieutenant commander had worked in the navy's ship-mounted HELIOS combat laser program. Getting the chance to fire a weapon with twenty times more power was a dream come true for her.

Boomer craned his head sideways a little to look over at Liz Gallagher. His copilot was busy monitoring their engine displays and navigation programs. "Ready to go looking . . for more trouble?"

"You ask . . . a girl . . . the nicest questions," she replied with a tight smile. "Oh, yeah, let's go get 'em." Straining, she reached up and tapped one of her multifunction displays. "Nav Program Two is laid in and running."

Boomer saw the steering cues on his heads-up display shift and he followed them, nudging the sidestick controller slightly to the left. The nozzles of the S-29B's five LPDRS engines gimbaled in response, and the spaceplane curved away from the still-distant Mars One—climbing toward an orbit that would converge with the second Russian Elektron and the fusion reactor module it was guarding.

"You know this approach is going to . . . run

our fuel tanks . . . pretty dry," Gallagher said, as conversationally as possible while feeling like an anvil four times her own weight was pressing down on her chest.

"Yep," Boomer agreed. "If we win this fight . . . we're gonna have to glide down the old-fashioned way, nose first."

"And if we lose?"

He fought the Gs to give her a wry grin. "The thought never crossed . . . my mind, Liz. See, I've already bailed out from . . . orbit . . . once. I don't plan . . . to make it . . . a habit."

MOSCOW
That same time

Leonov stared at his screen with a sense of eerie detachment. First, the EKS satellite warning of yet another American spaceplane launch had hit him like a bolt out of the blue. And then, only seconds later, the telemetry from Alferov's Elektron One winked out—signaling its sudden destruction by a laser weapon with frightening power and precision.

The battle in space was not turning in Russia's favor, he realized. While it was still possible that Strelkov and his men could defeat what now appeared to be an American attempt to board and capture Mars One, that was no longer certain. And based on the ease with which it had killed Alferov, the new S-29 Shadow already closing on the reactor module and its second Elektron escort was a deadly foe.

Slowly, Leonov reached out for his keyboard. He was running out of time to act. The inset message in one corner of his screen still read: *RAPIRA* SEVEN ON STANDBY. READY FOR TARGET SELECTION.

Carefully, he entered a new series of commands into the open fail-safe program, again routing them through one of Mars One's secondary communications antennas. Seconds later, the message on his screen changed: TARGET ACCEPTED. *RAPIRA* SEVEN LAUNCHING. WILL AWAIT FINAL ATTACK CONFIRMATION IN ORBIT.

Six hundred and sixty kilometers above the earth, an armored hatch on the underside of Mars One's central command module opened. A *Rapira* warhead with its attached rocket motor slid out into space with small puffs of gas from its thrusters. It separated from the station at ten meters per second and then accelerated away with a short burn from its motor—altering its orbital inclination by a couple of degrees to the north.

Once it was in position, the *Rapira*'s thrusters fired again, flipping the weapon over so that its rocket motor was pointed against the direction of orbit. One small antenna faced the earth, waiting for the final order from Moscow that would trigger its programmed deorbit burn and attack.

CHAPTER 47

IN ORBIT
That same time

Brad McLanahan watched the dark shape of Mars One grow with terrifying speed in his COMS display as he flew toward it at nearly seven hundred miles per hour. Numbers flashed through his neural link with the computer, keeping a running countdown of distance, relative velocity, and time to his planned braking maneuver. Through the link he also kept tabs on the positions of the other three robots. Nadia's Wolf Two was aimed at the Russian station's aft vertical module. Peter Vasey's Wolf Three had the forward vertical module as its target, which left the central horizontal module to Brad's Wolf One. Cub Three, their sole surviving unpiloted COMS, was currently flying using its own autonomous systems. For now, its chief task was to avoid colliding with any of the human-occupied robots or with Mars One itself.

"*Range to target is six thousand feet,*" his computer told him. "*Closing velocity is one thousand feet per second. Initiate rapid braking maneuver . . . now.*"

Brad activated his thrusters and felt a sharp jolt as twenty small rockets spread across the robot's outer shell fired simultaneously. His speed dropped.

"*Closing at six hundred feet per second. Fuel reserves at seventy-five percent. Continuing the braking burn.*"

More thrusters popped. Brad flew onward, slowing further. Even though they were still deep in Earth's shadow, he could see a lot more detail on the Russian station and its attached spacecraft now. Blinking green and red position lights indicated airlocks and unoccupied docking ports at several places on all three modules. Pieces of shattered weapons and solar panels drifted in a slowly expanding cloud above Mars One.

He frowned. If their robots collided with any of that space junk at speeds much higher than a normal walking pace, they could take serious damage.

"Watch that debris field at twelve o'clock high," he said to Nadia and Vasey.

"Copy that, Wolf One," the Englishman replied. "Wolf Three is going low."

"So is Wolf Two," Nadia said tersely.

Brad instructed his own COMS to alter its vector slightly, just enough to cross safely below the cloud of debris. Thrusters along the upper surface of his spheroid-shaped robot fired briefly. He curved downward along a gentle arc. More tiny rockets, these on the lower half of the COMS, popped—leveling out his approach so that he was flying straight at the middle of the central Russian module . . . aimed a little to the left of the docked Federation orbiter.

"*Range to target now two thousand feet. Closing at four hundred feet per second*," the computer reported. "*Fuel reserves at fifty-seven percent.*"

"Coming up on final braking burn," Brad said. He held his breath and then fought down a sudden wave of nausea as his perspective flipped. Instead of *flying* toward Mars One, he seemed to be *falling* right into it. But he had no choice: slowing down while in orbit meant going down. He could only hope that the maneuvering computer would do its job and control the thrusters with precision.

"*One thousand feet . . . six hundred feet . . . four hundred feet*," the computer intoned.

"Arm braking thrust routine . . . now!" Brad ordered.

"*Braking thrust routine armed . . . initiating . . . now.*" This time, every thruster oriented toward the Russian station went off in a sustained, maximum-power burn. He felt himself slammed forward, deeper into the robot's cushioning haptic interface. His eyes closed involuntarily.

The thrusters shut down.

"*Braking maneuver complete*," the COMS reported coolly. "*Range to target four feet. Relative velocity is zero. Fuel reserves at thirty-two percent.*"

Brad opened his eyes to find himself floating serenely within arm's length of the space station's outer hull. "Jesus," he said unsteadily. "Is everyone all right?"

"A bit shaken, but not stirred," Vasey replied.

"Wolf Two is in position and undamaged," Nadia said crisply. "Cub Three is in reserve one hundred feet below the aft module."

Brad looked along the curved surface of the central Mars One module, noting several communications and sensor antennas of differing sizes and shapes. Similar antennas festooned the forward and aft modules. "Then let's go! First, we make these guys blind and deaf. Understood?"

"Affirmative, Wolf One," both Nadia and Vasey said.

He activated a couple of thrusters and drifted toward the nearest antenna, judged by his computer to be the station's primary radio link. When he got closer, he grabbed its mast with one of the robot's manipulator limbs. Its fingerlike metal appendages curled tightly around the metal pole, anchoring him in place. Another limb uncoiled, this one equipped with a powered cutting saw. He spun it up and started slicing through the antenna mast. A stream of tiny flakes of glowing metal flew away into space.

Thirty yards away, near the bottom of the aft space station module, Nadia gripped the mast of another radio antenna. It would be faster to just tear the small dish right off the hull, she judged. She released another of the COMS' mechanical arms and flexed its appendages—

"Hostile at three o'clock! Range close," her computer warned abruptly.

Something crashed hard into the left flank of her robot—threatening to send her tumbling off into space. Frantically, Nadia caught at the antenna mast with a second mechanical hand. Her thrusters fired in the opposite direction, countering the impact.

Caught by surprise, she found herself staring at a monstrous figure, a ten-foot-tall humanoid machine with thin, agile arms and legs and a long torso. It was topped by an eyeless sphere bristling with antennas and other sensor arrays. A large pack equipped with maneuvering thrusters was strapped to its back. *My God*, she thought in alarm, the Russians had deployed one of their own KVM war robots aboard Mars One.

Quickly, Nadia lashed out at the enemy robot with a third metal limb—trying to shove it away.

Almost contemptuously, the KVM batted her riposte aside and then reached out and tore the arm off with its own mechanical hands. Trailing sparks from torn wiring, the dead limb sailed away into space.

Nadia cried out involuntarily. Through her neural link, she felt the loss of that COMS arm as a red-hot flash of pain. "Wolf Two is under attack!" she said desperately.

The Russian war machine reached out with one hand and grabbed hold of another of her limbs—securing itself to her COMS. Glittering crystals of frozen gas floated away from the KVM's backpack thrusters as they fired again to hold it stable. The metal fingers of its other hand probed at the stump of the arm it had ripped loose, trying to find a place where it could dig in and start peeling away her robot's protective hull.

"Hold tight!" Brad called out.

Obeying him, Nadia tightened her grip on the thin radio mast.

And then she felt another powerful impact as something slammed into the Russian war machine from below. Several mechanical limbs wrapped themselves around the KVM's torso and legs. Another COMS had grappled with the enemy robot. Now its thrusters fired at full power, burning through all its remaining fuel to wrench the Russian machine away from her.

Nadia felt fresh agony as the arm the KVM had been using as an anchor tore loose.

Still entangled, the second COMS and the Russian robot spun off into space—moving away from Mars One at a hundred feet per second. As they rotated around each other, she could see the KVM's hands flailing as it tried to pry itself free.

Suddenly there was a brief flash . . . and then the torso of the Russian war machine came apart in a cloud of frozen oxygen mixed with dark globules of blood. Splintered shards of composite armor floated away from the COMS. Locked together, the two wrecked robots fell into the endless void, shrinking rapidly until they disappeared from sight.

Inside the cockpit of her COMS, Nadia stared in horror. "No, Brad," she said brokenly.

"I'm fine," he reassured her quickly. "That was Cub Three and a strategically applied explosive breaching charge, not me."

Nadia swallowed hard. She could not cry, not in zero-G. If she did, her own tears would cling to her eyes and blind her. "Thank God," she murmured. Then she shook herself. This battle was not yet over.

Doggedly, she turned back to the small communications antenna and began prying it loose with her robot's remaining limbs.

A couple of minutes later, Brad finished cutting away another sensor dish. He tossed it away from Mars One as though it were the world's largest Frisbee. That was the last of them. The Russian crew inside the station no longer had any way to communicate with the world below.

He fired more thrusters and glided back around the central module until he came to a shallow bay that now lay open to space. The large, camouflaged clamshell doors that had sealed it previously were folded back against the station's outer hull. There was a standard-sized airlock on the inner wall. This was where the KVM that almost killed Nadia must have been lurking . . . ready to lunge out at them from ambush, he realized.

Well, it sure was nice of the Russians to leave at least one door open for him, Brad thought coldly.

"Wolf One to Two and Three," he said. "I am ready to enter Mars One."

"Roger that, One," Nadia said. Her voice echoed his own determination. "Wolf Two is prepared to breach the aft module."

Vasey spoke up from his position at the other

end of the Russian space station. "Wolf Three is ready to assault. But it looks a rather tight fit," he said thoughtfully.

Brad nodded. Their COMS were likely to find it difficult, maybe even impossible, to maneuver inside Mars One. They hadn't been able to get any intelligence on the station's internal structure, but the odds were that it was broken up into separate compartments, some of which might be too small to accommodate their large, egg-shaped machines. "Yeah," he agreed. "I guess we'll see. If necessary, though, we'll open everything up to space from the outside."

"Mr. Martindale may not be terribly happy about that," Vasey pointed out. "Since we're supposed to capture Mars One intact."

Nadia snorted. "Mr. Martindale is not here. *We* are."

"A fair point," Vasey allowed.

Brad shrugged inside his cockpit. "So we do our best not to break stuff unless we have to."

"And the cosmonauts?" Nadia wondered.

"They get one chance to surrender," Brad said somberly. "After that, all bets are off. Just make sure your short-range radios are set to the standard Russian frequency so you can talk to them if necessary. Is that clear?"

"As crystal," Vasey acknowledged.

"Then let's move." Through his sensors, Brad looked ahead. A bright glow lit the curved horizon of the earth. Mars One was approaching the dividing line between light and shadow.

He turned his attention back to the open bay

and glided inside. The airlock was a no-go, much too small for his COMS to fit. *So I'll make my own hole*, he decided. With his thrusters set to stabilize him, he powered up his saw and started cutting into the inner hull.

Mars One shuddered sharply.

"I have breached the aft module's outer hull," Nadia reported. "Moving on to the inner sections now."

Brad finished slicing an opening large enough to fit the powerful fingerlike appendages of two more of his robot's mechanical limbs. Bright white light, oddly flat in a vacuum, was visible through the gap. He gripped the edges of the slit he'd cut and then fired several of his COMS' thrusters at full power, pulling back and to one side.

For a moment, the section of hull plating held . . . and then it gave way—peeling back like tinfoil. Given the payload constraints involved in any rocket launch, no one built spacecraft like an armored battleship. Conduits and cabling running through that area of the inner hull ripped loose in a cascade of sparks. The bright white light he'd seen winked out, replaced instantly by dim red emergency lighting.

Instantly, Brad let go and maneuvered over to the breach he'd opened. He looked into a compartment full of electronic consoles and displays. A single cosmonaut in a white space suit was tethered by an umbilical to one of the consoles. Through the visor of his helmet, the Russian's eyes were wide with fear. The cloth name tag on his suit identified him as Lieutenant Colonel Pavel Anikeyev. A sign on one of the compartment's intact walls read: окружающая среда и техника.

"*Environment and Engineering*," his computer translated helpfully.

Brad swung the limb holding his powered saw toward Anikeyev and activated his short-range radio. "*Sdavaysya!* Surrender!"

Immediately the other man raised both hands.

The station rocked again.

"I'm inside the forward module," Vasey said carefully. "No hostile contact yet."

"Copy that," Brad said. He turned his attention back to Anikeyev. "Do you speak English?"

"*Yes, a little,*" the other man said shakily.

"Good. Then stay here and don't move," Brad ordered. "Do you understand?"

"*Da,*" the cosmonaut agreed.

Frowning, Brad used a short burst from his thrusters to enter the compartment. Hatches on either side opened up into narrow corridors. "No way is this thing going to fit through those," he muttered to himself. His robot's thermal sensors were picking up the heat signatures of at least two more Russian crewmen down the corridor to his right—the one that led off toward where the Federation orbiter and one of the Progress cargo ships were docked. Another sign over the hatch indicated this was the way to the station's command compartment. He spun the COMS in that direction, trying to decide what he should do next.

And through his rear-facing sensors, he saw the Russian cosmonaut suddenly lower his hands and grab a pistol that had been Velcro'd to the side of the closest console. It came up, aimed straight at his robot.

"Not cool," Brad growled. He lashed backward with the powered saw. Blood sprayed lazily across the compartment, already boiling away in the vacuum of space. Another of his flexible limbs grabbed the pistol as it drifted out of the dead Russian's gloved hand.

His COMS computer identified it for him. *"The weapon is a Vektor SR-1M 9mm pistol loaded with armor-piercing ammunition able to penetrate 2.8mm of titanium plate at one hundred yards."*

Or this robot I'm riding, Brad realized. His jaw tightened. These guys weren't going down easily. "Wolf One to all Wolves," he said tightly. "Stay sharp. This crew is armed." His computer transmitted pictures of the pistol to the other COMS.

"Roger that, Wolf One," Nadia replied. "The Russian I just encountered was similarly equipped."

"And?"

"He resisted," she said simply. "It was futile. I threw him out of the station. Major Filatyev should reenter the earth's atmosphere in approximately twenty minutes. He will have ample time to regret his error."

Harsh, but eminently fair, Brad decided. "How about you, Constable?" he asked.

"Captain Revin has opted for the better part of valor," Vasey answered. "I have his pistol."

Which left the two cosmonauts whose heat signatures he'd detected, Brad thought. It was time to put an end to this. He toggled his radio again. "Attention, surviving Mars One crew, this is McLanahan. It's over. Surrender and we'll spare your lives."

"*Yebat' tebya! Go fuck yourself,*" an older man's voice replied.

"*But, Colonel, maybe we should . . .*" a younger voice said hesitantly.

"*Shut up, Konnikov!*"

Based on its triangulation of the radio signals it had just received, the COMS computer tentatively assigned identification tags to the two thermal signatures. Brad studied their indicated positions and improvised a quick plan. It was probably insanely risky . . . so he decided not to waste any more time thinking it through. Pushing these Russians fast and hard was the surest way to beat them.

He released the robot arm holding his explosive breaching charge and swung it into position in front of the opening to the station's command compartment. "*Set the charge timer for thirty seconds,*" he instructed his computer. "*But deactivate the detonator.*"

"*The timer is set and running,*" the computer replied. "*The detonator is inactive.*"

Without waiting any longer, Brad disconnected his neural link and life-support umbilical. His awareness of the COMS dropped away, leaving him feeling fully human for the first time since they'd loaded aboard the S-29 Shadow several hours before. He squirmed around and punched the hatch release mechanism. It cycled open and he floated out into the environment and engineering compartment. The electronically compressed carbon fibers of his advanced Electronic Elastomeric Activity Suit protected him against vacuum and he had enough air to last at least thirty minutes.

He took the Vektor pistol out of one of the robot's hands. Its safety was off. He scooped up the rectangular breaching charge. A red light on its top winked on and off, counting down seconds.

With a crooked smile, Brad braced himself against the COMS. Then he tossed the breaching charge down the corridor toward Mars One's command compartment. It sailed away, flying straight and true.

One. Two. Three, he counted mentally. *Now!*

Brad pushed off hard with his boots. Holding the 9mm pistol out in front of him, he shot through the open hatch and along the narrow corridor.

The explosive charge flew out into the next compartment. Its red light blinked rhythmically, apparently signaling imminent oblivion.

"*Bombit'!*" the younger man screamed over the radio. "*Bomb!*"

And then Brad soared into the compartment right behind the dud charge. Out the corner of his right eye, he saw a cosmonaut desperately trying to pull himself down behind a bulky console. No threat there, he decided. At least not immediately.

But straight ahead, he saw another space-suited figure rising from cover. Time seemed to slow down, with single seconds seeming to stretch out into whole minutes. That other Russian's weapon was already swinging toward him, coming on target with frightening control.

Brad squeezed the trigger.

There was no sound. Only the sensation of a slight deceleration when his pistol fired, bucking back against his hand.

The other cosmonaut's helmet exploded.

Killed instantly by the bullet that drilled through his forehead and out the back of his skull, Colonel Vadim Strelkov drifted backward and then stopped, snugged up tight against the umbilical still connecting him to his console.

Screaming shrilly inside his helmet, Georgy Konnikov let go of his own pistol and frantically raised his hands.

Mars One had fallen.

CHAPTER 48

SHADOW TWO-NINE BRAVO
That same time

Hunter Noble felt the sensation of acceleration compressing his body vanish. Rapidly, he scanned the readouts flowing across his cockpit displays and HUD. "I show a good burn," he confirmed. "We're in the groove and closing on the predicted orbits of the second Elektron and the reactor module."

"I confirm that," Liz Gallagher said from her copilot's seat beside him. One of her displays pinged at her. She leaned forward, with her mane of red hair making a halo around her head in zero-G. "We have a radar lock on the Elektron. The range is one hundred thirty-five miles and closing fast." Her fingers tapped the display. "Passing the data to the OWO."

"I have it," Jill Anderson, their offensive weapons officer, said over the intercom from the Shadow's aft cabin. "Pinging the target with the laser radar now." There was a short pause while her small targeting laser hit the Russian spaceplane with pulses of coherent light. A sophisticated sensor picked up the reflected pulses—using them both to paint a 3-D image of the enemy spacecraft and to refine the range and closure rate established by the S-29's radar. "I have a good range. Now down to one hundred twelve miles. That guy has his nose pointed right at us, Boomer. Depending on how long it takes us to get burn-through, we may get a little cooked."

Boomer felt his stomach tighten. He'd known they weren't going to be able to surprise that second Russian pilot. "Copy that, Anderson. Zap the bastard and cross your fingers."

"Firing now," she replied.

He found the silence unnerving. His brain knew they really were using a two-megawatt gas dynamic laser to attack an enemy spaceplane so far away that it was still invisible to the naked eye. But his animal instincts kept shrieking that nothing was happening . . . since there was no sound, no vibration, no physical clue of any kind.

"We're hitting the Elektron," Anderson reported.

"Warning, warning, target-tracking radar lock," the S-29's computer said. And then, *"Warning, hull temperature rising."*

Boomer grimaced. "And he's hitting us." He felt hotter suddenly, though he knew that was an illusion. Before they truly felt the heat of that Russian Hobnail laser penetrating the Shadow's cockpit, they'd already be dead.

"*Lock broken. Hull temperature within norms,*" the computer said suddenly.

"Nailed him!" Jill Anderson crowed over the intercom. "Scratch one Elektron!"

Boomer allowed himself to relax a little, but not much. They still had one more task on this mission. He glanced at Liz Gallagher. "That was a little closer than I would have liked."

She nodded. "Yep." Then a quick, impish smile crossed her face. "But at least I won my bet."

Boomer raised an eyebrow. "What bet?"

"That we'd come through this in one piece," Gallagher said simply. "So you owe me dinner when we get back to the world. A really expensive dinner."

Boomer grinned back at her. "You're on." He spoke over the intercom to Anderson. "What's the score on that Russian reactor module?"

"I have good images and a solid lock," the OWO said confidently. "The reactor is in a stable orbit."

"Can you hit its communication antennas without damaging anything else?" Boomer asked.

"No problem."

He nodded. "Then do it. Let's make sure the Russians can't send any new orders to the module's guidance systems. We don't want them deorbiting that reactor before our guys get the chance to find out what makes it tick."

"Shooting now," Anderson assured him.

Several seconds later, their laser stopped firing—leaving the fusion reactor coasting silently in orbit, safe from any further interference by the enemy.

MOSCOW
That same time

For a long moment, Colonel General Leonov sat frozen at his desk, scarcely able to comprehend the speed with which all his years-long work and planning had collapsed. The Americans had captured Mars One . . . and it was only a matter of time before they took possession of the orbiting fusion reactor. By destroying the antennas aboard both the space station and the reactor module, the enemy had robbed him of any ability to activate the remaining fail-safe programs secretly installed in their software.

Not that many were left, he thought bitterly. Strelkov's attempt to evade the American attack by climbing to a higher orbit had completely drained Mars One's fuel supply—making it impossible for him to order a rocket burn that would have sent the station plummeting back into the earth's atmosphere. The destruction of the Scimitar missile launcher had been another blow, since he could no longer override its safety lockouts and fire directly into Mars One itself.

In a small inset screen on his display, Leonov could see Gennadiy Gryzlov's furious face screaming soundlessly at him. To avoid being distracted by the other man's increasingly unhinged ranting, he'd muted the president as soon as the disaster in orbit became clear.

At an adjacent workstation, he could hear his

deputy trying unsuccessfully to soothe Gryzlov. Tikhomirov might as well try to put out a forest fire with a spoonful of water, he thought dispassionately. Russia's leader had gone far beyond the reach of reason . . . and he would never acknowledge that his own impatience and overaggressiveness were at least partly responsible for this defeat.

Leonov's gaze moved to another small inset screen on his computer display. *RAPIRA* SEVEN IN ORBIT. AWAITING ATTACK CONFIRMATION. He entered a quick series of commands into his system, pulling up the hypersonic warhead's projected track. His eyes narrowed. Yes, there was still time. If nothing else, he could salvage something from this catastrophe by striking at Russia's most dangerous foe.

Decisively, he tapped more keys, sending a single encrypted order up into space. The message on his display changed: ATTACK CONFIRMED. DEORBITING IN 10, 9, 8 . . .

Calmly, Leonov took Gryzlov off mute. "Yes, Mr. President?"

IN ORBIT
That same time

High over Western Europe, the *Rapira*'s retrorockets fired. Decelerated just enough to drop out of orbit, the hypersonic warhead separated from its motor and fell toward the earth at more than sixteen thousand miles per hour. Seconds later, it entered the atmosphere and streaked eastward, trailing a plume of superheated plasma.

THE KREMLIN
That same time

Maddened almost beyond coherent thought, Gennadiy Gryzlov stalked around his office in a killing rage. Screens fixed around the walls showed Leonov seated placidly at his desk in his command post below the National Defense Control Center.

"You blundering fool!" he snarled. "Your unbelievable incompetence has snatched defeat from the jaws of victory!" For a moment, he stood breathing hard and fought for control over a rising tide of all-consuming fury. But then he gave in, yielding himself entirely to its red-hot embrace. "You'll pay for this, Leonov!" he snapped, delighting in the brutal orders he was about to give. "From this moment forward, you're nothing but a dead man walking!"

To Gryzlov's intense surprise, Leonov interrupted him. "As so often, you've got it exactly backward, Gennadiy," the other man said icily. "I'm not the dead man here. You are. Look outside your window, you asshole—"

Stunned, and suddenly terrified, Gryzlov whirled around . . . just in time to see a blinding flash as the *Rapira* screamed down out of the sky and slammed home only a hundred meters away. The enormous shock wave crushed him to death milliseconds before the following wall of fire and shattered concrete and steel ripped his corpse to pieces.

EPILOGUE

Silently, Brad McLanahan drifted down a narrow darkened corridor toward the space station's command compartment. Behind him, farther back in the module, he could hear the whine of power tools and murmured conversations. Several Sky Masters technicians brought up in the surviving S-19 Midnight spaceplane were aboard—fixing broken equipment and translating Russian-language controls into English where possible . . . or replacing whole systems if necessary. Computer specialists on the ground had already identified and removed a number of destructive fail-safe programs hidden in the station's operating software.

He felt bone-weary. The first days after they'd captured Mars One had passed in a blur of emergency work to seal hull breaches and repair some of the other damage caused by their boarding action. It would have been impossible without their COMS robots. As it was, they'd been forced to use the cramped Russian Federation orbiter as temporary living quarters until it was safe to bring the bigger modules back to life.

Electricity was still in relatively short supply, but that should pass soon. The captured fusion reactor module was in a parking orbit nearby, ready to dock and come online as soon as Jason Richter and a team of engineers were satisfied they knew all its secrets. In the meantime, to protect the newly renamed Eagle Station against a possible Russian counterattack, Hunter Noble's laser-armed S-29B spaceplane was docked and ready to launch against any threat they detected.

Brad floated through a hatch and out into the console-crowded compartment. Ahead of him, Nadia Rozek, anchored by footholds in an upright position, was intently focused on one of their computer displays. Images, bright in the half-light, flickered across the screen.

Suddenly Brad heard her swear viciously under her breath. *Oops*, he thought nervously. Someone was in big trouble. He hoped it wasn't him. Especially not right now, when he'd finally nerved himself up to take a step he'd been putting off for far too long.

"What's wrong?" he asked quietly.

Nadia turned her head and gestured at the screen. "This," she said tightly.

Brad reached out for a handhold and pulled himself closer.

She was watching a newscast from Russia. It showed a group of somber-faced government officials and military officers gathered outside the enormous triumphal arch of St. Petersburg's Palace Square. With the Kremlin Senate Building and others around it reduced to tumbled heaps of blackened rubble by the surprise *Rapira* strike, the Russians had temporarily moved their seat of government to Peter the Great's old imperial city.

Staggered by the sudden death of Gennadiy Gryzlov and hundreds of others in what Moscow claimed was a "treacherous attack carried out by Iron Wolf mercenaries when they illegally seized the Mars One space station," the Russians had only grudgingly agreed to a cease-fire on Earth and in orbit. Brad's suspicion, shared by Nadia, Martindale, his father, and others, was that they were just buying time while various factions inside and outside of Gryzlov's regime wrestled for power.

Reading the text crawl across the bottom of the television pictures, Brad frowned. It appeared that the different factions had come to an agreement. Russia had just announced the formation of a Committee of National Defense. While the office of president was vacant, pending a new election, executive power would reside in the hands of a select group of experts. Seeing their names, he realized most of them were holdovers from Gryzlov's council of ministers.

There was one exception, the newly promoted marshal of the Russian Federation, Mikhail Leonov.

Nadia stabbed her finger at the picture of the tough-looking soldier. "What if we've defeated a jackal, Gryzlov . . . only to see a tiger emerge from the shadows in his place?"

Studying a close-up of Leonov's hard-eyed Slavic face, Brad felt a slight shiver of dread run down his spine. Nadia's instincts were probably right. While the Russians loudly proclaimed that their new government was a committee of equals, he bet that Leonov would turn out to be, like the pigs in Orwell's *Animal Farm*, "more equal than others." Scion's intelligence pros said the Mars Project had been Leonov's inspiration from the beginning—and they strongly suspected he was responsible for launching the warhead that had nailed Gryzlov when everything went south in orbit. All of which indicated this guy was going to be serious trouble for the United States and its allies going forward.

Then he forced himself to set his fears aside . . . at least for this moment. The last thing he needed right now was Nadia in a dark mood. Instead, he deliberately lightened his voice and shrugged. "A tiger, huh? Could be, I guess. Then we'll just need to find ourselves a bigger gun." With a grin, he waved a hand at the space station around them. "Eagle Station and the Thunderbolt plasma weapon we captured sure look like a pretty good start to me."

Almost unwillingly, she laughed, though her eyes were still full of worry. "Perhaps you are right." She shook her head. "After all, we have won a victory and lived to fight another day. In this world of ours, what more can we hope for?"

Taking that as his cue, Brad cleared his throat nervously. "Well, actually, there is something else that I'm hoping for—"

Maneuvering carefully in zero-G, he gently pulled himself down to a kneeling position and hooked a foot under a nearby console to hold himself in place. Then he unfastened a pocket on his Sky Masters flight suit and pulled out a small gold ring with a diamond that glinted even in the dim light.

Swallowing hard against a sudden lump in his throat, Brad asked, "Nadia, *kochanie, wyjdziesz za mnie?* My dear, will you marry me?"

Caught off guard, she gasped. Then, for a long moment, the longest moment he could ever remember in his whole life, she looked down at the deck without speaking. But when she raised her eyes to his, she was smiling. Firmly, she said, "*Tak*, Brad, *zrobę to. Z całego serca i mojej duszy.* Yes, I will. With all my heart and soul."

WEAPONS AND ACRONYMS

AN/TPY-2—air defense radar system

BOHM—borohydrogen metaoxide, an advanced rocket engine oxidizer

CAPCOM—capsule communicator, person maintaining communications between a spacecraft and Mission Control

CID—Cybernetic Infantry Device, a manned combat robot

COMS—Cybernetic Orbital Maneuvering System, a manned or unmanned space transportation device

DEFCON—Defense Condition, an alerting system designating a particular war footing

DRAGON—manned space capsule designed by SpaceX

DTF—digital terrain-following, high-speed low-altitude flight without using radar

E-4B—airborne command and control aircraft

EA-18G GROWLER—carrier-borne electronic warfare aircraft

EKS—*Edinaya Kosmicheskaya Sistema*, advanced Russian early warning system

ELEKTRON—Russian manned spaceplane

ENERGIA-5VR—Russian heavy-lift rocket

ERO—Emergency Return from Orbit, a crew escape system capable of returning a crewman from Earth orbit

EVA—extravehicular activity; spacewalk

FSB—*Federal'naya Sluzhba Bezopasnosti*, Russian intelligence service that replaced the KGB

GAPA—Polish pilot's wings

GMD—Ground-Based Midcourse Defense, part of the U.S. missile defense system

GRU—*Glavnoye Razvedyvatel'noye Upravleniye*, former Soviet military intelligence service

HELIVERT AW139—AgustaWestland medium-transport helicopter

HK416—German assault rifle

HOBNAIL—Russian space-based laser attack system

HUD—heads-up display, a system that projects vital information to a screen in front of the pilot so he does not have to look down

HUMINT—human intelligence, using spies to gather intelligence

IKS—*identifikatsionnyy kod samolet*, Russian radar identification system

JP-8—military aviation gasoline

KA-52—Kamov-52, Russian armed scout helicopter

KIBERNETISCHESKIYE VOYENNYYE MASHINY (KVM)—manned Russian combat robot

KOŚCIUSZKO LAND FORCES MILITARY ACADEMY—Polish military academy

LEAF—Life Enhancing Assistive Facility, a mobile wearable life-support device

LPDRS—Laser Pulse Detonation Rocket System, advanced spacecraft propulsion system

MALD—miniature air-launched decoy, an advanced American aircraft defense system

MARAUDER—magnetically accelerated ring to achieve ultrahigh directed energy and radiation, experimental American plasma weapon

MARS PROJECT—Russian manned space station project

MIG-31—Russian high-speed high-altitude jet fighter

MOOSE—Manned Orbital Operations Safety Equipment, experimental American astronaut rescue system

MOSSBERG 500—special-purpose shotgun

OAK—FAA designation for Oakland International Airport

ORION   NASA manned spacecraft system

PKP—Russian special-operations machine gun

PLSS—Primary Life Support System, an American astronaut's backpack

RAPIRA—"Rapier," Russian space-based Earth attack weapon

RAZDAN—Russian electro-optical satellite

RD-0150 AND RD-171MV—Russian rocket engines

S-9 BLACK STALLION, S-19 MIDNIGHT, S-29 SHADOW—American single-stage-to-orbit spaceplanes

S-300, S-400, S-500—Russian surface-to-air missiles

SAM—surface-to-air missile

SBIRS—Space Based Infrared System, advanced American early warning system

SCIMITAR—Russian spacecraft defense system

SCT-2—thermal imaging gun sights

SERE—Survival, Evasion, Resistance, and Escape, training soldiers receive to prepare them for combat

SFO—FAA code for San Francisco International Airport

SPACEX FALCON HEAVY—SpaceX heavy-lift rocket

SU-27, SU-30, SU-35—advanced Russian fighter aircraft

THUNDERBOLT (*UDAR MOLNII*)—Russian space-based plasma weapon

WASP—Russian air-launched antisatellite weapon

WREN BRAVO—very light reconnaissance drone

XCV-62 RANGER—American stealthy short-takeoff-and-landing aircraft

XS-39—next-generation experimental American single-stage-to-orbit spaceplane

And don't miss

EAGLE STATION

Another riveting high-tech thriller
Coming soon from Dale Brown